Uncertain Heritage

also by Nora Robson
Pure Fiction: (Toronto: Fitzhenry & Whiteside, 1986)
"Searching for the Blue Heron"
"Nada"

ㄴ

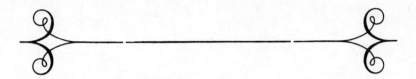

Uncertain Heritage

Helenora Gale

The Book Guild Ltd
Sussex England

*To John
and to Jack,
with love.*

This book is a work of fiction. The characters and situations are imaginary. No resemblance is intended between these characters and any real persons, either living or dead.

....

The Book Guild Ltd
25 High Street,
Lewes, Sussex

First published 1988
© Helenora Gale 1988

Set in Linotron Cartier
Typeset by CST, Eastbourne
Printed in Great Britain by
Antony Rowe Ltd
Chippenham, Wilts

ISBN 0 86332 275 1

PROLOGUE

It was in 1834, the year of the great emigration to the Americas. The decades following the Napoleonic Wars had brought change and economic hardship to the people of Great Britain. Traditional social patterns were falling before the Industrial Revolution. The more adventurous, or desperate subjects of the old world had converged on the ships which would bear them across the Atlantic to a new life. They came from all classes and from all corners of the British Isles, with courage and with hope.

The voyage across the north Atlantic had been long and tedious, especially for the lower class passengers who had been crowded into the ship's hold. The dreaded plague had already claimed some victims and the sick lived in fear of the medical examinations on Grosse Ile. The ship, already late due to storms at sea, had finally entered the waters of the St Lawrence and was sailing majestically into the gulf. Now the sun was shining high on a backdrop of blue sky and the passengers pressed together for their first glimpse of their new land, Canada.

A baby's cries rose above the babble of voices and the mother's voice became more urgent. "Please don't say no. Give my Catherine a chance at life, like your Darra. She'll be sure to die if I take her with me into that fever hospital." The grey-faced young woman stretched her hand in a pleading gesture towards the red-haired Irish immigrant she'd befriended during their storm-tossed voyage. "I can pay. I'll give you everything I have. Only promise me you'll take her to her father at Fort Henry, the military garrison at Kingston. He's expecting us."

Noreen sighed inwardly. There was no way she could say no. But the request troubled her. After all, she would be alone and friendless in a new land with a baby girl of her own. To take on the care and burden of yet another infant would only mean double trouble.

"Here, take this." The condemned woman pushed the dark blue velvet money-belt, which she had worn next to her body for so many weeks, towards Noreen. Its gold-embroidered letters, FRANCES KINGSLEY, shone with imperiousness. Before Noreen had a chance to protest, Frances pressed her advantage with the offering of a matching velvet jewelry case.

"This quilt was sewn by Catherine's grandmother from scraps of silk and satin gowns worn by the Kingsley women on important occasions, weddings, anniversaries and annual balls. You'll find it both practical and beautiful. Lieutenant Kingsley, my husband, will be sure to recognise it."

Her voice shook and her feverish thoughts carried her back to the home she had left and would never see again.

Reluctantly Noreen strapped the belt round her midriff and stuffed the jewelry case inside the worn knapsack she carried everywhere with her. It would be difficult but the money was tempting. She knelt beside Frances, held her hand for a brief moment and said, "Don't worry. I'll take both babes up river to Kingston. If Lieutenant Kingsley hires me as their nurse, everything should work out fine. I'll send him to Québec to fetch you as soon as the medical officers release you from quarantine." Inwardly she doubted that Frances would survive the trip to Grosse Ile where the sick and dying were exiled.

Frances smiled. Tears threatened to roll down her cheeks. She knew as well as Noreen that she was dying. Few recovered from cholera. She was already weaker than most because of her difficult childbirth and subsequent illness a bare three months before sailing from Liverpool. Noreen, a kind-hearted girl bred from stronger stock, had ministered to her throughout the voyage, even suckling both babes when Frances became so ill the milk in her breasts dried up. It had been an easy matter to arrange for Noreen to share her first-class cabin and it proved to the English lady something she had long suspected. Women of the lower classes, like Noreen, were often more generous and open-minded than those of her own social class. No one else on board ship had volunteered to help.

"Thank you, oh thank you, Noreen. God will surely bless you

and reward your kindness. I promise you my husband will be grateful too. Now I'll be able to rest at ease knowing that Catherine is being cared for."

Two attendants arrived at that moment, rolled the dying woman onto a stretcher and covered her with a grey blanket. Noreen, with one last look of horror, snatched up Frances' baby and deftly wrapped her with her own daughter inside the jewel-toned patchwork quilt.

Although the sailing brig reached Québec City during the first week of August, the weary immigrant passengers who were travelling to more distant parts still faced weeks before they would approach the Lake of the Thousand Islands. There had been delays in Montréal and later at Brockville, so by the time they docked in the port of Kingston, it was already September.

Kingston lay on low protected land on the north shore of Lake Ontario: long a strategic position, it had grown up beside the British garrison of Fort Henry which acted as a defence in the event of American aggression. To Noreen, however, Kingston meant only the end of her long voyage and the start of a new life.

The day was chill with an offshore breeze but occasional thin streamers of sunlight appeared from behind the clouds to encourage the disembarking passengers. Noreen had bound her bright hair in a kerchief but, with the constant necessity of tending her charges, ringlets kept escaping to bounce on her forehead with a pronounced coquettishness. She had fashioned the quilt into a sling of sorts in order to carry the babies in front of her, one peeking over each shoulder, and then she strapped her knapsack, containing all her belongings, to her back. Thus burdened, she marched, head held high, off the ship.

Crowds of people milled about the dock. They were mainly military but here and there she spotted groups of farmers and their families, men dressed in a way to suggest commercial trade and others who reminded Noreen of the tramps and drifters who hung around Dublin and Belfast. There were Indians too, but they didn't look the way she had expected them to. Instead of animal hides and furs, magnificent feathered head-dresses and bonnets, they wore dark grubby clothing just like the tramps, with blankets wrapped about their shoulders and battered felt hats on their heads. At least their hair was braided and not ill-shorn nor straggling like the drifters.

Noreen wondered where Lieutenant Kingsley might be and if he would recognise the family quilt. Her eyes searched one face after another looking for a friendly greeting or a questing officer. She had no idea what to look for. All Frances had told her was that she had been married for less than two years. Her bridegroom had received orders to report to Fort Henry and, since she was pregnant, he had sailed alone, promising to prepare a home for them. She had sailed eleven weeks after her daughter's birth, but Lieutenant Kingsley knew the ship she was on and was expecting her.

Time passed. No one came forth to exclaim over the quilt. It seemed like hours to Noreen, who was growing more and more restive by the minute. The babies were whining, their restlessness increasing as feeding time drew nearer. The number of people continued to dwindle. Still no sign of Frances' officer husband.

Finally Noreen singled out an officer who was engaged in conversation with a group of newly arrived men and women. She approached him cautiously.

"Excuse me, Sir?"

He turned, seemingly startled at being addressed by a stranger. "Yes, Ma'am?"

"I wondered if you would be knowing of a certain Lieutenant Kingsley? He's an officer at Fort Henry."

"Kingsley? I'm afraid not, but I've only arrived here myself from New York. Hold on a minute, and I'll make some enquiries for you."

"Oh thank you, Sir, I'd be ever so much obliged."

The young officer turned away and strode through the crowd, heading towards a group of about half a dozen military men. The people he had been talking to glanced at Noreen with ill-disguised curiosity. One woman, dressed in a smart city costume of russet-coloured wool and matching hat, examined her from her laced-up, mud-streaked boots to her red curls tied in a kerchief. At the same time, she took note of the two babies strapped to Noreen's chest and gave a knowing chuckle as she raised her eyebrows. She whispered something to her companion, turned her back on Noreen and the two women laughed as though they shared some private joke.

When the young man returned, his information did nothing to put Noreen at ease. "A couple of those chaps know Ed Kingsley, but they say he's not here at the moment. Captain Henderson sent him to Toronto with some papers for the Governor."

"But wasn't he expecting his wife?"

"Yes he was, but the brig was several weeks late. Kingsley had already made a trip to Montréal to make inquiries. Information travels slowly over here. Captain Henderson didn't have anyone else he could send, so Kingsley had to accept the Toronto assignment. He'll be back in a couple of weeks, three at the most."

On hearing this disappointing news, Noreen felt so discouraged she could have sat right down in the mud, where she stood, and given up. What should she do now? The gentleman was watching her carefully and with some concern.

"You were expecting to meet Lieutenant Kingsley?"

His tone was somewhat incredulous. Noreen knew she didn't look the type to be meeting an aristocratic English officer, as Kingsley obviously was, and felt obliged to explain.

'I'm supposed to go into service in his house."

The lady in russet wool, who had been listening in on the conversation, stepped away from her companion. "Lieutenant Kingsley doesn't have a house." She paused, staring at Noreen.

"At least, not yet he doesn't. He's having one built to be ready when his wife arrives, but it's still incomplete."

"Oh dear!"

If she weren't weighed down with the two babies and her knapsack, Noreen felt she would have been sorely tempted to teach that snobbish English lady a lesson in manners. As it was, she was simply too tired to fight back.

"I think the best thing, Ma'am, is to find rooms for you. Let me introduce myself. Lieutenant Wilder, at your service."

The young man felt sympathetic towards the pretty serving girl.

"Come, I have a buggy over here with a pair of horses. Not the most modern or comfortable, I'm afraid, but better than walking."

The Lieutenant picked up Noreen's knapsack which she had unstrapped on learning the distressing news of Lieutenant Kingsley's absence, put his hand beneath her elbow and escorted her to the waiting buggy. Just like I was as good as his uppity lady friends, Noreen thought triumphantly. Once the horses were in motion and the buggy began jouncing up and down, Catherine and Darra slept again and it was all Noreen could do to keep her eyes open.

Only a short time elapsed before Lieutenant Wilder drew up in front of a crude wooden structure which undoubtedly served as the inn for lower-class travellers passing through Kingston. Its proximity to the harbour suited the lieutenant and also Noreen.

"I'll only be a minute," he said, smiling at her as he hopped down from the driver's seat.

Noreen kept her eyes glued to the floor as she was conducted through a noisy, smoke-filled room which reminded her of the Irish pub where her mother used to serve draught ale when Noreen was a small child. The lieutenant, after placing her knapsack in the room, stood in the doorway.

"I've ordered hot water for you so you can bathe," he said, "and some supper. I reckoned you'd prefer to eat in your room. That crowd downstairs gets pretty rough at times. Is there anything else you'd like right now?"

"No, thank you. You've been too kind as it is."

She remembered suddenly that she must owe him a great deal of money.

"And how much would I be owing to you, Sir?" she asked, trying to hide her dismay.

He grinned. "Not a penny, Ma'am. A pleasure to help out. Think of it as my good deed for the day."

"I can't thank you enough, Sir." She meant to insist upon paying him but couldn't think how to go about it. She felt so terribly tired and surely Lieutenant Kingsley would settle it for her.

Three days passed by before Noreen was feeling restored and ready to resume life's adventures. She was eighteen, she'd survived the ocean voyage to America, escaped the dread cholera and death, and here she was in this new land. All the time she had been closeted in the room with her two babies; recalling everything that had happened to her, whenever she wasn't catching up on her sleep, that is.

Despite her deprived background (her mother had been a barmaid and she didn't have any idea of whom her daughter's father might have been), Noreen remained eternally optimistic. Even though her mother had put her into service at Castle-Blaine estates when she was only fifteen years of age, Noreen understood her motives. What else could her mother have done? The mistress had always been civil to her and so had her young son. He obviously favoured his mother's side of the family and not his father's. Noreen had observed the manner in which the cruel master of the estates ruled all the subjects who lived under his dominance, as though they were animals or slaves. He carried a riding crop wherever he went.

Noreen was seventeen when he raped her. She supposed she was lucky it hadn't happened sooner. The scars from the whip lashes and the pain when he violated her would remain forever to remind her of the incident, but she felt no animosity towards the child born of that union.

She managed to hide her pregnancy until she was fully eight months along. On the day of discovery, the mistress of Castle-Blaine gave her a jewel box containing an emerald brooch, after dismissing her, and demanded that her husband give the young maid a sum of money for the unborn child's support. Noreen had secreted the coins, already having decided to use them for passage to the Americas, and sought refuge in a nearby convent. The sisters, forgiving but sanctimonious, took her in, helped during her travail and presented the baby with a gold baptismal cross. Engraved on its underside were the letters, DARRA. It had been Noreen's Granny's name and meant "Charity is the heart of all God's commands." Courageously, Noreen planned the forthcoming voyage and kept her hopes for the future locked on the New World.

Now she tiptoed carefully from the bed, lest she wake the

babes, and gazed out into the starlit sky. Lights from a ship docked in the bay winked at her. They brought to mind elves and leprechauns, rosy-cheeked country maids whirling and twirling in circles to the music of fiddles, jews' harps and bagpipes. She recalled her mother's tale of an uncle who tapped out the fastest jig in the county. Loneliness descended abruptly on the shoulders of the young Irish immigrant.

I wish that Lieutenant would hurry up and get here, she thought, and then felt guilty about the distressing news she would have to give him. Noreen wondered if there was any chance that Frances would recover from the cholera and was forced to admit that she doubted it. Ghostly figures, wrapped against the chill wind, formed a steady stream going in and out of the tavern below. How good an ale would taste, she thought, but she daren't risk going downstairs – a woman alone.

The longer Noreen thought about convention, the more she longed to kick over its traces. Without consciously thinking of what she was doing, she straightened her gingham frock, brushed the red-gold curls that framed her pixie face and drew her shawl round her shoulders. Hesitating with one hand on the doorknob, she glanced fleetingly at the two little girls, one with fair hair so fine as to be almost invisible, the other like her own, flame-coloured. Both slept soundly.

When Noreen arrived at the tavern's inner entrance, she paused to take in her surroundings. Huddled around the bar in smoke-encircled clusters stood a crowd of men; young, old, military, civilian. They all appeared to be talking at once and each phrase was punctuated by much coarse laughter. Just like back in Ireland, thought Noreen. They're probably exchanging jokes. To her relief, she noticed that there were some women in the place. So, she supposed, it can't be too improper for a woman to enter the tavern unescorted.

Noreen stood straight, at first unaware of what a sensation she was causing with her pert features, her fine figure and high bosom, and her magnificent red locks. She advanced at an unhurried pace and, without looking left or right, moved to a small unoccupied table.

"What'll it be, Miss?" The barman stood before her, his ham-sized hands resting on a pot-belly covered by the stained apron. His little pig eyes dwelled at length on her bosom. Noreen refused, however, to turn aside from his insulting gaze.

"A glass of stout, please."

"Wouldn't recommend it, lass. It aren't like the stout back in the old country, you know."

"What should I order, then?"

"The local brew. It's good and a whole lot cheaper too."

"Fine. That'll do just fine."

After he had returned and placed a stein of amber-coloured fluid in front of her, she shoved a coin across the table towards him. He hefted it in the palm of his hand a moment and then set it back on the table.

"You got nothin' smaller than this?" he asked.

Noreen shook her head. She'd quickly used up all her pence pieces while travelling up the St Lawrence River. There had been so many things she'd needed for herself and the babies.

"Uh – you kin have as much as you want to drink. Beautiful wench like you. There be other ways of payin' than money, eh?"

"Please take my money, Sir, and bring me some supper too."

Noreen strove to copy the way she'd heard Frances talking on board ship, before she took ill, but the bartender just grinned lewdly at her.

"I know 'zactly which one's your room, Miss Uppity-Nose-in-the-Air." He leaned closer, put his hand on her arm and winked conspiratorially. His touch was loathesome, and Noreen jerked away from him.

"Go away."

"You lissen here, young jade, and lissen good. I know your type. So don't go putting on airs with me." Again he leaned across her but, as he did so, another hand grabbed hold of the back of his shirt and hauled him to an upright position.

"The lady has made it clear that she doesn't care for your attention, George." The voice was a low drawl and sounded like molasses syrup to Noreen.

"I'm sure you must have lots of work waiting for you at the bar, isn't that right, George?"

"Yessir." The bartender looked suddenly weaker and smaller.

He turned away, nodding and bobbing his head as he retreated.

"Allow me to introduce myself, Miss. Beaufort Powell." As he spun out his name, he bowed to Noreen, his broad-brimmed hat in hand, his jet locks springing like coils about his ears. "And you, my lovely?"

His shadow, magnified on the wall by the candlelight, caused the girl to start. "Noreen – Noreen Callaghan." She hadn't meant to tell him, but he was so handsome, so debonair. Careful, girl, she said to herself. This man could spell trouble.

"I don't believe I've seen you around here before," he continued, drawing up a chair and seating himself beside her.

"No." Noreen glanced at him, hesitating. "I've just arrived."

He grinned. "Right off the boat, are you?"

"Yes, I am, as a matter of fact."

"Where are you headed, Miss? If you don't mind my asking."

"Oh, I'm going no further, Sir. As soon as Lieutenant Kingsley comes back from Toronto, I'll be serving as nursemaid to his daughters."

"Daughters? Is that so? And where would these daughters be now? And how old are they?"

"They're only babies. You ask a lot of questions – for a gentleman, Sir."

"Well, Mistress Callaghan, I find I've taken a sudden compelling interest in your welfare, shall we say?" Beaufort Powell signalled for refills and, when the bartender drew near, he was ordered to serve supper for two in a separate room.

"Oh no, Mr. Powell, I mustn't. My place is with my charges. They was sleepin' peaceful-like when I left, the poor babies, but I must get back."

"We'll look in on them when we go to supper and then, later you can return to them. Surely your employer doesn't expect you to be in constant attendance on the babes, a young beauty like you. There'll be time enough when you've grown old and haggard to tend to children."

Noreen, somewhat befuddled by the heat and the unaccustomed local brew, which tasted stronger than the ale she remembered back home, allowed herself to be led by the gentleman to a deserted back room. First, however, he obliged her with a visit to her upstairs bedroom. Darra and Catherine were sleeping peacefully, their tiny fists clenched, their rosebud mouths breathing in unison. Noreen, her maternal instincts rising in her chest, experienced momentary twinges of guilt. Why had she pretended that both babies belong to the Kingsleys? It was impossible, as anyone could tell at a glance; Catherine, so fair, her skin like white rose petals, Darra, a tiny replica of her wild Irish-rose mother.

Seated across from each other at a rough-hewn table, Beaufort toasted his companion with yet another glass of ale. Supper consisted of an unusual game pie and Noreen ate heartily. She didn't bother to inquire about the ingredients and was quite unaware of the huge bounty of partridge in the wooded areas around Kingston. When they had finished eating, the handsome gentleman from Louisiana suggested a walk.

"It's a lovely moonlit night," he said, and his slow drawl was persuasive.

"I really ought to get back to my room," she demurred.

"Five minutes. A brisk stroll beneath heaven's stairway to the stars."

Noreen sighed and drew her shawl tightly around her shoulders. She thought his words romantic and seductive. They kindled a warm fire within her Irish heart.

The air was cold outside and they found it necessary to set a brisk pace. They headed towards the dark ribbon of the St Lawrence River. The wind had died down and the night was still.

"'Tis a beautiful land, to be sure," she said softly.

"You're a beautiful woman, honey chile." Beaufort put his arm across her shoulders in a more than friendly gesture. Noreen found herself unwilling to draw away. The voyage had been long and lonely. At last she had found a friend.

"Yes, the land is wondrous. There's so much more of it to be seen too. If you think this is beautiful, wait till you see the Mississippi. Yes, that's where I earn my living, on the Mississippi paddle-boats – and that's where I'm returning in just a few days."

He turned her to face him, fondled a ringlet in his hand, then drew her closer. She meant to protest but, when his demanding lips pressed themselves on her soft parted ones, she lost all sense of time and place. The world swirled about her. She responded with evident desire and he wrapped his arms around her body as though to unite them on the spot.

"Noreen, oh Noreen! My heart of hearts, come to me." He began to kiss her with more urgency. "Come, let us go to my room."

No one saw the pair re-enter the hotel and move along the hallway to Beaufort Powell's room except the bartender. His cruel little eyes took in the picture of them, arm-in-arm, and he tried to think what use he could make of this information. Noreen, however, was oblivious of all but the temptations offered by her virile cavalier.

Once inside the door, Beaufort carefully removed the shawl from Noreen's shoulders. Her frock had long sleeves, a high ruffled neckline and a seemingly endless row of tiny pearl buttons. Some men might have been daunted, but not Beaufort. He was skilled in the art of love-making and he was a hedonist, unusual in his knowledge of how to prolong the moment of surrender. Leading her towards the edge of the bed, he stroked her arms and shoulders, kissed the tips of her fingers, her earlobes, the corners of her eyes and lips, and only then did he allow himself to sink once again into the sweet moistness of her mouth.

When Beaufort had finished undoing the buttons from neck to waist, twenty-eight in all, he eased the gingham folds away from her arms. Noreen felt her whole body stiffen as the tension mounted. She moved towards him, placing both hands on his broad chest.

"Stop a moment," he murmured, his voice low. "Let me look at you."

As soon as she spoke, Noreen grew apprehensive. Conscious of the scars on her shoulders, she instinctively crossed her arms over her melon-shaped breasts. Moments later, Beaufort eased her onto the bed gently, pulling her on top of him, thus surprising Noreen, but she had no time for further thought. Finally, sated and exhausted, their bodies surrendered to the inevitable climax of perfect passion spent.

"Come with me to Louisiana, dear heart," he whispered.

"Yes, oh yes, Beau. I love you. I'd follow you to the ends of the earth. Don't ever leave me."

In the cold morning light, back in her own room, Noreen, huddled beneath the blankets, examined her night of seduction and surrender dispassionately. She knew she couldn't accompany Beau to Louisiana. It was impossible. She had sole responsibility for two small babies, and one was her own daughter. No. Wait a minute. No, it wasn't true. She remembered suddenly the easy falsehood of the previous evening.

The babies belonged to Lieutenant Kingsley. Twin daughters! Who would know? Frances was dead or dying back on Grosse Ile. Communication was notoriously bad between the old country and the new world. If Lieutenant Kingsley was presented with two daughters instead of one, he'd accept them. So what if they didn't look alike. It didn't matter, did it?

That evening, when Beaufort knocked lightly on her door, she raced to admit him. Inside, he wrapped her once more in his arms, covering her face with hot kisses and little sensual tongue licks. Noreen met him with unrestrained spontaneity. The blood boiled within her and she renewed her promise to go away with him.

"Now, dear heart, we must make plans for our travels. Tomorrow evening's game should bring in enough profits for us to make our departure."

"Game? What are you talking about, Beau?" She wished he hadn't taken his arms away. His strong masculinity made her feel protected, secure in their love.

"Why, Noreen, I thought you knew. I'm a gambler. I earn my living by making wagers, taking bets . . ."

"You mean at the races? Do you bet on the horses?" She thought immediately of the master of Castle-Blaine. He raised thoroughbreds, champions of the race-track.

"Well, occasionally. There aren't enough races over here yet to take advantage of alone. No, I play cards; poker, five card stud, any game that hands me a chicken ripe for plucking." Beau's teeth flashed merrily.

"Surely you couldn't possibly earn enough to live on by just playing cards, could you?"

"Depends on the stakes, dear heart." Beau chuckled deep in his throat. "I don't suppose you have any money, have you?"

"Well, no, none of my own, that is." She hesitated. Noreen was in love and wanted to do everything for this wonderful man who had stolen her heart. "Mrs Kingsley gave me some money to look after the babies . . ."

"Where is it?" Beaufort's tone had altered, but Noreen did not notice. She moved to the bed, lifted the mattress and withdrew the dark blue money belt. He took it out of her hands impatiently and began searching inside its hidden pockets. Gold coins, sovereigns and guineas cascaded onto the bed and, as quickly as they dropped, Beaufort shoved them into his pockets.

"No, no!" Tears glistened on Noreen's eyelids. "You mustn't! That money belongs to Catherine and Darra. Please!"

She flung herself towards him and tried to wrest the money belt from his hands, but he merely shoved her aside with indifference.

"It's alright, dear heart. Don't cry. I'll return every sovereign, every farthing, every penny. I promise you and more! I'll multiply what is here by two." He took her in his arms, held her close and buried his lips in her sungold hair. Noreen relaxed, eager to believe him.

"You promise?" she whispered.

"Of course," and drawing back, he stared straight into her sea-green eyes. "You know I wouldn't lie to you. Two days. Give me only two days and I'll double your money."

After he had left, Noreen stood in the middle of the room holding the velvet belt. The gold-embroidered letters stared at her accusingly. She searched its pockets, discovering one gold coin, inexplicably caught in a tight corner. When she moved to the bed, another, which Beau must have missed, flickered like a lone star in the candlelight. Noreen gathered both coins and secreted them inside her bodice. The cold metal quickly warmed to the heat of her flesh.

That night Noreen paced the length and breadth of her room for uncounted hours, hoping against hope for a visit from her lover. He never returned. Frustrated and frightened, she crept beneath the covers and slept fitfully. Darra wakened her at dawn with whimpering cries and Noreen picked her up quickly, praying that Catherine would continue to sleep. After a brief period of restless movement, the fair-haired baby drifted off again and Noreen turned her whole attention to her own daughter.

"It's not as though I want to desert you, baby Darra," she crooned, rubbing her cheek against the downy baby skin, "but Lieutenant Kingsley is a man of means. He'll be able to do much more for you than I ever could. You'll understand later and you'll thank me."

Darra threw her head back, waved her seashell-like fists in the air, striking her mother's chin a glancing blow as she did so, and uttered a musical scale of coos and oohs. She was a lively baby, quick to respond and had been "talking" to her mother for several weeks now. Noreen, knowing how responsive the baby was to songs, began to hum and sing an ancient lullaby she recalled from her own childhood.

Sho-heen, sholyoh, the soft shades are creeping,
Sho-heen, my heart's love, the angels are near.
Sho-heen, sholyoh, my darling is sleeping,
Marie's macushla, while Mother is near.

Beaufort didn't return for two days. Noreen was frantic. She vacillated between the extremes of hope and despair. He'd left her and was never coming back! He'd had an accident and was lying in a ditch somewhere, dead! He'd doubled the money and was making arrangements for them to travel south in a private carriage! He'd decided to keep the money and go to Louisiana alone!

What worried her most was how she would explain to Lieutenant Kingsley about the missing money. He'd be sure to know that Frances would pay handsomely to anyone willing to deliver his daughter to Kingston. Briefly, she wondered what had happened to Lieutenant Kingsley. Surely his work was finished by now and he was on his way?

It was that eerie time when the sky is neither dark nor light, a time when night blends into day and day into night. Noreen dozed restlessly and, when she heard a tapping on her bedroom door, she couldn't determine at first if she was still in a dream or awake. Since it continued unabated, she rose and, pulling a shawl around her, drew the bolt and opened the door a crack. The bartender stood before her. Instinctively, she recoiled.

"So, jade, you've not flown the coop yet, I see!"

"Ssssh! The babies are sleeping."

"Then, you'd best step outside – if you don't want to cause a ruckus."

Noreen, confused, glanced back at the babes, stepped into the gloom of the hallway and closed the door. The bartender leered at her unpleasantly.

"What is it? Please speak up and be brief." Again, Noreen tried to imitate Frances' imperious tones, hoping that George would be fooled. "You have no right to waken me in the middle of the night."

"It's morning. Here night's over at first light. I've come about the account. It's time you paid somethin' on it. Can't afford to keep you here for free, you know."

"When Lieutenant Kingsley arrives, your account will be paid in full." As Noreen spoke, she prayed for deliverance.

The bartender took a step closer. Noreen backed against the wall. Looking first left, then right, and satisfying himself that no one was stirring, he deliberately stretched his arm forward and, in one deft movement, loosened the shawl that Noreen held clasped in one hand. Before she could recover or cry out, he, as swiftly, yanked at her gown and, as the material ripped, one shoulder and breast tumbled forth. The bartender gave a lusty growl in the back of his throat and lunged with hands and mouth together towards the tasty morsel. Noreen, infuriated at the rude impudence of this filthy pig, raised her knee abruptly to collide with his jaw. A loud crunching crack could be heard in the silence of the hallway. The stunned man sank to his knees, cradling his chin. Blood poured forth from his mouth and, in a daze, Noreen noted that she had knocked out two of his teeth.

She moved swiftly in the minutes that followed, gathering her shawl and reaching for the doorhandle all at the same time. As she moved, George grabbed at her fleeing feet and managed to catch hold of her ankle, but only for a moment. Noreen was thoroughly enraged by now and, at his touch, she kicked out viciously, this time catching him on the bridge of his nose. He yelled and Noreen, like a lioness protecting her cubs, turned with teeth bared, eyes glinting gold and emerald in the half-light.

It was at this precise moment that Beaufort Powell reappeared. Taking in the scene at a glance, he rushed to her side, opened her door and shoved her inside.

"Heart of my heart, what a marvel you are!" and, just as swiftly, "Get dressed as fast as you can and let's get out of here. There'll be trouble over this. Mark my words."

Noreen said nothing, simply obeyed. Dashing water in her face from last night's washbasin and trying unsuccessfully to calm her laboured breathing, she threw on her clothes and crammed the torn nightdress, the money belt, and any other possessions not already packed, into her knapsack. Fastening her shawl with a magnificent onyx brooch she had earlier unearthed from Frances' jewelry case, she bundled the babies tightly into their patchwork quilt and turned towards the doorway.

"Leave the babies, Noreen! It's too late. They're sure to be cared for." Beaufort tried unsuccessfully to wrestle the bundle from her arms.

"No." Noreen stood adamant, her feet planted firmly on the floor. "I promised I'd deliver them to Lieutenant Kingsley, and I'll not be breaking my promise." At that moment, both babies began to howl in unison.

Beaufort looked at her, thinking how she resembled a vixen caught in a trap. He was unhappily aware that nothing he might say would cause her to change her mind; not at this moment, at any rate, and the babies would soon waken the entire inn.

"Come," he said, his voice low and urgent. "We'd best be moving. It's growing lighter by the moment, and for God's sake, hush those brats."

She followed, her babies clutched close to her bosom. She did not even deign to look down on the unconscious bartender. Quickly Beaufort got all three seated in a carriage with two horses which stood waiting outside the hotel.

"St Joseph's," he instructed the driver.

Noreen was still attempting to regain her composure, but she was at the same time very much aware of their danger and the unvoiced threat looming over the young infants who were her responsibility.

"Beau, tell me where we're going – and where's my money? All that money you went off with, to turn into double the amount that was there! That money belongs to Lieutenant Kingsley, you know – and don't you dare to forget it."

"Now, now, dear heart, calm yourself." He reached over to chuck her under the chin with his finger, but she angrily turned aside. Her eyes flashed like lightning. The Callaghan temper trembled on the edge of explosion.

Beau instantly changed tactics.

"Alright, Noreen. I can see I'd best level with you. The money's gone." Noreen's head jerked up. Her eyes changed from lightning to flame. "No point in getting yourself all riled up about it. I gambled with the money and I won, but then unfortunately, I was called for cheating and barely escaped with my life. Now there's no way you can go back. Be a smart girl. You know it as well as I do. I have some money, just enough to get us to the Hudson. Once we're in New York, I have friends and – then, we'll mosey on down to Louisiana."

Once Noreen learned of the loss of the Kingsley money, the fire went out of her. She knew about gambling. Those who were stricken with the disease were incurable. She'd seen enough in Ireland to know the facts. It was men who were the optimistic dreamers. Women were the practical ones. Her granny always said so, and she was right.

"What about Darra and Catherine?" she asked, brushing her lips against their dewy foreheads. Penniless, how much longer could she care for the babes?

"That's why we're going to St Joseph's. It's a fine upstanding parish. Father Andrew and his sisters, I'm afraid I don't remember their names offhand but their reputation is spotless. They run a small orphanage along with the church services in the parish. The babies will receive a good Christian upbringing."

"But Beau, what about Lieutenant Kingsley? After all, they're his daughters."

"Don't try to put that one over on me, dear heart. I'm not that gullible. One look at you beside that babe you call Darra ..." He laughed. "She's the spittin' image of you."

"Lieutenant Kingsley was going to hire me as the babies' nurse. Frances promised, that's his wife, but she got the cholera. The medical officers took her off the boat at Grosse Ile. She's sure to have died in quarantine. Those fever hospitals are dreadful."

"Not necessarily. She could have even recovered by now. Look here, my sweet love, I've got it all worked out. We leave the girls at St Joseph's, all wrapped up warm and snug in that quilt. The good sisters will care for them and, when Ed Kingsley comes home, he'll be able to collect them and – and when his wife gets better, she'll join him and your Darra will have a fine home, one far finer than you could ever provide. Isn't that the truth?"

Noreen was looking doubtful. Beaufort moved closer, sought her lips with his and, as his pointed tongue darted about inside her acquiescent mouth, she experienced yet again that exquisitely painful lurch which rapidly spread like molten wax through her loins and lower body.

"We must leave their names attached to the quilt," she whispered weakly.

"Of course, dear heart. Trust me."

The hour for breaking bread in the rectory had passed. The sisters had just completed their morning prayers with Father Andrew and the supervision of their orphan charges at breakfast. They were engaged in the removal of the dishes from the long wooden dining table to the pantry when strange cries began reaching their ears.

"Did you hear that, Sister? It sounds like a small animal."

"Or a baby."

"Oh dear! Is it possible? Whatever will Father Andrew say?"

"Never mind about that. Come, let us investigate."

Moments later, the two young sisters, clad in their dark convent garb, came upon a jewel-toned patchwork quilt with not one, but two babies who were screaming lustily for attention. The women stopped simultaneously, each plucking from the quilt's down-filled warmth a sobbing girl-child.

"Gracious Mary, Mother of God, bless this Thy child," said the older one and she drew the sign of the cross in the air.

"Thank you, Lord," said the other, kneeling on the hard ground, the babe held close to her starched habit.

"Blessed infant, may the light of the Lord Jesus Christ shine down upon thee and give thee His peace now and forever more."

"Oh Sister, look. It's a note." Once again she knelt and lifted the stained piece of parchment to the light.

"CATHERINE and DARRA," she read, "Oh dear, and no last name. What a shame!"

"How will we know which is which, do you suppose?"

"We'd best take them indoors and sort out their names later."

"Yes Sister, as usual, you're right." She leaned over to pick up the quilt and, as she did so, there was a flash of brightness.

"What's that?" Leaning over to retrieve what appeared to be a gold coin, she noted a second one and a child's gold bracelet fashioned in a circlet of tiny hearts, each with a different jewelled eye in its centre.

"Whatever will Father Andrew say?"

"Never mind about that. Leave it to me."

The sisters, each carrying one baby, walked quietly towards the kitchen door, and entered within.

1

25 November, 1849

Today is St Catherine's day, my Saint's day. It is also the day on which I turn fifteen. St Joseph's Orphanage lets us honour our special feast days and Sister Martha has released me from my usual chores. I had planned to go into the fields with my sister, Darra, and perhaps we would have slipped into the town, pretending to have some important errand to perform for Sister Isobel. It was obvious, however, first thing this morning, that Darra was in one of her contrary moods.

My sister, Darra, is also fifteen. She is very beautiful with curly reddish hair which she is forever twirling round her head in new styles when the sisters aren't looking. Today it was Darra's turn to illustrate the lesson of the day. We were reading about one of my favourite saints, St Francis of Asissi. Sister Martha was drowsing in the corner as I read aloud from *The Children's Book of Saints*. I wondered if I'd have the courage to leave my wealth and safety as St Francis did and I envied him his animal friends. Animals are put to a strictly practical use at the convent. Darra and I long to have a kitten, but all the cats must live in the barn. Sister Isobel is convinced that a kitten would bring fleas into the orphanage. As I read, I imagined myself surrounded by rabbits, foxes and wolves, while birds hopped confidently onto my shoulder. Darra was being unusually quiet. I had no idea what she was doing until Sister Martha suddenly woke up and, leaning over Darra's shoulder, exclaimed in annoyance.

"Darra! What do you think you are doing? You really can be very foolish and disrespectful."

Darra's eyes glinted and I glanced warningly at her. Sister Martha looked again at Darra's drawing and I thought I saw a glimmer of amusement, but it was followed immediately with great severity and a serious countenance.

"Darra, I am sorry to have to punish you on Catherine's Saint's day, but you really must grow up and take things more seriously. Go to the chapel, get on your knees and recite Hail Mary twenty times. After that, you can meditate on your mischief."

I sighed, hoping that Darra would go quietly without the pout which sometimes gets her into further trouble.

"Catherine dear," added Sister Martha, "why don't you go and write your first entry in your journal?"

The sisters had given me a large lilac-coloured diary for my feast day that very morning. Sister Isobel had instructed me, saying:

"It will be good practice for you to become accustomed to organizing your life. Many a wife has been thankful to be able to ascertain household costs and events by references to her records; you, my dear, may also keep note of your spiritual progress. It will soon be time for you to go out into the world and you must never bring disgrace on those who have given you a home. Now that you are fifteen and a woman, you must begin to think more seriously about these things."

"Thank you, Sister Isobel." I turned the creamy pages with delight. I've always loved books, even as a small child poring over the pictures of the saints and struggling to read the words. As soon as I had mastered the art of writing, I wrote down the stories Darra and I made up together when we were playing. Darra was fascinated by a huge volume, concerning the reign of our blessed Queen Victoria, which lies on a small table in the drawing-room. We always had to ask permission to look at it and together would whisper in admiration and surprise.

"I'm going to be an actress when I grow up. I'll perform in Queen Victoria's court," Darra announced on one occasion. She envied the freedom and luxury we had glimpsed beyond the walls of our experience, but we had long learned to hide our interest from all but each other. Although kind enough in attitude to us, the orphanage is strict and practical in planning for our future.

Darra and I consider ourselves twins, but in fact we are probably not related at all. My earliest memory is of Darra clinging to my skirts and screaming.

"Want to go with Cat, want to go with Cat." In the meanwhile, Sister Martha, red-faced and angry, tried to drag her up the stairs to the small room which we share. It has always been that way. We have eaten together, played together, studied together and slept together, huddled close for warmth and comfort. We were even found together, two small babies wrapped in a large patchwork quilt. The sisters heard us protesting our uncomfortable bed beneath a bush by the front gate. They carried us into the warm kitchen where they placed us ceremoniously on the long rough wooden table, the same one where today we help prepare our meals.

Sister Martha has told us over and over how the children crowded around, curious and delighted with the change in their routine. We were both fair-skinned. Darra was already crowned with a mass of copper curls, but I had only strands of straight honey-coloured hair which to this day falls in a sheet, resisting any curl. Darra's eyes had lit with smiles as soon as she noted the audience gathered around, so Sister Martha said, but I had gazed at them solemnly, blue eyed, considering the situation.

"Two dear little babies," Sister Martha used to say, "who should now be growing into two respectable young ladies."

"Where did we come from? Didn't you find out anything?" We used to wonder a great deal about this but the sisters either couldn't or wouldn't tell us more. Of recent years we have ceased to ask questions and have our own private ideas as to our births. For myself, I imagine a mother who is soft and kind, while behind her stands a dashing man, moustached and very proud of the baby in his wife's arms. This happy image, I must admit, is based on a picture which I have seen in St Joseph's Rectory. When I was still a child, I grew into the habit of whispering 'Good morning' or 'Goodbye, dear Papa and Mama,' each and every time I passed by. Now, of course, I am more sensible but I think that I still hold the same image in my heart. Darra, who is so easily carried away by the romantic, has a very different dream.

"If we are sisters, we must have the same parents," I remember telling her when we were about six years old.

"That is not my parents in the picture but you are my sister always. My Mama is like Queen Victoria." Darra used to scream

3

this at me. Now we laugh together about those dreams and it seems certain that we will never know the truth. Perhaps I can confide to the pages of this journal that we are now thinking more about our future and that any security in the future seems to include marriage. Darra and I have wondered endlessly who would come forward for our hands and how, separated, we would fare in the world.

I am afraid of leaving the orphanage and of assuming all the duties of a wife, but I have to agree with Darra that I do not have a strong enough vocation to give up all my chances of seeing the world. Father Andrew has often impressed on us the joys that sacrifice would bring, but Sister Isobel, who usually follows her brother's lead, has resisted adamantly any undue pressure on her charges.

"The Lord calls on each to do his duty in his own way," she has always maintained.

I hope that my way lies out in the world and will one day lead me to my earthly parents. It is my intention to record everything that is significant in my journal, partly for my own enjoyment but also for Darra, that we may not be divided in thought.

2

March, 1850

Hail Mary, full of grace, pray for us sinners now and at the hour of our death. Hail Mary, full of grace, pray for us sinners now and at the hour of our death. Sixteen. Hail Mary ... only four more to go. Sister Isobel is such an old stick. She always gives me twenty Hail Marys for my punishment. I'd have thought she'd be tired of the whole idea by now. I'm just not designed to be a saint. Hail Mary, full of grace. Oh, how I hate this life, hate, hate, hate! Cat thinks I'm only playing another game when I say I'm going to run away, but she's wrong. I'm going the minute I can plan a way to do it. I have to decide where I'm going, though. After all, there's no sense in leaving if I haven't a plan. All we ever do here is pray, pray, pray, kneel, kneel, kneel. When we're not kneeling for prayers, we're kneeling to scrub floors! The floors here are cleaner than anything else in the place. Hail Mary, full of grace ... nineteen. The moment my sixteenth birthday comes round I'll leave, even if I haven't a plan. Father Andrew keeps telling us we can stay and take orders but even Cat, who likes to please everybody, resists. The sisters are always praising Cat. She's so sweet-natured, so obedient. Obedience is Sister Martha's most important rule. Obedience to God, obedience to the church, obedience to Father Andrew. Hail Mary, Mother of God ... no no. Hail Mary, full of grace ... twenty. There, I've finished. These beads are pretty. I remember the year Sister Isobel gave them to me for Christmas. I was surprised and almost believed she must love me just a little bit, but I overheard her tell Sister Martha that she gave them to me because she thought if I had prayer beads it'd be easier for me to stop fidgeting during prayers! She said it worked with the Indians sometimes, so why wouldn't it work with me? Sister Isobel keeps warning me about being Irish. She thinks the Irish have a lot in common with the natives. Maybe she's right, that I'm Irish, I mean. After all, I do have red hair and a temper, and the sisters have decided that I can't help myself. Sister Isobel said I should meditate after I finished my Hail Marys. I love this little chapel, the bright stained glass windows, the exquisite needlework on the altar and the prayer stools, and the statue of the Virgin with Jesus. Meditating here is far better than scrubbing the kitchen floor again. Sister Isobel said I should try thinking devotional thoughts instead of conjuring up mischief all the time. These prayer beads, green and amber with a little silver cross at the end, I pretend they're emeralds and garnets instead of pieces of glass and that the cross is real silver. Of course it's not nearly so fine a cross as my own, the gold one I wear all the time with DARRA engraved on it. I was wearing it when the sisters found Cat and me by the garden gate. When I grew bigger and the chain was too short, Sister Martha suggested I put the cross away till I had grown up. I cried and cried and stamped my feet and refused to give up my cross. After all, it's the only thing I have that's my very own, really my own, that is. The result of my wilfulness was another twenty Hail Marys. All I want is to go out into the world and be someone important. The day I told Sister Martha I wanted to be an actress, I thought she'd faint. "Darra my dear," she said, "you are too well brought up to entertain any ideas of entering the theatre." She said the word theatre as if it represented the fires of hell. I don't understand why. As a matter of fact, I think actors and the visiting priests at St Joseph's have a lot in common! The actors get up on a stage and play parts and the priests get up at the front of the church, dressed up in their gorgeous gold-embroidered robes. They drone on in Latin. Last Easter, when the bishop visited us, he was all decked out, just like the pictures I've seen of some of The Shakespearian actors. It was marvellous. I told Cat, how I enjoy the drama of the church ceremonies. Right away, she said, "Don't say that to Sister, Darra," and she made me promise. As if I'd say such a thing to Sister! I told her I thought the bishop used make up too. I'd love to do that. She refused to listen to that sort of blasphemy, but he did. He had rouge on his cheeks and a spot of lipstick too. He probably gets very hot with all those heavy robes hanging on him. I hate kissing his horny old hand. It smells of dead leaves and spirits. He wears a magnificent ring though. It's gold with a huge red stone in it. It must be a ruby.

I wish I had a ring like that. It shines like the ruby glass collection on display in Henderson's goods store. Somebody bought that mighty quick. There's such a shortage of beautiful household goods in Upper Canada. If I ever marry, and I'm sure I will, I'll marry a rich man, one who will cover me in jewels and let me order silks and satins for my frocks. We'll have the grandest balls in the city, our dishes will be bone china from England and our cutlery real silver. The furniture will be brought over from the old country too and I'll have lots of maids to polish the rosewood and mahogany. I'm not going to marry until I've had my career in the theatre. I must be an actress. It's in my blood. If I ever find out who my parents are, one is sure to be a famous stage professional. I didn't dare tell Cat the first time I sneaked into town to Butler's Theatre to watch the acting. I've never seen a live performance, but I have watched actors rehearsing. It's so exciting. I heard one of them say that to work so hard in this rathole, you have to be born with the smell of greasepaint in your soul! I wasn't sure what he meant. I'd go to the ends of the earth if only I could act on the stage, even if it was only in a simple town hall.

Someday I'm going to New York. That's where the real theatre is. There's a famous actor coming here next week. I saw the pictures outside the hall when Cat and I were in town. His name is Trevor Vaughn. Oh, he's so handsome! He has black curly hair and a beard. And his eyes! How I yearn to meet such a man. If the truth be known, I simply yearn to know men.

I confessed as much to Cat about a year ago, after I disobeyed the sisters and went down to the barnyard to see the new litter of kittens born to Tassy. She's the prettiest barn cat with her long bluish-grey fur, her little white boots and the white rings around her yellow-green eyes. I was wondering who the father might be. There's only one Tom who lives around here but we've heard it said that Toms will travel for miles to find a female in heat. For years I used to wonder what that meant – being in heat. I said to Cat I thought it had something to do with making kittens or making any kind of baby animals, for that matter.

We'd all known for days that Tassy's time had come and I overheard Father Andrew tell his sisters that this time they'd have to be strong and destroy the latest litter, but Sister Martha spoke right up to him. "Murder would be against the Lord's holy commandments, Father Andrew," she said. So I knew that Father Andrew would be approaching the parishioners soon and looking for homes for the kittens. I longed to see them and I managed to steal away after matins. We were supposed to be studying and attending to our devotions. Once inside the stable I paused, listening to the snorting and stamping of Father Andrew's two carriage horses. I didn't have to search long before I found Tassy's kittens. I could hear their faint mewling cries. I dropped to my knees beside them, content to remain there and watch the little furry bodies nuzzle at their mother's teats.

I sensed rather than heard Burt, the stable hand. He's a young lad of about eighteen. He has corn-yellow hair and huge hands. "Evenin' Darra," he said, and I replied "Evenin' Burt," politely. He crouched down beside me and the closeness of his body to mine made me shiver, not in an unpleasant way, but in a way I couldn't understand. "How old are the kittens?" I asked. When he answered me, he put his hand on my shoulder. I started to pull away but he took hold of me with both hands and forced my body up against his own. For a few moments, my curiosity won out and I decided to allow Burt to kiss me, something I had never experienced. His whole mouth covered mine and I didn't like it a bit. His chin felt bristly and it scratched me – and he teased my mouth with his tongue. I couldn't decide whether to pull away and leave or to stay a little longer and see what would happen. I tried to loosen his grip but this only served to make him rougher. He pushed me slowly but relentlessly against the wooden wall of the empty stall. For a moment I thought it exciting, but then I realized what he was doing, and I felt embarrassed and ashamed. I began to struggle in earnest but my protests and my fighting back provoked Burt even more and, before I knew what was happening, he was lying on top of me and I could feel a hardness pressing against me. All of a sudden, I began to understand. I lashed out with both fists and fought so hard that Burt eased up on the attack. "Stop! Stop right this minute." I whispered in a choked voice, "or I promise I'll tell Father Andrew and the sisters." I knew I wouldn't. I'd never be brave enough, but Burt didn't know that. "Ah, Darra, you'd like it," he said. "I know you would, you're a woman now, Darra."

At that moment, we both heard the stable door creak. Burt leaped off me and pushed me into a dark corner where I was hidden from view. I watched Burt through a hollowed knothole in the wall as he walked cautiously across the stable floor. Sighing with relief, I jumped to my feet and sped towards the door. Burt tried to grab my hand but I was too quick for him and he didn't dare follow me. As I ran back to the rectory, keeping myself hidden among the trees by the barn, I thought how lucky I'd been to escape so readily.

When I burst into our room, Cat stared at me. "What happened?" she asked. "Now I know what men do to women," I blurted out, but the look on Cat's face was so shocked I decided not to tell her anything until later. When the day's schoolwork was finished and our final prayers had been said, I lay stiffly between the sheets and recalled in detail all the things that Burt had done.

How strange it all was. God must mean us to feel this way for some reason. As I relived the barnyard scene, Burt turned magically into Trevor Vaughn. I thought about his black curly beard and how differently I'd have behaved had it been Trevor instead of Burt. It was a long time before I was able to settle down and go to sleep. My head was whirling, my thoughts in upheaval. Every time I allowed myself to think about what I had done, I felt guilty until I exchanged Burt's face for Trevor Vaughn's. When I did that, I no longer cared.

I still haven't decided how to get away to Butler's theatre, but I'll manage somehow. If only I could persuade Cat to come with me, but she doesn't care about the theatre at all.

Considering that Cat and I are sisters and the same age too, there are many things about us that are different. For instance, Cat likes needlework. I'm too impatient to sit still for such a long period of time. Cat doesn't like to read the scriptures aloud nor does she enjoy reciting Latin poetry, but I adore Ovid and I translate his poems in my own mind quite differently from Sister Isobel. Memory work has always come easily to me and, even when the sisters are exasperated with me, I can usually charm them out of a mood by reciting their favourite psalms. Cat heard Father Andrew tell Sister Martha that it's a pity I wasn't a boy. Apparently he thought I'd make an excellent priest or missionary! Well, I wouldn't want to be a priest. I think I enjoy being a woman, especially now I'm beginning to learn about the spells women can cast over men. I wonder if I've been meditating long enough to please Sister Isobel? If I don't move soon, my knees will break in two.

At this point, my reverie was rudely interrupted by the sound of footsteps and I returned to the present.

"Darra? Darra!" It was Cat, come to fetch me. I rose hastily from my long vigil on the prayer bench.

"I said all twenty of my Hail Marys." I announced with pride.

"Never mind about that," she interrupted me. I could tell by the sound of her voice that she was excited about something.

"Sister Martha says we're to come to the parlour right away. Father Andrew has something important to tell us. Ohhh, Darra, I think they're going to send us away. I don't know why, it's just a feeling I have."

"Well, we're approaching sixteen, Cat. It's bound to happen sooner or later. Goodness knows, Sister Isobel has said often enough that it's time we were in service or meeting suitable men to care for us in the sacrament of marriage. Do you want to be married, Cat? I'm not sure if I do or not. I think not yet. Oh, how will I ever become an actress if Father Andrew decides I should be married right away to some lout or other?"

"Come! Hurry! They're waiting and we'll never know if we stand around wondering what they are going to say."

Feeling a sudden premonition of hardship and separation from my sister, I stood up, ready to learn our fate. At the back of the tiny vestry, I paused once more and, feeling unaccountably lonely and sentimental about our spiritual home, I genuflected and drew the sign of the cross before me. Then, grasping Cat's hand, the two of us raced across the field as though we were children again. Outside the rectory, we paused, straightened our blowing hair and skirts and marched, eyes lowered in a docile manner, into the parlour where Father Andrew, Sister Isobel and Sister Martha waited to inform us of our destiny.

3

It is just a month since I left Kingston to join the Dunne family, and this is the first opportunity I've had to confide all my thoughts and emotions in my journal so that I may share them later with Darra. I have missed my sister sorely and seek to comfort myself by unburdening my heart in these pages.

My greatest hope is that she is well settled and happy in her new home. I can no longer say that I wish she were in service with me at Tudhope, for I would fear for her safety here, but more of that later. Let me first recall, step by step, the last month as it carried me into the depths, and it is the depths, of the Dunne family. I will begin on the fifteenth of April, as Father Andrew and the sisters at St Joseph's bade me goodbye and I rode off along King Street, passing the city hall on my way to the eastern lots.

Despite the tears Darra and I shed, I must admit to a great deal of excitement too. It was the first time I had ever been outside of Kingston. At last I need no longer follow the dictates of the orphanage and I am free to find the future that Darra and I have so often planned. The prospect of riding out of the city on that bright April morning and of seeing hills, lakes and valleys that were all new to me, lifted the pain in my heart. Indeed I think I would have forgotten the sorrow of our parting for a while had not a strange little incident occurred.

We were an ordinary enough sight at first. I, riding along docilely on the horse provided, and profoundly thankful that I would have this freedom. Next to me bumped and clattered the cart full of provisions. It was packed perilously high by the Dunne's hired man, Jed, and left no seat for me. Indeed, I would have looked a ridiculous sight had I been perched above the boxes, crates, bundles and bags which had been bought for the return to Tudhope. Even before we left the streets of Kingston I noticed the casual lashing of the goods and how Jed's garrulous good humour increased each time he lifted the flask from his pocket to his lips. I longed to question him about the home in which I was going to work, to ask him about the farm and the new life awaiting me. He paid little attention, however, to my words, to the horses, or to the goods swaying behind him. What is more, he began to sing, but it was no song that I've ever heard before and I was much embarrassed as people began to look at us and laugh.

"One night they went to bed together,
There they lay till cocks did crow,
Then they sport till daylight is breaking,
Now it's time for us to go."

"Sir," I began, hoping to distract him. At that moment, two officers from the fort rode towards us. A small dog ran out and began barking and yapping at my horse's heels. I pulled on the reins, but the silly little cur ran next at the cart. Jed, in full song, paid no attention. His horse reared, upset the cart and all the goods went flying over the road. My bundle containing our treasured patchwork quilt burst open on the ground. Confusion abounded. People appeared from everywhere; Jed lay on the blankets which fortunately had cushioned his fall, seemingly quite addle-pated and droning on.

"Up and down, up and down . . ."

I wished I could sink into the ground. Imagine my feelings on hearing peals of laughter! Looking up, I saw the two officers, serene and confident on their horses, surveying the assortment of pots, clothing, farm utensils and broken shards that adorned King Street. Quickly dismounting, I threw the reins at one of the officers.

"Must you laugh?" I berated him. "Can't you help me, Sir?"

I hastily ran to pick up my quilt, I can't explain the unusual rage I felt. There was a sudden silence and one of the officers got down from his mount. As I shook out the quilt and folded it over my arm, he approached me. I looked up, angry, shaken and now feeling the shock of the whole event. Hazel eyes, flecked with green, gazed into mine. I resented the suspicion of amusement that still lingered there, but I could not deny his charm. He was tall, lithe and easy in movement. His straight nose and firm mouth looked as if they had been chiselled from the granite which abounds in the area, but his hair was very curly. Something about the chestnut gleam made me think about Darra. My eyes filled with tears. It was unfortunate as it provoked further indignity.

"Don't cry, allanna, I liked you better when you scolded me," said the officer and kissed me full on the lips.

For a moment I stood there, dumbfounded. What would the sisters say? Obviously, they are correct in telling us there is no end to the wiles of men! I gathered myself up to reproach this man; I cannot call him a gentleman, because he used me so casually.

"Sir," I cried out, "I am no tinker! You're mistaken if you think you can treat me this way."

This brave statement was the less effective in that my limbs were shaking and strange shivers were running through me. With reddening face, I turned from him to regain my composure and then towards Jed, the cause of all the trouble. The unfortunate man was now sitting up regarding the scene around him with interest. Fearing that he might seek to gain further enlightenment from his flask, I urged him on.

"Pray do get up! With help from these good people we can surely repack our goods and be on our way."

At this point, my unusual Samaritan again joined in. "Old man, shame on you! Your poor daughter is trying to get you and your provisions back on the road and you lie there like a grand potato that's fallen out of the basket!"

Hard pressed not to laugh at this apt description of Jed, but furious at being taken for his daughter, I rounded on the officer again.

"Sir, it is most kind of you to concern yourself with my affairs but, doubtless, duty calls and it is time you returned to it. Jed here, who is no kith nor kin of mine, will soon be able to collect himself. I beg you not to delay on my account."

At this point, Jed arose, fortunately, and, brushing himself down, began swearing at the horse.

"Enough of that, man," said the officer, ignoring my dismissal. "Gather up those goods and I will teach you how to make a lashing that will stay in place."

Several spectators joined in and, more quickly than I had dared hope, all was soon back on the cart and most securely bound. Thanking those whose efforts had stirred Jed into action, I reluctantly turned to the officer.

"Indeed Sir, I must thank you for your assistance. We will now be on our way without further delay."

As he stepped towards me, I backed hastily, removing my horse's reins from the urchin who now held them. I was not quick enough. Taking my free hand, the officer held it a moment and searched my eyes with his. My composure fled. Nothing in the orphanage had prepared me for the emotions which suddenly overwhelmed me.

"Why, allanna, you are lovely," he murmured. "Will you not give me your name that I may hold it in my heart?"

I was silent and, before I could answer, the second officer spoke up.

"Cavan, for mercy's sake, will you stop plaguing that lass and let us be on our way. An act of charity need only take so long."

Laughing, Cavan answered, "I am coming." Then, leaning down, again he put his lips on mine. I did not, could not, resist. For a minute, his arms encircled me and then he swung me onto my horse.

"Till we meet again, allanna."

Leaping astride his mount, he and his companion rode off rapidly in the opposite direction, but not before I again heard the sound of their laughter.

I barely noticed the countryside during the next hour as we travelled eastwards along rapidly worsening roads. My mind was in a turmoil. We had small contact with boys or men at the orphanage and we had been well supervised during the times we met at church functions. In order that we might gain better positions, we had been educated as much as possible in all proprieties. I had accepted this régime far better than Darra who could not be blamed for her tendency to flirtatiousness. Her unusual charm, her natural liveliness of manner (unhappily referred to by the sisters as her Irish temper) and her lovely colouring attracted attention from early days. How could so affectionate a girl not respond to the sometimes unwise attentions given to her? I tried to discourage her excessive fancies and to argue that, by learning all the housewifely skills, she would find a good Christian husband. Now, however, I began to think there was more to Darra's fancies than I had realised.

Missing my sister and anxious to direct my thoughts to a more sensible course, I began to look around the countryside opening before me. The bright April sun was now high in the sky, warming me. I loosened the grey cloak which I had been given just before my departure. I promised myself that, when I received my first wages, I would buy some soft cloth of blue. Surely I would have the opportunity to return to Kingston and then I would observe the fashions and use my skills to cut and sew. I certainly didn't want anyone thinking I was a child of Jed's and I hoped I could dress the way I liked on my time off.

The road was rough, but I still rejoiced in my new freedom as we left the St Lawrence to the right of us and began to ascend a small hill. The cart was creaking alarmingly and Jed muttered to himself. Ahead of us, there appeared some buildings which gave hope of a farm and a store where we could stop to water the horses and buy ourselves a drink.

"Jed," I begged, "Let us break the journey for half an hour. I have need of a draught of milk and the horses will make better time for the rest."

"You'll have to wait, little mistress," he grunted in answer. "There's naught between here and Tudhope."

Opening my mouth to question him, I observed with surprise the ramshackle appearance of the farmhouse. The gardens, once lovingly laid out, were now overgrown and untended. Windows were broken and the barn door hung open. No human life or even animal life was evident. As we drew nearer, I could read the sign above the store. SMITH'S GENERAL PROVISIONS. The paint was chipped and again empty window frames stared at us in a state of neglect.

"What has happened? Where is everyone?" I demanded.

"Dead or gone." Jed relapsed into silence once more.

"Jed, please tell me. Was it the plague?" I shuddered. Three years before, Kingston had been hit with a widespread outbreak of typhus which had been brought in by the immigrants. Some 1400 deaths had occurred and Kingston had suffered greatly. Many children had been orphaned and St Joseph's had taken in as many as possible. Sister Isobel and Sister Martha, however, had always considered their girls a family and could not easily accommodate many more hungry mouths. Darra and I had been designated as older girls, in charge of the new and desolate influx. Fortunately Mother Bourbonnière opened the doors of Hôtel Dieu Hospital and we were able to transfer many of the destitute children Father Andrew had brought to his sisters' home. I had never thought that the illness could travel farther to the farmlands.

"Maybe 'twas the plague, maybe not," responded Jed. "Times has been very bad for the farmers with Britain turning her back on our wheat." He spat into the road. "Many-a-body has had to run afore the debt collector got there."

That sad prospect silenced me and we rode on without further conversation.

Not all farms were in the sorry state of the one that had attracted my attention. Accustomed as I was to the elegant and well-built houses of Kingston, I could still appreciate the love and care that had gone into the solid log homes of the settlers. As I gazed at the strong weathered walls, often surrounded by a verandah, and admired the small gardens filled with sprouting plants, I began to wonder about Tudhope.

I had been engaged to act as companion and help for Mrs Dunne, who was in poor health. Her husband had appealed to Father Andrew for a young woman who was a cut above the regular serving girl for, he said, his wife suffered sorely from homesickness. Her constant complaints of loneliness and boredom were contributing to her malaise. Father Andrew had chosen me for this position.

"Well, Catherine," he said, "perhaps your bookishness will now come in useful. Thanks to my sisters' good care, your manners are refined and you are well-skilled in all the household arts. Always do your duty, remembering that the Lord is your protector."

"He weighs you up as if you were a horse at the auction. 'Your bookishness will come in useful, your manners are refined, my dear,'" mimicked Darra rudely as soon as our good guardian had left the room. I had to laugh for somehow she could pout her mouth and peer forward, taking on a strong resemblance to the priest.

"As for myself," she added, "I certainly do not wish to be confined to a life in the bush acting as companion to some mopish woman."

"Quiet Darra, I am looking forward to meeting poor Mrs Dunne. Perhaps she is only needing some companionship such as we have always enjoyed with each other. I hope in time to become part of the family. Above all, I am longing to live and be away from charity."

Now, approaching Tudhope, I recalled our innocent conversation and, when Jed lifted his whip and pointed to the far right, saying, "There be Tudhope," my heart pounded with anticipation.

My first sight of the cabin was scarcely reassuring. The building was smaller than many we had passed. This I could willingly overlook, but my eyes were drawn to the neglected heaps of discards, offal and dirt that were scattered widely over the area. Remembering that Mrs Dunne was hardly in a position to supervise the exterior property and that her husband may have been compelled to tend her and the children, I withheld judgement. It was obvious that Jed required supervision. The land had been roughly cleared around the log frames and led to a shed at the right. A few pigs, a cow and several hens were wandering freely in the area, eating from the gardens and adding fresh droppings to the turds already underfoot. Not even the entrance to the front of the cabin had been cleared. As I stared at the unkempt lot, the door before us burst open and some four children rushed out.

"Look, look! The girl is come. Ain't her pretty? Jed, Jed, what did you buy in Kingston? Jed . . . pig got into the store and ate the potatoes. Lady, what's your name? Lady, Mama is sick but she says to come right in."

Dear Mother Mary in Heaven! I said to myself, Sister Martha

called Darra a little wild Indian, but I have never seen such unruly children.

At this point an older boy emerged and, cuffing one of the smaller ones, he set to unloading the cart. The cuff was received with an infuriated shriek and the younger child threw himself on the ground, making as much ado as Darra ever did. While I watched all this in consternation, a determined pull on my skirts drew my attention. Looking down, I saw a cherubic face, though grimed and dirty, beaming up at me. Big brown eyes peered through a mass of tangled brown curls and fat little hands grimly used my skirts as a lever.

"Cherry wants up. Cherry wants up." I gathered up the little thing and was almost suffocated by a pair of arms round my neck, my face moistened with sticky kisses.

"Gerry too, pick Gerry up now. Gerry wants up now." Unbelievable as it may seem, the same clamour began again and the same pulls restricted my free movements. Disentangling myself from Cherry's embrace, I looked down and saw her double at my feet.

"Gerry wants up now." The second child raised her voice even more emphatically.

At this, my armful opened her rosebud mouth and yelled, "No, pick Gerry up. My lady!" While my mind and body reeled under this assault, a new element was introduced.

A stentorian bellow came from the direction of the house and a short stocky figure emerged, crop in hand. Though walking with a pronounced limp, there was a ruthlessness about him that made all the children scatter. Sergeant Dunne, for it was he, cleared a pathway to the cart and, with a few shouted orders, directed the older children to their duties.

When he finally turned to me, he stared for a minute and said, "So you're the young miss they've sent to care for the missus. I hope you last a bit longer than the last one. Get in with you and Mrs Dunne will fix you up." He did not remove his gaze and a quiver of discomfort ran through me.

My body, so recently awakened by the touch of the lieutenant, was responding already to some instinct of self-preservation. There was a certain predatory feel to the man which I sensed but did not yet understand. Once Darra had run in from the stable, where we were not supposed to go without good reason, and had pulled me into the parlour. Her face was flushed and she seemed unusually elated.

"Cat, Cat," she had whispered, "I know what it is men do to women."

"Darra!" I was scandalized. Then my natural curiosity getting the better of my sense of propriety, I begged, "Tell me!"

"Tonight," she whispered back.

I didn't know how much of Darra's story was exaggerated, but I was much aware of the strange animal magnetism that flowed from her as she whispered her tale in my ear. Now I felt this force in the man before me but, where in Darra it had been untainted, here I sensed evil.

August 27, 1850

I begin to despair of ever finding the time to write in my journal. I am up with the hens in the morning, often after a restless night with little Cherry and Gerry who toss and turn in our bed beside me. The stove must be prepared for the day's baking and, if Jed has failed to bring kindling and logs to the kitchen, I must send young John to the woodpile. This young lad is a great joy to me. He will often lend a hand and spare me some heavy task, in pleasant contrast to his father who seems to delight in watching me struggle. John's sweet temper is also markedly different from that of Eddie, now eight years old and strongly resembling Sergeant Dunne in mood. James, Charlotte and the twins often feel their brother's blows and pinches.

I am proud of the changes to the interior of the cabin since my arrival, but it is a far cry from any building I entered in Kingston. I do believe it must be close in spirit to the log homes first built by the settlers, but lacking the improvements which care and hard work gain as their reward. The first floor has three rooms; a small parlour, a bedroom used by Mrs Dunne and a roomy kitchen with a windowless pantry which resembles a cupboard. I have a particular dislike for this pantry where the floorboards are uneven and, even carrying a lantern, it is easy to trip or stub a toe. At my urging, John and his father constructed shelves; the younger children and I then scrubbed vigorously until all was clean and ready to store our goods.

The open hearth and oven occupy one side of the kitchen and I am now gaining greater skills at using this monster. A clay chimney draws the smoke or, I should say, it usually does. When it billows through the house it causes Mrs Dunne to choke and wheeze, thus exaggerating her symptoms. I am filled with guilt on these occasions, though the dear soul never reproaches me. Indeed, if she would perhaps show less resignation to her lot, her weak constitution might receive some reinforcement.

"Madam," I ventured one day, "let me help you dress and you can enjoy the sun from the porch, and I'll brush out your hair so that you'll be pretty for your husband's return from the fields. We can occupy ourselves planning next season's garden and I will persuade the children to help me with the weeding."

"Catherine, if you knew what I do of marriage, you would not wish to doll me up and to encourage any matrimonial attentions." Tears and outrage shone in her eyes. "I wish I had never been persuaded to come here, had never married. Surely any trials a spinster faces must be mild compared to those duties the church imposes upon a wife."

I gazed at her in horror. What could I say? Unsure of the nature of the intimacies she described, I could yet imagine so close a proximity to Sergeant Dunne and it was distasteful to me. The man had never touched me but his eyes followed me constantly. He seemed to gain some perverted pleasure in watching me perform the lowliest of tasks about the house.

I remembered the time I was at the well. The children and I were drawing water. It was very hot that day and I was wearing a light but serviceable cotton frock. Darra had helped me make it before we went into service. It fitted to my waist trimly and included discreet frills unusual to a working frock. The soft pink blended with grey and, so Darra insisted, enhanced my fair colouring.

The Dunnes had received notice that the priest from the nearby parish was riding over to pay a duty call and Mrs Dunne had insisted that I receive him in her stead.

"I am not well enough to have to put myself out for Father Anselm," she complained. "It is not I who fail to pay the yearly tithe and it is no easy matter to make regular church attendance."

Uncertain as to the time of his arrival, I had cleaned the house, baked, and prepared myself for his arrival. Just as I counted myself ready, a great howl was heard and Cherry toddled into the house clasping one of our best layers to her small chest. The incensed fowl struggled wildly, squawking and screeching.

Cherry was weeping bitterly. "Bad, bad henny! Bad henny has eaten all Mama's seeds in the garden and henny dirty my frock."

"Oh dear," I exclaimed. "Who let henny out of her run?"

Since my arrival, we had fenced the hens and all the animals out of the front area. Hastily removing the clucking fowl from Cherry's embrace, I ran to the yard and restored the indignant hen to her roost. It was then necessary to scrub Cherry and this, in turn, meant a trip to the well to replenish the water I used to clean the soiled child.

Leaning over to lower the bucket, I became aware of being watched and turned abruptly to see who was there. It was Sergeant Dunne, his eyes glued to my breasts as I strained at the handle. He said nothing, but his gaze lifted without embarrassment to my face and moved to inspect my mouth and to stare into my eyes. His expression was morose and he lingered seemingly to no purpose. My innate distrust only deepened. Awareness of my body and of my vulnerability quickened and I hastened to dispel the mood.

"Oh mercy, Sir," I exclaimed, "you startled us. We're hurrying to prepare ourselves for Father Anselm. Come, Cherry, my sweet, let us run back quickly to Mama."

Since that day, I have been careful never to be alone with the sergeant. In daylight hours, I am always in the company of one or more of the children and in the evenings I seek refuge in the smallest of the three upper rooms which I share with Cherry and Gerry. There, I wrap myself in my patchwork quilt and dream. I dream of being back with Darra, of finding my lost family and sometimes of the lieutenant, Cavan.

Pulling myself back to the present, I stared helplessly at Mrs Dunne, not knowing how best to answer her unseemly confidences concerning her marriage.

"Oh, Madam," I stammered, "I'm sorry to hear you speak this way. Please God, with restored health you will be better able to reconcile yourself to your life."

Mrs Dunne sighed heavily and, pulling herself lower in her bed, asked me to draw her shades, which I did, whereupon she lapsed into a silence I was unwilling to disturb. Quietly, I left the room.

September 15, 1850

I am beginning to lose heart. It is now three months since I left Kingston and no word has come from my sister. I have sent letters with Jed, who swears that they have been delivered. I was comforted in receiving a sweet note from Sister Isobel who tells me that we are remembered daily in their prayers and that the younger children often ask for us. She added, "You will, of course, have had news of Darra who, please God, is happy in her new employ. We take comfort in knowing that she has been placed with a respectable and God-fearing family." How much more I need to know!

I long to consult with my sister. Her worldliness caused the dear sisters great anxiety but, without knowledge acquired by experience, I find myself on an unknown road without directions. There is no one to advise me nor to lift me from the low spirits in which I find myself. I have taken to walking in the woods behind the house where I delight in the autumn colours. There are dark pines, in stark contrast to the flaming tints of red, orange and yellow which adorn the glowing maples. Underneath, the tamaracks turn red, tawny and rust-coloured. I dread the winter when I shall be forced to stay closer to the house, to the constant tears of Mrs Dunne and to her fears. These will surely become worse as her husband perforce spends more time indoors.

I would ask my sister how is it that I shrink from Sergeant Dunne who seems to me to embody all the things that the sisters warned us about. Yet, when I think of Cavan, as I dare call him to myself, my heart softens and I wonder about his body. His lips on mine were so soft and yet, when he lifted me to my horse I felt his lean hardness. His certainty and strength comforted me. I have made up my mind that I will never engage in marriage unless I am certain that I shall be happy. I now understand that there is much we did not learn with the sisters.

September 30, 1850

I am crouched beneath my quilt still shivering and sickened. The morning light is just giving faint colour to the walls. I am writing that I may gain control of myself, that I may collect my thoughts and decide what to do. I can no longer stay here! It is painful to write, not only because my body is bruised, but also for the nausea that had me retching into the slop pail for an hour after I finally dragged myself up the stairs.

I had retired early last night as is my custom, having seen to Mrs Dunne and leaving her husband by the hearth. He usually works on the repair of his tools or plays tunes on his fiddle if his mood is favourable. Often he will drink from his flask and reminisce on earlier better days, blaming this one or that one for his wrongs. I fell asleep to the sound of the fiddle, thankful that the house would be the happier for his melodies. It was, therefore, with shock that I woke to the sounds of deep moans and sobs.

Throwing my robe around me, I ran from my room to the stairs and, looking down, I saw the sergeant bent over in his chair, weeping like a woman. My first thought was that there must be something amiss with Mrs Dunne. I ran down the stairs.

"Ah, dear Lord in Heaven," I implored. "What is it? Is it my mistress?"

He raised his head and looked at me with glazed eyes. In my sleepy state, I wondered if his wife was dead. Returning to her room, I saw she was sleeping peacefully. I closed her door and turned to the sergeant.

"For pity's sake, man," I begged him. "You will wake the children and your dear wife, who has need of her rest."

Still he stared at me, his eyes inflamed, unfocussed. I began to fear that he was ill. He rose uncertainly and moved towards me, his empty flask clattering to the floor.

"Ah, Catherine . . . you caaaan he-lp me . . ."

Thinking that he wanted assistance in reaching his room, I stood there, reluctant to touch him but feeling it my duty. He lurched forward quite suddenly and fell against me, causing me to lose my balance. We slipped to the floor and I struck my arm on the wooden bench which gave me great pain and weakened my efforts to protect myself. He lay, sprawled across me, suddenly ripping my gown and exposing my breasts. Twisting and turning within his grasp, I wrenched myself from him, my gown falling to my feet as I tried to escape. Undoing his belt, he lashed at my legs. Terrified, I screamed and ran for the stairs but, before I could make further headway, he tripped me and I sprawled on my face. He grabbed at me and, reacting unconsciously, I turned and raked his cheeks with my nails till the blood flowed. Aghast, I ran up the stairs to the safety of my room and fell shaking on the bed. Nausea welled up in my throat. At least he had made no further attempts to follow me. During the next minutes, as I lay exhausted on my bed, I vowed no man would ever touch me again.

Unable to sleep, I waited impatiently for the first light. Now that I have written this, a plan has come into my mind and I shall leave today. When Jed prepares to leave for market with the cart this morning, I'll seek a reason to accompany him. I will be up and about my duties so that no one may suspect my intentions, and I shall hide my bag in the cart before anyone is about. It is imperative that I go to Darra. She is the only one who will never fail me. She is the only one I can trust.

4

I cannot imagine why I was so critical of our treatment by Sister Isobel and Sister Martha in the orphanage. In retrospect, I see that Cat and I were almost spoiled in comparison with what I am experiencing in the Kingsley household as the most junior member of the serving staff. Major Kingsley is kind enough and polite, I must confess, but since he is almost never at home, it all goes for naught. It's Mrs Kingsley, his second wife, who gives us all our orders and she's forever cancelling our days off.

It seems that the major suffered a tragedy which haunts him to this day. Oonagh, the other serving girl, told me the story. Oonagh is nineteen and has been here a year longer than I have. She's from Ireland. It would appear that scores of potato famine immigrants end up in service in Upper Canada.

"Ooooh," Oonagh wailed one day as she burst into the kitchen, her eyes red-rimmed from the tears she had been shedding, "Miz Major Kingsley says I may not, may not, I repeat, have my afternoon off. The fine lady is giving a tea and she wants everything to be just so. Now, we're to wear the uniforms she brought back from New York on her last trip and – ooooh, Darra, I needs to meet my Terry. If only we could save up enough so's we could be married and build a little cabin somewheres."

"There there, Oonagh, there'll be other afternoons. I do agree. It does seem unfair. I wonder why she's so thoughtless ... there must be some reason."

"There is. Don't you know the story? Why, 'tis common gossip. The major doesn't love her. He's still in love with his first wife, at least, so they say."

"His first wife?"

"Yes, a beautiful, fair young lady. They'd only been married a year and, when he was posted to the Canadas, she was big with child and couldn't sail with him. When she did finally come to join him, she was stricken with the plague and he never saw her again. She died, and so did his baby daughter. Well, they say he never recovered from the tragedy. It's so sad, aren't it?"

"Yes, it is, but when did all this happen? Do you know any more of the story?"

"No, that's all. I think she died 'bout fifteen years ago; they say the sailings was somethin' fierce. Storms and illness. Every ship that come in, they took off great numbers of sick and ailing passengers and left them in the fever hospitals. It was just like here in Kingston, but it were earlier. Very few survived the quarantine."

"When did Major Kingsley marry Mrs Kingsley?"

"You mean this one? Only 'bout five years ago. I hear tell he was so shaken with the news of his first wife's death, he didn't take kindly to the idea of marrying again. Then his house, the one he was building for the first Miz Kingsley, it burned to the ground. So he had to start from scratch and build a new one. He moved into barracks for a while but, finally, some of the officers' wives persuaded him to start attending their social events again and he decided to build another house. More of an interest than anything else at the time, or so they say. He was a very handsome man ten to fifteen years back and lots of gentlewomen were anxious to see their daughters make his acquaintance."

"Yet you say he remained a bachelor, or a widower, for a whole ten years?"

"That's the story, although I did hear that he had a little arrangement on the side with a French lady in Montréal. But nobody knows if that's true."

"How did he meet Mrs Kingsley?"

"Agatha."

"Is that her name?"

"That's what he calls her, Agatha, and he met her in New York. She comes from a very refined background, so they say. She's a real social type. So she's good for him in that way. But we hear she's barren, poor soul, and that's why there's no babes."

"Well, we can sympathize with her then, Oonagh. At least, she

27

seems to enjoy planning parties; she's been trying to persuade Major Kingsley to have a ball in the spring and she wants to decorate the gardens and have it outside."

"It'll probably rain."

I picked up the silver tea service which I had been polishing for the past half hour, set it on its large ornate tray and prepared to return it to its position on the tea wagon. If only I didn't feel so down all the time. I knew I should be grateful to the Kingsleys for giving me the opportunity to work in their beautiful home, but my heart wasn't in it. I missed Cat too much. I'd written her letters and I knew she must have written to me too, but somehow the deliveries must have been delayed. I knew that Tudhope, where Cat was sent to care for Mrs Dunne and her brood of children, was in a remote farming area quite distant from Kingston, but I didn't expect this sort of irregularity in the messenger service.

I even inquired of Mrs Kingsley why I hadn't received a letter from my sister, and she replied that any number of things could have gone wrong. She also reminded me that there was no rural mail delivery and, therefore, I would simply have to wait until someone from the farm came into town before I could expect news of my sister.

The Kingsley house is quite magnificent compared to the orphanage where we were brought up. The rooms are large with high ceilings and long rectangular windows. Mrs Kingsley had crystal chandeliers shipped from New York for both the dining room and the parlour. Downstairs there is a bigger than average foyer with a cherrywood wardrobe by the door to hold the outer clothing. There is also a long low parson's bench on which sits a silver dish where Mrs Kingsley collects her neighbours' calling cards.

The parlour houses all the best furniture, every piece imported from England, I think, and there are several oil paintings on the walls too. There is a fireplace in the centre of one wall with a marble mantelpiece. Mrs Kingsley ordered it from New York but originally it came from Italy, she says. The dining room table is long enough to seat twelve people for a formal dinner party, and it has an enormous buffet and hutch to match. Mrs Kingsley's bone china with the gold band around the edge is the best, naturally, and her heavy crystal glassware, which she keeps locked up in a corner cupboard with glass panels, looks perfect when set out on one of the damask linen tablecloths.

The kitchen, where Oonagh and I spend most of our time alone with the cook, when we're not working elsewhere in the house, that is, is vast with two open fireplaces for the cooking and preparing of meals. The maids' quarters are attached to the rear side of the kitchen, so we're close enough to be always on call.

Upstairs are three bedrooms, two of enormous size and one smaller. Oonagh told me that the third one was meant to be the nursery. Since Mrs Kingsley hadn't gotten in the family way during her first three married years, she turned it into a sewing room. Although there are two double beds, one in each of the two larger bedrooms, and another extra single bed in Mrs Kingsley's room, she always refers to the major's room as his dressing room. That's becuse she wants people to believe that they share the connubial bed. Oonagh and I know, however, that, most of the time, Major Kingsley sleeps in his dressing room because, when he's at home, his bed is in constant need of making up.

I feel very sorry for Major Kingsley. It must be terrible knowing that your wife and only child perished at sea or died of the plague somewhere along the St Lawrence River. Then, when he finally got around to remarrying, he managed to choose a woman who couldn't carry on the family line. No wonder the poor man never smiles.

I've been here with the Kingsleys for nigh onto three months, the same time Cat has been at Tudhope. Now that the end of September is nearing, I am hopeful that she will come to town for supplies and we will see each other again. I have never known time to pass so slowly. Especially since I've received no word from her. If she doesn't come soon, winter will overtake us, she'll be snowbound and I shan't see her till spring.

I don't know how much longer I will be able to tolerate this way of life. Next week is my half day off and I want to go to the theatre again. I'll go backstage and this time I'm determined to meet Trevor Vaughn and find out how I can become an actress. Yesterday, when I was dusting in the parlour, I looked in the

Literary Garland for theatre news. It was an out-of-date issue, as might be expected, but, although there was nothing about the travelling actors, there was some of Mrs Moodie's poetry in it. I memorized some of the verses and practiced a recitation on Oonagh in the kitchen later. She loved it. I hope Trevor Vaughn will be as impressed by my delivery.

Whenever I read any of the stories and poetry in the Kingsley's parlour, I think of poor Cat, hidden away in rural Tudhope. She went off so optimistically, but I can't believe she could've been properly prepared for the hardships of caring for a farmer's sick wife and his brood of children. I'm certain she must be starved for books and I suspect that by now she will be thoroughly exasperated.

September 28, 1850

Major Kingsley arrived back this afternoon only a half hour before I left the house on my day off. Since he wasn't expected, Mrs Kingsley was instantly thrown into a pique. She cannot bear to allow alterations to her plans.

"Edward, couldn't you have managed to let me know you were going to be coming home a day earlier than expected? You know how it upsets me to have to alter the arrangements for the day."

"I've already said I was sorry, Agatha. But you needn't put yourself out for me. I shall make no extra demands on your time nor on the dining schedule. Please don't excite yourself."

Oonagh and I could hear her exaggerated sighs right out in the kitchen.

"Oh-oh. Watch out for the sparks now. You'd best hurry up, Darra. Get your bonnet on and fly, or you'll be held back for sure."

As she spoke, the door to the kitchen opened and a red-faced Mrs Kingsley entered.

"Darra. Oh, there you are. Thanks be I caught you before you were gone. The master has arrived home unexpectedly. You'll have to stay. The dinner menu must needs be changed. Now, what was on the list for tomorrow?"

"Agatha." It was Major Kingsley and his voice was unusually angry. "Don't be foolish. I beg of you. Let the girl go. Is it your afternoon off, Miss? I'm so sorry. I seem to have forgotten your name."

"It's Darra, Sir," I said and made him a pretty curtsey.

"Yes, Darra. Well now, you just run along and enjoy yourself."

"No, Edward. I won't have it. You simply must not interfere with my household staff. Go at once Darra, and change back into your uniform."

I hesitated, looking from one to the other.

"Off you go now, Darra. There's a good girl." As he spoke, Major Kingsley stepped forward with determination and clamped his hand on his wife's arm. "Come, my dear, we must needs talk," and, as she struggled to take over and resume her command post, he propelled her from the kitchen. "Agatha, when will you ever learn not to raise your voice or disagree with me in front of the servants?"

Oonagh looked at me and giggled. I giggled too.

"Hurry up, Darra," she said, and I picked up my bonnet and fled out the back door.

I was already late when I had begun my preparations to leave and now I had been delayed again. I would have to run all the way to the theatre if I was to arrive before curtain time.

Butler's rarely gave matinée performances. This was an exception and it was only because all the tickets had been sold out for the evenings. The play was one I'd never heard of before but the British Whig said it was a closet drama, whatever that might be, and that Charles Maire had first been popular in it. I knew also that Trevor Vaughn was acting in it. The newspaper critic had given a glowing account of his acting, comparing him to Charles Heavysedge, who apparently used to be famous for his imitations of Shakespearean characters.

By the time I arrived at the theatre and claimed a seat as close to the stage as possible, I was breathless and flushed. I tried to control my breathing and to look as unconcerned as the rest of the audience, but it was impossible. For me, the stage and the drama acted upon it were the most exciting events in life. I balled and unballed a small cambric handkerchief, a gift from Sister Martha, between the palms of my hands. All of a sudden, the heavy stage curtain parted and rolled away. I leaned back and prepared to bask in the fairytale atmosphere unfolding before me.

Trevor Vaughn stepped on the stage from the left rear entrance and the audience fell into a frenzy of wild applause. I sat bolt upright in my seat, staring at the magnificence of the actor. He was bowing to the left and bowing to the right, acknowledging the adulation as his due, and then he looked straight at me. I gasped. My hands rose to press my burning cheeks and Trevor Vaughn smiled right into my eyes.

The drama from that moment onwards passed in a blur of ecstacy. I felt certain that Trevor Vaughn was acting for me alone. I held onto his every word, savouring his voice inflections and drinking in his poetic speeches. He was far superior to the visiting priests or even the bishop! When it was all over, I continued to sit, drained of every ambition and of all will. Long after the rest of the audience had risen and staggered out of the theatre, I sat on, trying to exit from my dream and return to reality.

"Excuse me, Miss." A young boy stood before me, a bit of paper held in his hand. I started, at first not seeing him, so lost was I in my imaginary world.

"Oh, I'm sorry," I said.

"Mr Vaughn sends his compliments and says will you be so kind as to visit him backstage." Again, the boy proffered the message towards me.

Somewhat more aware of my surroundings by this time, I accepted the paper and thanked the boy.

"Exquisite one, be assured that I await your presence in my dressing room. Your beauty, your hair like the sunset, your lips like the rose at dawn, your fair form have combined to stir my heart to everlasting admiration. Yours, Trevor Vaughn."

I was astonished. I read it again and felt my cheeks grow warm once more, this time with blushing. The great American actor, Trevor Vaughn, and he wanted to meet me, Darra!

I folded the note carefully, tucked it inside my bodice next to my heart and stood up.

"Will you please direct me to Mr Vaughn's room?" I asked the boy.

"Right this way, Miss."

Trevor Vaughn was undeniably handsome. It wasn't just his shoeblack curly hair and beard, nor was it his mellow Shakespearian voice either. He turned out to be not nearly so tall as I had thought from his pictures or from seeing him on the stage. Nevertheless, he did have broad shoulders and an appearance of strength.

"Ahhh, so you've come." The moment I stepped inside his doorway, he crossed the space between us and took my hands in his. As he gazed down on me, fixing my eyes with his own, I understood what it was about him which was so compelling and I had a dangerous feeling that led me to believe that I would do as he asked, no matter what the request might be.

"Your hair is like spun gold with a blood-red sunset kindling it to flame." As he spoke these romantic lines, he held a lock of my hair between his fingers and stroked it. I stood stock still, not daring to move so much as an inch.

"I enjoyed your performance, Mr Vaughn," I finally managed to mumble. "I've been waiting for a long time to see you."

"Thank you, my dear. Never were words so comforting to an old ham like myself," and he chuckled. "Now, tell me your name that I may remain in ignorance no longer."

"Darra is my name, Sir."

"Darra? Darra who?"

I gazed at the floor for what must have seemed long minutes. I did not wish to tell this handsome stranger that I was an orphan and, therefore, had no legal surname, so I said what I had been practising since the first moments of embarrassment.

"Darra St Joseph," I said.

"What a pretty name. Indeed, I like it muchly."

"Thank you, Sir," I said aloud, and to myself, "Please forgive me, Father."

"I would be happy if you would share my midnight supper with me, Miss St Joseph. Do you think that might be possible?"

"I regret to say that I do not believe so, Sir." My heart was pounding as I tried in vain to think of some way in which I might escape the Kingsley household and thus join Trevor Vaughn.

"My mistress would be much distressed if I were to be absent from the house at such an hour."

"Then we must make special arrangements. I have another performance to give this evening. So, as you see, I cannot be free until past eleven." He spread his hands in a helpless gesture. "Be independent, Miss St Joseph. Tell your mistress that you must, simply must join Mr Vaughn at midnight; better still, say nothing and come away in secret. How will she know if you do not tell her?"

He smiled persuasively and, before I was able to answer, he stepped forward and took me in his arms. Seeking my lips with his, he kissed me urgently and I knew that I would be powerless to deny him his request. The thick expanse of hair surrounding his mouth and mine surprised me with its softness. Somehow I had expected his beard to be scratchy, the way the stable boy's chin had been. Caught within the circle of his arms, I thought for a moment I might swoon, such was my excitement. Trevor Vaughn, however, loosed me quickly and, setting me on my own two feet, he asked me again to join him at midnight. It was then that I made the decision which was to alter my entire life.

"Yes," I whispered somewhat hoarsely. "I'll come. I don't know how I'll manage but, somehow or other, I'll meet you."

"Come to Iron's Hotel on Ontario Street. Do you know it? Slip in the side entrance and speak to Stephan Irons. He's the proprietor and a friend of mine. He'll conduct you to my private room where I entertain after theatre performances. I'm so pleased you can come, Miss St Joseph. I look forward to furthering our acquaintance."

"Thank you, Sir," I managed to say, all the while wondering how I was going to contrive the scheme.

Trevor Vaughn kissed me once more, lightly on the cheek, before sending me off. I rushed home as quickly as I had sped to the matinée earlier, my head bursting with new ideas and emotions. Arriving at the Kingsley house, I ran round to the back and hid beneath the overhang of the carriageway long enough to assure myself that Mrs Kingsley was nowhere about. The last thing I wanted was for her to discover that I had come home early.

Quietly I let myself into the house and tiptoed into the room which I shared with Oonagh.

I had not been there long before Oonagh entered our room.

"Whatever are you doing, Darra?" she gasped, seeing me stuff a packsack with clothing.

"Ohh, Oonagh!" I hadn't heard her come in. "You frightened me. Where is everybody?"

"Major Kingsley had a disagreement with Miz Kingsley. I thought for a few minutes they was going to have a real drag-down fight, but the major's a gentleman, you know, and before Miz Kingsley could get things going too much, he announced that he was leaving. After he'd gone, Miz Kingsley got into a real tizzy and retired upstairs. In about half an hour, she rang her bell, told me she had a frightful headache and for me to bring her some camomile tea. She's still up there now."

"Praise be. Then I won't have any difficulties with her."

"What are you talking about?"

"Oonagh, I'm so excited. I simply can't tell you. I met Trevor Vaughn - you know, the actor - and he invited me to have midnight supper with him at Irons' Hotel."

"But Darra, you can't! The missus would never stand for you to be out past midnight."

"She's not going to know, Oonagh - that is, I'm certainly not going to tell her, and I don't expect you will."

"Well, of course not," she replied indignantly. "Ooh, Darra, what will you wear? Have you got anything grand enough?"

That was a problem, I had to admit, but I had no intention of letting it stand in my way.

"I'll wear my best worsted. It's all I have and it's too chillsome to wear cotton."

"If Miz Kingsley weren't in her bedroom, you might have sneaked one of her gowns." Oonagh ventured.

I was aghast.

"I wouldn't wear anything Mrs Kingsley owns. I'd rather just wear what I have."

"The doors'll be locked up when you return, Darra. I'll unbolt the back door before I retire for the night but you can always knock on the window if you run into any trouble."

"Thank you, Oonagh." I didn't tell her that it was not my intention to return. Ever. It was too great a secret and would be too much risk for her to be burdened with.

When I had finished dressing and styling my hair in an elaborate manner, I picked up my bag, kissed Oonagh fondly and bade her farewell, letting myself out into the dark night. As I ran along Brock Street past all the fashionable houses which stood side by side with the Kingsleys', I could not prevent a shudder from passing through me. I was leaving the security of the Kingsleys' home for I knew not what, and if, for some reason or other, Trevor Vaughn refused to allow me to accompany him on his theatre tour, I had no idea what I would turn to next. I knew I was stretching my luck but saw no other means of accomplishing my ambitions. The hardest thing about it was to keep the faces of Sister Martha and Sister Isobel resolutely chained in the back of my mind.

My arrival at Irons' Hotel coincided with the departure of a coach and four, so I hastened to make inquiries of the freckle-faced lad who was handing the reins to the driver as he made ready to leave.

"Excuse me, Boy" I called.

"Yes, Miss. I be Caleb McBaine. May I help you?"

"You may, if you please, direct me to your master, Mr Stephan Irons."

"Yes, Miss, right this way, please," and he led me by a side door into the warmth of the inside.

After I had made Mr Irons' acquaintance and explained my purpose at this late hour, he led me silently through the inn to a room situated near the rear of the hotel. A table was laid with fine linen, silver and glassware. Elaborate candelabra and a bowl of late roses graced the table's centre. Wicker baskets filled with flowers and greenery stood in formal array in one corner of the room. A settee upholstered in royal-blue velveteen and two leather armchairs lined the walls and, off at one end, was an archway leading, I had no doubt, to the bedroom and the usual four-poster bed.

"Thank you, Mr Irons," I said and placed my valise on the floor beside me.

"I'll light the fire for you," and so saying, he kneeled to set the logs and coal aglow. "Is there anything I can bring you while you're waiting the arrival of Mr Vaughn?"

"Oh, no, thank you. You're very kind."

"Not at all. Then, if that will be all, Miss, I'll return to my duties."

As he turned to leave, I could not help noticing how he stared at me with curiosity, in that strange manner men have when they are calculating in their minds what the situation might be. I knew that he thought I was a paid harlot, but I didn't care. I was going to join the theatre and nothing was going to stand in my way.

It was past midnight when Trevor Vaughn finally made his appearance.

"Ahhh, my dear, you are a delight to this tired old man," and with that introductory statement, he placed his hands on my two breasts and kissed me on my forehead. If the sisters could see me now! I lowered my eyes that I was able to restrain a smile at the thought.

Fast on his heels, a serving cart arrived and was wheeled into the room. I could not help but note the large number of covered dishes and the savoury odours emitting from them. A short, slight waiter with polished hair and a skinny moustache drew the cork from a champagne bottle. Trevor Vaughn deftly filled two fluted glasses with the golden bubbling wine and handed one to me.

"To a perfect evening," he said and clinked his glass with mine.

I tasted cautiously, having never experienced such an exotic luxury and, to my surprise, found it slightly acid but not unpleasant. It reminded me of ginger beer, not that I had had that more than once. Still, once tried, I was not likely to forget it. By the time I looked up from my wine, Trevor had dismissed the waiter, filled his own glass once again and was standing before me, bottle in hand.

"Drink up, my lovely," and he gestured towards my scarcely touched wine goblet.

I took a sip, and then another and finally, a gulp. Trevor smiled and refilled my glass to the brim. He then sat down beside me and, placing his once more half-empty goblet on the table beside mine, began to trace the contours of my face with his forefinger.

"You are a beautiful sylph," he exclaimed, stroking the bones which outlined my eyebrows and my cheeks. "Your eyes are orbs of green crystal dotted with flecks of cinnamon. Your lips? How can I describe your lips adequately? Cherries? Strawberries? The wine of Mount Olympus? Ah . . . , permit me to drown in their dew." Having uttered all these nonsensical and poetical phrases, he settled his lips on mine as though intent on drawing from me a response filled with I knew not what.

As abruptly, he drew back. "Drink up," he said. "Let us eat."

There was enough food to feed a family of eight: a tureen of heavily peppered cabbage soup, potatoes, carrots, turnips and creamed onions, all served in separate bowls, and the main dishes: a stew of venison, squabs surrounded with more carrots, and some coarse white fish. I was taken aback when Trevor Vaughn began filling my plate, piling it with large servings from each of the dishes and set beside it a bowl of the soup. I averted my gaze lest he catch the look of amusement which flickered across my face. Never had I been served such a vast amount of food, all at one time. I could only suppose that acting was an appetite-building activity.

The fact that I merely nibbled on the portions allotted me did not appear to concern my dinner partner in the least. He tucked a large napkin round his shirt collar and, without undue haste, shovelled bite upon bite into his mouth, chewing thoughtfully as he did so before scooping up more. I watched with fascination the pattern emerging on his beard as stray bits of food settled there. All the while, he continued to fill and refill our glasses. When the first bottle of champagne was emptied, he promptly opened another which was chilling nearby.

Hours seemed to pass before we had finally done with the food. Cheeses, a steam-pudding and some autumn fruit appeared after the first courses. To my amazement, Trevor Vaughn managed to eat some of each dish. He leaned back against his chair at last, mopped his mouth and beard with his napkin, and sighed. Indeed, if more gaseous exclamations had escaped from his lips, I would not have been taken by surprise.

"There," he said, smiling roguishly at me, "that's better. And now for a digestive." He reached beneath the serving cart's covering and drew forth a bottle of cognac. Again, without asking me, he poured equal amounts into two brandy snifters and handed one to me. By this time, befuddled as I was with all the food and drink, I did not even attempt to refuse the offering. I had never tasted brandy, indeed, I was under the impression that it was a beverage consumed by men only.

At that moment, Trevor rang a bell, discreetly hidden beneath the table. A waiter appeared as if by magic to wheel away the cart and, all at once, we were alone.

"And now, my precious girl," he spoke slowly, deliberately, staring straight at me, "it is your turn."

"My turn?" I was bewildered.

"But of course! I have performed. Now it is your turn. You did not think I was merely a kind old gentleman who had decided to feed you a meal, did you?"

"I ... I ..." I was at a loss as to what to answer. "I am very flattered, Sir, that you deigned to invite me to your table."

At that, he roared with laughter. "You didn't think I meant to seduce you, perhaps?" Again he looked me straight in the eye.

"I, I – hadn't entertained that idea," I replied, although I knew, as I said it, that it was untrue.

"First, Darra, that's your name, isn't it? Darra, now tell me, and tell me true. Why did you come here? What are your motives?"

In that moment, I had made up my mind to confess all. After all, what did I have to lose?

"When I told you that I had always dreamed of seeing you on the stage, I meant it, Mr Vaughn."

"Call me Trevor," he interrupted.

"Yes, Trevor. Well, I first read about you two years ago, when I was an orphan girl in St Joseph's convent school. I always wanted to be an actress. That's why I came to your room at midnight."

"Aha, so you want to be an actress, do you? But can you act? That, my pretty one, is the question."

"Oh yes, Sir, I can act. I know I can. The sisters always said I read the scriptures and our Latin studies well, and I can memorize readily. Shall I recite for you, Sir?"

Trevor was looking at me as though he was thinking up some kind of devilish scheme to test my words. Frantically I racked my brain to seize upon a poem or quotation which might please him and convince him that I was not lying.

"My dear little baggage, I am going to give you a test, a test to determine your acting abilities. Now do you agree to my suggestion?"

"Most certainly, of course, Sir, anything!"

"Do not forget, Darra, what you have just said – anything. Was that what you said?" He chuckled with amusement.

"Yes Sir."

"Yes, Trevor."

"Yes, Trevor," I repeated obediently.

"Good. Come closer." I rose from my chair and complied with his request. "That's better. Now, Darra, you must remove all your clothes for me, but you must do it in a provocative manner. Think of it as an acting test. Convince me as you disrobe that you harbour a deep desire for me. By the time you stand naked before me, I should feel that your only wish is to be ravished by me. You must accomplish this without touching me. You may touch yourself, of course, any way you think will inflame my ardour. I shall be both audience and critic for your one-act drama. How you conduct this test will signal failure or success."

Trevor smiled in that devastating way of his when he addresses his public, leaned back in his chair and sipped from his brandy snifter.

I was speechless, so amazed was I at what had transpired in the last few minutes; I was unable to think whether I should fly from this spider's web or attempt Trevor's shameless test. My ambitions decided the matter. Since I was still a virgin and had little or no experience in the art of seduction, I would have to use my imagination (of which I had much) and trust my natural instincts. Surely it would be an improvement over being Agatha Kingsley's maid. I took a swallow of brandy to bolster my spirits and prepared to abandon the moral upbringing of my youth.

Hail Mary, full of grace, pray for us sinners now and at the hour of our death. As I turned my back on Trevor, the familiar rosary repeated itself in my head. Then I pivoted slowly, slid my palms upwards till they rested on my bosom and, hands shaking, began unhooking the fasteners which held my bodice together. Once my cotton camisole with its pink-ribboned laces was revealed, I turned to unfasten the hooks and eyes that held the sleeves of my frock in neat array. It was then an easy matter to wriggle out of the upper half of my clothing. Oh, whatever would Sister Isobel say if she could see me now?

Dallying over the unlacing of my camisole, I planned my next move: to dangle the garment provocatively before Trevor's eyes, then to drop it into his lap. That evening I was girded with more petticoats than usual, the reason being that wearing them proved more practical than carrying them in my bag. When I left the Kingsley's, my idea had been never to return although, if I were to fail in my present act, all would be lost. Placing my hands at the back of my waist, I proceeded to unfasten the first of my five petticoats. Each time one dropped to the floor, I stepped gracefully aside and allowed it to flutter onto a heap with my other clothing. The moment soon arrived when there were no more petticoats to remove.

Now I stood before Trevor Vaughn in naught but my long ruffled drawers and immodest camisole and, if the truth be known, I sincerely wished there were some way I could conclude this play other than stripping further. I paused, but Trevor gestured for me to continue. It was the first sign he had made to indicate that he was paying any attention. So began the finale and I soon stood tall before the famous man, cupping the curves of my naked breasts with my hands to prove I was not ashamed of my womanliness. That left only my pantaloons. I untied the tape at my waist. Nude, the candlelight flickering brightness and shadow across my skin, I attempted to hide my flaming bush beneath my hands.

Trevor was sitting up straighter now. He crooked his finger at me. "Well done," he said. "You might succeed, after all." As he beckoned, I knelt by his side and held my breath as he stroked me with his tapered fingers, never lingering longer in one area than in another.

"The bed's yonder," he said, pointing in the direction of the archway.

Hastily, I gathered up my discarded garments, bundling them in front of me. Once inside the bedroom, concealed by curtains across the doorway and a canopy over the bed, I pulled a high-necked, long-sleeved flannelette nightdress over my head. Hastily I crept beneath the coverlets which were piled high on top of the mattress. I should have been warmed from the food, the wine and my emotional performance but, to my surprise, once I lay prone on the bed, my body shook and shivered as though I had contracted the ague. I wondered how soon Trevor would join me and hold me in his manly arms.

The minutes crept by and, at every creek and groan of the hotel's walls and joists, I stiffened, alert to the sound of his footsteps which would signal my initiation into womanly maturity. Briefly I surrendered to an overpowering fatigue, but a loud bang brought me back to my present situation. I waited, tossing and turning, trying to imagine what might have delayed him. Finally, unable to keep my eyes open any longer, I succumbed to sleep.

The room was still dark when I awoke in the early hours and, thinking that I was back in the Kingsley household and that it was time to rise and prepare the morning tea, I forced myself to sit up and throw the blanket back. Instantly I recalled my whereabouts and the events which had led me to my present position. I breathed deeply and glanced around the room. Where was Trevor Vaughn? Fearfully I searched beside me in the bed, thinking that he must have joined me after I had fallen asleep. But the bed was empty of any presence on the opposite side. Still tired, I curled up once more and allowed myself the luxury of extra slumber.

5

Were it not for the disappearance of Darra, which took place just before my arrival back in Kingston, I should be truly happy. I am now employed, surprisingly enough, in the home of Major and Mrs Kingsley. On my arrival early on the morning after my flight from the Dunne's, I found the Kingsley household in an uproar. The young maid, Oonagh, greeting me at the servants' entrance, was quick to fill me in.

"Ooh, Cat," she wailed, "if only you'd arrived yesterday." I had just finished explaining my appearance and she told me of Darra not returning from her day off.

"The mistress is right vexed, what with company expected and the new girl not arriving as promised. She has boxed my ears and told me to do Darra's work and me with only my two hands."

I grasped at the straw offered me. If only I could stay with the Kingsleys for a while, I could perhaps learn what had happened to Darra. It would also spare me from having to beg charity at St Joseph's until I found a suitable position.

"Oonagh, I'll stay. I'll help you. I had the same training as Darra and I can do the work. Please tell Mrs Kingsley that I am a friend of yours. Don't let her know that I am Darra's sister. It might prejudice her against me."

So it came to pass. Oonagh was delighted to have me and, after the solitude of the Dunne's, I enjoyed her company, even if at times I could wish her to be less common in her conversation.

I do not care for Mrs Kingsley, but I am studiously avoiding trouble with her as I wish to keep this position until the spring next year. There is also the advantage that I am learning many social skills as I help her in her plans and in the execution of her entertainment. She is a lavish hostess and is eager to be among the best in Kingston. After her functions, she enjoys telling me of the company present and I am the repository of much gossip. As I become more experienced, she seeks my advice, as she did today.

"Catherine, lay aside your dusting for a minute, girl, and come to the sewing room with me that I can make preparations for the luncheon next Wednesday." I followed her to the sewing room where she usually settles to plan her menus and to make out her lists of orders.

"You realise that this is to be in honour of the young Mrs Gildersleeve? There will be eight of us all told."

I was looking forward to the occasion myself as there could not be anyone in Kingston who is not familiar with the name Gildersleeve. The family have been shipwrights for generations. The old man, Henry, arrived in Kingston shortly after the 1812 war and is living still. Since then, his two sons, Overton and Charles, have continued working in the Lake Ontario and Bay of Quinte Company which runs the steamships between Kingston, the Thousand Isles and the Bay of Quinte. In the summer, visitors come for miles to admire the beauteous scenery and I long one day to make an excursion myself. Mrs Kingsley wishes to be accepted in the social circle of the Gildersleeves and the coming luncheon was quite a feather in her cap.

"Madam," I suggested, "you will perhaps wear your bottle-green velvet? The underskirt is so cunningly fixed with the loops of Brussels lace and there are those shoes of latest fashion that you brought back from New York."

"Do you think so, Catherine? I had thought of the more elaborate purple and pink satin."

"No, Madam. It seems a little excessive for the luncheon and you would not have Mrs Gildersleeve think you overly eager to entertain her. After all, it was she who sought you out, asking you to contribute to the Mechanics Institute."

"Indeed, yes, it was, Catherine, and I cannot really see why we should be contributing to the working classes."

"For sure, Ma'am, it was you who told me yourself! It is better that men should occupy themselves with books and learning to improve themselves, rather than spend their earnings in the taverns."

I hid a smile for, on her return from her last meeting with Mrs Gildersleeve, Mrs Kingsley had been so elated with her contact that she had willingly donated to the library. Personally, I envied the members who could settle down in the large room above Mr Dumble's confectionery store and, were they free, read from ten o'clock in the morning to ten o'clock at night. Of course I could not, but I often had reason to visit the confectioners and on one occasion I had met with Terry, who was walking out with Oonagh.

"Morning, Cat," he greeted me, his arms full of books. I looked at him enviously and he took me up the stairs to see the library. One day, I vowed, I will read every book I can put my hands on. I had already examined the books belonging to Major Kingsley while I was dusting, but I had not yet ventured to ask the officer if I might take one to my room. Major Kingsley daily reads the newspaper, the *British Whig*. I find it rather dry and difficult but am persevering, as now that I am privy to so much of daily gossip, I try to make sense of the news.

I must describe Major Kingsley as he is so kind and it gives me much pleasure to work for him, especially after Sergeant Dunne. I had thought never to trust men again, but I realise that a gentleman such as Major Kingsley would never force himself on a woman. I feel sorry for him in that his remarriage has obviously not brought him the happiness he deserves and he is saddened by the lack of children in the home. My first real meeting with him occurred thus.

At the end of September, the staff was called in for payment of wages. Being the most recent appointee, I was the last the major called and the others had returned to their duties.

"Catherine," he said, "I must congratulate you. You have pleased Mrs Kingsley well. She finds you eager to learn and well skilled."

"Thank you, Sir," I said, meeting his eyes rather timidly. They were vivid blue and the kindness in his gaze reassured me. His hair was greying at the temples and he had the moustache so common to military men. I noticed that his face was lined as if sorrow had become familiar to him.

The poor man, I thought, remembering Oonagh's story of his

losses. Of course, many men are forced to take a second wife, indeed, I knew Mrs Dunne to be step-mother to the older Dunne children. Yet surely Major Kingsley had earned happiness in his second marriage. He showed himself considerate to all his household and even though his wife tried him sorely, he never lifted more than his voice. At this point, he disturbed my thoughts by saying, "Where do you come from, Catherine? You look like a rose, fresh from an English garden, yet I can tell from your voice that you were brought up in the province."

I found myself unable to lie to him.

"Sir, I was brought up by the kind sisters at St Joseph's. Father Andrew is the only father I have ever known."

I hoped he would not question me further, for what could I tell him? One of my reasons for wanting to remain longer in Kingston was that I hoped somehow to gain more information about the arrival of the two small babies at St Joseph's sixteen years ago. Of course, Darra and I were not the only foundlings, but we were the only children who had come with the two gold coins wrapped up with us in our quilt. Furthermore, the gold cross that never leaves Darra's neck is valuable and so is the small bracelet that I keep hidden with my clothes. The fact that we were twins should also help me in my search. Did one of us resemble one parent and one the other? I suppose we must be love-children, but does this make us less valuable in the eyes of our Father in Heaven? We know it does not.

Major Kingsley looked at me compassionately. "You do the sisters much credit. I can only think you come of good stock. I hope you will be happy with us."

I could not, however, leave the good man believing that I would be serving in his home past a few months, so I ventured to say, "Sir, I am not entirely alone. I have a sister whom I wish to join when I am able. I am anxious to save my coins so that I will be prepared. Could you advise me, Sir? I have thought of approaching Glassup's Savings Bank, but I am inexperienced and I hesitate to enter."

"Bravo, Catherine, how wise you are. I will take you myself and arrange things for you to your satisfaction."

This he did that very week, but I was sad that Mrs Kingsley

mocked me, saying, "Come, Catherine. Aren't you the canny little thing? We have a capitalist in our house, I do believe."

I did not let her words disturb me, however, for my savings will enable me to reach Darra and to support her if she is in need. Naturally, on my arrival, I turned over every stone in seeking news of my sister. Oonagh told me of her interest in the theatre and how she suspects that she has gone to follow the players. Mrs Kingsley, still unaware that she was speaking of my sister, remarked unkindly of her.

"I am glad you are not as flighty as that red-headed young miss I had before you. As soon as I saw her, I knew that one was going to make trouble, she had all the boys looking at her and making sheep's eyes. When she started getting letters as well, I knew enough to hold them back."

My attention was caught instantly and, hoping to draw her out further, I questioned, "Madam?"

"Yes, she had several thick letters addressed in an educated hand. Now why would some threepenny-piece girl be receiving those? I just threw them in the fire."

Blazing with anger and resentment, I turned my back on the woman on the pretext of straightening a damask cloth on her bureau. So Darra had never received my letters! What must she have thought, longing and hoping for news as I had! I was certain she had written to me, indeed, Oonagh had assured me that Darra frequently talked of me and then put pen to paper. What had happened to her letters?

"She was real educated for a serving girl, like you, Cat, always looking at a book or reciting, Darra was. And she could put on a grand show. Why, she could be the Madam herself, she could, true as life and me laughing so much I feared to lay hands on the dishes."

I would never forgive Mrs Kingsley for her arrogance, but I turned a bland face towards her. Little by little the clues would come in and I promised myself that I would find Darra.

December 15, 1850

This past week I have had an unexpected encounter which I believe gives me some clue as to Darra's whereabouts. I have noticed, while about my errands in the shops, that at times a young man has been paying me attention. I learned from Oonagh that he was an ostler in Irons' Hotel.

"Ooh, Cat, you have an admirer," she confided. "My Terry tells me that young Caleb McBaine be asking about you."

"And who might Caleb McBain be when he is at home?" I asked her. I had no interest whatever in followers.

"He is the ostler at the Irons'. You must know, the lad with the freckles. He says he knows something you'll be wanting to hear."

"And what could that be?"

"Listen, Cat, he'll be waiting for you on your next day off at Moore's tearoom."

I tossed my head. "Well, that's as it may be," but I resolved to be there, for the tearoom was a busy place and no harm could come to me.

Caleb was already there and waiting when I arrived. It was cold and the ice on the ground was slippery and treacherous. The snowfall had begun only the previous week and as yet we did not have the raised banks which had to be flattened by the horses' hoofs and the runners of the sleighs. I had bought myself a warm muff and a smart matching hat, at which Mrs Kingsley looked askance, being accustomed to seeing her serving girls cover their heads with a scarf. My cloak was dark blue and the dry air caused the lining to crackle and cling to my flannel skirts. I pushed it into place with irritation.

Caleb looked at me admiringly.

"Oh Cat, you look a proper lady."

I smiled and thought that, with his freckled nose and bright, friendly eyes, he looked like the brother Darra and I had often imagined. I hoped he wouldn't spoil it by touching me. I kept at a safe distance from him as he opened the door of Moore's tearoom and led me to a table at the back. I was relieved to see that he was scrubbed and clean, his clothes, though rudely made, were also clean and patched. He had obviously taken immense care to prepare himself for meeting me and I was touched and grateful.

"Well, Caleb, speak up," I urged him when the hot chocolate he had ordered was put before us. "What is it that you want to tell me?"

"It's about your sister, Darra," he replied. "I just happen to know that she was with that actor, Vaughn, and she was meeting with him at Irons' Hotel. Then I saw her get on the morning stage-coach with him, all dolled up she was, but I knew her when I saw her. She was with all the actors, all laughing and talking and they was going to Toronto."

"Caleb! Are you sure?"

"Sure as the Creed, Cat. Honest."

I questioned him closely and was convinced at length that he was telling me the truth. I have now written to the acting company in Toronto, both to the actor, Vaughn and to my dear sister. I do not want to have my letters intercepted by Mrs Kingsley, so I went to Father Andrew and took him into my confidence. At first he was shocked and grieved that I should have been forced to leave Dunne's but, seeing my distress, did not press me for reasons.

When he learned of Darra's sudden departure from Major Kingsley's household, he spoke angrily. I managed to persuade him, however, to regard Darra with all charity until we heard her story from her own lips. Our dear Father has promised, with true Christian love, that he will hold Darra in his prayers and ensure the safety of any letters that come for me. Indeed, I do believe he is as anxious to hear as I.

To return to Caleb. I thanked him heartily for his news and, on his pressing me, accepted an invitation to drive in a cab which a friend of his owned. This was certainly a rare treat for me. Caleb helped me onto the single seat and the black horse started off at a merry trot. The runners hissed as they traversed the snow-covered roads and the clip-clop of the horse's hoofs was muffled, enabling us to talk easily, without raising our voices.

I was bundled in a huge woollen blanket that Caleb's friend had provided and, although our breath whitened the air, I was too exhilarated to notice the cold. We passed the redoubts, one by one, and I saw that at last the Martello towers, as Major

Kingsley calls them, are completed. It seems they have been building these round forts with the pointed tops for as long as I can remember.

"Caleb, do you really think there is danger that the Americans will attack us again?" I asked, looking admiringly at the solid stone walls of Fort Henry rising above us. Caleb had stopped the cab and we gazed past the fort across the water towards the distant shores of our powerful neighbour.

"Naaa," said Caleb scornfully. "I've heard tell how we put them to the run last time they came. My Da was a boy then in 1812 and he has plenty of tales to tell. Oh no, they won't be taking us on again."

I hoped that he was correct. I had heard Major Kingsley mention the land hunger of American settlers and the idea of war alarmed me. Putting the thought from me, I snuggled into the warmth of the blanket. Caleb shook the reins, calling out, "Giddy-up, giddy-up," and we were on our way, past the fashionable houses with their limestone faces and on to the Kingsley's home where Caleb let me out, laughing and bowing as if I were indeed a lady. As the horse's hoofs clattered off and I ran through the carriageway to the back entrance, my heart sang. This was surely the happiest day of the year, I thought.

January 4, 1851

I give thanks to the Lord for seeing me begin this New Year in such favourable conditions. I daily expect to hear from Darra. My small savings are mounting in my account at Glassup's Bank and I am in very good favour with Mrs Kingsley.

The Christmas season was full of good cheer and festivity and Major and Mrs Kingsley seemed more at ease with each other. Many guests were in and out of the house and the kitchen staff, Oonagh and I were kept fully occupied. Mrs Kingsley hired a young maid from St Joseph's to help, saying that she must have a full staff in order to entertain according to her station. Our Christmas table was a joy to behold with pies, roast goose, a ham and a turkey, and many sweetcakes, confections, fruit pies and fresh fruit. Mrs Kingsley arranged for the fresh fruit to be sent from New York at great cost. Little Eileen from St Joseph's could not believe so many delights could be gathered at one time. We in the kitchen did well, as Major Kingsley ensured that many delicacies came our way.

It was also a time for gifts, no one being forgotten. Caleb sent me a box of candies, tied in a huge blue ribbon which I folded and put in my chest of drawers. From Oonagh, I received some warm stockings she had herself knitted. Mrs Kingsley, with much ceremony, gave me a book of psalms. The major, who has somehow learned of my interest in Charles Dickens, gave me a bound copy of *Dombey and Son*. It is the first really new book I have ever owned.

I must explain how it is that Mrs Kingsley has taken me into her favour. It always falls to me to dress her hair. It's long, of course, and of a rather indeterminate brown colouring. One day I suggested that I should fashion it in a different style and, finding her amenable, I washed and rinsed her tresses carefully. I used a preparation of rosemary which, when steeped in boiling water, brings a shine and light to the hair. When Mrs Kingsley arrived at Mrs Gildersleeve's afternoon Christmast party, her modish appearance enchanted her new friend. On learning that it was I who was responsible, the young hostess begged to borrow me. Her own carriage would be sent to fetch me. Mrs Kingsley was much set up and told several of the young matrons that dear Mrs Gildersleeve had sought her advice on her coiffure and now asked for me several times a week.

"Of course," Mrs Kingsley said, "Catherine is much needed at home, but I am always one to put my friends first."

As a token of her pleasure, my mistress gave me one of her gowns which she no longer wanted.

"Catherine, I think this will do you very well. My figure is somewhat more womanly than yours and I find the style rather too plain."

I could not believe that anything so lovely could be mine. With a darker overskirt of daffodil-coloured silk, the underpanel and bodice are of a lighter shade and embroidered with white and yellow daisies. The frilled sleeves and bodice neckline are discreetly subdued in delicate lace. There are matching gloves which Mrs Kingsley generously added to the gift, making sure that Mrs Gildersleeve knew of her kindness.

"Catherine is quite valuable to me and absolutely devoted. At times it is necessary that she accompany me to functions and she must do us credit. Sister Isobel was begging me to take another of her girls last week, saying she has never known a better employer."

Mrs Gildersleeve smiled pleasantly and, the next time I completed her elaborate hair style, gave me a small gift, saying, "Well, Catherine, I hope you will enjoy wearing this in appreciation of your skill."

The small velvet box contained a necklace of yellow and white stones and is enchanting with the dress. I was wonderfully happy and before I fell asleep I prayed to the blessed Virgin Mary that I might not become too fond of the pomps and vanities of this wicked world, for it seems to me that they be very pleasant.

I must now describe our evening at the New Year's concert which took place at the garrison. I would not give the occasion too much value so have left the account towards the end of my entry. I was not expecting to accompany Major and Mrs Kingsley to Fort Henry, but my mistress felt somewhat unwell and desired my presence. Since it was an important event with many social dignitaries present, Mrs Kingsley told me to wear the dress she had given me. I was delighted to do so and heartily wished I might dress my hair in one of the latest fashions.

In the servants' room, I wound my heavy flaxen tresses in one style after another while Oonagh and little Eileen "ooohed" and "aaaahed" beside me. Finally, time running out, I hastily wound it into a neat chignon and pinned it carefully. When I arrived at the carriage with Mrs Kingsley, who was wearing her purple and pink satin with several strands of amethysts around her neck, the major was waiting for us. He saw me and started, then quickly smiled to cover his surprise.

"Catherine," he exclaimed, "for a minute I did not know you. You take me back to my youth in England. How well that dress becomes you." He then turned to his wife.

"Will you be warm enough? There will be a blazing fire, but

you know how cold those stone walls can be."

"See to it that we are well seated, Edward," she responded. "I would expect as much consideration as the non-military people who are going. I am not the mayor's wife but you are an officer and we are well-known in the city."

"Of course, my dear," he replied absent-mindedly and we turned to our various anticipations of the entertainment.

What a magnificent performance it was! We were entertained first by the band. The players were most colourful in their dress uniforms. This was followed by several songs, the audience rising to applaud one fine young baritone. Next we were invited to partake of some refreshments.

Mrs Kingsley rose in high good humour and said, "Let us take a turn about the floor, Catherine. I am weary of sitting in one position, but I forgot all else as I listened to the songs."

Soon we were being greeted by numerous acquaintances and exchanging many good wishes for the coming year. Major Kingsley stood with us and I looked and listened to my heart's content. A newcomer approached the group and, as I glanced his way, I started with surprise. It was the young lieutenant who had helped me when Jed's careless behaviour had resulted in our cart overturning.

His eyes were on me and he smiled. Suddenly remembering his lips on mine, I turned pink and then I think white, and my limbs betrayed me in a traitorous manner. I wanted to escape, but there was no justification whatever for my leaving Mrs Kingsley at that time. Major Kingsley, catching sight of the lieutenant, greeted him gaily.

"Welcome, Lieutenant O'Hara, I have not seen you for some weeks. I believe you are currently posted to Toronto. What brings you here?"

"Sir, I have leave over the holiday and I made arrangements to spend it with friends in Kingston." The young man's eyes left my face momentarily, only to return again.

I cast a cautious glance at him from beneath my eyelashes and then hastily looked away. Would he reveal the humiliation of our meeting? I prayed not. I met his gaze imploringly. Meeting my eyes and realising that I was asking something of him, his look changed from interest to surprise.

Turning to Major Kingsley, he said most courteously, "Sir, I have had the honour of meeting your good wife but I do not think I have the pleasure of your daughter's acquaintance."

Mrs Kingsley opened her mouth to protest. I drew a sharp breath, my colour now rising, ready to explain my position, but Major Kingsley answered him easily and with a pleasant smile.

"Lieutenant, this is Catherine, my wife's companion, and she is thoroughly enjoying this delightful evening's entertainment. Catherine, allow me to present Lieutenant O'Hara, recently of Ireland."

To my relief, the conversation became more general, but all too soon Cavan made his way to my side.

"You little sorceress!" he said. "The last time I saw you, you were a tinker's child and now you look as if you'd stepped from some enchanted palace. Who are you?"

"Sir, Major Kingsley told you no lies. I am Catherine."

"Catherine! Do you know you have haunted me? I've seen your face in my dreams and I have given you a hundred names. Catherine, and what is your family name?"

I looked at him, not willing to acquaint him with my tale.

"Catherine St Joseph," I said firmly. To my relief, the Kingsleys were moving to return to the entertainment. I was about to follow when Cavan caught my hand in his.

"I must see you again. Have I your permission to call on you, Catherine?" I remembered the warmth of his kisses, and then I recalled the horror of a man's body forcing himself upon me.

"No, no, I don't know. I must go."

Pulling my hand from his, I ran after my employers and sank hastily into my seat. I have no idea as to what took place in the second half of the concert. Sometimes, I reproached myself for dismissing Cavan so rudely; at other times I took great fear in the thought that he might ignore my words and appear at the Kingsley house. In the carriage going home, I was flushed and preoccupied.

"Catherine, I do hope you are not getting a fever," remarked Mrs Kingsley and added, "you seem in quite a dither, girl."

Major Kingsley came to my rescue. "She is naturally excited

54

after so stimulating an evening, my love, there are no signs of fever."

That night I tossed and turned and struggled with unruly feelings. Once I dreamt that Cavan pulled me into his arms and that I ran from him only to find that I was lost. My breasts tingled and strange vibrations shook my body as I slowly turned to look for him again.

Catherine, I reproached myself, have you taken leave of your senses? What good could come of your seeing Cavan? Why do you suppose he seeks you out? Have you not learned your lesson? What would a young officer like that want of a charity girl? With those words, I put him from my mind and it is my resolution not to allow him to return.

January 6, 1851

I have never felt the effects of too many glasses of wine, but I have observed the women at the Kingsley's dinner parties with their flushed faces, the tinkling gay laughter and the provocative looks cast at the most handsome men. Tonight I, who have prided myself on my sense and reason, feel intoxicated without ever having raised a glass to my lips. My heart lifted with a curious delight and, as I gave my hair the required hundred brush strokes tonight, the mirror reflected lips curved in a smile.

"Cat! Cat! Cat, what is the matter with you?" It was Oonagh standing at the door.

"What do you mean, Oonagh? Nothing is wrong."

"Cat, I've been waiting on you downstairs to help me lock up. You know how I hate to go about in the dark. You promised to come right down."

To lock up? Oh yes. It seems like a dream. It is night-time, but there is sunshine. The kisses on my lips overwhelm me. . .

"Cat! Cat, will you come?"

I laugh. I am unlike myself, almost wild. I who am thought beautiful.

"Yes, Oonagh, yes, I'm coming."

This morning began badly and I was much put out with Mrs

Kingsley. Her complaints began with my taking in the breakfast tray and I was forced to return to Cook, asking for a fresh plate of eggs to be prepared. My Lady also wanted chocolate in place of the usual camomile tea. Cook took this much amiss and gave me the blame. On my return with the breakfast tray, there were complaints as to the hour at which the repast arrived, Cook and I being held responsible.

The good woman's head was sensitive to the touch and she suffered much as I dressed her locks and prepared her for the day. Oonagh had scorched the linen collar required for Madam's worsted frock and I had mislaid the ribbon to lace the bodice. I gave thanks as the task of dressing my mistress neared an end and promised myself some luxury when I dusted in the parlour. I hoped to be able to spend at least fifteen minutes reading the latest romantic serial printed in Mr Lovell's *Literary Garland* which Mrs Kingsley received regularly. This time, the ornaments could be spared the flick of the duster.

But just as I had settled on this happy plan, Mrs Kingsley cried out, "Oh Catherine, my dear, tell Oonagh she must do the dusting today and pray put on your coat and go on an errand for me – and a little less of the sulks, please. I cannot abide the sulks."

Finally, I was out of the house and, shivering in the bitter January cold, I hurried indignantly to Mr Dumble's confectionery store. Upon exiting from the place, I braced myself against the wind and prepared to continue on my errands, the next being the haberdashery. The sound of horse's hoofs caused me to look up.

A cheery voice called out, "Good morning, Miss St Joseph. Whatever brings you out in such unkind weather?"

It was Lieutenant O'Hara bearing down on me, snowflakes decorating his uniform, his chestnut hair unruly in the wind with his cap pushed down at an unusual angle to prevent it being blown away. Explaining that I was hurrying to perform errands for Mrs Kingsley, I made to be on my way.

"Catherine, may I call you that? Please. I have to leave tomorrow and I have been racking my brains as to how I might best go about seeing you. Let me hire a cab and escort you on your errands. It is far too inclement for you to be out. Afterwards, in the time saved, perhaps you will come to the tearoom with me."

"Sir, I cannot go to the tearoom on my mistress's time."

"Then at least let me only accompany you on your errands. Catherine, you are shivering and blue with cold."

Indeed I had begun to shiver and it was not entirely the cold. I was tempted by his offer, but I feared the impropriety. The numbness of my toes and fingers, however, decided me.

"Sir, you are most kind. But what about your horse?"

The fine animal tossed his head at that moment, snorting and filling the air with a white mist.

"I will leave him at the inn. Come."

I had hardly realized his intention when the lieutenant leapt down and, putting his arm around my waist, swung me onto his mount. Jumping up behind me and pulling my body close to his, he flicked the reins and we proceeded at a brisk pace towards the inn. I was becoming acutely aware of the firm, lean body behind me, his warmth reaching me through the layers of clothing between us. Switching the reins to his right hand, the young man's left arm encircled my waist completely. With the movements of the horse, I felt his hand move upwards, as though by accident, until it supported my breast. I moved slightly but his hand caressed me only more firmly and he tightened his grasp, thereby pulling me so close that I thought I felt his heart beating against my back. Waves of embarrassment, mixed with an extraordinary elation, swept through me. It was as well that we reached the inn shortly for I was fast losing my common sense.

Lieutenant O'Hara soon rented a closed-in cab and had me safely installed. I was careful to sit well to the side and, though the officer looked sharply at me and was obviously aware of my intention, he merely seated himself on the opposite seat.

"Indeed," he said, "it is amazing how warm it becomes after a short ride, Catherine. I myself have lost all sense of the winter's chill."

I did not deign to answer, pointedly looking out of the window. Cavan, as I still privately called him to myself, had spared no expense in hiring the cab.

I reproached him, saying, "I had no idea that officers had so much cash in excess. We hardly need such luxury." Once having

57

made my protest, I settled down to delight in shopping in such a luxurious manner. After we had completed all my undertakings, I regretfully said that I should now return home.

"My little love, am I to have no payment?" Cavan leaned towards me, smiling teasingly.

"Sir, what can you mean?"

"Thanks to my great charity, you have finished your duties at least an hour before time. Now would you not say that the hour belongs to me?"

"Mercy, Lieutenant O'Hara, I do believe you are blackmailing me!"

"Catherine, my name is Cavan, and my heart longs to hear you say it. Say, 'Yes, Cavan, I will come for a drive in this fine cab, for which you have impoverished yourself, hiring it for the love of me'."

"Cavan! I swear you've kissed the famed Blarney stone."

"Well, yes and sure I have, and I'm to be telling ye all of my doings." Switching abruptly from his exaggerated Irish accent, he called to the driver.

"Drive for an hour and avoid the bad roads." With a lurch, the cab leapt forward and I turned to Cavan timidly.

"Sir, I think you have misunderstood my position in the Kingsley household." I then told him of my history and of my lack of social background.

"Why, allanna, my little love, did you think I was after your dowry? Major Kingsley has already told me all he knew about you, at my urgent request, and he respects you for the sweet, lovely girl you are."

Taking advantage of my surprise, Cavan moved beside me and slipped his arm around me. It felt so comfortable that I did not think to resist.

"Tell me about your home. Tell me about Ireland. Do you know that I have only once left Kingston? I so long to travel and see the countries that I read about. I often beg Mrs Kingsley to tell me about New York and she has promised to take me with her should she be visiting her family there."

Cavan drew me closer, taking one of my hands and putting it to his lips, drawing each finger across his mouth and kissing it in its turn.

"My home is a great house called Castle-Blaine and all around it are green Irish fields full of little streams. There are flowers and birds and small paths leading to the tenants' cottages. We have beautiful oak trees planted by my great-grandfather, and there is a peat bog where I was forbidden to go as a child. But I went there, playing with Rory and Patrick and Larry an' all." For a minute, Cavan seemed lost in memory and I realised with surprise that he was homesick. Without thinking, my fingers touched the curves of his mouth and moved in a gesture of comfort to rest on his cheek.

"Tell me more. What about your father and mother? How wonderful it must be to know and to have grown up with them."

Cavan laughed and placed a kiss in the centre of my palm, keeping my hand imprisoned.

"My mother is a good kind woman. She is saddened that I am her only child and have left home. My father is a hard man and we have had some grand quarrels. We breed horses at Castle-Blaine and our stock is famous in all the English-speaking world. I was nearly born on a horse and have never remembered a day when I could not ride. Like my father, I love all aspects of breeding, the waiting for the birth of a colt, the anxiety and the triumph if the new arrival shows promise."

I listened in fascination. I could not visualise such a world nor such a life. I looked into his eyes, hazel and sparkling with green as his enthusiasm rose. There was a comfort and familiarity in the acquiline nose and the chiselled line of his cheek.

"Why did you leave, Cavan, when you love it so? Doesn't your father need you?"

"I object to his running my life. I did not welcome the marriage he proposed for me. Finally, we agreed that I would do a stint in the army and also try to further his sale of horses on this continent. At the same time, if I see any promising stock here, I have my father's consent to act in his name."

Catching me unawares, Cavan put his arms around me and showered my face with kisses. A burning flame leapt in my body and my lips parted as his mouth found mine. I pressed myself to him for a moment, forgetting everything. Cavan's hand busied itself at my coat buttons, slipped in, and found my breast. With a groan, he slid my coat from my shoulders and reached for the buttons at my neck.

"Cavan, no! No! Cavan, the driver may look round." Oh, shame on me: So lost was I in the new and thrilling sensations that swept over me, that I thought only of the coach driver and not of my behaviour.

Cavan's lips were on my neck, on the cleft between my breasts and then, oh, sweet Mary in heaven, forgive, I was exposed to his gaze.

"My little love, my sweet, how lovely you are. Do you realise your breasts are like the curve of some rare shell?"

Hardly taking in his words, I saw him bend his head and I felt the delicate touch of his lips, light as a feather. For a moment, my hand went to the head bent in homage before me and I ventured to touch the untamed chestnut curls. I sighed, and it was almost with relief that I felt him turn to the other neglected breast. An unexpected maternal impulse filled me and I held him close.

After what seemed an eternity, Cavan raised his head. "Heart's dearest," he said, "you must be getting cold and I must not take advantage of you. You make it difficult for me not to claim you utterly and this is not the place – nor the time. Sweet love, help me with these cursed buttons and I will take you back in good order to Mrs Kingsley.

My hands were shaking so much and I was so dazed and lost that I could scarcely do up my buttons. Laughing, Cavan tenderly restored me to propriety and set my cloak to rights. Pulling me beside him, he called directions to the driver and we set back towards the Kingsley home.

"My love, I leave for Toronto tomorrow. I will not be able to see you before I go, but I will be in touch with you. Farewell, allanna."

He handed me down decorously and planted a kiss on my lips for all to see. I ran from him to the coachway, waving as I entered its shelter.

"Good-bye, Cavan, good-bye."

Would I ever see him again?

This morning I was surprised to find Mrs Kingsley still in bed, tear-stained and very quiet when I answered her bell.

"Madam, are you not well? Shall I fetch your smelling salts?"

"No, no Catherine. I have just had some news that has cast me down. Major Kingsley has been assigned on a mission to Montréal for a few months and I shall be left a grass-widow in Kingston."

"I do not understand the expression – a grass-widow – Madam. Will you explain it to me?"

Mrs Kingsley favours new and fashionable terms and sometimes leaves me quite mystified. As I hoped, the opportunity to instruct me cheered her immensely.

"It is the latest in our Anglo-Indian coinage, Catherine. The major explained to me that the term is used for wives whose husbands have temporarily left them. I really do not remember what grass has to do with it. At all events, it is now my lot."

At this point, Major Kingsley entered the room and, seeing me, said, "Ah, Catherine, I was wanting to speak to you. Mrs Kingsley has told you that my duty takes me to Montréal for a couple of months? I hope that I have your assurance that you will not leave my employ until my return. I should like to know that my wife has your companionship."

I hesitated. At any point I hope to hear from Darra. Major Kingsley seemed to grasp my concern.

"Look, my girl. Stay with us till the spring. Then I will finance your journey to visit your sister. You may take a month's holiday and should you wish, return to our employ. If you really insist on leaving us for the capital city, perhaps Mrs Kingsley and I can be instrumental in obtaining a position for you."

His unexpected kindness brought tears to my eyes. "Thank you so very much. Of course I will be glad to stay with Mrs Kingsley till your return. Thank you."

Indeed I do find that I can tolerate my mistress more kindly these days. Her barren state has made her self-conscious and she seeks appreciation and esteem for her social status, hoping to shine in the womanly skills of entertainment. I pity her and wish to help ease her pain.

Since it was my afternoon off, I put on my little blue coat and, wrapping a woollen kerchief round my face to ward off the biting wind, I set forth to visit Father Andrew. I found him poring over his books in the rectory. Upon noticing my presence, he shifted his spectacles and peered vaguely at me.

"My dear Catherine! What brings you here on this most inclement day? Come up closer to the fire, my dear."

"Father," I hesitated, "I must know, I really want to know who I am. I've asked you before, and now I wonder if there is anything you held back from me. You see, if some young man – well, if anyone asked for my hand in marriage . . ." To my alarm, I found my words were fading and my face warmed in embarrassment.

Father Andrew looked at me with sudden interest and removed his spectacles to regard me more closely.

"But this is very good news, Catherine. Am I to understand that some young man is asking for your hand?"

I was overcome and near speechless. "Oh no, no, Father. It's only that if ever I should marry, I'd wish to marry a gentleman," my tongue tripped over my explanations. "And – well – how could a gentleman. . .?" I stopped in confusion.

Father Andrew was looking at me with some concern. "Surely you are not looking above your station, Catherine? No good can come of that. I am sure that many a young workman would be proud to have you for a wife and not ask for information that no one can give."

I felt utterly dejected, but raised my head, nevertheless, and said, "Was there nothing? Surely Darra and I must come of good stock? The jewelry and the quilt are not the possessions of a labourer. Without a doubt the fabrics used in the quilt were most expensive and exquisite. No one from the lower classes could afford them.

Father Andrew looked at me sadly.

"Catherine, my dear child. Our Heavenly Father knows who you are and, if it is His wish, it will, in time, be revealed. Your only duty is to obey His commandments and to have faith. Heed my advice. Do not romanticise your birth any longer."

Rising to give me his blessing, he escorted me to the door.

How I long for Darra. As for marriage, I really am not at all interested.

6

Dear Cat,

Christmas is past and so is New Year, but today Trevor presented me with the best gift I have received in over twelve months. A letter from you! I simply can't believe it – and to think that I was about to give up. Why, at one point, I had even convinced myself that you had fashioned a new life and no longer had need of your scatterbrained sister, Darra. I cannot tell you how indignant I was when I read of the actions of that scurrilous woman, Agatha Kingsley. To think of her destroying the loving letters we wrote each other, especially when you and I are all the family we know in this cruel world. I still refuse to believe that we will never learn the identity of our true parents.

When I think of Mrs Kingsley's cruelty, my cheeks turn the colour of my hair! You are correct, however, in your assessment of Major Kingsley. He is kind and I am happy to know that you agree.

What irony that you should be working in the Kingsley household, taking my place, so to speak. Do give Oonagh a hug for me. I must confess that she was responsible in part for keeping me calm, at least as calm as it was possible for me to be. You know how I tend to let my emotions take over from time to time.

Now you tell me that we will not see each other till the spring. Before your letter's arrival, I'd have angrily declared that I could not, would not wait that long, but now that I know you are safe and reasonably contented, I suppose I can contain myself.

Can you forgive me for taking off with Trevor Vaughn in such an unprecedented manner? How can I explain it to you? Were I to confess the entire story, I feel sure you would think I had gone mad! At least I know you are fully aware of my shameless feelings

63

for that handsome actor. Do you recall how I mooned over him when we were at St Joseph's, promising myself to meet him backstage at the first possible opportunity? Well, unbelievable as it may seem, when I went to Butler's Theatre, Trevor himself sent me an invitation to visit him. We had supper in his rooms that very night after the performance and I knew there'd never be a more felicitous time to pursue my ambitions than at that moment. He invited me to audition in a one act play and . . . well, my dear sister, I left with him the very next morning to come to Toronto.

We broke the journey on the last day at Montgomery's Inn, on the corner of Dundas and Islington in Toronto. Such a lovely building with what Trevor tells me is Georgian architecture. How I wish I could have stayed there! The players, who aren't all that economically secure, however, live in Mrs Cooper's boarding house, where Trevor brought us on the very next day. Mrs Cooper's is conveniently located as far as Frank's Hotel is concerned. The upper floor of the hotel has been used to present plays since 1820 when the city was still known as "muddy York", and some of the actors, including Trevor, have sentimental feelings about it. Now there is a much grander theatre called the Royal Lyceum which was built by a Mr Ritchey only three years ago on King Street. Naturally, any actor of stature wishes to perform there and Trevor is already rehearsing for the opening date of *School For Scandal*.

Everyone has been anticipating the arrival of Mr John Nickinson to take over the management of the Royal Lyceum but to date he is still in Montréal. It seems that he set out from Albany to come to Toronto but, somehow or other, found himself in the wrong city! But I suppose he will turn up in time.

In the meantime, dear Trevor has secured the part of a maid for me in the play. I know it doesn't sound much, but a career isn't something you attain overnight. It's not the only part I'm working on either. I am understudying the role of Maria, but would far sooner play Lady Teazle, the young bride who is married to an older man of prosperous means. Do see if you can lay your hands on a copy of *School For Scandal*, Cat, that I may discuss it further with you. As for the plot, when you stop to think about it, that's what all young women should do! Surely it's just as easy to fall in love with a rich man as with a struggling poor one.

If ever I have the opportunity to play the role of Maria, I think it will be not the least bit difficult. You see, Maria is the ward of Sir Peter Teazle and, in a sense, my position in the company is somewhat similar. I am learning so much from Trevor. His knowledge of the theatre is unlimited and, fortunately, he was born into wealth and position long before he discovered his attraction to the theatre. I can't tell you how pleased I am to have made this decision and come away with the actors.

Of course, eventually I will have to go to New York if I want to enjoy any success worth speaking of. The most important theatres in North America are there. In the meantime, however, I will remain under the guidance of Trevor in Toronto, and hope that when the group goes on its springtime road-tour I will be offered a more important part.

George Skerett, a famous British actor, played in *School for Scandal* and also *The Taming of the Shrew* during his Toronto visits in the 40's. How I would love to play the role of Kate with some famous actor. I can just see your face as you read this. Wouldn't I be a splendid Kate?! I wouldn't need to practice her tempestuous temper tantrums at all, would I? The actors say they feel sure that, once Mr Nickinson arrives in Toronto, Mr Skerett and other famous players too will visit the city.

Just last evening, when Trevor and I were having a midnight snack in Mrs Cooper's vast kitchen, Mr and Mrs Prentice, freshly arrived from Galt, requested permission to join us. Mr and Mrs Prentice are part of the Galt Thespian Amateurs and, like many ambitious actors, move from city to city in search of better roles. I must confess that I wasn't much taken with Mrs Prentice from her opening questions which I considered far too personal.

"How are you enjoying your life in the theatre, Miss St Joseph?" she began curiously, "Are you and Mr Vaughn related?"

"Oh no," I replied, elevating my chin somewhat as I spoke, "I come from an established family in the old country. Trevor is my sponsor and advisor," and then I deliberately turned my head aside from Trevor's warning glance.

"How interesting," Mrs Prentice continued. "And Mr Vaughn,

I assume, is an old family friend?"

Trevor firmly prevented me from replying that time by grasping my hand and signalling me to be quiet.

"Thank you for your concern, Mrs Prentice," he said smoothly, "but I have appointed myself to be entirely responsible for Miss St Joseph's career."

"Ooooh," she gushed. "Such a lucky little girl!"

It's funny. Cat. Although she didn't say anything mean, I sensed that she was trying to make me feel ill-at-ease. She reminded me of Tassy the day she sneaked into the kitchen at the parsonage and licked the cream from the top of the bowl of rice pudding.

From that moment on, Trevor dominated the conversation and, although Mrs Prentice looked rather put out, Mr Prentice was as nice as could be.

"A fine playwright, Richard Brinsley Sheridan," said he, "and some fine roles in this delightful comedy. I take it you agree, Mr Vaughn?"

"Comedy involving old age, the senex, is always timely," Trevor replied. "Surely you recall the *Canterbury Tales*? The Merchant, January and his young bride – and Damion, who caught her fair and square up in the pear tree? Oh, 'tis a fine comedy, and it contains the same moral. As Sir Peter says in *School For Scandal*, 'When an old bachelor marries a young wife, he deserves – no – the crime carries its punishment along with it.'"

"Why, gentlemen," I protested, "surely the bargain brings joy to both sides."

At this, we all had a good laugh and soon retired for the night. As usual, Trevor was asleep the moment his head touched the pillow but I lay awake for some time thinking of all that had been said.

Well, dear Cat, I shan't bore you further with the conversations of actors and actresses. I miss you so. Be assured that you are in my thoughts every day and in my prayers too. It is not so easy to attend mass regularly, being part of the theatre group, but I sneak away as often as possible, usually in the early hours to seek a quiet time. And when I do, I think of you often and of St Joseph's, Father Andrew and the sisters.

Do write and tell me all that occupies you. Love, Darra.

Dear Cat,

You will be shocked and horrified, as am I, when you note how long it is since I have written to you. It's not as though I haven't begun, truly I have. I cannot say how often. Dear Cat. Dear Cat. Then I'd get no further.

January rushed by in a swirl of activity. There were rehearsals, performances and after-theatre suppers. Every evening, it seemed as though I'd meet more and more admirers; young military officers, old monied-Americans, prissy politicians and married men seeking mistresses. It caused me to think more seriously about my own future. We've always known, you and I, that in the end, our careers must become matrimonial endeavours. One day some kind soul will keep us in the manner to which we wish to become accustomed! But not too soon, I hope. Dear sister, after observing what's available here, I've decided to close my eyes to men's physical attractions.

Some of the lads who come mewling round the stage door are boisterous and comely. Why, just the other evening, a handsome cavalier was pressing me for my favours.

"Delighted to make your acquaintance, Miss Darra," he began and, scarcely allowing me time to answer, his arm crept round my waist.

(I need not, indeed, must not tell Cat how attractive I found this particular gentleman, Ian MacLaren by name, and that the dalliance went on much longer than I confessed.)

Knowing that I must not entirely discourage my admirers, I smiled at him and gently disentangled myself from his persistent embrace. What a pity they are so often young and penniless. The younger they are, the more their interest seems to lie with seduction. So I try to bear in mind that these beautiful young men will age in time. Why not simply fall in love, if that's what your determination be, with an older and, therefore, richer gentleman? My ideal is one who can provide me with all life's little luxuries; satins and silks, fashionable bonnets, costumes and soft suede boots; large country estates and exquisite town houses too, all staffed abundantly with servants.

(Once more, I pause in my letter writing. It is many long months since I have seen my sister and I find it difficult to put into a letter all that I might confide to her in person so readily. I feel sure she must be wondering about Trevor and me, as well she might. Cat no doubt visualises me, her own sister, as a scarlet woman. After all, I did run off with Trevor and it's true that I was prepared to sacrifice my virginity in order to become an actress.

Things have turned out quite differently, however, and I am as lily-white today as I was on the evening when I first disrobed before him. Oh, we share the bed on occasion and Trevor fondles me for a few short minutes before falling asleep. It is my guess that he suffers from some illness or other which prevents him from being capable of completing his masculine role. Despite his shortcomings, Trevor makes sure I do not flirt long with the young men at the stage door. Unfortunately, Sister Martha herself couldn't do a better job as my chaperone!

Alternately, I feel sorry and glad. I am very curious about the feel and contact of a real live man. At the same time, I'm not sorry that my introduction to what must be joyful ecstacy is not to be made by Trevor. Until I saw him up close, I thought, of course, that he was youthful and vigorous. He is not. He is an old man whose clever stage make-up merely disguises his wrinkles and ageing skin. He is fortunate still to have a full, thick head of hair because I fear baldness would be his undoing.

How can I tell Cat all this? Committing the words to paper would seem blasphemous. Were she here, though, I'd whisper it all in her ear without a moment's hesitation.)

Did I ever tell you, Cat, that Trevor wanted to know when my birthday was? Well, that was a difficult question, wasn't it? Yours was easy enough to settle, with St Catherine's Day to celebrate, but it was another matter with a name like Darra? No Darra ever got sainted, nor is ever likely to! I know the sisters let me choose a saint of a different name, but she never seemed to belong to me. Their main concern was that I chose a day which fell during the summer.

"Children who have their birthdays during the months of the Christmas season are always disappointed – having the celebrations so close to one another," I recall Sister Martha remarking.

I remember there was St Mary Magdalene on July 22 and St Margaret on July 20. St Barbara's Day turned out to be December 4, so she was rejected. Finally, I decided on Theresa, and the drama of her story about the excruciating pain she suffered in her side, which she claimed was caused by an angel, who plunged a flaming sword repeatedly into her heart. Her feast day was August 27. However, when I repeated the story to Sister Martha, her face got all tight with frowning and I could tell she didn't approve of my unusual choice. Rather subdued, I accepted July 22. After all, who could be more blessed than St Mary? Half the girls in the world must have Mary for their second name, perhaps because they are told they should honour Immaculate Conception. The whole matter is rather strange, don't you agree?

Ah, yes, I was about to tell you what I said when Trevor asked me about my birthday. I suspected that he wanted to buy me a gift and, since it was obvious that Toronto was in for an unusually cold winter this year, I hoped for a warm coat or a fur piece. Cannily I made up my mind to have my birthday during the month of February.

"Why Trevor dear," I answered him as sweet as pie, "my birthday is very soon, as it happens."

"Really?" he exclaimed, rolling his eyes roguishly at me, since we were within earshot of several people he wished to impress. "Out with it, Darra, my sweet. On what cold wintry day were you brought into this cruel world?"

"Just one day before St Valentine's Day, 13 February," I said thinking it was a fine choice. On the 14th, our troupe had been hired to perform a revue skit at the home of some Important People. Rumour had it that one of our government leaders, Mr Robert Baldwin, might be on hand. Trevor was most interested because of the political unrest in the country.

For my part, I am interested in searching for clues leading to information regarding our family. Surely one of our parents must be red-headed. At any rate, I intend to keep my eyes open and my ears alert.

I can't remember offhand the name of the street where the party was to be held, but I do recall that it was way out in Yorkville and there's only one city omnibus which travels there hourly from central Toronto. I was so glad when Trevor announced we would hire a one-horse cab.

However, I'm getting ahead of my story. After I announced the date of my supposed birthday, Trevor looked surprised.

"Pray what does your pretty little heart desire? Since your anniversary falls so near to the feast day of St Valentine, we can incorporate two gifts into one. What do you say?"

Since it hadn't occurred to me that Trevor had been planning a St Valentine's gift, I regretted for one short moment my devious decision. I smiled, nevertheless, assuring my benefactor that I would be delighted with anything he might decide to bestow on me.

Imagine my delight when he bade me come with him the following morning to Yonge Street.

"Don't keep me in suspense, Trevor, where are we going?" I asked, as we swished through the streets over the frozen snow.

"Never you mind now. You'll find out soon enough."

When the driver drew up in front of a smart store-front, bearing a fresh sign in bold black letters, I drew in my breath sharply.

"James H. Rogers," I read. "Furs."

Once Trevor and I were inside the shop, a short, pudgy man, dressed in a morning suit, approached us. His round face beamed with pleasure.

"Good morning, Sir, Madam. May I help you with something this fine morning?"

"Would you be Mr Rogers, Sir? Mr James Rogers?"

"Mr Rogers is not in this morning, Sir, but I am his assistant, Mr Cohen."

"Then I hope it is safe to assume that you may help us. I sent you a message yesterday. I am Trevor Vaughn."

"Ahhh," said the little man and rubbed his hands vigorously together. "I received your message, Sir, and feel certain that I can provide a coat for the young lady or anything else she may fancy."

Oh Cat, don't think me foolish, that I exaggerate what happened. Those are the exact words Trevor and Mr Cohen used and that is exactly what took place. After that introduction, Mr Cohen seated us and disappeared into the rear of the shop. When he returned, he was carrying three coats, and a younger assistant who was following, was weighed down with three more fur garments.

"First, I must explain," Mr Cohen began, after he had hung up his load of pelts. "Most of our trade is accomplished through order and specifications; therefore we do not keep on hand a great number of ready-made coats and jackets. If Madam would prefer to give us an exact order, we would, of course, make for her the finest garment possible."

"Madam needs a fur coat now," Trevor interrupted patiently. "Winter is upon us with a vengeance and Madam must be kept warm."

Cat. Can you imagine how I felt? Madam (that's me) must be kept warm!

When Mr Cohen said he had very few garments ready-made on hand, he was certainly telling the truth. Happily, he did have some; two muskrats, a black seal, a man-sized lynx coat, a raccoon and a magnificent mink with which, of course, I fell instantly in love. One by one, I tried them on and modelled them for Trevor, who waved them aside disdainfully.

"Well, Mr Cohen, you seem to have failed," he said. My heart sank instantly into the toes of my boots. No fur coat? After all this?

"One moment, Sir. There is one more item in the back of the shop. Not specifically what you requested – but perhaps – you will allow me? One moment please."

When he returned this time, it was with a treasure. I gazed at the full-length cape, fashioned in midnight-blue velvet. I imagined myself wearing it with my newly discovered family to the opera and the theatre in large European cities. Its beaver lining was soft and the hood was trimmed in a ruff of white ermine. Mr Cohen was explaining that it had been made for a British colonel's wife who changed her mind after the cloak had been completed.

The moment he placed the cape on my shoulders, I knew it had been meant for me, not for any British colonel's wife. Can you picture me? I pulled the hood up over my hair so it framed my auburn curls and lit up my sea-green eyes. I paraded and modelled, delighted with the vision I caught in the mirror.

"Happy birthday, Darra," said Trevor, and to the clerk, "We'll take it."

I threw my arms exuberantly around him and almost knocked him over in my enthusiasm.

On the evening of the Valentine's Day fête, I dressed myself in a flurry of excitement. I had, of course, already decided on a gown for the evening. In view of the celebration, it should have been red. Do you remember how red clashes with my hair? I thought long and hard about what I should wear and finally decided on white, sprigged all over with little hearts and forget-me-knots. I had decided also that, if I felt the least bit chilly, I would not hesitate to keep my new cloak about my shoulders.

The hall was already packed when we arrived. Mrs Kelly, our hostess, had decorated the entire foyer and ballroom with festoons of hearts and flowers which looked so real that, until I got up close to them, I could not believe they were artificial.

Mrs Kelly is a cheery soul, stoutish and good humoured, still unused to the quite miraculous fortune into which she and her husband seem to have fallen. Perhaps some would refer to her and her husband as "nouveau riche". Be that as it may, her hospitality should not be scorned, for she made great efforts to please us.

On the drive over to the Kellys, Marcus was telling me all about the famous people I would be sure to meet. Have I told you about Marcus? Marcus Denby. I don't believe I have. Well, he's the youngest actor in our group. Actually, I don't know whether you'd call him an actor or not. He doesn't do much acting. What he does is handle the details that nobody else is willing to attend to; stage directions, lighting, scenery, bookings in other theatres and small towns; I guess you could call him a sort of impresario.

Marcus is very nice. He's only 26, but he's grown a beard to make himself look older. At least, that's what I think. When he saw me in my new cloak, his face betrayed his admiration.

"For sure Darra," he said, "you look like the young Queen and make no mistake about it."

To tell the truth, I believe that poor Marcus is somewhat smitten with me. It's unfortunate, because I am unable to reciprocate the feeling. He's handsome enough and he's not poverty stricken, but there are no answering sparks.

Very shortly after our arrival, both Trevor and Marcus were obliged to desert me to ensure that the prepared revue would run smoothly. I was left in the safe hands of Mrs Kelly and some of the other city ladies. At least, "safe" was the way Trevor described it. I would have called it their clutches rather than safe hands myself.

"So, Miss St Joseph," beamed my hostess. "I understand you are Mr Vaughn's niece and have come all this way from Kingston to care for his needs."

I smiled pityingly. "Not at all. Dear Papa was in failing health at the time of my departure and Mr Vaughn, being an old family friend, was selected as my guardian."

Trevor had instructed me to smile if I was asked any questions which I was unable, or didn't care to answer. Privately, however, I disagreed with his solution.

"Are you also an actress then?" asked a woman whose nose was shaped exactly like a hawk's and had a large warty-looking growth on one side of it.

"Why, yes I am," I answered.

"Don't they have a part in the play for you tonight?" she pursued.

"I lean to more dramatic roles," I replied, determined to impress her.

"Oh, and what precisely have you acted in?"

"I am in constant rehearsal for my Shakespearian debut which will take place in New York. I was to have opened in Toronto, but Trevor changed his mind."

"Are you related to the Devlins in Niagara?" The rude interruption and most unexpected question came from a fat, young dimpled creature with blonde, sausage curls who had been staring frankly at me for some time. "Shelagh Devlin is a close friend of mine and I swear you could pass for her sister with that hair of yours."

Remembering to continue my role as a British lady, I murmured discreetly. "Papa did mention distant connections in that area. To date, I have not found the time to send out any cards."

There was a momentary silence and fortunately, before one of them could question me further, the curtain rose on our Valentine's Day revue. Everyone's attention was riveted on stage, even mine, despite all the rehearsals I had sat through already. I knew all the lines by heart and, had someone suddenly taken ill or passed out, I was prepared to rush up and take over.

There were love duets, popular with the ladies, comical skits which had everybody laughing, and a blackface routine.

"How I enjoy those clever minstrel shows," exclaimed Mrs Kelly. "I saw my first ones in New York."

There was something to please everyone. I was so excited, I almost wished I might fall in love to complete the evening's success.

After the actors had taken their final curtain calls, Marcus approached me, accompanied by a familiar figure.

"They say it's pink lemonade," he said, handing me a glass, "but I saw at least two bottle of wine being poured into it. Have you met Mr McLaren, Darra?"

"Of course she's met me. We're good friends, aren't we, my sweet?" interrupted my admirer.

"We have seen each other on occasion," I allowed, wishing he could be less effusive.

"Well, I'll leave you to your own devices, in that case," said Marcus. "They need me backstage."

After his departure, Mr MacLaren leaned forward and seized my hand. "I've just had a marvellous idea, Darra."

"And what may that be, Sir?"

"Come, come Darra. You've been calling me Ian for long enough. Why put on this high and mighty act all of a sudden?"

"I'm sorry, Ian. It's just that I don't want to give Trevor anything to reproach me for later," I apologised, "but tell me, what is your idea?"

"Well, I know you've not been in Toronto very long and I thought perhaps you might be interested in seeing Niagara Falls."

"Ohhh, Ian, indeed I would," I replied, keeping secret from him the most recent information I had gleaned about the Devlins, who might be related to Cat and me in some manner. "When are you thinking of making the trip?"

"Whenever it would be convenient for you, Darra. Do you think you can escape Mr Vaughn's scrutiny?"

"I cannot imagine Trevor having the slightest interest in visiting Niagara Falls, but I don't see why I shouldn't go there and see them in all their splendour."

I laughed, and immediately began to wonder whatever Ian must think of me. He probably wonders about Trevor's and my relationship, even if he'd never ask. I almost needled him on the spot – it would have seemed an amusing dare – but we were interrupted by the arrival of Trevor in the company of our host.

"Darra, my dear, have you met our fine host, Mr Kelly?" Trevor asked.

I nodded to assure him that I had and quickly dropped one of my daintiest curtsies. Oh Cat, how I long for the day when I am presented at The British court in London, England. I practice and practice and, although I am all but perfect in the execution of a curtsy now, I feel certain I will be able to add extra grace and finesse on my presentation day.

The fine gentleman grasped my hand lightly, murmured, "Are you enjoying yourself, Miss St Joseph?" and turned immediately to Trevor, respect evident in his eyes.

"Your niece is indeed a beauty, Sir. I had heard it said before tonight."

This time I knew better than to refute the relationship. Trevor could be quite possessive. I do believe I blushed, however, but everyone pretended not to notice, putting it down to my modesty.

Soon the men returned to their talk about what is on everybody's mind these days, when they're not talking politics, that is; building the railway. While they droned on, I listened, and it all sounded exactly the same as the conversations I've heard so often before.

The ride home under a starry sky, with the bells ting-a-linging on the horse's harness, was exhilarating. I leaned back against the bearskin rug in my glamorous cape, drank in the pure night air and dreamed about the projected trip to Niagara.

Later in bed that night, I had a dream in which I was riding a horse with a golden bridle. He was pure white and galloped as fast as the wind. I could hear a tumultuous roar of what I thought must be thunder. It was coming from afar and I peered ahead of me into the darkness to try and distinguish what it could be. As the din increased in volume, an enormous abysss opened up in front of us. My horse tried to halt but, finding himself unable to, we hurtled into space. I tightened my hold on the reins and clasped his beautiful milky mane with desperation.

Below us, what looked like several mighty rivers plunged over an embankment onto myriads of sharp, slippery rocks. The air was filled with a shining mist and I felt bathed in rainbow sprays. Thinking to smash at any moment on the craggy landscape beneath us, I was amazed to discover that my magnificent steed had sprung wings like Pegasus and we were flying, higher, ever higher, over what I realise now must have been the Falls. As we circled that fairyland once more, I leaned farther to gain a better view. At that moment, I woke up.

Dear Cat, when did I last tell you of my dreams? And now adieu, sister mine. As soon as I have visited Niagara, I will write you a more sensible report.

With my own true love, Darra.

March 18, 1851

Dear Cat,

I'm late again, but this time it's not really my fault. I have been laid low with an undiagnosed illness. It began with stomach cramps and fever and whatever it may have been, I most heartily pray that it will never strike me again. I remember when we were girls and caught cold, the sisters would dose us with something horrible; castor oil, goose grease, mustard plasters: Ugh. Unwelcome memories. Still I do not recall being very sick then, not as sick as I was this time. It struck me while still away at Niagara Falls. Oh Cat, I haven't told you about the Falls. Patience!

My cold began with my feeling too hot and then too cold, and almost at once, too hot again. My bones ached from head to toe as though I had been beaten. As if that weren't enough. I had bouts of diarrhoea coupled with spasms of vomiting. Soon my fever chased all sense from my mind, and I called for you, for Sister Martha and Sister Isobel. I was racked with pain. I didn't know whether to lie down or sit up. Nothing helped.

Eventually, of course, the fever subsided, but it was weeks before I returned to my normal state. I grew so thin and shrivelled. You cannot imagine. My skin hung on me in loose folds. I looked like an old hag of 30! Trevor nursed me and tended to my wants himself, and he was as tender as the sisters always were.

Ian was frankly dismayed by my sudden illness and embarrassed for me as well as for himself. After we had returned to Toronto, however, he sent me flowers, which must have been expensive since it is the middle of winter.

Now, Cat, you shall hear about the Falls. I have been to Niagara and it is quite unique among my experiences in life. To begin at the beginning so that you may see it all through my eyes. As soon as you come to Toronto, we must go together.

Ian warned me that we should be making an early start, and, accordingly, pulled up with a sleigh and two horses at 8 a.m., an hour when it is barely light at this time of year. Naturally, I was dressed warmly and held my cloak tightly around me. Ian helped me get settled on a mound of bearskin rugs which he arranged about me like a cocoon.

"To shelter you from the wind, Darra," he explained. Then, just as he was climbing agilely in beside me, Trevor appeared, a broad smile on his face, bag in hand.

"Why, Trevor," I quaked. "I thought you were asleep."

"I am quite aware of that, my dear Darra," he answered.

"Good morning, Sir," Ian broke in at this point. "How thoughtful of you to come to see us off."

"My intention, Mr McLaren," stated Trevor firmly, "is to accompany you. I have never viewed the Falls in their winter garb."

"Oh Trevor, you mean you're coming too?" I gasped, completely taken aback.

"Well, of course, my dear. Surely you'd not wish to leave me on my own," with which remark, he placed his bag in the rack and climbed aboard, placing his bulk carefully between Ian and me.

Ian's face was a study of confusion; however, he quickly recovered himself and, with a smart crack of the reins, we were off.

"We should make Beamsville before dark," he said gloomily. "They say it's as good a place as any to put up for the night. I also hear tell the local inn is a good one."

Everywhere I looked I saw snow, snow and more snow, but the air was so fresh and tingling, I grew intoxicated on the sheer beauty of the landscape, despite my disappointment at Trevor's abrupt appearance.

For a while, we were able to sight Lake Ontario, the wind blowing loose twigs and debris against its frozen shores. Being such a large, beautiful lake in the summer, it is difficult for me to fathom the difference in winter. We galloped past the iced-up Credit River and through the village of Springfield. Despite our speed, it was noon before we arrived at Oakville which is situated on the lake at the mouth of Sixteen Mile Creek.

The landlady at the inn produced steaming bowls of bean soup, thick slices of bread and a nice bird pie. There was also a whisky punch placed in the centre of the table which I declined, (and Trevor drank much of), for I was convinced that one glass, combined with the frigidness of the air, would overcome me. The idea of missing any of the sights filled me with determination.

Soon we were off again, through Wellington Square and Port Nelson, then headed towards the narrow isthmus which divides Burlington Bay from Lake Ontario. At that moment, I leaned across Trevor towards Ian, calling out with delight, "Wouldn't it be fun to skate there?"

He smiled and nodded his head. It was far too difficult to make conversation when the air and the wind caused such shortness of breath.

When we reached Stony Creek, a village which was the site of a gruesome battle between the English and the Americans, Ian was keen to make a stop so I could see it. It was getting dark again, however, snow was beginning to fall once more, and Trevor insisted that we push on to Beamsville.

I must confess, Cat, that I was happy when we arrived for I was growing weary of sitting in the same position and my limbs were cramped and numb. After an ample supper of fried pork chops and fish, accompanied by boiled onions and turnips, coffee and the inevitable "traveller's punch" Trevor, Ian and I settled down before the open fireplace. It had been Ian's and my intention to spend an intimate evening becoming better acquainted, but Trevor's presence altered our plans. Soon we bade each other good night and retired to our separate quarters, I with my protector.

In the morning, we woke cold and ravenous to discover Ian up and ready to be on the way. As I drank cup after cup of strong tea, I soon found my appetite diminishing in the wake of the excitement ahead of me. How would I be able to locate the Devlins without confessing all to Trevor?

The next place we came upon was St Catherine's, a pretty town near the Welland Canal. The name, of course, made me think of you, Cat, and I wondered which of the six Saint Catherines it is named after.

"Only another twelve miles, Darra, and we will be at Niagara," Ian announced, peering round Trevor's girth in a vain attempt to catch my eye. The horses' hoofs flew across the frozen snow, the rhythmical jingling of the bells sending out messages of our arrival.

The town of Niagara lies at the mouth of the Niagara River, but it appeared to me as all small towns. When Ian suggested a brief halt, Trevor firmly shook his head.

"On to the Falls," he ordered, pulling himself into a more erect position.

Just before we sighted our destination, Ian stopped the sleigh and, once more turning to me, said, "Darra, I hope you won't be disappointed with your first sight of Niagara. Many people are, you know. Personally, I have never understood why. Perhaps it's because they've heard too many superlatives about the Falls. Sometimes the reality cannot equal the imagined. Remember also that it's winter and the Falls in winter are quite different in appearance from that in summer."

"Nonsense, Ian, I could never be disappointed in Niagara." I was incredulous at the thought. Believe me, I wasn't disappointed in the least.

We came upon the Falls from above and, although not so spectacular a sight as looking upwards, it is, nevertheless, awe-inspiring. I had anticipated hearing the roar of the water falling ceaselessly on the rocks below but, of course, all that sound was muffled in the sheets of ice and huge suspended icicles. The spray which I had been told was like a million garden hoses all turned on at once, condensed as soon as it rose and the frigid air turned the water drops into instant ice sculptures.

"Ohhh," I sighed. "Words can't describe it. Please, can't we get closer?"

"Yes, of course we can. I've brought along two pairs of crampons, so we should be able to walk out on Table Rock at the base of the Crescent Falls."

After minor protests from Trevor, we descended, leaving him behind. Once below, we found ourselves surrounded by the crystal artwork and I cried out in delight. Reaching out for Ian's hand and pulling him closer, I deposited a warm kiss on his eager lips.

It was like standing inside an enormous cave filled with stalactites and stalagmites composed of clear ice. Some of the icicles were gigantic, larger than a man's body. A filigree of ice covered every tree in sight. I thought that when the wind blew, the shard-like branches would set up a sound resembling the music of wind-chimes. From time to time, huge blocks of ice formed on the lip of the cataracts, then abruptly, as if it were nature's whim, they would be swept over the falls to crash into the boiling cauldron below.

I moved closer to Ian; his arms pulled me against him and he covered my face with passionate kisses. What a backdrop for romance, I thought.

(I move onward with my tale, omitting Ian's insistent explorations beneath my cloak. I did not want to leave. Even as we became aware of Trevor's shouts, we lingered, pressing our bodies against each other with teasing delight. Eventually, for the ground was constantly shifting and unsafe, I tore myself reluctantly from his embrace).

As we turned, the sun burst forth more brightly than it had shone all day. Instantly a rainbow splayed itself like a bow across the expanse of the Falls.

"Ohhh, just look, Ian." I was shivering, not so much from the cold but from the thrill of the moment. He put his arm around me and I was happy, thinking that such a monumental miracle of nature should be shared with another of God's creatures. It is impossible to describe adequately. The awesomeness, the magic, the beauteous perfection, shared with a loved one. You will have to see it for yourself.

As for the chill, it prevented me from seeking out the Devlin family for, that very evening, the illness came upon me and was well advanced by the time we arrived back at Mrs Cooper's. She took one look at me and ordered me to bed. Soon I was wrapped in heated blankets. Alternately, I shivered and sweated. Two weeks passed before I was able to rise from my bed and, even then, I was so weak that I required assistance to cross the distance from the bed to the chair; but I refuse to bore you further with my ridiculous ailments. The days did pass and eventually I mended, just in time for the annual St Patrick's Day celebrations.

March 19, 1851

Dear dear Cat,

It was my intention to write on and on until I had told you about every occurrence in my life to date. Sleep overtook me, however, which only goes to prove that I still haven't regained all my strength.

I knew St Patrick's Day would be busy so I went out quietly in the early morn to mass. St Michael's is a fairly new cathedral and I enjoy the spaciousness inside. I gave thanks for my regained health and prayed for wealth and true love. Quite a change from the days when the sisters used to order me to chapel to repent for my sins by saying Hail Marys.

After lunch, Marcus persuaded me to walk with him to Yonge Street to see how the arrangements for the parade were progressing. Beneath my blue velvet cloak, I was attired in green and I also sported an emerald-green bonnet which I thought very smart.

"I see, Darra," said Marcus, "that you're a true daughter of those who believe in the wearing of the green."

"Oh indeed," I agreed, thinking it seemed that the only thing certain about my lineage was my red hair, which suggested an Irish background.

The weather is milder now, not warm nor springlike, but not freezing either. The sun was shining that afternoon and that helped enormously. As we arrived on the scene, some pipers and runners were in the process of organizing the top-hatted Irishmen into a semblance of order. It was only two o'clock in the afternoon and already several had visited the taverns more than once.

As the parade was about to commence, I heard shouts of "Marcus, Marcus," from just behind us. We turned to see who was there and I noticed the broad grin on Marcus' face as a handsome, chestnut-haired officer joined us. The two men shook hands like old friends and then turned to me.

"Faith and begorra, mavourneen, but you do look like a bit of Ireland itself," said the officer impudently, without waiting for proper introductions. "Are you a native of that fair isle?"

"No Sir," I replied, forgetting my past pretences. "I am a daughter of the New World and have lived in the colonies all my life."

"What? Born and bred in 'muddy York'? I'll not be believing it."

"No, not Toronto," I conceded. "Kingston."

"Well, I'll be . . ." but then he grew silent.

"Is there anything wrong with Kingston, Lieutenant?" I pursued.

"Oh no, it's just that you are the second pretty girl I have met recently from that town."

"Perhaps Kingston has a monopoly on pretty girls," I teased.

"It's remarkable. Why, if I'd not already lost my heart to a temptress with gold hair and cornflower blue eyes, I swear I'd lose it to you."

With that, I stepped closer to him. His eyes looked so familiar to me, but I could think of no reason why.

"If we are not destined to be sweethearts," I mocked him, "then, let us pledge to be brother and sister."

"Why, 'tis a fine idea. Sister, what is your name?" As he spoke, he took my hand in his and made a long, low courtly bow.

"Darra," I began, "and what. . ."

"Well, I must confess I'd as leave have the two of you joined in a brother-sister relationship," broke in Marcus. "It's been a long time since our last meeting, Cavan. I didn't know you were in town."

"Just arrived, Marcus. Tell me, for I mustn't linger – Colonel Thompson is expecting these dispatches – is there some entertainment in town tonight?"

"To be sure! *Ali Baba* is playing at the Lyceum."

"Good," he interrupted before Marcus could tell him that I had a part in it. "I'll see you tonight then."

So saying, he strode off in a great hurry, and Marcus and I turned our attention back to the parade which was moving smartly down the street. Not only were the bandsmen and the members of the St Patrick's Association organised to march along the designated route, but most of the assembled crowd joined in with them a few blocks before they arrived at their lodge hall.

"We must return, Marcus," I said reluctantly, and we hastened back to the stage door where a bevy of admirers were hanging around.

"Darra," one called out, "tell us what part you are playing tonight."

"Oh," I laughed. "I'm only a harem girl."

My reply was met with widespread amusement, and I quickly ducked inside.

"I wouldn't mind being one of the thieves, Darra," I heard from afar as I dashed towards the dressing rooms, "and I know just which sweets I'd steal."

Mr Besnard had planned a gala evening performance of *Ali Baba* which is one of the favourites. There was a part for everyone; in most cases, we did not have much to do, but the fact that I'd be on stage was enough for me. All I need do was dress up in a harem costume with veils hanging about me and slink around the stage. Actually, it was necessary to keep on the move and be lively because the theatre was cold and my bare arms have a tendency to turn blue and get covered with goose bumps.

When I spotted Marcus backstage just before my entrance with the other harem girls, I stopped him to ask, "Marcus, please tell me who the handsome lieutenant was who joined us at the parade this afternoon, and how do you come to know him?"

"Why are you interested in him, Darra? Perhaps I'll satisfy your curiosity after you've danced for me."

I knew he was teasing me, but did not feel in the mood for such frivolity.

"Please, Marcus," I pouted, "don't be that way."

"Very well, Darra, but it will have to be later. Mr Besnard is signalling."

The audience was merry and receptive, as a matter of fact, at times too merry. They even revived the old theatre game of tossing. Have you heard of it, Cat? All the seats in the house had been sold except for some of the cheap front ones. Two men wandered into the Lyceum off the streets (no doubt straight from the alehouses) and insisted that they be tossed up to the cheap seats. Whereupon, some of the stronger men in the back picked up the lads and, swinging them back and forth to get some momentum tossed them over the heads of the audience in the general direction of the front rows. Needless to say, it was necessary to toss them more than once! A man's body, hurled through the air in that manner, tends to clear only a few rows at a time. One of the men made the trip safely, but the other one took a bad fall and dislocated his collar bone. He had to be removed from the theatre, moaning all the while and, simultaneously, Ali Baba carried on with his adventures on stage!

Mr Besnard and Mr Skerett were hosting a cast party and everybody was expected to come and meet the actors. By the time I had changed out of my harem costume and climbed into my new pale green silk gown of Dresden shepherdess design, with shamrocks dotting its surface, the scene looked as though all Toronto had turned out. Mr Skerett had one of Mr Nickinson's daughters in tow. There were a few representatives of the Galt Thespian Amateurs and, everywhere you looked diverse uniforms. There must have been at least one officer from every regiment in the country and maybe a few Americans too. Everyone appeared to be in good humour. Several of the gentlemen were drinking green beer, brewed especially for St Patrick's Day.

"Darra! Darra!" I could hear my name being called from two different directions. I turned my head to see who had spotted me. There was Trevor on one side with two portly but distinguished looking gentlemen. On the other side was Marcus with what appeared to be an entire contingent of young men, some of whom were army officers. I knew I should go straight to Trevor but mischief pulled me in the opposite direction.

"Good evening again, Marcus," I said, searching the faces of the officers for a familiar face, "How can you bear to drink that revolting concoction?"

Marcus looked down at his stein of green beer, and laughed. "Why, 'tis the custom, Darra. May I be so bold as to inform you that you are looking especially beautiful this evening?" he said. "And may I present to you these good gentlemen who, after watching your performance as a harem girl, have begged to make your personal acquaintance?"

Having asked permission, he proceeded to reel off the names of each one and, as he did so, each in turn snapped his heels together and bowed. I reciprocated by giving them a curtsy in the manner of the stars at the Garrick Theatre. As for their names, however, I promptly forgot them.

At the same moment, Trevor made his appearance with the two portly gentlemen, and the officers and other gentlemen backed away, leaving me to the designs of the older men.

"Darra, my dear, I am sure you remember Mr Besnard? And may I present Mr Basil Levishon from New York?"

"Good evening, gentlemen." Once again I went into my curtsying act, but this time it was meant only as a gesture of respect and formal pleasure.

Mr Levishon, however, was not to be dismissed as cursorily. He advanced on me and, taking my hand in his, said, "Good heavens, my dear girl, you have nothing to drink. Come, let us go together to the punch bowl." Hastily, before anyone could protest, he led me firmly by the elbow away from Trevor and Mr Besnard.

"Please do not think ill of me, Miss St Joseph, but I must have you to myself for a few moments."

"Why Sir, you flatter me."

Frankly, I couldn't think what this old man wanted of me. However, as he spoke, I began to understand vaguely. He's rich, Cat, oh not just comfortably rich but ostentatiously so. He lives in New York and he told me (can you imagine?) that he thought I could have a fine acting career there.

"You have the makings of a great dramatic actress, my dear," he said.

Now how could he predict whether I could act or not from watching me parade about on stage in a harem costume? I wonder when men make some exaggerated statements.

"When you come to New York, contact me," he continued. "I can move mountains. You'll see. Ask, and it shall be yours." Have you ever heard such blarney?

I'll probably never see Mr Levishon again, but it's rather amusing to dream of what he could do for me if I ever do meet him a second time. Thinking about New York and its possibilities almost made me forget that I didn't see the handsome lieutenant again, nor did I learn his name from Marcus. What's more, Ian wasn't on hand for the party tonight. I wonder why.

At any rate, it was an extraordinary day and the excitement seems to linger. Towards midnight, I sought out Trevor to inquire when he intended leaving. I am still tired from my illness and need extra rest.

So now I must go to sleep. How I long to be with you once again, dear sister.

With love from your own Darra.

7

April 22, 1851

I am writing by the window in the small room assigned to me at Spalding's Inn where the stage-coach breaks the journey between Kingston and Toronto. After all the confusion of leaving, it is good to collect my thoughts. When I finally heard from Darra, my instant impulse was to catch the first coach and to join her, but I was bound by my promise to Major Kingsley to stay by his wife till his return. Even then, Madam took most poorly to my departure.

"Catherine," she complained. "What a foolish girl you are to go running off. I have just trained you to my satisfaction and you leave like a silly goose heading for the woods."

I didn't know whether to laugh or to take umbrage. "Why, Madam, I scarcely think that joining my sister will offer me the dangers a goose may find in the woods."

Remembering my experience at Tudhope, I knew that I would always be on guard for dangerous encounters. No, I am no longer the child who left St Joseph's and nor it seems is Darra. Her letters have left me longing to see her in person and have caused me some anxiety. Her early success on the stage seems only to have increased her love of worldly goods. While all her old affection comes through the words she pens so conscientiously, so does a new Darra. It is as if the old impetuosity has hardened to a resolution to absorb all life offers, as if the child, who so longed for excitement and colour, is trying to capture all of life itself. But to return to my departure.

I have become fond of the Kingsley family and my departure was the point of much emotion. Oonagh cried loudly in the background, making me promise to write and pressing a small St Christopher medallion on me. Mrs Kingsley unexpectedly gave me a smart leather travelling case and the Major passed a purse, generously filled, into my hands, saying, "Be sure to let us know how you are, Catherine, and remember you have friends in us if ever you are in need."

Confusion reigned about the stage-coach, what with the pile of luggage and the milling around of passengers and those who saw them off. At first I did not notice that Oonagh had forgotten to put one of my bags onto the Kingsley's coach and I now searched for it frantically. Where was the roll with my quilt? After consulting with Major Kingsley, I realised that it was still in the small room I had occupied for the last seven months. Even worse, there was no time to go back for it. My distress was so obvious and seemingly so disproportionate to its cause that Major Kingsley asked the reason. Diffidently I explained that my sister and I regarded this link with the past as one of our most valuable possessions, whereupon he promised me to see personally that the quilt should be put away safely for me. Somewhat comforted, I hastened to take my seat in the coach.

Caleb, who had been hovering nearby, rushed up and put a small package in my hands. "A pie from the kitchen," he said. "The kind the travellers order, but I lifted it when Cook's back was turned."

"Oh, thank you, Caleb. I'll miss you, but I'll never forget it was you who helped me find out where Darra had gone."

Looking at the cheery, freckled face, I blew him a kiss. This fine gesture was, however, lost in the sudden mêlée just outside the window. An elderly woman, all in black, and a ragged youth were valiantly struggling to drag a barrel, wrapped in cloth, into the coach. The driver was equally determined that the ungainly piece of baggage should remain outside and be strapped with the rest of the passengers' baggage. The old woman shouted and wept; the driver swore, and the lad gave a final heave and deposited the container in one corner of the coach. He hastily sat down, using the parcel as a footrest.

Two men of the cloth, one old and one younger, pushed in and made themselves comfortable on the seat opposite. Both ignored the unseemly commotion concerning the other passengers. Unexpectedly, the driver gave up on the dispute and the old woman jumped in agilely. With a bang and clatter, we were on our way. I eyed my companions with some interest.

I guessed that the men across from me must be Methodists or Baptists. Kingston boasts a variety of religious orders and Anglican and Presbyterian churches already have a place along with St Joseph's. A new church is currently under construction for the Wesleyan-Methodist congregation and it is to have the tallest spire of all the churches in Canada. Probably because they need God's attention most, Darra had irreverently suggested. Father Andrew had warned us often of the heresies of these misguided souls and called for us to pray for all sinners. As small children, Darra and I had been careful to walk on the opposite side of the road when passing these dangerous areas. Up until now, I had never had contact with any of the adherents and, gazing cautiously at the two before me, I decided that they looked staid enough.

At that moment, the older gentleman smiled pleasantly and said, "Allow me to introduce my companion and myself. I am Benedict Harding, recently of the Bay of Quinte and this is Everard Dulwich. We are on our way west to join the new mission station."

Assuring me that, should I need any assistance during the journey, I had only to ask, he turned a dubious look on the woman and boy in the opposite corner.

The former spoke up at once. "I be Mrs Fern Jubb, a widow woman and this be me boy, Willie. Me poor husband being dead and under the ground, we be going to my darter. She be at Peterborough and – "

Mr Harding interrupted hastily. "Yes, yes, my good woman, of course, of course."

Silence prevailed for a while and was soon broken by Mr Dulwich enquiring of his elder, "Does this posting not remind you of your days as a circuit rider?"

"Oh yes, indeed," was the enthusiastic response. "I was but twenty when I first set foot in this country, bringing the word of the Lord. What days those were. We rode round the outlying areas and stopped in small villages. We'd set up in a hall or a barn or even under canvas if not welcome in the town. After work, the families drifted in and we'd preach and sing . . ." He paused reminiscently.

At that point, a subdued and impertinent comment came from the corner.

"Holy kicker! Holy smoke. Hold your – "

Stunned, we all turned towards the lounging boy just in time to see his mother aim a kick in his direction. Mr Dulwich's eyes met mine in shock and we both hastily turned our courteous attention back to Mr Harding. Visibly startled, he had wavered but gradually regained full spate.

"The crowds came, eventually they came, first the young and curious and then the families as the good news spread. Sinners that they were, drunks, fornicators, the Lord's lost ones seeking redemption."

For a moment, Mr Harding paused and looked sharply at the corner of the coach. Mr Dulwich's eyes and mine swivelled warily in the same direction, but all was quiet. The lad was gazing out of the window and the widow had settled for a nap apparently.

"Yes," continued Mr Harding. "Then came the glorious moment when these outcasts opened their hearts to the – "

"Holy kicker. Holy kicker. Hold your luff. Scraaaam." The last word was uttered in an outraged shriek. All eyes were again on the corner. The widow was a strange puce colour and the boy was shaking with laughter.

"Mam," he finally spluttered, "I told you Polly would take on." Finding a crust of bread in his pocket, he opened a hole in the container. Instantly a beak appeared and the crust disappeared.

"Dash my buttons," laughed Mr Dulwich unexpectedly. "My uncle had a parrot and it said the deucedest things. One doesn't see many of them these days. Where did you get this bird?"

"'Twere my Dad's. He did get it from the West Indies. He was a sailor afore he took poorly. He took lumber and fish down wid him and he brought back molasses and rum. And Polly did go where he went."

Encouraged by the interest, the lad pulled more of the wrapping from what turned out to be the parrot's cage. A curious yellow eye peered out as the occupant hurriedly clambered into a better position to view his surroundings.

"Tickle your tail," he shrieked.

The boy, Willie, rebuked him, handing him another crust which he eagerly accepted. Admiring the vivid green feathers and the red head cocked so saucily, I asked, "What is his name?" then added, "Is he very old?"

Mrs Jubb gained courage and explained. "My husband did say he be 30 or 40 years old when he did buy him and that's when Willie here was but a babby. I calls him Polly but young Willie is always talking with him and he calls him Toff."

"He be a real toff too," added Willie, laughing. He went on to say that his mother refused to have the precious bird endangered by travelling on the coach roof, but had not dared to bring him openly into the coach, Toff's manners not always being up to scratch.

"People do say birds bring vermint," he confided.

Mr Dulwich was obviously captivated and I much excited at my first contact with so amusing a bird. Mr Harding looked as if he considered the outdoors a much more suitable place for poor Polly, but he charitably made no complaint. So the trip passed quickly and pleasantly. Despite the bumping of the coach on the road, we reached Spalding's Inn before we suffered any undue discomfort.

After a good meal I shall settle down to rest, for surely Darra and I will be talking till all hours of the night tomorrow. I pray the Lord and His merciful mother, Mary, that I shall find my sister in good health and spirits.

April 29, 1851

My arrival in Toronto was so different from my expectations. Indeed, it was such a disappointment that I have had no heart to write in my journal. Far from finding Darra at Mrs Cooper's, I was greeted by an empty room. As I stared around disconsolately, a knock sounded at the door, and a young man entered.

"You must be Miss St Joseph's sister, I think. I have a letter for you explaining why you have not had a better welcome. I assure you that Darra was really in quite a pickle to know what to do. Please do read this and then I am at your service. Marcus Denby is my name."

Still I stared at him, bewildered despite the fact that I remembered his name from Darra's last letter. The young man smiled kindly at me. His thick brown beard and longer than usual hair gave him a rather rakish look and I recalled that he was one of the actors in the company Darra had joined. His mobile face changed expression quite suddenly.

"Look, Miss Catherine," he said, "you can trust me. We in the troupe help each other out and I promised Darra that you could turn to me. Now you unpack and rest up from your journey. Read that letter. I will take you to dinner at 8 o'clock." He then gave me a sweeping bow. "The honour is mine, Ma'am."

I was laughing as he left the room. On reading Darra's letter, however, I fell into gloom.

April 23, 1851

Dear Cat,

I write in haste and with abject apology. Mrs Perkins, the lady who was playing the role of Mrs Teazle in School for Scandal, has decided at the very last moment that, because of her pregnancy (which grows more noticeable daily) that she is unable to tour with the company. So her role has been assigned to me. Oh Cat, it is the opportunity I have been waiting for all these long months and, although it breaks my heart to leave just on the point of your arrival in Toronto, you must see that I have no choice. Marcus has promised faithfully to care for you until my return and Trevor has sworn that the road run will not be of long duration. So, please, dear sister, forgive me and be patient with my flightiness. This opportunity may be the chance of a lifetime. I regret to inform you that the decision has been made so hastily that I do not even have a schedule of the towns we will be visiting. Marcus assures me, however, that he knows all the movements of the cast. Everyone tells me that when one is on the road there is absolutely no time for personal commitments such as writing letters. We shall see. Somehow I shall endeavour to communicate with you, Cat. At any rate, Marcus presented me upon our departure with a pretty diary bound in yellow linen and instructed me to keep accounts of all the theatres and towns we visit.

Be brave, dear Cat, and believe me when I say my heart is with you. As always, Love, Darra.

Here I was in a city I did not know and far from all my friends. With the memory of Tudhope not entirely erased from my mind, I dreaded looking for employment on my own. Above all, the longing to see my sister overwhelmed me and I began to cry bitterly.

Common sense finally reasserted itself and I made good use of the jug of warm water brought by the serving girl. Stripping to the skin, I washed the road dust from my body, shivering slightly as the sponge trickled cooler water from the tips of my breasts, down my abdomen to the hay-coloured curls below. A heavy mirror hung beside the washstand and I glanced into it. A rather slight girl, some five foot five, a neat waist and two generous breasts, the latter somewhat hidden beneath the long fair hair which fell in a heavy sheet. My hair reaches below my waist which makes it a heavy burden when pinned up. I have always been reluctant to cut it.

As I looked at myself critically, a voice from the past forced itself to my attention. It was Sister Martha's. "Do not look at your body in the mirror, nor when at your ablutions. Hold a towel before you."

Darra and I had been early acquainted with the fact that it was sinful to spend thought on your appearance. We had speculated on the reason for this. Darra had asked unfortunate questions as well.

"Why did the good Lord give us bad bodies?" she inquired when still small. Later she and I decided that our bodies were in fact very interesting. Ah, Darra! Where would I have been without your lively, independent mind? If I had not been needled by your obstinacies, I might now be at St Joseph's, taking a vocation. Instead, I have met Cavan – and so has Darra. Instantly I recalled her last letter and the words Cavan spoke to her of "the temptress with the golden hair and cornflower blue eyes." How I longed to tease each of them about the other.

I dried the water on my breasts and my stomach and wondered what Cavan would think if he were to see more of my body than he already had. Would he find me lovely? I could not reconcile what had happened at Tudhope with the possibilities Cavan offered. What would he demand of me? Darra was the only person to whom I might venture to talk on this intimate subject – and she was gone.

Cavan has written two short affectionate notes to me since his departure and I placed them in a sachet and pinned them to my bodice. He called me "dear one," "my sweet" and "allanna" and I delighted in the words. I longed to see him now that I was finally in Toronto and nearer to his garrison. His last letter had set me wondering with the comment, "I have recently heard from my father, who is on his way to the provinces. I fear that the two of us will be at odds again, if I read his letter aright." If I could not see Darra, at least perhaps Cavan and I might meet without undue delay.

Somewhat cheered, I was dressed and ready when Mr Denby arrived punctually to escort me to dinner. As we walked along the streets near Mrs Cooper's boarding house, my new companion filled my head with information. Toronto had now surpassed all other cities in population, attaining 30,000 and was I not impressed with all the new buildings? I would surely find life in the capital city exciting and did I know that there was likely to be an election this year? I admitted that I was ignorant of politics and, fearing that Mr Denby might choose this moment to enlighten me, I remarked on the large number of taverns and beer shops we passed.

"Kingston does not lack for centres of hospitality or vice, whichever you prefer, but I swear we have seen at least three in the last street," I commented.

"That is true," laughed Marcus, which was what he insisted that I call him. "I have heard that we boast 152 taverns and over 200 beershops. As you can imagine, there are often brawls and the streets are not safe at night. To counteract this, we have the same

Temperance Societies that you must know in Kingston."

I had, of course, heard of these groups but had no real knowledge of them. I began to feel very inexperienced and was thankful that at least I had the friendly advice of Marcus until I found a position and permanent lodgings. From what I had seen of Mrs Cooper's establishment, I should not wish to remain there longer than the week for which Darra had so kindly arranged.

We stopped at a small hotel where Marcus ordered an excellent dinner. After we had relieved our appetites, he told me of Darra and of her life in Toronto. For the first time, I began to see that my sister had braved many hardships to reach the position now open to her. The pain that her departure had left in me was eased and I felt less resentful. What else could Darra have done? If this is really the life she wants, she had to grasp any opportunities that came her way.

By the time we had returned to our respective rooms at Mrs Cooper's, I was exhausted. I fell into a deep sleep, hopeful that the next few days would bring me news from Cavan and that I might find congenial employment.

In fact, the next four days were most discouraging. A letter came from Cavan with the news that he would be in Montréal for a few weeks and planned to travel back to Toronto with his father. His letter struck me as being guarded, although he ended affectionately thus: "It seems that fate conspires to keep us apart, my little love, but I beg you to keep me in your heart till we can meet again." The news that his father was arriving filled me with dread. How could Cavan introduce a girl of unknown parentage to his parents and would he even want to? For the first time I began to ask myself what I would do if Cavan were to ask me to become his lover.

How I envy those women who know their place in society. Darra and I do not have the certainty that we are or are not fitted to any situation. I long to know that my birth gives me the right to stand at Cavan's side. Conversely, if it does not, then need I feel shame to be his love should he choose me? Darra is so certain and so confident. She does not seem to hold St Joseph's training in her heart, as I do. She does not seem to be pulled both ways.

"Cat, don't be so missish," she'd say. "While you're agonising like some old nun, all the world is waiting for us."

Now at least I do have a position awaiting me. It only came about today and I am still incredulous and a little nervous. Writing about it will perhaps give it more reality for me. Indirectly I have to thank the Gildersleeves for this unexpected rise in my fortunes.

I was on my way to the haberdashery, planning to spend a sum from the purse Major Kingsley had given me. It might lift my spirits, I thought. As I entered the large emporium, two women were standing at the counter. They were engrossed in ribbons and laces and, thinking this a useful area to start my purchases, I moved towards them. The nearest looked up and I recognised her as the older Miss Ashe with her sister, Beatrice, at her side. I had met the two women at Mrs Gildersleeve's home on several occasions. Miss Ashe looked surprised and greeted me kindly.

"Good day, Catherine. I had no idea that the Kingsleys were in Toronto at this time. Do tell me where they are staying?"

I explained that I had come to join my sister and was now looking for a position as companion. On these words, Miss Ashe exchanged a sudden look with her sister. "Now that is most interesting, Catherine. I do believe that I might be able to help you. Will you wait with us while we complete our purchases and then join us in the carriage?" Of course, I was only too willing.

We settled in the elegant carriage summoned by Miss Beatrice. This blushing young woman was now affianced to Mr Gordon Smythe, with whose brother and wife she was staying. The brother, Mr Alastair Smythe, worked for the government as one of Mr Robert Baldwin's secretaries in the Baldwin-Lafontaine ministry. His wife, Jean, was recovering from childbirth and still lacked in strength. Her social duties were onerous to her, especially since she lacked in confidence. Additional entertainment would now be necessary with the forthcoming wedding.

"So you see, my dear Catherine, falling on you is just providential."

I was alarmed at the value set on my services. "Oh, Miss Ashe, I do want employment, but I am far from experienced in social entertainment on such a level. Mrs Kingsley and Mrs Gildersleeve taught me a great deal but it would be presumptious to think I could help in this situation." I was stammering with nervousness.

"Do allow me to know what I am saying, Catherine. Mrs Smythe is very knowledgeable and capable of social entertaining. It is just that she is low of spirits and needs someone to carry out her directions. It is difficult to find good help these days. So many women consider themselves above service or refuse to take instruction. I know the Kingsleys consider you quite one of the family."

I did not know what to think. Would another ailing wife present me with another lecherous husband? On the other hand, Darra was right. If we want to be of good standing, it will take all our efforts. Perhaps if I learned to move in government society, that would somehow bring me closer to Cavan. I would watch all that happened and I would learn all the arts. Miss Ashe watched me silently.

"What is the problem, Catherine?" she asked. "Most young women would be delighted with this offer."

"Miss Ashe, I am extremely pleased. I wonder, however – perhaps I should wait until I have met Mr and Mrs Smythe. The gentleman might prefer to see whom he will be paying." I laughed lightly to cover my lack of ease.

"Oh, please do not concern yourself about that," cried Miss Beatrice. "Alastair is no ladies' man and he is devoted to dear Jean. Anything she wants is all he asks for. Not like my naughty Gordon. I'd have to keep my eye on him." She tittered provocatively.

"What nonsense you do talk, my dear," her sister reproved her.

We arrived at the Smythe's residence, a charming home built in recent years to house the influx of government officials. While I waited in the parlour, I looked around, suspecting that there would be greater formality in the great houses of Toronto than in Kingston. While I felt rebellious at reminders of 'my place' in society, I decided to control my feelings until I had achieved all I could.

"Those who would dwell in court must needs curry favour." Was that one of Darra's speeches that she would declaim so ardently when trying out some part on me? It sounded like it.

Enough to say that I am now installed in the bosom of the Smythe family and that I find it rather intimidating.

May 15, 1851

My dearest Darra,

I cannot tell you what a blow it was to arrive in Toronto and to hear that you have left on the tour. Of course I know that it will further your career and I am happy for you. I had so longed to see you, however, and to exchange all our news. I had looked forward also to seeing you on the stage and to sharing some of the glamour of the boards with you. I still find it hard to accept the fact that our lives seem to be drifting so far apart. Do you find me a dullwit now, I wonder?

Darra, will you credit fate with some kindness? Believe me, I can scarcely get used to my new circumstances. I am now companion to Mrs Alastair Smythe, whose husband is in the civil service working for Mr Robert Baldwin. Imagine your sister meeting and talking with the leaders of our government. For I have said "Bonjour, Monsieur" to Mr Louis Lafontaine as well.

I can even give you some political gossip. You remember how highly Father Andrew has always spoken of the Baldwin-Lafontaine government, saying that these leaders of Upper and Lower Canada had achieved a miracle in easing tensions between the French and English provinces? Well, there is a rumour that they may be stepping down as leaders and Mr Smythe is extremely angry about it all. It seems that the radicals are putting up a great fight and are demanding further reforms. Mr Dorion of the Parti Rouge seems to consider himself more a leader of the French-Canadians than Mr Lafontaine, and it is reported that he says some shocking things about the Church. Canada West is also complaining and the Clear Grits are demanding "rep by pop". Of course, in the Act of Union, the two Canadas were given equal representation, but now with all the immigration, Canada West has the bigger population and wants more representatives.

I was quite carried away by all the argument over this and, forgetting my shyness, I cried out that it didn't seem just. When

French-Canada had the bigger population, they accepted equal representation and no one heard Canada West complain.

We were at a dinner party, rather informal, with the Baldwins, Lafontaines and some of their department. I was sitting next to a friend of Mr Louis Lafontaine's, a Mr Roger de la Haye. He is a big laughing man with a most charming accent. On hearing me, he turned a very direct gaze my way saying, "So the little demoiselle beside me is really a politician in disguise?"

I excused myself and was much discomforted for, Darra, I really know so little about politics, but it is so interesting. Mr de la Haye forgave me very readily, however, and said that he will explain anything I should like to know. He is here as advisor and friend to Mr Lafontaine, but says he will be happy to return to Montréal where he has his home. Do you think your tour will take you to Québec? I long to go and plan to practice my French.

A friend of mine, someone I want to talk to you about, is in Québec now. I think I am in love, Darra. But I was waiting to tell you about it in person and even now I find I cannot put my feelings in a letter. I am, however, still keeping my journal and find that there I can record my most intimate thoughts. Come back as soon as you can, my dearest sister, for I have need of your counsel. Meanwhile, I think of you and wish you all good fortune.

Your sister, Cat.

May 17, 1851

Dear Mrs Kingsley,
It was a delightful surprise to have your note, with Major Kingsley's kind postscript. It was so good of Oonagh to wrap up my quilt and just unfortunate that I forgot it. I do apologise for the space it is taking in the armoire. As soon as I am able, I will make arrangements to collect it.

I do indeed miss you and the Major, but I am enjoying Toronto and all the new events in which I participate. I am always grateful to you for sharing with me your skilled training in social graces. Mrs Smythe considers you to be a most talented hostess and longs to make your acquaintance.

My sister unexpectedly left Toronto and I am awaiting her return. It was a bitter disappointment but I try to bear it with fortitude.

I do hope you and the Major are in good health.

I remain yours in respectfulness,
Catherine St Joseph.

May 19, 1851

Dear Lieutenant O'Hara,

I received your long letter from Montréal with much joy. It must be a most fascinating city, almost like being abroad. I do remember hearing about the Tories being so angry with Lord Elgin's Rebellion Losses Bill that they set fire to the parliament buildings! Except for that, I suppose that Montréal would still be the capital. I was shocked at the damage the great 1849 fire did to the parliament building in Toronto. However, the new building is proceeding apace. You will be surprised when you return. With the advent of warmer weather, the workmen are to be seen about and busy.

I am far from sure what you mean when you say that your father is bringing unwelcome company with him. Of course, I will wait for explanations until I see you, but the delay in his ship's arrival has made me very impatient.

I am not, as you suggest, causing devastation among the eligible bachelors in Toronto. I am far too busy mastering the art of entertaining large groups of government officials and occupied in sorting out the men from their parties. Mrs Smythe has impressed upon me that it is not the responsibility of a good hostess to hold political opinions, but I must confess I find it very fascinating.

Since you ask, it was a friend of Mr Louis Lafontaine's who escorted me to the spring ball, a Mr Roger de la Haye. He is much older than I and a most kindly gentleman. No sir, you may not ask what transpires when I go in a carriage with him. I assure you I have suffered from only one indiscretion in a cab and that in Kingston. I hardly recall it now, but the guilty party was a young lieutenant.

I do look forward most eagerly to your return ... although perhaps you will think me very bold to confess to such a feeling.

Allanna

May 25, 1851

Dear Mr de la Haye,

Thank you most kindly for the exquisite bouquet which arrived this morning. I really cannot think what prompted it as it is not my birthday. I fear your generosity is causing some raised eyebrows in the Smythe household and I do beg that you will not repeat it. Again with my deep appreciation.

Yours most respectfully,
Catherine St Joseph

June 1, 1851

I am longing to hear from Darra. I mailed my letter to Kingston on the advice of Marcus. He tells me that the strain of these tours is very severe and that I must not be harsh in judgement should I not hear often from my sister. I find that I am concerned about her. A fever can be debilitating and I do not think she has taken sufficient care of herself since her illness. I ventured to mention this to Marcus.

A rather sad expression swept his face and he answered, "I do not think you need worry unduly, Cat. Mr Vaughn cares for her as a miser would for a gold coin he found on the shores of an uninhabited island. No matter if there is naught he can buy with it."

I thought that remark passing strange. It renewed my anxieties about the relationship between Mr Vaughn and my sister. It seems that she is not concerned that he doesn't make an honest woman of her. I could not discuss this with Marcus and made haste to change the subject. We do not often meet these days as Mrs Smythe does not consider it seemly. Ladies may enjoy the theatre and entertainment and it is well known that the gentlemen associate with the women of the boards. We, however, must be careful of our circle of acquaintances.

It has become certain that Mr Baldwin and Mr Louis Lafontaine are stepping down this month. It will not affect the Smythes as Mr Baldwin will still require his services. Mr de la Haye will be returning to his Montréal home in the fall. I have learned that he is a lawyer and left his practice to be of service to Mr Lafontaine. Mr de la Haye has three young children and he has shown me miniatures of them. It is obvious that he loves them dearly and would prefer to be with them. At this time, they are under the care of their grandmother. Their mother died after a tragic accident last year.

Mrs Smythe explained that the poor woman had slipped on one of the icy side-paths. Falling awkwardly, she broke several bones and was in great pain. When it was found that the physician could do little for her, Mr de la Haye called in a renowned herbalist. Despite her tisanes and the rounds of prayers said by the Grey Nuns, his wife passed away a few weeks after the accident. I have heard of so many cases of tragedies following breakage of bones, it is no wonder that many fear the winters.

Railways are again the talk of the town and it is said that building for the Northern railway will commence here in the fall. I cannot wait to ride in one of these exciting machines. Imagine the speed! They must be so smooth after the bumping of the coaches. Miss Beatrice Ashe, whose wedding is to be on June 15 was discussing her honeymoon last night.

"I vow," she said, "I am so nervous to think of our train journey from New York to Boston to visit Gordon's grandparents that I can hardly put my mind to the wedding."

"Oh," I cried out, "I envy you the experience. I must have been born in the wrong province for I should so love to travel by railway."

"It seems unnatural, all that speed. They say the passing distraction of railways causes the cows to lose their milk." She tittered. "Gordon will have to hold my hand."

I find it difficult to be charitable to Miss Beatrice, perhaps because Sister Martha always impressed on us that we should make some contribution to daily life. I think both Mrs Smythe and I will be delighted when the wedding is over and the self-indulgent young bride is in her husband's hands.

How fortunate are those who can find their love and settle in holy matrimony. I am so disturbed by Cavan's latest letter that I have not known how to answer. Mr O'Hara has arrived in Québec City and has in his company a Mrs Parnell and her daughter, Moira, old neighbours to Castle-Blaine, so Cavan tells me. The voyage having been arduous, they are resting and sightseeing in the city of Québec before continuing their journey to Upper Canada.

I am filled with misgivings and feelings of jealousy that I have never known before. Why have Mrs Parnell and her daughter accompanied Mr O'Hara? Surely this must be the same young woman that Cavan's father saw as a suitable bride for his only son. Cavan tells me that he loves me and on his return to Toronto, he will explain all the problems caused by his father's arrival. He begs me to wait for him. As if I wouldn't! He does not, however, mention marriage.

If only Darra were here and I could pour out my feelings of impatience, of anxiety and longing. Time does not seem to move and I do not know how to wait until Cavan's return. I reproach myself for my lack of generosity, but I find all the preparations for Miss Beatrice's wedding a source of great pain to me. I will take myself to work on a small water colour of the Smythe's garden that occupies me, hopeful that it may calm my emotions.

June 10, 1851

Darra should be in Kingston by now. Our home! I wonder if she will visit St Joseph's and the dear sisters. I know she must miss them but they would surely be grieved by her way of life. Yesterday, while on an errand to the post office, I met Marcus. He asked me eagerly whether I had yet received mail.

"No," I responded, "and have you no news of my sister?"

"I have instructions from Mr Vaughn, who mentions that the tour has been tiring but so far successful. He says that he has been troubled with his health and that he may have to change future plans in order to take the waters. Meanwhile, Darra's performance as Lady Teazle has exceeded his greatest hopes and far surpassed that of her predecessor. The company is well into rehearsals for *The Taming of the Shrew* which is the highlight of the Kingston run. That's all I can tell you."

"How excited Darra must be! If only I could see her in person. Will she be Kate? Surely she will."

"Without doubt, our Darra will have that honour."

"Oh, Marcus," I said impulsively, "I can tell that you care for my sister. I am so worried about her. I wonder what will come to her without a family's protection. She is so thoughtless of the proprieties in her passion for the stage, which is a risky way of life for any woman."

Marcus was silent, then spoke again. "I wish I could take care of her. I would marry her if I could. She is so warm and such a creature of fire and passion, but she holds me off and I have not dared venture telling her of my love."

"Write to her, Marcus. If Mr Vaughn is ill, she may come to realise how little she can depend on him to give her a future. Who knows what foolish impulse she may follow. Do let her know of your feelings. Surely she is not so unnatural a girl that she will not value a proposal?" I smiled rather sadly.

"I will think on it, Cat, that I promise," with which Marcus hurried on his way.

June 20, 1851

How glorious it is to feel the sun upon my face. I have had to be careful not to allow it to brown my skin while working on my sketch in the garden. The wedding is now behind us and we are free to resume our usual activities. The May bushes are in full bloom at last and there are many rose buds on the stems.

"Catherine, you had best soak your hands in buttermilk," Mrs Smythe remarked last night when she looked at my brown hands. "Do it before you go to rest. Your skin has definitely darkened while you were out with your water-colours. You don't want to look common."

Dutifully, I went to follow her advice, thinking that my sun-tinted skin had probably been the result of my afternoon at Jabez P. Speier's Travelling Menagerie.

In the morning, I finally heard from Darra. Having received my letter, which I mailed to Kingston some time ago, she was relieved to know that I am comfortably situated. I am less sanguine about her and was brooding on this when the doorbell sounded. It was Mr de la Haye.

"Mademoiselle Catherine, I am at your service. You look a little downcast. Would it amuse you to accompany me to Speier's Travelling Menagerie?"

I was delighted. Of course, these menageries were not strange to Kingston but, as children, we were not permitted to attend them. On one occasion, when Darra was taken on as nursemaid to the children of a family of the parish, she was included in their family outing. I, being less forward, missed the sights. When Darra came back to St Joseph's, she was wildly excited and told me all about the animals she had seen. She was horrified also by the sight of a lamb with two heads. I began to cry and Sister Martha scolded both of us.

Unfortunately, I had forgotten the unpleasant aspects of the menagerie, so I set out with Mr de la Haye full of anticipation. The drive to the grounds just beyond the city was most agreeable. The air was fresh and the countryside green and full of flowers. We saw a small deer run across the carriageway. My mood lifted and, under Mr de la Haye's tactful questioning, I found myself telling him about our upbringing and even certain of my concerns about Darra. At that point, however, we arrived at the fairgrounds. Tents and stalls were spread around and the noise of a megaphone boomed across the area. Vendors of various foods, drinks and souvenirs called out and children ran in all directions. I paused and gazed about me with interest.

Mr de la Haye took my arm in his. "What would you like to do first?" he asked.

I was attracted by a juggler who was tossing numerous balls into the air and catching them nonchalantly at the last minute. A cheerful tune was playing nearby where a small monkey was collecting money for his master, a fiddler. I gazed at the small wizened face and little, almost human hands. Of course, I had seen pictures of these animals, but had never seen one before. How alarming and frightening the large apes and chimpanzees must be.

We moved on to the bear-baiting ring, but the whole activity repelled me and, despite the short time since our arrival, I begged Mr de la Haye to take me away.

"There has been much cruelty in the world of entertainment," he told me.

"Do you know that at Niagara Falls, rafts of dogs, cats, horses, bears and even buffalo were sent over the Falls and money was bet on which animals would survive?"

I cried out in horror, hurrying away from the animals.

The next tent was adorned with a large sign saying, "This baby has the biggest head in the world."

"No!" I cried out emphatically.

Fortunately, at that moment, our attention was drawn to a lad who was winding a snake around his neck. I had seen small snakes from time to time in Kingston, but never such a large one as this.

"It's a python," said my guide. "If he is well fed, he will be langorous and do no harm."

We stopped next and bought a basket of flowers, then paused by a tent which advertised, "Winona, the witch woman will tell your fortunes with astonishing accuracy". I looked at the doorway hesitantly and Mr de la Haye handed me a silver coin.

"Go and have your fortune told, and may it be a good one," he said.

My heart pounded and I slipped into the gloomy interior. A large woman was seated in the corner. Her skin was swarthy and she was clothed in black with a red kerchief round her neck. A stale smell of perspiration surrounded her.

"Sit down, my beauty, sit down," she said. Taking my hand in hers, she looked closely at my palm. "Ah, my little lady, there is mystery here. I see heartbreak and I see joy. You are separated from your other half, who is not your other half, but who will always be your other half. A man searches for you, but you have passed by him. He who loves you will not claim you until the cloth is unrolled and the colours seen. Be of courage, my child, for life is hard."

I could not understand any of this and I looked into her face, asking, "Tell me, good woman, will I know love?"

"You speak like the child you are. You will know life. That is all I can tell you."

Puzzled and silent, I left the tent.

Mr de la Haye handed me into the cab. "If you are sure that you have seen all you wish, we will drive to one of the teahouses and refresh ourselves."

I agreed willingly, knowing that I had seen more than enough of the travelling menagerie. As we drove, the silence became more tangible. I looked up to find Mr de la Haye's gaze on mine.

He leaned over and took my hand in his. "Chérie," he said in a tender tone which I had not heard before. "These are early days, but I want to tell you how dear you are becoming to me. If ever you feel that you would be comfortable with me, I should like to share my life with you. Do not answer me now. Just keep these words in your heart and we will speak of it later."

I gazed at him incredulously without answering. Darra's words came to my mind. "I will choose an older husband who will care for me and give me all I want. I want a man who will stand behind me and not leave me alone as we have been."

Ah, Cavan! Will you choose me, against the will of your father, with the loss of Castle-Blaine as my bride price?

Without moving my hand from under Mr de la Haye's, I replied slowly, "You are too kind, Sir. You must not hurry me in this." Gently, he moved away from me and, until we reached the tea house, diverted me with tales of Montréal.

8

May 3, 1851

Dear Diary,

No, it won't do. My dear sister, Cat, might enjoy confessing her most secret thoughts in a diary, but it will never have appeal for me. Dear Diary – whoever heard of calling someone Diary. I shall rename you and begin anew.

Dear Daffodil,

My friend and confidante; Daffodil, and that is exactly what the ground should be covered with instead of this wretched snow. Whoever could have imagined a snow storm the first week of May? It's springtime, the green time of the year, and I long to enter the woods and seek out the first wild flowers.

So, Daffodil, I am in Peterborough and I suppose you might say I'm fortunate to have arrived unharmed. We left Toronto ten days ago, all twelve of us, divided into two lots of six. I travelled in one of the hired carriages with Trevor, the Prentices from Galt, and two gentlemen actors who have recently joined our group.

Mr Ashley Percival is quite elderly and portly; his nephew is a mere stripling, with hair the consistency of straw and a high-pitched voice like a girl's. His name is Sydney Farrell. Trevor tells me he was signed on because of his connection to Mr Percival. How wonderful when birth alone provides the key! The others left earlier in the other carriage and, fortunately for them, made a reasonably safe and comfortable trip.

Once we were on the road, Trevor began to worry as usual about the extra actors we would have to recruit in each of the towns we plan to visit.

"The last road trip I took in this area was a disaster," he was saying. "Peterborough, Cobourg, Port Hope, Belleville and

Bytown were on our itinerary. We planned to stage an even more ambitious play than *School for Scandal*; *The Merchant of Venice*, with its nineteen major roles, not counting courtiers and servants, meant picking up amateurs en-route. Each town provided its own piece of bad luck! In Peterborough, there were many actors willing to volunteer, but none could act! Needless to say with all those extra bit parts, everyone had to assume double roles. Dreadful! I can't tell you." Trevor paused and coughed several times before continuing.

"In Port Hope, where we were invited to present one act in the church hall, we were cancelled out. So humiliating! Belleville was somewhat more civilised. We got through one performance without too many scandalous interruptions. Would you believe me, I remember Belleville best for its bedbugs!"

Once again he was seized with a coughing fit. "Bytown was almost our undoing. Upon our arrival, we were told that the theatre was on the outskirts of town." Trevor became even more melancholy in reflection.

"Worse than that, we couldn't persuade the driver to take his horses one yard further, the mud from the spring floods was so thick. Finally we had to walk. We tripped and slid – the conditions underfoot were abominable. The so-called theatre turned out to be even worse. A rat-trap not to be believed. When a mere handful of people turned up to receive us, I was almost ready to cancel."

Here, he rallied, sounding more like his old self. "Nevertheless, the wonderful call of the theatre prevailed. As they say, 'The show must go on!' We acted that evening as though our audience was royalty. But it was a disgrace! I do hope this tour will be better."

"Uh – when was that, Mr Vaughn?" piped up young Sydney.

"Er . . . ah, let me see now . . ." Trevor looked vague, put his handkerchief to his lips and cleared his throat noisily. Of late, he has a tendency to mix dates and years in his mind, and I fear his confusion is worsening. Of course, the last time he was on tour was the occasion of our meeting in Kingston.

"Well, it was probably at least five years ago," he continued, taking charge of the situation once again. "No doubt things have altered greatly in that time . . . progress – can't stop progress!"

"From what I hear," said Mrs Prentice, pouting. "Peterborough is a most civilised town. I doubt we shall experience any horrible repercussions. My relatives, who live there, are close friends of the newly elected mayor, Mr Thomas Benson, and he's a fine man for the task. It must be difficult to be the first in any position, especially a political one. Why, the population is almost 2,600 inhabitants already; they have three churches and their one-room, log schoolhouse has already evolved into a grammar school."

"Yes, I am sure you are correct, Priscilla," said Mr Prentice, nodding his head in perfect agreement each time his wife offered a new fact.

At that very moment, our carriage began bouncing and shaking mightily, I made to peer out the window to see what was going on, but the snow had increased to such an intensity that the landscape appeared to be a giant blurred cotton field.

"Whoa! Whoa there." I could hear the driver trying to coax the horses to slow down, but it was in vain. Abruptly, the whole body of the carriage lurched to a sickening halt. We were all thrown heavily against the door and crushed in a heap.

With difficulty, we extricated ourselves and, opening the door, learned the worst. One of the wheels had come off. The weather, being so unpredictably snowy, made us all feel wet and chillsome; however, it is May and the temperature cannot have been too wintry. How I wished I had not left my beautiful fur-lined cape in Toronto, but who wears winter clothing in the spring?

Once it was ascertained that the repairs could not be attended to instantly, the driver suggested that we walk on ahead and seek cover in the nearest farmhouse. Fortunately, there was one less than a mile away. The news buoyed me up considerably until Trevor intervened.

"My dear, I could never make it on foot," he moaned.

I had forgotten the breathing difficulties he encounters in the wet open air. Finally, after a brief consultation, it was decided that Sydney and I, being the youngest members, would set out to seek help – another carriage, that would be best.

As I look back on that distressing day, I recall wondering if it would ever end. It did, of course. Sydney and I, more elated than

110

concerned, set off at a brisk pace. A change in routine always affected me in this manner and it seemed to act similarly for Sydney. The owner of the next farmhouse was a neighbourly, Christian man and, after taking us into the vast, warm kitchen to meet his wife, he harnessed up his two carriage horses and set out to fetch the other four travellers.

Mrs MacGowan, for that was her name, poured large steaming mugs of tea for us and plied us with fresh baking.

"Tell me, where would ye be heading?" she asked, cocking her head enquiringly and folding her floury arms across her ample bosom.

"Indeed, we're on a stage tour," I explained. "We were to have been in Peterborough this very evening."

"You? An actress?" She looked more closely at me, then nodded her head. "Well, I must admit you're certainly pretty enough to be Jenny Lind herself."

"Oh, I'm afraid I haven't the gift of a beautiful singing voice," I protested, pleased with the compliment.

"Would you take it amiss if I was to ask you to recite something for me?" As she spoke, she blushed beet-red.

"It would give me a great pleasure," I assured her. So, for the next half hour or so, Sydney and I entertained Mrs MacGowan with poetry and lines from Shakespeare and Mr Sheridan's comedy.

Several hours passed before all was put aright once more. The MacGowan family bade us farewell and wished us luck in Peterborough. As we climbed back into the carriage, only one thing troubled me, and that was Trevor's condition. He appeared to have taken a chill and was coughing more fitfully. I determined to dose him with Ayres' cherry pectoral the moment we settled in Peterborough.

May 4, 1851

Dear Daffodil,

I discontinued my writing with our journey unfinished, didn't I? However, you must know by now that I am easily irked with matters of ill health, so I shall skip along past those tiresome events. Suffice it to say that, once we had arrived and booked into McFadden's Hotel, I got Trevor settled, dosed him with the pectoral and left him to his sufferings.

Our hotel is nothing out of the ordinary, just the usual sort of firetrap Trevor warned me to expect on tour. But I don't mind. The food is wholesome and everyone is quite polite. I must admit that I was really worried about being snubbed. Why, to hear Mrs Prentice tell it, unmarried actresses are no better than prostitutes. She flaunts the fact she has Mrs in front of her name! I suppose that's why she told me all those tales!

Peterborough is most attractively situated on the Otonabee River. Such a pretty Indian name. An old wooden bridge caught my attention as I slipped out of the hotel. I headed straight for it.

"At last," I heard a voice whispering over my shoulder, as I stood gazing down into the river. Starting at the familiar, deep intonations, I found myself clasped in Ian's firm grasp. His devilish eyes and mischievious smile caused my heart to skip a beat.

"Ian," I gasped. "Whatever are you doing here?"

"Following you, my pretty maid." He doffed his cap and the spring breezes ruffled his raven locks.

"Oh, Trevor mustn't find us together." I recalled the angry words we exchanged after the Niagara trip.

"Then come, my pretty. Let us walk along the river path."

Taking my arm, he led me away from the bridge, oblivious of the mud beneath our feet. At last we were shielded from the view of the townspeople and we halted by a grove of budding trees.

"Oh look, Ian," I cried, bending down to a cluster of trailing arbutus. The tiny pink blossoms peeked out from their snowy bed, proving that winter was at last on the wane.

As I rose, Ian took me in his arm once more and sought my lips.

"Did you really follow me to Peterborough, Ian?" I asked when I was able to catch my breath.

"I'd follow you to the ends of the earth, my sweet," he answered, running his hands across my back and pulling me closer to him.

"I mustn't be absent long," I said fearfully. "Trevor is very jealous of admirers."

"Darra, Darra my sweet, surely the time has come for you to learn what real love is. Let me teach you." All the while, he continued to caress my eagerly responding body.

"Oh yes, Ian," I breathed, "but at this moment, I must return lest Trevor be suspicious. He always expects my company at lunchtime."

With that, I turned determinedly away from Ian's blandishments.

May 5, 1851

Dear Daffodil,

Sydney has taken to following me lately, eager for my attention, ever since our walk through the snow to the MacGowan's farm. At first, I considered his presence a nuisance, but lately have used it as an excuse to meet Ian secretly.

"Uncle Ashley says that the ladies of the Literary Society are trying to arrange the rental of a hall where we can give our performance," Sydney told me.

"Oh, I am pleased," I answered. "Experience is essential if you want to act on the New York stage."

"New York?" He looked askance at me, as though I had taken leave of my senses.

"Yes, of course. That's where the real theatre is."

"I suppose you're right – I'd just as leave remain in Toronto myself."

'What a dullard,' I thought, but aloud I said, "Ian's late again."

We had just arrived at the grove on the Otonabee where our daily meetings had been taking place.

"Oh, Darra, are you sure you're not making an error seeing so much of this MacLaren fellow?" Sydney enquired.

"Why ever do you say that?"

"Well," he looked off into the distance as though suddenly unsure of what he was about to disclose.

"Tell me, Sydney," I insisted.

"It's only that I've heard some unsettling stories about that chap, Darra. Perhaps he's not all you suppose him to be."

I tossed my head, thinking that Sydney, like Trevor, was jealous and, before I could say anything in my defence, Ian mounted on a fine steed, was seen galloping towards us.

"We'll meet you in an hour, Sydney," I announced, after Ian had tethered the horse to a limb of a nearby tree.

Meanwhile, Sydney nodded his head to Ian and scuffed off, a petulant scowl marring his features.

Hidden by the grove of treetrunks, Ian began fondling and kissing me, as was his custom, but I pulled myself from his urgent embraces sooner than usual.

"Sydney tells me that a place has been found for our rehearsals," I told him. "I'll be rehearsing, and it will be necessary to curtail our rendez-vous."

"In that case, my sweet, it seems our plans dovetail nicely. As it happens, business affairs necessitate that I leave you once again."

"Oh, and where are you going this time, Ian?"

"Probably north, my inquisitive one."

"North, Ian? When will I see you again?" I asked, by now quite distressed.

"Oh, one of these days I'll turn up, like the proverbial bad penny." As he spoke, he grinned at me mockingly.

"How can you say such a thing?" I threw myself into his arms and allowed a tear to squeeze out the corner of my eye.

"Dry your tears, my love. I'll return with a pretty bauble before you can say 'Jack Robinson'."

May 10, 1851

Dear Daffodil,

I thought I would be miserable without my secret meetings with Ian, but the last week has been full of excitement. Trevor rallied to rise from his bed, dress himself with my help, and visit the Literary Society ladies. To my amazement, he returned to the hotel at the end of the day to inform us that his plans had been brought to fruition and we would have a hall where we could rehearse. The actual performance was set for the evening of the

8th; we would rest and pack on the 9th, and be ready for departure on the 10th.

It was wonderful. A hall, oh, not a theatrical stage, but a roomy space and, after our enforced 'rest period', a new enthusiasm seemed to permeate the group. Numbers of amateur performers turned out to read for the roles, and those who couldn't be given speaking-parts were offered the chance to be servants. One sweet young woman with brown hair and eyes was ecstatic when informed she would be playing the role of the maid. It reminded me of my own first stage appearance.

Rehearsal was riddled unbelievably with forgotten lines, mis-cues and wrong entrances and exits. Trevor was wringing his hands at the end of the day, and coughing more than ever. Fortunately by the performance, everything seemed to come together. We had a fair to middling audience and the actors gave it their best effort.

After the play, many members of the audience found their way back to our dressing rooms, and, since the night was springlike, we decided to engage in conversation outside.

Several young men eagerly introduced themselves – farm lads, bankers' clerks, a newly licensed doctor and a fledgling lawyer. I stood in the centre of the circle, watching them vie for my attention.

"Have you seen much of the countryside roundabout?" one inquired. "I've a buggy with a fringe on top if you desire to take a ride with me."

I smiled kindly at him. "Thank you so much, Sir, but I fear we must pack tomorrow and leave with the dawn on the following day."

"'Tis a fine comedy, and you were a splendid lady throughout," said another. "I should have thought your throat would be dry after all them speeches. Would you care to accompany me to Bailey's Tavern for a draught?"

"You are very thoughtful," said I, "but the hour is late and I must confess to fatigue."

"I could run over to the tavern myself right now and bring back a drink for you," he offered, and then turned red in the face, having been so bold.

Once again, I smiled but shook my head to discourage him.

Later that night, Trevor climbed into bed with difficulty, meanwhile coughing mightily. Once more, I suggested Ayres' cherry pectoral, but he informed me gruffly that whisky was a far better remedy than "that overly sweet syrup."

"Very well, Trevor," I replied and poured him half a tumbler of the strong rye-based drink.

"I notice that roustabout, MacLaren, wasn't around, gawking down your bosom tonight," Trevor said, taking a great gulp of whisky.

"Trevor," I protested. "Please."

He looked chagrined and moody, but, since I didn't want to argue with him, I said nothing further.

"Well, Miss, I'm sick to death of seeing him mooning about you. Doesn't the man work for a living?"

"Why, Trevor, you know as well as I that Ian works for the government, as a land surveyor," I replied indignantly.

"Huh! I wonder."

I decided to ignore the implications of his comments and turned aside to gaze out of the window. A heavy silence fell between us and when I looked over towards him, I saw that he had fallen into an uneasy sleep. He was lying on his back and, with his mouth open, he looked an old man.

May 16, 1851

Dear Daffodil,

We left Peterborough on time and made as good speed as possible in our light carriages to Cobourg, Trevor having decided to omit all other planned readings. There were no mishaps en route and we arrived two days later in fine form.

No sooner had we settled back in our beds, however, than Trevor woke me.

"Turn on the lamp, Darra. Quickly! The bed is full of bugs!"

At the sound of his voice, I leapt from the bed and immediately became aware of an itchiness and irritation of my skin. Scratching my midriff, I examined my ankles and discovered, to my horror, patches of reddened welts.

In the moments which followed, we were fully occupied with mass murder of the wretched vermin. Trevor, to my surprise, knelt by his trunk and brought out a box containing a greyish white powder which he proceeded to pour over the sheets.

"Whatever are you doing, Trevor?" I asked, not having encountered such an action before.

"Roach powder, my dear! The solution to all our problems," he replied, shaking another round onto the bed.

"You mean it's poison? Will it kill bedbugs?" I asked incredulously.

"I discovered this roach powder at a travelling medicine man's show many years ago. I can't swear it will kill the beasties, but it will deal with them temporarily and it will stop the itching, my dear."

With that, he settled himself back in bed and soon was sound asleep again.

I was wide awake by now, however, and quite revolted by the invasion of the nasty bedbugs. Not that it was the first time I had met up with them. I will say, however, that I do not recall ever having seen them at St Joseph's. Of course, the sisters would never give such filthy creatures house room. Of a sudden, I saw myself a small girl, down on my knees, scrubbing and scouring. Proverbs popped into my head. "Cleanliness is next to godliness. Familiarity breeds contempt." At times, this unfamiliar Darra awakes and takes over. I sound like Cat now.

In the morning, Trevor berated the landlord soundly, threatening to withhold payment for our rooms. Frankly, I don't believe that the landlord took him seriously, but nonetheless it was exciting to watch Trevor assume the role of injured traveller as though acting on stage. Given a dramatic situation, Trevor is not easily bested.

Cobourg is a town not unlike Peterborough, except for its being located on the shores of Lake Ontario, as is Toronto. Since Ian's disappearance, I had taken to walking with Sydney, but did not care much for promenading on the upraised wooden sidewalks of the town. Since it was a gloriously sunny spring day, I was eager to explore the woods for spring flowers. Sydney was an escort of sorts and I'd have to make do with him.

Trevor has lately become a real task-master over what seems, to me at least, small details in the staging of *School for Scandal*. He has also determined to have us perform *The Taming of the Shrew* and, in his enthusiasm, has us reading lines and preparing ourselves already. I do not in the least mind, of course, because he has promised me that I shall have the role of Kate ... if I behave myself.

When he speaks of my behaviour, I feel he is being unfair, for I know that since Ian's departure, I've been leading the life of a most saintly nun. Some days I feel so bound in convention that I long to throw off all my clothing and ride naked like Lady Godiva through the streets. To be convincing, I should have to grow my hair longer, yet I fear, since it has such a stubborn tendency to curl, it would never reach a length to cover me like a cloak. Cat's hair must certainly be the right type. I do recall, while still at St Joseph's, how she was able to sit on it. Oh Cat, when ever will we be together again?

Ah, but I was about to write of my adventure with Sydney.

We had set out briskly and, as we traversed the main street, a lounging figure caught my attention.

"I've been waiting for you for the past thirty minutes, my sweet." His voice was tantalising and his lips curled in a teasing manner.

"Ian! Where have you come from?" I was totally taken aback.

"Hither, thither and yon," he replied.

Sydney sniffed disparagingly.

"Still trailing that puppy around with you, I see, Darra."

"Be a dear, Sydney, and leave us for a while," I said and patted him on his arm reassuringly.

Sydney, however, pulling himself to his full height, refused to accept orders from me.

"We were about to take a walk in the spring sunshine," I explained to Ian.

"Very well," he agreed, taking my arm possessively and striding forward, leaving Sydney to follow as best he could.

Soon we found ourselves on a country lane. Civilisation seemed far behind and I felt a sudden urge to blend with the surroundings. Untying my bonnet with it stiff sides which framed my view as blinkers do a horse's, I shook my hair from its pins. A heavy head of hair may be a woman's crowning glory, but come the warm weather, it drains the spirit from her.

At that moment, we heard unearthly noises coming from around the bend in the path.

"What can it be, Ian?" I asked, meanwhile moving closer to his side.

"We should know in just a minute, my pet," he answered sensibly.

"Indeed, as soon as we round the bend."

Sure enough, we were met with a crowd of rowdy drunkards standing aimlessly in the front yard of a small white-washed cottage. They were carrying on an uproar to wake the dead.

"Can it be a wake?" I enquired, thinking that, if it was, it was surely not the kind of wake I had ever encountered.

"Not likely," said Sydney. "Look, Darra, those men have guns, and horns and drums."

As he spoke, the din began once more. The beating of drums rolled out like thunder. The bleat of horns rose with strident insistency. Men ran in circles, shooting upwards towards the sky. Several dogs appeared, as if by magic, and added their howling and barking to the commotion.

The three of us stood speechless, wondering what possessed these savages to behave in this strange manner. Suddenly, one of their number noticed us. Separating himself from his companions, he weaved his way towards us.

Sydney took a step backwards, but Ian held his ground. No drunken jackanapes would intimidate him.

"How-ja-doo?" the black-bearded giant roared. "Have a slug, li'l leddy," he continued, and offered me a half-full whisky bottle.

A drum was slung over his shoulder, fastened to a long tasselled cord on the end of which he had tied a horn. Pistols jutted from both his pockets. In one hand, he carried his whisky bottle; in the other, he held a pair of drumsticks.

"No thank you, Sir," I replied politely as Ian moved his body between us. "We were just passing by and were curious about the strange celebration," I added.

At my words, the man guffawed, dropped his drumsticks and slapped his knee.

"Cel–ebb–ray–shun, is it?" Once more, he laughed loudly. "That's a good one, that is." He peered at us more closely, blinking his eyelids several times as though trying to clear his vision. "Ain'tcha never seed a shivv–urrr–ee, girl? Ain'tcha?"

"Of course," said Ian. "I should have remembered. It's a charivari." He laughed and addressed himself to the bearded tosspot. "Tell me, my good man, and who might the bride be? Is she a pretty lass?"

"Aye, mon, and I be tellin' youse that she deserve lots better than old Zachariah. He be all of 70 years and the lass be but 18."

"And I suppose he's had many young wives? Lucky fellow."

"Ye be right, Sar, ye be right."

I'd heard of charivaris, of course, but had never before witnessed one. I knew that they were most common amongst newlyweds who were not of a similar age; an old man and a young virgin, for example, or an old widow who had grabbed off a young husband.

On such occasions, the village roustabouts decked themselves out in disguise. They blacked their faces, wore their clothes back to front, put dunce caps on their heads and decorated themselves with bells and feathers. No wonder, when we first spotted them, that I had thought of a band of wild Indians. Once costumed, they set out in a band, beating on their kettles, drums and horns – even sour fiddles.

Their purpose was to disturb the newly married coupled with discordant music, to beat upon the doors until the bridegroom showed himself and acted the part of merry host. It was a well-known fact that, if the newlywed husband desired peace and quiet, and time to consummate his marriage, he would distribute liquor and money lavishly. Then the band of charivariers would go away and leave him be.

"Is this Zachariah a friend of yours, then?" Sydney was asking timidly.

"Zach? A friend, you say? Naah. That ol' bugger he ain't got no friends, he ain't. We be fixin' to spend the night; it be our plan to chivvy the ol' miser till the morn and then some."

At this point, I decided that it would be best if we took our leave, but now Sydney was thoroughly intrigued.

"Yuh wanna join in, young blood?" the man was asking.

"Oh, uh, that's very kind of you, Sir, but no thank you, we must be getting on." Put on the spot, I wasn't surprised to see Sydney back down.

Before we could take our leave, two mounted men, sporting half-uniform and half-civilian clothing, rode into our midst. Shiny badges were affixed to their breast pockets, so I assumed they represented the law.

Dismounting, the nearer officer approached. At once, to my utter amazement, Ian turned violently on his heel. With a bound, he leapt into the saddle, jerking the reins from the officer's hand and galloped off.

"Who was that man?" demanded the officer, but all I could do was stare into empty space.

"His name, Sir, is Ian MacLaren," Sydney said, with unexpected boldness.

"Hah! That swindler," and with that, the mounted officer took chase in the direction of Ian's disappearance.

"I don't understand," I ventured.

"Don't worry, young lady. Sergeant Bates will deal with the scoundrel. And now, if you'll excuse me, I must deal with this lot."

With that, Sydney took my hand and urged me away. For a moment, I wondered if we would be allowed to depart so easily, but the officer had lost interest in me.

"Let us go, Sydney. Quickly."

Back in town, we wondered about the outcome and later, at supper, after yet another rehearsal, Sydney related our experience to Trevor and the rest of the actors.

It was not until the following day that we learned of the untoward incidents which took place after we had taken our departure. Apparently, the remaining officer realised instantly that he would be no match for the unruly crowd. He, therefore, returned to town seeking assistance.

The husband, Zachariah, it seems had made up his mind to ignore the men who had gathered for the charivari. However as the men grew noisier and more drunken, he came down to speak to them, hoping to persuade them to go away. Unfortunately they were in no mood for persuasion or blandishments.

In a sudden impassioned moment, the atmosphere turned from mere annoyance to violence. The men rushed Zachariah, dragged him from his doorway and bore him off to the barn. There they tied him hand and foot to a post and whipped him with his own horse whip. Zachariah, instead of keeping silent and acting passively, fought them and cursed in foul threats. His attitude infuriated them even more. Eventually, and no one can explain how it happened, least of all, who was responsible for the act, he was shot in the leg and left, still tied.

In the meantime, the young bride stole down the stairs, terrified by all the turmoil. As soon as she was spotted, one of the younger men in the group, who was rumoured to be besotted with her fairness and beauty, grabbed her round the waist and began kissing her.

"Kiss the bride! Kiss the bride!" was the cry.

After they had all kissed her soundly and she was in floods of tears, it was decided to spirit her off. No sooner said than done! The men drove her to the docks on Lake Ontario, paid for her ticket, and sent her off to Toronto.

"Wait, Sydney," I begged. "You haven't explained about Ian. What about him? Where did he get to? And why did he run off like a criminal?" I was desolate.

"Try not to be too upset, Darra. Ian MacLaren is a bounder and he has a criminal record. I tried to tell you. Put him out of your mind forever."

"You might as well tell me the whole truth, Sydney," I said, sighing as though defeated.

"Very well, Darra. If you insist." Sydney looked temporarily embarrassed, but cleared his throat and continued with the story. "Part of it is a rumour but a lot of it is fact. MacLaren comes from Scotland and, while still living there, he married a wealthy widow, absconded with her fortune and sailed to New York. After gambling away most of her money and her treasures, he made a second wealthy marriage. Since that time, his illegal activities on both sides of the border have caused him to be on the Wanted

List for some months."

"Oh! He said he was a government land agent," I objected.

"I'm sorry, Darra. It was only a cover-up."

I was aghast. I didn't want to believe Sydney, but my heart told me that everything he said was true.

May 20, 1851

Dear Cat,

The moment I reach Kingston, I shall rip the pages of this Daffodil diary from between its covers, package it up and send it post haste to you in Toronto, that you may know all that has befallen me. I long to give you my news.

Our performance of School for Scandal was going along excellently. We had reached the very last act, right in the middle of Sir Peter's speech, [the one that goes thus: ". . . you would give your hand to no one else; and now that he is likely to reform I'll warrant you won't have him,"] when Trevor collapsed on the floor in such a fit of coughing that the play was forced to come to an abrupt end. Trevor, I fear, is ill indeed. The cast was obliged to pull the curtain on the scene because he had begun to spit blood.

Belleville has been cancelled. We are making immediately for Kingston. I feel strongly that Trevor should be sent back to Toronto promptly but he will not hear of it. He says he knows a doctor, an herbalist actually, whom he trusts implicitly, and the man lives on the outskirts of Kingston. So we are off to our home-town.

We are to open with The Taming of the Shrew and Trevor says that, if he is unwell, he has an acquaintance in the military who will play his part. I had quite forgotten that there are many gentlemen in the military who are professional dramatists. The man's name is Captain Kendall Warrick. Quite a romantic name, don't you think?

Perhaps once I have played Kate to the Kingstonians, Trevor will take me back to Toronto and we shall be together again. Please believe me when I say I truly miss you and think of you often. Of course, you are in my daily prayers, but nothing can

take the place of our being together again.
Love from your sister, Darra.

May 31, 1851

Dear Cat,

Now that we are once more settled in Kingston and staying at
Irons' Hotel, I feel much relieved. Trevor's cough has somewhat
lessened, although he is much weakened and, last week he hired a
coach to take him to visit the herbalist, Dr Winterberry. When
he returned, however, he was so fatigued, he collapsed onto the
bed. He is taking all his meals in our room.

"What did Dr Winterberry do for you?" I inquired anxiously.

"Not much," muttered Trevor. "He said I must seek the advice
of a certain specialist in Albany and, if that doesn't work, I must
travel to France and take the waters."

Well, dear sister, surely you can imagine how I felt about that.
I've relied entirely on Trevor ever since I left Kingston with him
last fall. It seems so long ago. He has cared for me kindly in turn
and provided me with all manner of luxuries, to say nothing of
offering me financial security. I needn't have worried, though,
because, in the next breath, Trevor informed me that he had set
up a fund for me at Glassup's Savings Bank. Indeed, he said that Mr
Glassup would see to my wants personally.

". . . and when I return from Albany," he continued, "I shall
know my fate and you will have become famous in the role of
Kate."

"Supposing you must travel to France . . . what then, Trevor?" I
ventured.

"Let us not look too far into the future, Darra. There are other
considerations to discuss, more pressing matters."

"Whatever do you mean, Trevor?"

"The theatre. Captain Warrick is meeting us for tea tomorrow.
You will have to become closely acquainted, learn your lines and
rehearse together. I think you will find the good captain a
satisfactory understudy for Kate's domineering husband."

So, as the old saying goes, whatever will be, will be. Tomorrow

I meet Captain Kendall Warrick and two days later, Trevor travels to Albany.

In the meantime, I have ventured cautiously round to the Kingsley's house, hoping to see Oonagh, but the place is closed up completely; blinds and curtains drawn. Why, there's no one except for the stableman who tends to the horses and the groundsman who is preparing the gardens. Do you suppose they have moved? I thought, from the way you spoke, that you'd remained in correspondence with Mrs Kingsley, although I could never understand why.

I have also sought out the young man, Caleb McBain. Didn't you say that he worked at Irons? He seems to have moved also. It's so strange! Only a few months have passed and I have as yet seen no familiar faces.

I feel sure you are wondering why I haven't flown instantly to St Joseph's to reunite myself with the sisters and Father Andrew, and I don't know how to answer that. I suppose it's that I wish to avoid the chiding and reprimands which I know full well I richly deserve. How can I explain my ambitions to Sister Isobel, or to Sister Martha, or least of all to Father Andrew? It's too much for me to attempt. Perhaps later – after I have been in town a while longer.

My thoughts whirl round my head these days. It's as though I have become addle pated. Only one thing seems to help and that is taking long walks. Even then I am thwarted, for, despite my slipping out unannounced, Sydney invariably joins me. He, of course, believes that I enjoy his company, for he was useful as an escort in Peterborough and Cobourg. Now, however, I feel the need to be alone. I cannot explain this, not finding it within myself to behave cruelly towards him. How very trying life can be in times of stress.

So, dear sister, until I next put pen to paper. Good night.
Darra.

June 7, 1851

Dear Cat,

Time fleeth, whether it be friend or foe. The weather has turned hot and sticky, most unusual for early June. My escape is, of course, the banks of the St Lawrence, for seldom is there a time when an offshore breeze does not blow to cool the cheeks.

Trevor has gone to Albany. I bade him farewell on the second of June, the day after my meeting with Captain Warrick.

(Here is the spot where I paused, pen still in hand, for I do not know how to confess to Cat the emotions which gripped me when Trevor introduced me to the man who will be my constant companion for the following days and possibly weeks.

Kendall, for that is what he has told me to call him, is a giant of a man. Why, the top of my head reaches only to beneath his shoulder. He is dark of hair and eye, with a swarthy complexion and a compelling virility. His uniform emphasises the broadness of his shoulders and the muscles of his powerful arms and legs. When I offered him my hand in greeting, he held it for an overly long period of time. I became aware of a strange light-headedness as his index finger titillated the inside of my palm with soft, feathery strokes. Simultaneously, his eyes held mine. Just before releasing my hand, Kendall ran the tip of his tongue lightly round his lips and I found myself wondering how his whiskers would feel brushing against my own mouth.

In bed that night, I felt as though I were a young, inexperienced girl once again. I tossed and turned. Sleep refused to overtake me and, when it did, I was plunged into a series of dreams which threw me back to my girlhood. Not for months had I dreamed of flying horses, corridors and staircases through which I ran in vain. As a fifteen-year old, I had told myself that, during my dreams, I was running away from all the knowledge I lacked. Today I am more aware and know that I long to embrace it all. I have accepted already the inevitable fact that Kendall will be the man to woo, seduce and teach me the ways of men and women. It is simply instinct on my part and, moreover, I am eager to have it happen.

Cat's letter still lies on my desk. Not another word have I

penned, for what can I say? In just a few hours, Kendall and I will commence rehearsing the roles of Kate and Petruchio. Yesterday, in one of our scenes, he picked me up in his arms and almost crushed my bones. When Petruchio turns Kate over his knee and spanks her to teach her discipline, Kendall moves the flat of his hand on my buttocks in the strangest manner! The slaps sting me and yet, at the same time, they cause stirrings and flashings such as I have never before experienced. When the scene is finished, I find myself almost shaking, wishing we had to rehearse it again.)

June 10, 1851

Dear Daffodil,

I am a woman. No longer am I in ignorance of the mystery of man. And it is wonderful, nay, miraculous. My limbs and body feel butter soft and I now understand why men are sometimes compared to tempered steel; for it is right. Men are, and should be, hard. And women? They should be melting and acquiescent. Ever since my seduction, I have been living and reliving the moment over and over again.

We had just finished rehearsing, and Kendall suggested quietly to me that we should work further on the scenes between us. I was surprised for I believed that all was going along splendidly.

"Come, Kate," he said, casually placing his hand on my shoulder. "Let us walk down by the river to cool ourselves. We can discuss the scenes as we walk. Then I'll order supper for us at Irons."

The evening was warm, the air soft. A bit of moon shone down on us and the sky was buttermilked with a million stars. I felt excited in a way that is impossible to explain and the more I tried to calm my mind, the faster my heart beat.

"Is there anything amiss in my interpretation of Kate?" I asked tentatively.

Kendall chuckled and clutched my shoulder more tightly. "No, no, Darra. It was only that I wanted to have you to myself tonight."

"Why's that, Kendall? We normally take supper with the rest

of the cast, although I doubt they'll miss our company."

"Exactly. Don't pretend, my little minx. You know as well as I what is happening between us." He stopped and drew me into the shadow of a large tree. "Can you deny our desire?"

I shivered. What could I say?

Kendall wasted no time taking me in his arms and, when his mouth crushed down upon mine, it was with savage insistence. I felt his whiskers brush against my upper lip and was pleased to discover that the hairs were silky, not wiry as I'd feared. While his tongue sought its way inside my surrendering mouth and moved about in probing exploration, his hands busied themselves caressing and stroking my back and waist. I felt a fire kindling within me, and moaned slightly when he moved his investigations to my bodice.

The lacings gave way easily to his deft fingers and soon he was cupping my breasts in his large hands. He stared down at me and, shyly, I glanced at him to see what he next planned.

"Just as I suspected," he said, holding me at arm's length. "You are dazzlingly beautiful."

"Am I, Kendall?" I asked him, for I had often wondered about my attractiveness.

He did not answer, occupied as he was in exploring the contours of my breasts. The sensation? How can I describe such bliss? Just as I was near swooning from the petting his tongue was bestowing, unexpectedly I felt a needle-sharp prick. I started, and was amazed to hear Kendall's laugh, deep in his throat. Once again, that stinging stab. What could he be doing? All at once I realized. He was using his teeth, and gently biting – just enough to produce discomfort, yet not pain. Indeed, the sensation reminded me of the stirrings he had forced on me when Petruchio spanks Kate.

As though he'd guessed my thoughts, Kendall's hands dropped to my skirts and, abruptly hauling them up, he began pinching my buttocks and hips. Still he held me tenderly between his teeth, his fingers wandering in many surprising ways. The soft stroking of the furry cap between my legs caused me to lose all sense of time and place. I felt myself in constant movement and ultimately my body was seized in a maelstrom of emotion. I held my breath, tension rising, and then experienced the most exquisite release. All the while, Kendall rocked and stroked and pinched and nibbled while I whimpered, unable to help myself.

Finally, he eased me onto the ground beneath a full bush and, sorry as I am to admit it, I do not remember if we were lying on the earth or the cloak which Kendall had earlier carried across his arm.

"There, there now, that's good, my sweet. Enjoy yourself. It's good, isn't it?"

As I nodded, assuring him of my agreement, he hoisted my skirts above my waist and knelt, preparing to mount me. I was in a daze, caring no longer what happened to me. All I recall is a quick glimpse of his manhood, straight and engorged, before he raised my hips with his hands and thrust himself inside me. After that, time roared in my ears, our movements increased in ferocity, and I heard him cry out as though in agony.

How we returned to Irons' Hotel, I know not. My introduction to love and bliss beneath the bushes was not the only time that night that Kendall made me his own. Throughout the dark night, between brief moments of sleep, we kissed and embraced, fondled and teased, all of which ended in passionate consummation of our insatiable desires, time and time again.

In the morning, when I woke at last, it was to find Kendall gone from the bed and my body stiff and sore. Upon examination of myself, I could not explain the scratches, bruises and abrasions which covered my shoulders, breasts and lower body. Swiftly, rejoicing yet ashamed, I covered my nakedness with a gown.

June 15, 1851

Dear Cat,

We have just ended a straight run of three performances of *The Taming of the Shrew* and, according to Kendall and the rest of the cast, I am a success. Naturally I am happy, but find myself of late wondering what lies ahead.

Trevor has written to inform me that his chest condition is not improved and the specialist strongly advocates a trip to Aix where he can enjoy the waters. He has said nothing about my accompanying him, not that I should wish to do so. As you are well aware, I have a strong aversion to illness and prefer the company of healthy companions, especially where gentlemen are concerned.

Truth to tell, I fear that I have let my heart take over my head in matters of romance. Captain Kendall Warrick has captured me in quite the same manner that Petruchio enslaved Kate. At the moment, in a mood of trembling love, I would gladly follow him to the ends of the earth. I would cook for him, clean his house and generally do all those things which wives are instructed to do. Whatever has happened to my decision to wed a rich philanthropist?

(Oh, Daffodil, how I wish I could confide in my dear sister as I am able to in you! I can no longer send your pages on to her. Do you suppose she will guess my misdemeanours from reading my letter? Say nay, for I must write on.)

I have received a letter from Marcus also and, because of what he has written, I hasten to address myself to you, Cat. The dear boy believes himself to be in love with me and, although he does not come right out and propose marriage, it is evident that the idea is on his mind. Dear dear sister, I cannot bear to wound him. Please, please break it to him gently. Let him know, in that elusive manner you affect so well, that he must not think of me romantically or in terms of marriage.

Mr Percival, Sydney's uncle, has kindly offered me letters of introduction to strategically placed gentlemen in the New York theatre world. I have not yet thought of going to New York, and I do not know if I would have the courage to travel there alone. One of the names that Mr Percival mentioned to me was that of Mr Basil Levishon, whose acquaintance I have already made, as you may recall. I shall think on it.

I have not as yet visited the dear sisters, and am well aware that you will be shocked at my behaviour. Fear not, however, for I plan to make a pilgrimage to St Joseph's next week – just as soon as our play closes. I must confess it frightens me for I feel sure that Father Andrew will berate me for my life in the theatre.

Kendall has promised to take me out on the river tomorrow

evening and I am anticipating the voyage with great excitement. The breezes do much to cool one on a hot June night. He has business, or so he hints, with some gentlemen who are anchored a mile or two offshore.

It is almost time for the post and, since I would like to send you my letter immediately, I shall make haste and seal it with a kiss, as they say, and much love and affection.

Your sister, Darra.

June 20, 1851

Dear Daffodil,

Only to you Daffodil, am I able to pour out my adventure on the river, and when I have done so, I must remember to lock you away. Your key I wear round my neck with my gold cross.

Kendall called for me, as promised, and a hired carriage sped us to the dock outside town. Arrangements had been made for a small skiff to propel us to the watery rendez-vous. When we first cast off, the weather seemed bright and pleasant but, as we neared the larger ship, the wind was picking up and clouds were moving in to hide the moon and stars.

"Oh, Kendall," I said, "do you think we are going to have a storm?"

He looked briefly at the sky. "I doubt it, love. Don't worry, I shall keep you safe from harm. If we do encounter rain, we can always spend the night aboard the *Gambling Queen*."

"*Gambling Queen*?" I repeated, surprised. "Why does she have such a name?"

Kendall chuckled in that amused way he has. "Why indeed, my innocent one? Because she's a gambling ship, that's why."

"Really? And why would you have business with gamblers, Captain?"

"Don't you worry your pretty little head about that," he said.

At that moment, another skiff, bearing lights fore and aft, appeared almost directly in front of us. A man was standing in the bow, trying to attract our attention.

"Must be Powell," Kendall said as though to himself. "Wonder why he's come out to meet us. I hope there's not been any trouble."

"Oh, Kendall, surely you're not in any danger," I said.

"Hush! Certainly there's no danger. Just sit still and stay quiet."

Since I had no other occupation, I made to do as bade. Sitting perfectly still, however, didn't stop me from thinking long and hard. What sort of business could Kendall have out in the middle of the St Lawrence with an officer from a gambling ship? I hesitated to give any credence to my musings, but couldn't keep from wondering if the handsome officer and actor might be involved in some criminal act.

Soon the skiff drew alongside us, and Kendall stood to greet the hidden man. "Ahoy there. Is that you, Powell?"

"Right y' all may be, Warrick," answered a drawling voice from the shadows.

"Anything amiss?" Kendall asked.

"'Twould seem necessary to close our operations for the time being. I made the ride out to tip you off."

"Pity. I was looking forward to an evening of wagers."

"The word came down that the sniffers are out. Our sister ship was attacked last week. These pirate frigates will ruin us yet."

"Lose much?"

"Everything," the man answered, his voice on edge. I tried to catch a glimpse of him in order to see what manner of man he might be. By chance, just as I looked up, he waved his lantern full in my face. With a start, I lifted my arm to ward off its brightness. As I did so, I heard the man called Powell gasp in surprise. The lantern swayed back and forth dangerously, but finally was righted.

"What's the matter, Powell?" asked Kendall as the lantern again turned full on my face. "What are you trying to do? Blind the lass?"

"Who is she?" Mr Powell demanded in a hoarse voice.

"Lower your light, man, and I'll introduce you." The brightness was turned aside hesitantly and Kendall's hand dropped to my shoulder. "May I present Miss St Joseph? This ruffian is Captain Beaufort Powell, my dear."

"How do you do, Sir?" I murmured and lowered my eyes in

embarrassment. Suddenly I was the centre of attention.

"A pleasure, Miss. Do forgive my behaviour but, for a moment, I'd have sworn I'd seen a ghost." So saying, he placed the lantern lower so I could barely discern a tall man, giving me a bow from the waist.

"A ghost, Powell? Pray tell us more." Kendall's voice was full of disbelief.

"Yes, Warrick – a ghost. It must be almost twenty years ago. A woman I met in Kingston." He paused. "Never have I seen hair the colour of hers again till tonight. Who was your mother, girl?"

"Never mind all that. This wench is flesh and blood, no ghost, I can assure you." Kendall laughed wickedly. For a moment, I felt wounded, for there was something in his voice which sounded boastful and, yes, degrading. I decided to ask him about it later.

"Well, Powell, shall we make another time and place for our meeting?" Kendall was saying. As he spoke, I felt a drop of rain on my face.

"Tomorrow night, near the abandoned alehouse beyond the town's outskirts. You will recall the place. We've met there before."

"Fine. Midnight then?" The wind was blowing more steadily now, and several more raindrops had fallen as the men talked.

"As you wish. I'll be there."

"Good then, and we'll conclude our business fairly and squarely," said Kendall with what sounded like a veiled threat. "Now we'd best make haste before we're caught in the squall."

"Yes, 'twould be wise. Goodnight to you, Miss St Joseph. I look forward to meeting you on a more fortuitous occasion. Perhaps, at that time, you might enlighten me about your background. Goodnight to you, Warrick. God-speed."

With that, his skiff took off with double the speed he had approached us. Kendall wasted no time in urging our own craft and we headed for the shores whence we came. By the time we docked, the waves had doubled in size and what had started out as a light shower was now a proper rainstorm.

Back at Irons' Hotel once more, I hurried to change from my dampened clothing and was surprised when Kendall bid me goodnight with undue haste.

"Kendall," I pleaded, as he headed towards the door, "won't you tell me what all this is about? Why are you having secret meetings in the middle of the river and outside of the town? Indeed, it sounds sinister to me. And what upset Mr Powell so much when he sighted me?"

"Darra, calm yourself. My meetings have nothing to do with you, so put them out of your mind. I wish to hear no more about the matter, do you hear?" As I nodded my head obediently, he continued. "As for your appearance and Beau's notion that he was seeing a ghost, I know nothing of it. Probably an old flame of his. When he saw you in the half-light, he imagined that she'd come back!"

Kendall then folded his arms around me, kissed my lips tenderly and suggested that I not wait up for him. "I may be late for I still have some business to attend to, and you must be fatigued from our boat ride in the rain."

With that, he turned aside and I found myself alone with nothing to occupy my thoughts other than the mysterious rendez-vous we had almost kept on the *Gambling Queen*.

June 25, 1851

Dear dear Cat,

I scarcely know where to begin or how to tell you of the ordeal I have been through. If only you were here so we might console each other. Never have I needed your companionship and comfort more sorely.

I shall tell you the whole story. Though it will take longer to relate this way, it will ease my burden somewhat to tell it all as it happened.

The Taming of the Shrew closed last week after our final performance. I know you would wish to know of my triumph, dear sister, but now is not the time to speak of it. Suffice it to say that the audiences were kind and I drew much applause and many curtain calls.

It was last week also that Kendall took me with him in a small skiff to meet a man in the middle of the St Lawrence River. At the time I thought it odd to be doing business in such a spot and at that hour, but odder still that Mr Powell, the man Kendall arranged to meet, should live on a steamship called the *Gambling Queen*. Today I am wiser. I have learned that Mr Powell is a renowned gambler, what some would call a card shark, and that he plies his trade mainly on the Mississippi paddle-boats.

Kendall, as you may have guessed by now, was in debt to Mr Powell and, therefore, had become more and more associated with him in criminal activities. The night we met on the river, Kendall left to go and attend to further business. Oh Cat, I have not seen him since. He has disappeared and I dare not make inquiries in case I find myself implicated in the gambling investigations which are presently being carried out in Kingston.

The rest of the acting group has broken up for the remainder of the summer. This is the usual case because, during the hottest months of July and August, people are not anxious to be indoors. The Prentices have returned to Galt. Sydney and his uncle left for Albany and plan later to visit Buffalo. They invited me to accompany them but I did not care to do so.

Trevor has left for New York to take a liner to France. He wrote me a letter with instructions to return to Toronto, where he expects to settle a few months hence.

Since I have been living very frugally here, and spending as little as possible of Trevor's settlement, I made the decision to visit St Joseph's and, if Kendall has not turned up by the first of July, I shall take the coach and return to Toronto. I do not know what I would be fit for there, but at least I would be with you.

Now I come to the difficult part. I dressed myself carefully on Sunday and headed for St Joseph's. I cannot tell you how homesick and frightened I was as I approached the fence with its white gate. Once inside it, I stood for several minutes beside the bush where the sisters found us as babes so long ago. Thinking back to our mysterious start in life, I was overcome with sorrow and tears began streaming down my cheeks.

Eventually, however, I was able to take charge of myself and I headed, just as we had in former times, for the door of the kitchen. I peered inside, but no one was about. Without thinking, I put my hand on the doorknob, turned it (as you know, the sisters have never locked a door in their lives) and let myself inside. Everything was silent. It was so very eerie.

Walking across the kitchen floor, I began a thorough search of the familiar surroundings. It was in the little chapel off the parlour that I finally discovered Father Andrew. He was kneeling before the Virgin Mary and his hands were clasped before him. Quietly I moved closer and knelt beside him.

"Father," I said in a choked voice, "it is I, Darra."

He turned to look at me, and a strange look passed over his face. At once I knew that something was amiss but before I could stammer out another word, his arms reached out and he clasped me with such fatherly love that, once again, tears came unbidden to my eyes.

"Oh Darra," he said, "praise the Lord. You've come home." It was only then that I saw the tears in his eyes also. "Come, child, let us go to Sister Martha. She will be so happy."

"Oh yes," I said, "and Sister Isobel. It has been so long, or so it seems."

"Sister Isobel is ill, my child, gravely ill."

"Then I shall nurse her, Father, until she is well once again."

Oh Cat, I cannot go on. When I saw Sister Isobel, lying on her cot, her hands so thin and blue, and the pallor of her skin so grey, I understood that Father Andrew was correct.

Sister Martha sat beside her, as though willing her to recovery. When she saw me, she held out her arms and I knelt to embrace her. I cannot tell you, what strong emotions gripped me. Sister Martha is also skin and bones. I fear she and Father Andrew have been grieving so and spending so much time in prayer that they have neglected the food they need to keep up their strength.

I must not write longer. The moment I appraised the situation, I determined to stay and care for them all. I have been here five days now.

Both Father Andrew and Sister Martha are eating again and resting for longer periods. I have hired a girl to clean, but am attending to the cooking myself. Whenever I am idle, I spend the time with Sister Isobel but am afraid we must expect the worst. She suffers and there is so little we can do. Yesterday she recognised me for the first time and I thank God for that.

136

If only I might persuade her to eat a little, to gain strength.
Love from your sister, Darra.

June 30, 1851

Dear Cat,

Sister Isobel has gone to her reward and I feel certain she must
be in heaven, sitting with the rest of the saints on the right side of
God, don't you agree? The end came suddenly but quietly when
we least expected it. As a matter of fact, I was out of the manse
when it happened, but Sister Martha was with her. Arrangements
had to be made quickly, dear Cat, so I fear there will be no time
for you to travel here for the funeral. The heat wave we have
been enduring shows no sign of letting up and it is for that reason
that poor Sister Isobel's burial must be carried out with such
undue haste.

During the following days, I plan to visit the sisters at Hôtel
Dieu and move the few small children from St Joseph's back into
their home. Both Father Andrew and Sister Martha were so
distressed over Sister Isobel's illness, they felt quite unable to keep
the children here while they nursed and fretted over her. There
was also some concern over an infection that Sister Isobel had
contracted. You know how careful the sisters always were when
it came to the protection of the children. They were fortunate to
secure a place in service for the older girls and only half a dozen or
so of the younger ones will be returning at this moment.

I do hope you will agree with me that Father Andrew and
especially Sister Martha should continue their good work with
orphaned children, despite their ageing years. Otherwise, I fear
they will fall into depression the moment I leave. So I am making
arrangements that they will have their hands full with attending
to God's duty.

The atmosphere at St Joseph's is oppressive and it has not been
lightened by the massive amounts of food and flowers brought in
by the sympathetic, yet good-hearted parishioners. The scent of
lilies is overpowering and last night my head ached when I
dropped into my bed. I look foward to hearing the voices of

children about the place, just as I remember it.

You are ever in my prayers, dear sister, and I trust I am in yours also. Surely the time will not be long before we are together again.

With love from your own sister, Darra.

9

I have just returned from confession and am stinging and somewhat repentant, for the good father scolded me severely. I had hoped that the Holy Sacrament would bring my mind to a more submissive state, but I am still unaccepting of the blows of fate.

My heart sorrows for my friends at St Joseph's and for dear Darra in the loss of Sister Isobel. For all our childish plaints, we knew full well that we were fortunate in the care and training we received at her hands. If I remember the sharp slaps that recalled us to our duties, so do I think of the many kindnesses. It was sister Isobel herself who soaked and bathed my foot the day I disobeyed her and ran barefooted in the orchard, chasing Darra round the trees. The noxious poison ivy caused a red rash over which I could not put my stockings. I hobbled back to the house, my guilt obvious to all. Disregarding Darra's tale of the 'big spider that got into Cat's stocking and bit poor Cat all over,' Sister Isobel sent the child to gather the big leaves which we applied to these burns. May her soul rest in peace.

I am not easy over the news I receive from Darra. Marcus is mooning and downcast. We met again at the post-office. "Good morning, Marcus," I cried. "How often I find you in this area."

"Good morning to you, Cat. Have you no word of your sister's return?"

I did not feel free to disclose my doubts to Marcus and merely answered, "She busies herself about her affairs in Kingston. I await further word from her myself."

I wonder anxiously why Darra cannot settle for a good man and a secure future? Has she lost her virtue to the young man she calls Kendall? Surely not! What will become of her with this restless chasing after fame?

It seems nothing suits me these days. An inflammation has settled in one of my teeth and I have suffered much pain. The swelling is somewhat eased by poultices but I was recently unable to attend an evening concert. Miss Fanny Kemble arrived in Toronto to give her Shakespearian readings. These entertainments are very popular and I longed to go, for Darra's sake. I have never heard a famous entertainer read Shakespeare and I hoped to learn more of the great bard's genius. The Smythes had obtained tickets and I was to be of their party. I missed it all, however, being confined to bed on account of my swollen face.

Apparently a dilemma befell poor Miss Kemble. On her arrival, her trunk was found to be missing. The heat-wave we have been suffering perhaps had made the carriers careless. At all events, Miss Kemble was forced to give her reading in her travelling dress of simple calico, which bore the stains of her journey. Her performance was greatly praised, as she rose above her afflictions, her vivacity being much admired. I thought of my dear sister and her experiences of the mishaps of travel. I had eagerly looked foward to the evening's performance, hoping to experience some of the excitement which Shakespeare's work brings to all acting companies. I waited to hear the words of Mistress Kate and to imagine Darra, as she acted the part. Well, it was not to be.

Of all the troubles that have descended on me, the one that is the most painful is Cavan's continued absence. I had expected his return this month and tore open his last letter eagerly. Alas! Cavan has had difficulty in concluding the military assignment which was concomitant to his leave in Québec. His father, accompanied by Mrs Parnell and her daughter, are on their way to Toronto, to be followed by Cavan as soon as possible. He sends his love, begs my patience and assures me that I alone rule his heart. I both long and dread to meet Miss Parnell as she enters into Toronto's social life. I had hoped to have the encouragement of Cavan's presence at this time.

In openly confessing my fears and discontent, Father Michael declared that I showed a heart "reluctant to accept the will of the Lord." My penance was to be more time-consuming and arduous than usual. It seems to me that the pain in my heart is sufficient burden and the penance remains undone. I go to rub whisky, kindly supplied by Mr Smythe, upon my aching gum and then take myself to bed. May tomorrow dawn more kindly.

July 15, 1851

My dearest sister Darra,

It is more than a year since we were together, yet I feel closer in spirit to you than ever. Forgive me for the doleful letter of reproach I sent you two days ago. Surely there is nothing you tell me that I will not understand. It is only my great fear for your safety and my longing for your happiness that make me warn you of dangers that you may not see. I always acted as if I were the older sister, you were so wilful, such a hoyden. Now I must remember that we are both women of marriageable age, who have been seeking our fortunes for past a year.

I am relieved to say that the abscess on my gum broke and the pain has now subsided. Can you imagine my terror at the prospect of having a tooth drawn? Do you recall when old George, the stable-hand, Burt's father, had a tooth drawn by the travelling apothecary? A ripe infection set in and he was at St Joseph's in great suffering. Father Andrew said that, for once, the man had an excuse for all the spirits he downed! Oh, Darra, how I grieve for Sister Isobel. Knowing that she rejoices in everlasting rest, I try to find comfort in the thought that her work continues at St Joseph's.

A letter from Oonagh tells me that the Kingsley family are in New York, visiting Mrs Kingsley's relatives. Major Kingsley will only spend a couple of weeks there, but she will stay on and see the shows. Oonagh also tells me that the Major will be sadly out of pocket by the time they return as Mrs Kingsley is set on acquiring all the very latest in fashion. Major Kingsley is surely a most kind and courteous man. According to Oonagh, he approached her one day and asked, "Have you had any recent news of Catherine, Oonagh? I regretted seeing that young woman go off on her own to join her sister, whom I understand did not stay around Toronto in any case."

"I took the liberty," said Oonagh, "to tell him that you are doing very well for yourself and keeping company with all the very best in Toronto. Why, I told him, Catherine has even sat at table with Mr Baldwin himself, and her just learning her comportment with Mrs Kingsley this past winter."

Major Kingsley sighed and said, "Catherine has great appeal, Oonagh. Let me know if ever she is in need." And said Oonagh, "He's a real gentleman, Cat, weren't nothing funny about it. He really wants to help you as if you was a lady."

Inside, Darra, I am still unsure and wondering who I am, but outwardly I think I do more and more become a lady in demeanour. You and I both know how unkind society can be to those without background, yet I have found a powerful protector. I have most exciting news for you. Oh, how happy you will be to learn of my good fortune, for if I rise, I will always hold you to my side. This is what has transpired.

All conversation lately has been of the Fête Champêtre which is to take place at Government House on July 28. The best of Society is very pleased that the centre of government was moved to Toronto after the burning of the city hall in Montréal, and it is said that Lord Elgin himself has remarked how much at home he feels among the Upper Canadians.

The women of the Smythe family are all absorbed in designing and planning their attire for the eventful day. Dress-makers are sore-pressed with all the new orders.

I'd been attending a most trying fitting with Mrs Beatrice Smythe, who is now returned from her honeymoon. She and her husband remain with us until the building of their new home is completed. Her robust bosom, barely restrained by the border-line of frills the dress-maker endeavoured to secure, heaved and fell as she simpered. "I vow I will be quite frightened to put this on when Gordon is around. Of course, Cat, you have no knowledge of men, but Gordon can be a very naughty boy. I'm sure I must already be in the family way."

I did not deign to answer, but the fitter snickered. Mrs Beatrice really has very little refinement. I am now deeply appreciative of the lessons of deportment we mastered at St Joseph's, almost as if we were the Sister's own children. We would never have had this advantage if we had been in the crowded orphanage started by the Hôtel Dieu.

I was reflecting on this when Mrs Smythe entered the room. "Catherine," she said, "I have news for you. You are greatly honoured. Indeed, I begin to think you have won a heart."

I looked at her, questioning and uncomfortable. She held out an envelope addressed in my name and I recognised it at once as similar to the invitations to the Fête Champêtre. How could my name have been included? Imagine my surprise.

"I think, my dear, that Mr de la Haye has used his influence and would enjoy having you on his arm to stroll the grounds." Mrs Smythe laughed kindly and the ready pink rushed to my cheeks. "You will need a dress," she added.

Oh, Darra, I wonder if indeed I am the girl who left St Joseph's just over a year ago. So that you may imagine me strolling the grounds of government house, I will tell you about my gown. It is a white tarlatan, very fashionably made. My gloves and shoes are matching. How I hope the weather will be clement.

Mr de la Haye made me a gift, a charming French parasol of white silk, lined in pink with an ivory handle. I was hesitant as to whether it was proper to accept so extravagant an article, but he assured me it was given in the spirit of a family friend. I thanked him, but begged that he would not again befriend me in this way.

I am much excited about this garden party. My only regret is that Cavan will not be here. To be truthful, I long to know if he still cares for me. A flower among the others at the Fête, would I be the one he'd pluck? Pray for me, Darra, for you have guessed my secret. It is Cavan who rules my heart, since he first placed his lips on mine.

I accept your decisions, my dearest sister, and send you my prayers and my love. May the sweet Virgin guide you always.

Your Cat.

July 31, 1851

No matter how our spirits soar, it seems that always we are brought hurtling to the ground. Only I know how I am wounded.

The talk is still of the Fête Champêtre, surely the most successful event of the year.

The day dawned sunny and fresh, without the close heat which our summers sometimes bring in their wake. The men, in uniforms or formal dress, and pretending indifference to the importance of the event, were ready long before we descended the stairs, in all our elegance. We were greeted with calls of surprise and admiring comments: Mrs Smythe in lemon yellow, Mrs Beatrice Smythe following, billowing puffs of rose-coloured silk, and I in the soft white tarlatan. Straw hats are the fashion this year and are neat and close-fitting. I had chosen a more traditional soft-brimmed white bonnet.

Outside, the Smythe's best carriage was drawn up, the two chestnut horses with gleaming coats. The gentlemen handed us in, amid many injunctions not to crush our gowns. A mood of excitement and geniality prevailed, in pleasant contrast to the recent gloom in the Smythe household over the resignation of Mr Baldwin and Mr Louis Lafontaine.

On arrival at the grounds, colour and music welcomed our eyes and ears. We joined the reception line of gaily dressed belles and their escorts, who were waiting to be greeted by Lord and Lady Elgin. Many, of course, were well-known to the Smythes and, as the men greeted each other, we covertly eyed each new vision of silk, satin, cambric, lawn, lace or tulle. The dress-makers had excelled in fitting those Torontonians who couldn't afford imported gowns, but many a robe came straight from London or even Paris.

My attention was drawn to a trio who were just ahead of us in the line. The man was heavily-built, his skin somewhat ruddy in tone. As he turned, I noticed the arrogant gaze which he ran over Mrs Beatrice's swelling breasts. His gaze lingered on her cleft in a most ungentlemanly way, then rose to her face. Having caught her attention, he smiled slightly and again scanned her curves. Mrs Beatrice tossed her head, smiling provocatively at her husband. Then, turning artlessly aside, she leaned over, flicking a speck of dust from his jacket and allowing the unknown stranger an intimate view of her bosom. Scandalised, I turned my attention to the two ladies of the party.

The older woman, presumably his wife, was short and dumpy. Discreetly robed in violet and white, she nevertheless had a certain elegance. It was the daughter, in a cascade of green, who really held my attention. Slightly taller than her mother, she was dressed in the height of fashion. I was certain that her clothes were from some famous couturier. Her shining hair was dressed in an elaborate series of curls and, to my surprise, I noticed that her hat seemed to be held by a long pin. No troublesome ribbons to irritate her skin which was clear and delicately-coloured. Her manner was vivacious and she was chattering to the coarse-looking man beside her.

"Yes," she was saying. "I met connections of Lord Elgin while I was enjoying the season in London. I was invited to their country estate several times, in fact."

Was she not the man's daughter, I wondered? At this point, we reached Lord and Lady Elgin and I heard the former say, "Welcome, Mr O'Hara. My good friend, William Hume Blake, tells me that you may have some tips for me for the races. Later we will speak on this."

At his side, Lady Elgin was smiling, adding, "Mrs Parnell, how pleasant to see you. Moira, my dear, you look quite lovely."

I smiled and made my curtsy almost unknowingly. So the arrogant-looking man was Cavan's father, and the beautiful young woman, Moira. They must be staying with Mr Hume Blake, Chancellor of Upper Canada. Of course, he had originally emigrated from Ireland. I had met his two sons on one occasion. Samuel, who was slightly older than myself, had been most kind to me, sensing my lack of ease as a newcomer to society.

At this moment, Roger, as I must learn to call him, appeared at my side and asked Mrs Smythe's permission to take me to the refreshments. Long tables were set among the trees, covered with snowy damask cloths; their surfaces covered with every imaginable delicacy, cold meats, aspics, canapés, cheeses and fruit. Champagne flowed. Several regimental bands were situated at different areas of the gardens, attracting me with their cheerful melodies.

"Oh," I cried. "Pray do let us go over to the band. I am not really hungry yet." Unfurling my parasol, I tilted it gaily behind my head. I must not, must not think of Cavan.

We listened to the medley of tunes for some time. I was beginning to relax when Roger left me to select our refreshments. He returned with these in the company of Samuel Blake and Moira Parnell.

My throat dried and my heart disturbed me with its violent beating. Moira's elborately embossed green satin skirts shimmered as she moved towards us. Her big pansy-brown eyes gazed at me with certain acuity. I felt sure that Moira assessed all women in comparison to herself and was seldom disappointed. How does a woman always know these things? I knew.

Ah, Sister Isobel, I am not worthy of your training. Forgive me. You never received the sacrament of marriage, never knew the pain of love. Would my own unknown mother have passed this knowledge to me, in forming my body? But I digress.

Miss Parnell and young Mr Samuel Blake settled themselves beside me and Roger handed me my glass, asking me if I were acquainted with the newcomers. Miss Parnell's melting gaze fixed itself on Roger and then wandered speculatively towards me. She was, however, far too sophisticated and poised to allow herself any questions. The conversation drifted easily from her life in Ireland to the world tour she had just undertaken. Warm and with a natural gaiety, she was accustomed to masculine admiration and took it as her due. I fell increasingly silent.

"Miss St Joseph," she said sweetly. "You will have heard of the Black Virgin? She is a most popular tourist attraction. So unusual to depict our Holy Mother in black. Some say it is the smoke of all the candles that has darkened her, but of course this could not be so."

"No," I replied. "I have never heard of this holy image. Pray tell me more."

Smiling winsomely at Roger, she continued. "I have no doubt that you from Québec have many a tale of miracles performed to tell us, but since Miss St Joseph begs me, forgive me if I repeat a well-known story."

She went on to recount her visit to the church Saintes-Maries-de-la-Mer in Southern France where the statue is kept. Smarting at her hands, I ceased to pay much attention to her words. The narrative continued and her gay laugh rang out from time to time.

"Our party was joined by such a delightful group of Germans – Frau Schmitt – Herr Doktor – Herr Professor – together – festival for the Black Virgin – Herr Doktor an antiquarian – annual gypsy pilgrimage in May – Frau Schmitt – Herr Doktor – "

At last she fell silent. Realizing that I had been discourteous in allowing my attention to wander, I sought for something to say.

"Was Mrs Schmitt perhaps taking a cure? You kept mentioning her doctor."

Samuel Blake laughed, then hastily passed me another canapé. Roger turned quickly to me saying, "Catherine –," but he was interrupted by Moira's trill of amusement.

"Oh, Miss St Joseph, you are the most amusing child. Herr is simply a German title of respect. In French I'd say Monsieur le docteur."

I was filled with chagrin. How could I, a parentless girl from St Joseph's orphanage, be expected to know these things? For all my lovely clothes, I was but an unwanted child, who could never be accepted by those of true blood.

Again I was silent and Roger took my arm, saying, "Catherine is becoming an excellent French linguist, and now I must return to her to Mrs Smythe." As we walked across the green lawn, he tried to offer me words of comfort, but he could not know the real source of my pain.

If I really loved Cavan, I would not hold him to a few promises, for it was obvious that Miss Moira Parnell was far better able to grace his estate than I. Dear Mary, Mother of Sorrows, help me bear the pain. I was hardly conscious of the passing of the rest of the afternoon, but finally we said our farewells and walked towards the Smythe's carriage. We could not, however, depart, as Mr Gordon Smythe had gone in search of his wife.

"How could she have disappeared?" demanded Mrs Smythe angrily. "Surely you did not leave her, Gordon?"

"I left her, Jean, for a short time in the company of Mr Hume Blake, his son, Samuel, and their guests, the Parnells. I went into the house to see the constructions being carried out, but Beatrice expressed herself unwilling to go indoors. When I returned, I could not find the group. I hope there is no need for concern."

Roger was waiting to hand me into the carriage, he and I exchanged glances. I looked away quickly, ashamed of my thoughts. At this point, Mrs Beatrice was seen approaching us most hastily, without escort, from the direction of the shrubbery. Her face was blotched and unusually flushed and she was quite out of breath. I had the impression she was holding back her tears with difficulty.

"Beatrice." Mrs Smythe hurried towards her. "Whatever have you been doing? Where were you? Gordon has gone to find you."

Beatrice answered somewhat incoherently. "Please, Jean. It was nothing. I was overcome with a sudden nausea. I withdrew for a minute." Sobs defeated her. I noticed that she was holding her hand to her bodice and that her lace ruffles were bunched in her hand, which was shaking uncontrollably. Reaching into the coach, I drew out the light shawl I knew was inside.

"Perhaps you are getting a chill," I suggested, handing it to her. She grabbed the shawl eagerly and drew it round her. As she dropped the lace frill, I saw it to be torn and that her voluptuous white breast, momentarily exposed, had marks that resembled scratches or bites. My horror and suspicions temporarily drowned the pain in my heart.

Both Mrs Beatrice and I were very quiet on the way home and we both retired early to our rooms, pleading a case of too much exposure to the sun.

August 15, 1851

I have written a long letter to Darra, hoping that it will catch up with her. It was a letter full of small things that do not count in my life, for somehow I find I am moving through the paces of daily living as if in a dream. We were always taught that work was the answer for an uncontrolled imagination, as prayer is for a troubled soul. So I try to follow these precepts.

At times I wish I could consult with Father Andrew, since I find it difficult to pray as I should. If the good Lord in His infinite wisdom has decided to say 'no' to my heart's desire, all I can ask for is a spirit of acceptance. This is extremely difficult. I doubt that Darra would be of much help as she has always been a rebellious soul, yet at times she is very practical. What would she advise? It seems I fill even my journal with useless musings, so will go out and busy myself with errands.

Mrs Beatrice is still with us, expecting to move into their new house in East York at the end of the month. She has lately been overcome with nausea and is thought to be breeding. Since the Fête Champêtre, she has been quieter and more subdued. Little more was said of her absence, it being put down to her condition, one quite usual in a young wife.

The heat has been unbearable, our clothes repressive and clinging to us. Even the lightest voile is too much. The humidity is very high. We enjoy picnics on the shores of Lake Ontario, or we drive into the country to seek the shade. Fortunately the insects are discouraged by the lack of rain. Even so, we are careful to annoint ourselves with oil of citronella, this being distasteful to the pesky creatures.

I have been working on my water-colours and have ventured to send one of my efforts, St Michael's Cathedral, to Darra, for, whenever I attend mass there, she is first in my prayers. In fact, I much prefer my garden sketches, finding the delicacy of the blossom to be more responsive to my palette than the austere stone of St Michael's. Roger, however, claimed my latest nature scene.

August 25, 1851

I am so ashamed of myself. Today I received the following letter:

> Dear Miss St Joseph,
>
> I take my pen in hand on behalf of Lieutenant Cavan O'Hara. He is unable to write himself at this point. He dictates with difficulty from his bed in l'Hôpital Hôtel Dieu, where he recovers from a case of concussion.
>
> On our returning home from an evening at our favourite tavern a few nights ago, three of our officers were set upon in the alley. We resisted our scurrilous attackers with good will, but they were

six to our three. Cavan received head wounds and has been forced to rest abed.

He begs me tell you that there is little amiss. I would suggest, nevertheless, that you do not expect him to correspond with you for a few weeks. The Sisters inform me it may be some time before he returns to active duty.

I have the honour to remain your humble servant,

Lieutenant George Delaney.

No wonder I have not had any letters. In my silly jealousy, I had assumed that my love's attention had been directed to Miss Parnell. I have spent this month in the doldrums and realise now that, as the old saying tells, while there is life, there is hope. I have written a letter of good cheer to the invalid. I also lit two candles in the cathedral; that will grant him our Lady's precious intercession.

September 20, 1851

The weather has been astonishingly hot for much of this month and, being unseasonal, has brought increased attacks of fever and liver complaints. Now we sense the coming of the fall and trees begin their seasonal display. My life goes on in the usual round of charity and entertainment. Mrs Smythe and her coterie have been occupied in working for the Children's Orphanage of Toronto. We hope to have a fine purse to present to them for the Christmas season. A ball was given, the proceeds of which were all donated to the cause. I wondered, being the only person who had actually passed her childhood in such an institution, why so much should have been spent on the ball itself.

Roger has returned to Montréal, having resigned from his work as advisor to Mr Louis Lafontaine. He asked me to return with him. Despite my ready affection, I know that he is as a father to me, and I could not imagine myself in the position of his married wife. Yet I find I miss his companionship. He offered a security I do not know when in the company of the young men I meet under Mrs Smythe's roof.

He will be here next month as he is returning for the sole delight of hearing Miss Jenny Lind. After months of speculation, we now are to be honoured by her presence. She will have completed her tour of the United States and will grace Toronto for a week. I long to hear her. Darra was looking forward to this privilege in New York and even hoped to be in the position of speaking a few words with the Songbird.

Cavan, alas, has made slow progress and is still in Québec City. He writes a few lines himself but admits to headaches. Mr O'Hara and the Parnells are still in Toronto and, from time to time, we meet at social events. I have avoided personal contact, which has not been difficult. Miss Parnell is belle at all events and is said to be courted by several young men. How I wish to hear of her acceptance! Instead, rumour has it that she is privately engaged to Mr O'Hara's son and only awaiting his return to make it all formal. I cannot write of this to Cavan and must turn a deaf ear to the words that come my way.

October 16, 1851

Yesterday was the celebration in honour of the commencement of the new Northern Railway, which is to traverse Simcoe County and to extend as far as Georgian Bay. All of Toronto turned out to see Lady Elgin turn the first sod. It was also the day I shall remember forever as the turning point of my life.

October weather is often crisp and golden and, so it was, as we gathered across from the parliament buildings, in the roped-off sections reserved for dignitaries. The open area was soon filled with people. Ragamuffins and urchins were running between the ropes. Groups of school children stood quietly with their teachers and the Toronto Orphanage had their young ones, in tidy drab uniform, waiting to cheer the official party.

The Elgin's carriage drew up in good time and the couple was greeted by the railway officials and representatives of the government and of the city of Toronto. Speeches were made and the crowds, in excellent humour, cheered long and loud. Lady Elgin, looking most charming, but a trifle earnest, was handed a spade.

Major Bowes, in official costume, stood to her side, his cocked hat and sword reminding me of tales of highwaymen. With knee-breeches, silk stockings and shoes with steel buckles, he almost drew more attention than did our First Lady.

The sod she was to dig had naturally been prepared for her and, as she lifted out the earth, the grouped bands broke into music and the crowd into further prolonged cheers. The official party moved over to the roped section, speaking with various of the onlookers. While we chatted, waiting for them to approach us, I heard a voice behind me. It was impatient, cutting and decisive.

"The engagement will be announced very soon. My son is not so foolish as to lose his inheritance at Castle-Blaine for some chit of a girl. No, no! Mark my words! Moira assured me . . ."

The voices were drowned out at that moment as the Elgins approached. I tentatively turned my head to see Mr O'Hara and Mr William Hume Blake in deep conversation. For a moment, I was utterly numbed, refusing to believe what I had heard, refusing to believe that it related to myself. A slow chill overtook me and I began shivering uncontrollably. It attracted the attention of Mrs Smythe.

"Catherine? Whatever is the matter? Are you taking a chill? Why did you not wear your blue merino today? It is the fall, you know, and you cannot trust the wind off the Lake." Chattering and concerned, she led me to the carriage and bundled me in the shawls we kept to put across our knees. The chill did not leave me as the coach rattled along the road to our home.

Once in my bed, drinking the hot tisane prepared for me, I thought long and painfully of my future and made my plans.

October 26, 1851

Last evening was the long-awaited concert given by the Swedish nightingale, Jenny Lind. How beautiful and sweet this young woman appears. While singing with the voice of an angel, it seems she is also charitable of disposition. She has given a vast sum of money for the establishment of schools in her native land. She has set up funds to help the fishermen's children. Now she modestly took her turn with the other soloists, who gave performances on clarinet and violin and pianoforte to allow her to rest her voice between numbers. All feelings except joy left me as her voice rose in the wonderful song, "The Echo." St Lawrence Hall was on its feet as we applauded and called her back, again and again.

During the interval, Roger said gently, "Catherine, ma petite, have you given any more thought to the suggestion I made you? My mother longs to extend her hospitality. Staying with her, you would get to know my children and to become familiar with our way of life, without a final commitment."

The moment had come. Looking up at him, I spoke gently. "Yes, please, Roger. I will come." For me, this meant forever, for how could I hurt this tender man?

Roger gripped my hand, his eyes glowed. "Catherine! Do you really mean it?" He reached into his pocket and drew out a small velvet box, which he handed to me. I looked at him wonderingly.

"Open it," he said.

I did so and drew out a delicate friendship ring, a golden band with a semi-circle of minute pearls, rubies and sapphires. Each small stone a perfect well of colour. He slipped it on my smallest finger, where it rested as if at last at home. My eyes filled with tears and I lowered them as we returned to our seats for the conclusion of the concert.

Now, as I write this in the parlour, my eyes stray to the circlet on my right hand.

I hear the sounds of horse hoofs, so suppose the Smythes are returned from their errands. I must conclude my entry in haste as, from the ringing and banging on the front door, it would appear rather that guests have arrived.

The maid is speaking, and footsteps approach . . . Cavan!

10

Dear Cat,

I do want you to know how very pleased I am for you. Your world appears to be full of successes, one after another; parties, balls, indeed a veritable social whirl. The fête champêtre must have been extremely fashionable. My own world is obviously not in the same style as yours, nevertheless, I move from one event to another.

Cat dear, may I ask a favour of you? You will remember my cloak with the fur lining which was stored at the furriers when I left on tour? Well, now that the air is becoming chilly, I feel the need of it. Would it be too much trouble for you to arrange its delivery to me at the above address?

Your affairs of heart sound complicated and, although you speak of Cavan with love and longing, Roger appears to offer many advantages. After consideration, I think you perhaps erred in refusing Roger's proposal of marriage. Were you to marry a man of his social background, you'd never have to worry again about security or acceptance in society. Suppose Cavan's head injury were to linger for years, indeed for ever? Surely you do not care to spend your years caring for an invalid! I say no more.

Dear Daffodil,

It seems to me that the longer my sister and I are apart, the more difficult it is to confide in her. Before leaving Kingston in August, I wrote to her in detail concerning all the events of at St Joseph's. I am sure she was pleased, just as pleased as I, that Father Andrew and Sister Martha were able, within a few weeks, to take up the labour of the Lord once more; such sweet apple-cheeked children, six of them between the ages of four and ten; quite a handful. Father Andrew and Sister Martha are not as young as they once were. Seeing them with those wide-eyed innocents took me straight back to the days when Cat and I were in their charge.

Of course I was incapable of confiding to Cat my horror when I discovered Kendall's involvement with the crime world. When I first learned of it, I made a vow to put it out of my mind completely, to do penance for my own fallen state, and to act according to Christian concepts from that day forth. You at least will bear with me, Daffodil, for I dare not share this burden with dear Cat. As you are well aware, I have never even written of it, but the shame has never left my mind. Perhaps if I confess once and for all, I shall be able to hold my head up one day.

In late June, I had written to Cat that it was my intention to return to Toronto if I hadn't heard from Kendall by the month of July. Fate had other plans for me. July began hot and oppressive and, because of my concern for St Joseph's and the return of the younger foundlings. I determined to remain for some weeks yet. It was in the middle of the month, when my monthlies failed to arrive, that I began to suspect that my dalliance with Kendall had led to something more than I desired. On turning the thought round in my head, I came to a decision. I would make a visit to headquarters and inquire of the commander of the regiment as to the whereabouts of Captain Kendall Warrick.

Dressing carefully, and telling Sister Martha that I had errands to run in town, I set out on foot. I was not long on my way when I realised the foolhardiness of my actions. The heat from the unrelenting sun made me faint and squeamish. My steps slowed to a faltering gait and I looked for a spot to rest. Within minutes, however, I set forth with determination again and, upon my arrival in town, made for the tearoom.

"Tea with lemon, please," I ordered, "and would you have a copy of today's newspaper?" At St Joseph's, I seldom saw a journal since Father Andrew considered such things unnecessary.

Soon the smiling waitress appeared with a small earthenware pot of tea, a china cup and saucer and slices of lemon on a plate. Under her arm, she carried a folded copy of the *Whig Standard*, which she quietly placed on the table before me.

The moment I had finished pouring my tea, I opened the newspaper and glanced at the headlines. That was when I realised the serious difficulties which lay ahead of me.

BODY IDENTIFIED AS MILITARY OFFICER, the headline screamed. I read quickly, anxious to know all immediately. It seemed that the naked body of a man had washed up on the shores of the St Lawrence River a week ago. There was a bullet hole in his chest and one above his right ear. At first the authorities were baffled, however, within days they linked the case to the gambling ship which had been anchored outside of the city for some weeks. As Kendall had been on extended military leave, his absence had not been reported and it had taken almost a full week to identify the corpse. Nevertheless, it was proved to be the remains of my lover and actor friend, Kendall Warrick.

"Excuse me," a voice spoke directly beside me, startling me with its suddenness. "Miss St Joseph, I believe?"

I looked up into the expressionless face of an officer who looked vaguely familiar. He smiled, but it seemed to me that, when he did so, it was only with his lips.

"I'm afraid I don't . . ." I began.

"Captain Hayworth," he introduced himself. "I met you after your charming performance in *The Taming of the Shrew*, at a party given by the cast one evening. You were, I believe, in the company of my dear departed friend, Captain Warrick."

"Ohhh." I could think of nothing further to say.

"May I join you?" he asked, pulling out the chair next to mine.

"Why yes, certainly. Please do." I wished he would disappear, for I feared I might be ill at any minute. My sense of propriety prevailed, however, and as it turned out, it was just as well. Captain Hayworth was just the person to supply me with details concerning my former lover.

"You were aware of Captain Warrick's disappearance?" he asked. I felt that his eyes were capable of seeing right through me.

"I haven't seen Kendall for some time," I replied smoothly, grateful for my abilities as an actress. "I have been sorely occupied with the loss of a close and dear family friend."

"Please accept my condolences, Miss St Joseph, and who might that friend be? If I may inquire."

"Sister Isobel of St Joseph's Orphanage and parish," I said.

"I was not aware that your talents spread to considerations of a religious nature as well as dramatic."

"My sister and I were foundlings and brought up at St Joseph's," I responded guardedly, wondering all the while at his interest. "We are both devoted to the good sisters and Father Andrew. Indeed, we are forever in their debt."

"Of course. Forgive me." I could tell I had caught him off guard by speaking of matters religious, but he pressed on. "It is tragic, the death, er, the murder of Captain Warrick."

"Yes, Captain, I agree. When you arrived at my table, I was just reading about it, and I am still in a state of shock."

"You did not know?"

"Of course not. How could I possibly have known?" I knew I sounded indignant, but felt no concern.

"I was under the impression that you and Kendall were close acquaintances. You may correct me if I judged wrongly." He stared appraisingly at me.

"We were of necessity in each other's company much of the time, what with rehearsals and all." I waved my hand in such a way as to dismiss the matter as one of no import.

"He was in fact seriously involved with a criminal gambling element. It is thought that he had a quarrel with someone, possibly an American. The authorities know of one or two who are highly placed. You were not aware?"

"I know nothing of gambling and certainly nothing of criminal activities, Captain. I am surprised at your impudence, Sir, in even daring to question me." My voice and actions remained aloof and I was determined that they would continue thus.

"I beg your pardon, Miss St Joseph. I thought you would perhaps care to hear of the scandal, of the foul play which concern an officer and gentleman."

"Indeed I would, Captain," I assured him much too quickly. "Please speak on."

"Yes, I rather imagined you would," he murmured insinuatingly. "Kendall owed a great deal of money, not only to the gamblers, but also to the bank and to certain private creditors.

You knew nothing of it?" I shook my head and he continued. "Yes! Well, it is suspected that he was shot in a fight over money and his body thrown into the river. Whoever committed the foul deed is no doubt far away from Kingston by now."

"No doubt," I whispered, wondering if the man, Beaufort Powell, was in any way responsible.

"It will be hard on his wife."

"Wife?" My voice rose an octave. Kendall had been married and I hadn't known! I resolved to mask my emotions more carefully.

"But of course. She has been visiting her relations in New Orleans. What a shock for her to come back to this. She will be responsible for all his debts, of course. A tragedy."

"A tragedy indeed," I repeated, lowering my eyes to my lap. "Surely the regiment will help her out in some way?"

"It's doubtful, but perhaps some of the officers will endeavour to pass the hat for her. I only met her once. She is not the sociable type, more of a homebody, I should think."

I could think of no rejoinder, so I gathered my belongings together and rose to my feet.

"Please forgive me, Sir, but I must be returning to St Joseph's." I knew instinctively I should leave before my true feelings betrayed me. Captain Hayworth was instantly on the alert and kindly ordered a cab.

"Thank you," I said, knowing that I would be unable to make the return journey on foot, feeling as I did, ill and full of despair.

October 25, 1851

Dear Daffodil,

I am still much concerned over my sister, Cat. She speaks of her feelings for the handsome Irish lieutenant who is suffering from concussion in a Québec City hospital. I am afraid she will be hurt if she counts on his love. He had not proposed marriage, after all, and her French gentleman has. Also, her letters seem guarded and reticent. Of course, I cannot blame her for that. No doubt my letters seem the same to her. When and how will we meet again?

Moreover, when we finally meet, will we able to confide in each other as we used to? I wonder.

I must force myself to complete my letter to Cat, explaining that I am now, quite unexpectedly in New York. Trevor sent for me, to my surprise, as I was under the impression that he had already set sail for France. Of course, once I knew he was too ill to travel, I set out post-haste to his side.

What a trip it was! In the first place, I was not in the best of health and, since I was forced to make all my plans at the last moment, I suspect I may have taken a rather roundabout route. After bidding farewell to Father Andrew, Sister Martha and the little children, I took a carriage to the docks where the ferry crosses to Watertown. The weather was fair, but the decks were crowded with people, all desirous of enjoying the breezes on the open water. At Watertown, I boarded the coach to Rome which joined up with the steamships plying the Mohawk River and the Erie Canal to Albany.

Much to my surprise, the coach trip was speedy and not nearly so jolting as some I have taken. Since I felt too fatigued to make conversation with my fellow passengers, however, I feigned sleep for much of the journey. My trip along the Erie was more pleasant than I might have hoped, despite my protesting innards. By the time we arrived in Albany, I had made up my mind to rest a few hours at a travellers' inn.

Albany is, of course, the hub of all the canal trade and I have been told that it is not uncommon for as many as fifty canal boats to leave within a day. I determined, therefore, it would not be difficult to book passage on one of the most modern and up-to-date steamships running between Albany and New York. The boards advertised all manner of ships, some boasting a time of only seven hours and a bit. It was almost not to be believed.

Once I had registered at a modest but clean inn on South Market Street, which was the closest location to the departure point, I removed my outer garments and lay down to rest. Surprisingly, I fell asleep immediately. I say surprisingly because usually I am full of vitality and anxious to extend the day's length rather than shorten it. Upon awakening, I was instantly aware of my plight. The monthlies were upon me. At least that was my first thought until I took note of the abnormality of the situation. My flow was unusually heavy, coupled with clots of blood and knife-like cramps in the abdominal area. Within minutes, I knew that what was happening to me was what happened to all women in the throes of miscarriage.

Oh Daffodil, how can I write of this to dear Cat? What would she think of her sister were I to confess all? Added to the turmoil of my thoughts, the physical disability of my body seemed fitting punishment. I was most confused. Had I been sane and sensible, I would have accepted instantly the freedom from unwanted pregnancy, but something made me sad. Was I a maternal type after all?

As circumstances would have it, I was compelled to keep to my bed and room for several days. The chambermaid kindly arranged for a midwife to call upon me and help with my adjustment to the tides of fate. I was weak, without appetite, and feared I might succumb to an attack of the vapours. For the first time, I admitted to myself a longing for Kendall. I found it almost impossible to accept his death. In my fevered state, I dreamt of him and of our romance; for that was how I remembered it, a foreordained love, one such as that shared by Romeo and Juliet. I mourned for the tiny son I might have borne him; somehow I was convinced I was carrying his son, even though it had been a short eight weeks.

November 1, 1851

Dear Cat,

I am addressing this letter to your Montréal address in care of Madame de la Haye and I trust it will find you well settled in. Somehow I feel that you are closer to me in Montréal than you were in Toronto. I hope that is true.

At last, my dear sister, you are taking the sensible course. I highly approve of your acceptance of Roger and the lovely friendship ring which you described. You are right in putting Cavan from your thoughts. He could only bring you sorrow and hardship. From what you have told me, sad as it may seem, Miss Moira Parnell appears to have the young lieutenant well and truly netted. I think you must accept your fate, dear Cat.

Thank you so much for sending me my cloak. It arrived safely and it looks as pretty as the day Trevor bought it for me.

With love, Darra.

(I seem to be unable to break the habit of writing to Cat, but must somehow discourage her letters.)

November 13, 1851

Dear Daffodil,

Yes, it's true, Daffodil. I am happy for Cat! She will be far better living in the busy port of Montréal, married to the gentleman, Monsieur Roger de la Haye, than she would be settling for Cavan O'Hara, disowned son and heir to Castle-Blaine. How I longed to tell her of my invitation from Basil Levishon. I wonder if she would understand were I to explain how it all came about.

When I boarded the *Francis Skiddy* on that August morn in Albany, I was still feeling faint and giddy. While preparing my toilet, I pinched my cheeks in the hope of producing a bit of healthy colour; when that didn't work, I carefully applied the slightest amount of pink greasepaint as I had learned to do on the stage. My travelling frock had been carefully cleaned and pressed and, before leaving the hotel, I distributed generous tips to all the people who had been so helpful during my travail. On deck, the steward provided me with a lounge chair and I prepared myself to enjoy the trip down the Hudson River.

Just after we were underway, I was surprised to discover a gentleman hovering over me. "Miss St Joseph?" he inquired after some time.

I nodded, wondering how anyone could know my name.

"Please forgive me," he continued, "but I thought, as soon as I spotted you, that it could be no other. Beaufort Powell, at your service, Ma'am."

I drew in my breath. Beaufort Powell – that sinister man who had met Kendall and me out in the middle of the St Lawrence River. Was he following me? I looked up at him, and was unable to deny his handsomeness. For an older man, he had kept himself trim and fit. Indeed, I must admit he had a certain charm.

"You do not recall our meeting in the month of June? On the river?" He smiled at me. I could not decide whether to admit my memory or not, but how could I have forgotten? Once again I nodded my head. Beaufort Powell drew a wooden stool close beside me and sat down.

"I suppose you would find it difficult to trust me, in view of the unfortunate demise of Captain Warrick," he said.

I longed to demand of him if he were Kendall's murderer. "It caused a great scandal in Kingston," I said instead.

"In case you are wondering if I was the cause of his mishap, Miss St Joseph, let me assure you that I was not. I am afraid that the good captain had many enemies. When it came to handling financial affairs, he was without scruples. His debts were staggering."

"I had heard that," I ventured. "Yet someone must have killed him."

"Indeed, you are right, my dear, but I promise you it was not I. And now, let us put that gruesome subject from us. Tell me, what are you doing on board the *Francis Skiddy*?"

"Well, Sir, I am travelling to New York," I answered. "What else?"

"A wise answer, Miss St Joseph. Have you friends in that city?"

"Yes, I have. A dear old friend, Mr Trevor Vaughn. He is famous in acting circles. Unfortunately, he is ill and has requested that I come and care for him. I owe him much and do not hesitate to hurry to his side."

"Ahhh yes, I know old Trevor. So he's unwell, is he? And what might his trouble be?"

"It started in his chest, but I fear it has worsened. He was leaving to take the waters at Aix, on the advice of his specialist, but was unable to board the ship when the time came."

"I am sure, Miss St Joseph, that the sight of you will do much to restore his health."

"Thank you, Sir, and what, if I may be so bold as to inquire, are you doing on the *Francis Skiddy*?"

Mr Powell grinned broadly. "I am in charge of the wagers on the speed of the steamships and on the time it takes to make the voyage. I am sure that Kendall must have at least informed you of my gambling career."

Embarrassed, I indicated that he had. "Do you mean to say that men bet good money on such daily events?"

"Indeed yes, my dear. Men will bet on anything. You may count on it. I've been in the business a long time. Would you care to wager a small amount yourself? I could advise you, and you might win a great deal of money."

Temporarily, my flighty side, what the sisters used to call my Irishness, rose, up but I managed to calm myself. "No thank you, Sir."

"Then allow me to escort you below. The rococco drawing room is palatial, as you may have heard, and is not to be missed. The stewards are serving all manner of food and drink on demand. I believe you will enjoy it."

I agreed. With his strong arm to lean on, it would be a pleasurable experience, I knew full well that I was not strong enough to manage the walk alone. Once inside, I stood still and gaped. Mr Powell was quite correct. The interior was like a palace, extravagant with elaborately carved wooden beams and furniture, columns decorated with Corinthian curves and arches, and enormous hanging gaslight chandeliers.

"Oh Mr Powell, I must thank you for bringing me in to see this magnificent sight. It is true that I had heard something of the splendours, but the actual sight is overwhelming."

"I thought you would be impressed," he said, "and now what can I fetch for you?" He led me gently to a leather covered banquette and seated me. "A glass of champagne to celebrate your voyage on the Hudson?"

As I nodded my head in agreement, I could not stop myself from thinking of Cat at her fête champêtre. Minutes later, Mr Powell was presenting me with a long-stemmed goblet filled with amber bubbly which fizzed and sparkled like a fountain.

"To a happy sojourn in New York," Mr Powell saluted me.

"Thank you," I answered, but secretly drank to my sister's fortune.

The hours which followed passed swiftly. Mr Powell and I made light conversation, that is to say, he talked about the history, commerce and trade plied on the Hudson River, and I listened. From time to time, however, I found myself losing the 99end of what he was saying and realised that I was still fatigued from the past events of my life. My inattention became apparent eventually and, in my embarrassment, I spoke the truth.

". . . would you say?" It was all I caught of the long sentence that Mr Powell had just uttered.

"Oh, pray forgive me, Sir. The champagne is making me giddy. I must confess that I did not hear your question."

"I asked you, Miss St Joseph, what your Christian name is, and how you came to Kingston."

"Darra," said I without thinking and, seeking the cross which I always wore, I showed it to him. "I was a foundling, abandoned as a babe by the gate at St Joseph's orphanage. This gold cross was round my neck at that time, and I have worn it ever since. It is the one possession I have which links me to my unknown past and uncertain heritage."

Mr Powell leaned close, and fingered the cross lightly and read, "Darra."

"It's strange, isn't it?" I continued. "I was not left alone. I have a sister who is in Toronto. Her name is Catherine. When the nuns found us, we were wrapped in a most distinguished quilt, sewn from beautiful bits and pieces of silk, satins, velvets and finest lawn. There were some gold sovereigns also, so I expect my sister and I come from a fine, aristocratic family."

"No doubt," Mr Powell murmured politely.

"Of course, it doesn't solve the question as to why we were left at St Joseph's. Father Andrew and the sisters told us everything they knew. When Cat and I left the orphanage, we determined to find out somehow about our background. However, we've been so occupied with other affairs, time has passed and it no longer seems so important as it once did.'

"I'm certain the circumstances were such that it was absolutely essential for your guardian or your mother to entrust your care to the good priest and his sisters," my companion answered.

"That's what I tell myself." Privately, I thought it was true, but still it wasn't enough. The mystery would always trouble me.

Upon arrival in the port of New York, Mr Powell helped me

with my bags, escorted me off the ship and hired a carriage for me. His courtesy pleased me greatly.

"You have the address, Miss St Joseph," he inquired. "Where are you going to meet Trevor?"

"Oh most certainly, Mr Powell. Thank you so much. You've been very kind, and a good companion. I'm meeting Trevor at some hotel. Wait, I have the name written down someplace. Astor House. Do you know it?"

Mr Powell looked amused. "Astor House? Oh yes, my dear, I know it well. You will be well looked after there. It's most elegant."

So we made our farewells and the driver took me smoothly and safely to my destination. As we drove up in front of the hotel's imposing entrance, with its tall architectural columns, a gentleman in fancy livery appeared as if by magic to take charge.

At the desk, where I signed the check-in card, I also made inquiries about Trevor's whereabouts.

"Mr Vaughn, Miss? Mr Trevor Vaughn?" the clerk asked and I thought his face bore a slightly blanched look.

"That's right. He's staying here. He's an actor and he was about to sail for France when his chest ailment worsened." Somehow I felt uneasy as I explained myself, although there was no reason to feel thus.

"Er, uh, Miss – Miss St Joseph. One moment please." The embarrassed young man disappeared rapidly into the room behind the desk area. Almost instantly he reappeared, followed by an older man with florid cheeks and whiskers.

"Miss St Joseph?" He bowed slightly to me. "Allow me to introduce myself. I am Rudolph Corona, manager of Astor House. Would you kindly step this way, please?"

Startled, I followed him into an office nearby and, when he had seated me, he turned aside and closed the door.

"I have some – er – quite unfortunate news to give you, Miss St Joseph." As he spoke, he strode, hands clasped behind his back, up and down, down and up, round and round the room. "Some rather regrettable news – uh – ah – er – which concerns, I am afraid, Mr Vaughn."

"Trevor? Oh dear, tell me quickly. Has Trevor taken a turn for the worse?"

"Yes, I'm afraid he has. Yes, you might say that. He has indeed taken a turn for the worse. He has, in fact, passed on."

I stared at the man, for it seemed to me that what he was saying could not be true. "Trevor? Are you quite positive?"

"Oh yes, Miss, I am absolutely certain. The maid, when she took his tray up to him at breakfast time – there he was, so still and not moving at all. Lifeless. Departed from this world. God bless his soul, gone on to a no-doubt more angelic existence."

"When did all this take place?" I asked, wondering why the man couldn't have simply said that Trevor had died. There was nothing immoral or wrong with the word 'dead'. "When did Trevor die? And who made the funeral arrangements?"

"It must have been fully a week ago, Miss. All the instructions were with his lawyer. You must understand. Mr Vaughn knew that his time was not long on this earth. I believe his body was shipped to Albany. It was his home."

I had not known. It all seemed a mockery. Here I had travelled all this way, simply to be at Trevor's side, to nurse him in his final hours. To think that while he was dying, I was resting up in Albany, gathering strength to travel to him in New York. Why, we might have passed en route, going in opposite directions. Trevor, a corpse in his coffin travelling to Albany for his final rest. Me, Darra, sailing along the Hudson to New York harbour, coming in answer to his call.

That night, as I lay in the middle of a large, sumptuous four-poster bed, I thought that I must soon come to a decision about my future. As for my financial state, there remained an adequate sum in my savings account in Kingston. In New York, however, I must seek other accommodation, and soon.

Who could I call upon in New York? Which acquaintances might aid in revitalising my acting career? I pulled forth the names and addresses so kindly given to me by Mr Percival and his nephew, Sydney, glanced down the list and suddenly, I knew. Basil Levishon! I had met him once briefly in Toronto. His name and address were on Mr Percival's list of recommendations. What's more, the thoughtful gentleman had penned a letter of introduction for me to each of the men in the world of Broadway and the stage.

November 15, 1851

Dear Daffodil,

I press on, for I will confess all to you and, since destiny has determined that I may no longer write to my once-sister Cat, you are the only one left in my confidence.

It was still summer when I learned of Trevor's untimely death and, therefore, I made the decision to seek out the assistance of Mr Levishon. It was worth a try before admitting defeat and returning north again. So one day in late August, I sent my card accompanied by a note to his address, informing him of my presence in New York and of the circumstances which led to it. When no answer was forthcoming for an entire week, I despaired of hearing, and felt embarrassed that Mr Levishon might think me less than a lady for bringing myself to his attention.

Once again, I drew forth Mr Percival's list of Broadway acquaintances and studied it. All the names were unknown to me and, therefore, looked hostile and unapproachable. Perhaps I would be better persuaded to leave this expensive city and return to Kingston post-haste. Or Toronto? Surely someone would aid me there. I had already determined not to go to Montréal lest I be an encumbrance and complication to Cat, who has enough problems at the moment.

During the following week, since I was feeling much more lively and less fatigued, I decided to set forth and view New York City from a traveller's angle. My fondest hope had been to hear Jenny Lind but she had already departed. I did not know then that P.T. Barnum was a friend of Mr Levishon and I might meet her later. So I made my way to Castle Garden at the Battery that very day and, although all I could do was admire the posters outside, nevertheless, it was an enjoyable visit. I have heard that there are many similar gardens of pleasure and later, when I am more at home in this city, if that is possible, I will visit Niblo's or Vauxhall or one of the others.

I have never seen so much traffic as New York boasts. Indeed, it is a major effort to cross from one side of the street to the other, and it is extremely hard on one's boots or shoes. The atmosphere seems very bohemian and picturesque, mainly because of the variety of vendors who shout their wares constantly. Of course, it is necessary for them to pitch their voices to compete with all the other metropolitan noises. The hucksters include butchers, sellers of salted oysters, hot roasted corn and even ice, which I understand is shipped from upstate Rockland Lake. How I wish I had been here in the strawberry season. It is, however, harvest time for corn and I confess to having enjoyed a hot cob, dripping with butter.

After wandering around the theatre district in Union Square, I was feeling tired once more, so hired a carriage to drive me, after which I requested of the driver that he return me to the Astor. Once inside, I approached the desk to claim my key.

"Miss St Joseph," the clerk addressed me. "I have two messages for you," and he handed me two envelopes. I was, of course, instantly on the alert.

"Thank you," I said, and retired to my room to read them in privacy.

> Dear Miss St Joseph,
>
> Please forgive me for not replying to your welcome letter sooner. I was unavoidably out of town on business. May I have the pleasure of escorting you to dinner on Saturday evening of next week?

It was signed Basil Levishon. Just as I had finished reading the message, there was a knock on my door. When I opened it to learn who could be wanting me a young, uniformed busboy, almost invisible behind an enormous bouquet of long stemmed roses, was revealed.

"These arrived for you, Miss," he said. "May I bring them in? Please?"

"Oh yes, of course," and I moved quickly out of his path.

Soon they were sitting in the corner in a huge vase. Two dozen late roses, all brilliant red with a mix of feather fern. After the busboy had left, I knelt before them and all but smothered my face in their perfume.

The discreet note accompanying them said,

> "To a lovely lady, more beautiful than a red rose. May our acquaintance bloom into a lasting memory. Basil."

For a moment, I was annoyed with the foolish message. What

could he mean? I hoped that whatever he had in mind would be instrumental in furthering my career. Perhaps I had reached a turning point in the course of my life, I tried to convince myself.

The second letter was as brief as Basil Levishon's.

Dear Darra. It is imperative that I see you as soon as possible. Please give me a time and date when I may call upon you. Sincerely, Beaufort Powell.

Whatever could Mr Powell want with me? His message sounded so urgent that all my worries instantly returned to plague me and put me on the defensive. Could it be something further about Kendall? I determined to make an appointment to meet with him as soon as possible.

Dear Mr Powell (I wrote). It would be agreeable to me, if it is satisfactory to you, for us to meet tomorrow at teatime. Please inform me if that date is convenient. Darra St Joseph.

I dispatched it immediately and turned my attention to preparing myself to meet the gambler. I surveyed my wardrobe critically and, deciding upon a costume of fine lawn with many ruffles and bows about the hem and neckline, summoned the maid to iron it so it would be fresh for tomorrow's meeting.

At four o'clock sharp on the following afternoon, I received a message from the clerk that a gentleman awaited my company in the main lounge. Checking my costume and my hair, which I had at the last moment decided to dress on top of my head, I walked slowly to my rendez-vous with Mr Powell.

His appearance had not changed and, when he spied my approach, he strode across the remaining length of lobby to greet me.

"Dear lady," he said, "but you look ravishing. Just like . . ." but at that juncture, he paused.

"How do you do, Mr Powell? I trust you do not think me overly hasty in setting our appointment. Your urgency set me to worrying and I thought it best to learn whatever you have to tell me as quickly as possible."

"Most wise, I can assure you," and he led me, hand tucked beneath my elbow, into the tearoom. "A quiet corner," he instructed the waiter. "We have need of privacy for a discussion of much import."

Once the silver tea-service was placed on our white linen-covered table, and the scones and rich tea cakes had been served, I turned towards Mr Powell.

"Pray do not keep me in suspense, Sir. Your message indicated news of an imperative nature." I kept my hands folded in my lap and tried to curb my tendency to twist and braid my fingers in and out. Why I was so nervous and apprehensive, I was unable to explain.

"Yes, my child," he agreed. "The sooner the better. First, however, allow me to offer my condolences regarding the passing of your benefactor and my friend, Trevor Vaughn."

I felt temporarily taken aback; Trevor was far from my thoughts. I nodded my head and responded quietly, "Thank you," and waited for him to continue.

"After I left you, at first I thought it best to say nothing, but I have been persuaded now to change my mind. Let us return to our first meeting on the St Lawrence River. Do you recall how startled I was when I first saw your face and hair?"

"I do indeed, Sir, but pray continue."

"It was in the month of September in 1834 in the city of Kingston." He paused. "One evening, I met a young woman – she would have been just about your age at that time. She had just arrived on an immigration ship from the old country. Noreen, her name was, Noreen Callaghan, and she was exquisitely beautiful, and she had hair exactly like yours; red like the sunset, red gold like the portraits of the Old Masters. Titian!" Once again he hesitated, and sipped the steaming Indian tea. "She was staying in the same waterfront wayfarers' inn as I and when I met her, we fell in love. However, there were several problems. For one, she had two small baby girls in her charge. She was supposed to meet with a military gentleman, one Lieutenant Kingsley."

I gasped. Could it be the same Kingsley? With a swift gesture, Mr Powell held up his hand and bade me keep silent.

"It seems that Kingsley's wife had been detained at Gross Ile but, before leaving the ship, she had begged Noreen, who was merely a penniless Irish immigrant, to take the Kingsley baby on to her father in Kingston. Mrs Kingsley entrusted Noreen with a small fortune in gold sovereigns and jewelry, also an heirloom quilt from the family."

"The babies! They were Cat and me, weren't they? So we're sisters as we always thought. What happened? Why were we at St Joseph's?"

Mr Powell hushed me once again. "When Noreen arrived in Kingston, the good lieutenant was away. He had gone to Toronto on an official assignment. There was some confusion about the ship on which his wife had sailed, in all events, he wasn't there to meet her."

"She died?" I knew she must have, for how else the second Mrs Kingsley?"

"Yes, almost certainly she must have, and now, Darra, may I call you Darra. . ."

I nodded my head. I didn't mind at that particular moment what he called me, just so long as he got on with his story.

"Now Darra, I must beg forgiveness. In my passion for Noreen and in the necessity of returning to New Orleans immediately, I confess that I persuaded my love to accompany me. We decided to abandon her two charges at the portals of St Joseph's Orphanage. I realise it must seem inhuman to you, but try to understand. We were young and unthinking. I assured Noreen that Father Andrew and his sisters would care for both of you well and that undoubtedly Lieutenant Kingsley would claim the two of you on his return to Kingston."

"How could he do that? He didn't know about us. Just think. There we were living in the same city as the good officer and not knowing that he was our father." I was stunned.

"Not you, Darra. Catherine. Catherine is his daughter."

"But – but Cat and I are sisters. We've always been sisters."

"Noreen was your mother," he said.

"Noreen? The Noreen you are telling me about? Where is she and why didn't she keep me? I don't believe you." How could I? Who did he think he was, marching in and turning my life upside down?

"Noreen came with me, believing that Lieutenant Kingsley would give you a better upbringing as Catherine's sister than she could as an immigrant. I thought I was doing the right thing. I tried to make Noreen happy but, even in that, I failed. My business took me away too much, leaving her all alone. She was desperate to have another baby but every time she was in the family way, she miscarried. She considered it a punishment for having abandoned you. Finally after the eighth try, she managed to carry for six months. The babe was stillborn and my lovely colleen died from an infection."

"You're telling me a long drawn-out tale, Mr Powell; for what reason, I wonder?"

"I thought it only fair that you should know, and I suppose that, in my old age, I am suffering from pangs of guilt. Is it possible that you can find it in your heart to forgive me?"

My emotions were on the boil and it was exceedingly difficult for me not to give way to them. It would have been most satisfying to tell this man to be gone, to deny him forgiveness, to let his soul rot in hell. At the moment, my life seemed finished.

Repenting of a sudden, I thought, 'What good will it do me to vent my wrath on this old man?'

"You must understand, Mr Powell, that I am shaken and in a state of agitation. You've just confessed to me that you have knowledge of Cat's and my parentage, and you tell me that my own mother is dead. What of my father then? I don't suppose you are my father? No, you said you met Noreen after she had birthed a baby, didn't you?"

"Yes, Darra. Your mother was Noreen and she's dead, but I can assure you, if it's of any help to you, that she was an angel. I loved her always. As to your other question, I'm afraid I must disappoint you. I do not know who your father was. Noreen never divulged that information to me."

"Are you saying I am a bastard, Mr Powell?" My voice was low and it was difficult to refrain from bursting into tears. I was nevertheless determined to wait until I was alone in my bedroom to surrender to such sentiments.

Beaufort Powell said more, much more, how sorry he was, how distressed my mother, Noreen, had been, what a beautiful woman she was, how he missed her. Not surprisingly I was numb. I sat there, sipping my tea, shredding a tea cake to bits, nodding my head. After what seemed an eternity of time, Mr Powell announced his departure. Before he left, however, he proferred a small jewel box to me. I accepted it with sadness.

"This was Noreen's; a brooch which she brought with her from Ireland. I believe it was given to her by her mistress, at the place where she worked. It was in compensation for some wrong done to her. She always wore it."

I said nothing, merely accepted the box. We walked together to the lobby and, as he was about to leave, he turned once more and looked at me.

"Try to be compassionate, Darra. Try not to be too harsh in your judgement of your mother. Pray for her, if you can, and forgive me for the wrong done to you and to Catherine Kingsley." His voice was unusually hesitant.

Slowly I turned towards him. "I forgive you, Mr Powell, and when I go to mass at St Peters', I will light a candle for Noreen – for my mother."

"Thank you." Those were his parting words. I watched his broad shoulders as he walked through the doors into the crowded street.

At this point, I put away my journal, the memory still being far too painful to me.

November 24, 1851

To pick up my sorry tale again. After my distressing rendez-vous with Mr Powell, I spent an anxious day and night weeping and praying. I cursed my ill-luck and my low-born self. I determined to do all manner of things and then did nothing. Slowly I came to myself and began to perform the tasks which were due. I lit a candle for my dear mother, now dead and departed, sorrowing that I never knew her. I confessed all my past vanities, my abject thoughts, my envy and all my errors. I confessed them to the strange priest at St Peter's where my candles still were burning. I felt surprise and gratitude at the leniency which he showed me.

This morning I plan to finish these confidences, Daffodil, and when I do, I shall put my past from me forever and move on to a new life. It will be a life without Cat, for the following note was long ago sent to Major Kingsley to inform him of his daughter's identity, which my conscience would not allow me to keep secret.

> Dear Major Kingsley, (This is what I wrote)
> Go to the cupboard and remove the parcel which Catherine left in your care. Inside you will discover the quilt. Unroll it and you will regain what you believed was lost to you forever.

I addressed the envelope carefully, but put no return address on it. Neither did I sign the letter. Revelation of anything but Catherine's true birthright was unnecessary. Once I had mailed it, I felt a burden lift from my shoulders. How I longed to tell Catherine myself, but she must never know I wrote the letter nor must she know of my base background.

November 25, 1851

Now I may write of my encounter with Mr Basil Levishon. I pick up with the gift of the beautiful red roses which he sent me on that most eventful day, surely the last roses of summer, never mind that September had arrived. It was with a heavy heart and subdued hope that I began my preparation for our dinner engagement. Pinning my mother's emerald brooch, surely reminiscent of Ireland's shamrocks, to my bosom, I felt a reluctant surge of love and sympathy. She also had known hardship.

11

I am sitting in the parlour of the old stone manor house owned by Madame de la Haye. There is a bright fire blazing in the hearth, although the weather is not yet very cold. Two of the children are sitting with me. Marie-Louise, who is eight years old, is a solemn child. She is carefully and silently embroidering a sampler which reads "Le bon Dieu nous protège." She labours on the border which is adorned with flowers and candles.

Sitting beside her is a miniature feminine version of Roger. Brown hair in a tousle, big brown eyes, the solid little figure statue-still in concentration. Marie-Claire is engaged in stringing a series of bright beads. Her eyes twinkle with Roger's look of amusement.

"Pour Minou," she explains.

Minou, the family cat, is with us also, his tawny coat gleaming in different shades of rust in the firelight. Roger's son, Jean-Jacques, has not returned from school. He is ten and occupied with superior masculine affairs.

I have been here for just over two weeks. The flow of French becomes slightly less foreign to my ears, but at times I long for English voices. Roger's father died many years ago, and his mother is the centre of the family. She has welcomed me kindly but I find her a little intimidating. Always in black, her white hair in perfect order, she moves serenely, arranging her household affairs. I have never seen her ruffled or in a temper. She is never other than courteous and warm in manner to me, but on my arrival I heard her murmur to Roger, "Elle est belle, la petite Anglaise." Then she added, ". . . but she is just a child, Roger."

I do not feel a child. It is a woman's despair that rends my heart every time I remember that evening in Toronto, when Cavan stood before me. He was thinner than I remembered him and looked older, more drawn. His face was, however, lit by the joy in his eyes.

"Catherine," he cried out and, before I could do more than gasp with shock, he pulled me into his arms.

His warm kisses showered my face, my eyes, my cheeks, then with a laugh, my nose. Our lips blended. I felt his muscular body pressed to mine. A surge of joy swept me and, my arms around his neck, I clung to him.

"Cavan, I can't believe it. Is it really you at last?"

"Of course it is I, my little love. I hope you would not be expecting this of anyone else?" Putting me from him, he looked at me attentively, "Catherine, you have grown up, I do believe. You have a stylish air, a certain poise that is new to you. Why, my love is now a society belle!"

These words brought me to my senses and I pulled myself from his arms. As he sought to recapture me, I gasped, "Cavan. No! You have forgotten Moira Parnell."

"Indeed I have forgotten her. Why would I be thinking of her at a moment such as this?"

"But, Cavan, you are going to marry her."

"No, I am not going to marry her. I'm going to marry you." His arms now encircling my waist, he lowered his head to kiss me again.

My mind turned and twisted. Castle-Blaine, Castle-Blaine. That was it. Castle-Blaine and Moira. They went together. I pushed his arms away and backed off from him.

"Cavan. You forget," I stammered. "Your father will disinherit you. You know that. I cannot marry you."

He looked at me in surprise. "Allanna. I thought you realised that I am not one to be intimidated by threats. I have chosen you over Castle-Blaine."

Stupidly, I thought he had not understood. "You cannot lose the home you love so much. Cavan, you know how much it means to you. I am not a fit bride for your estate."

Terrible sobs rose in my throat and I struggled desperately to hold them back. He looked at me wonderingly.

"Of course you are, Catherine. You are gracious and beautiful.

You're all I desire – I love you."

"Cavan. I have no background. What will all the gentry in Ireland say when you come back with an orphanage girl? How would your sons be received? Anyway, you forget. Castle-Blaine would not be yours."

He was silent. My heart contracted, but I pressed on, seeking any excuse to bring my agony to an end.

"Cavan. Roger has asked me to go to Montréal with him to stay with his mother. I have promised to go with him. Please leave me now. Please go to Moira and think what you should do. I cannot be the cause of your alienating yourself from your family. A family is too great a gift to lose."

Cavan's face darkened suddenly and he spoke coldly. "I can't believe it. You have made arrangements to go to Montréal with that wealthy lawyer? Why, he could be your father! Have you promised to marry him? Have you, Catherine?"

He grabbed my hands and looked for a ring. "Did he give you this token, Catherine? Is it that you do not want me without Castle-Blaine?"

I could not credit that he could be so cruel, nor think so poorly of me. I looked down without answering, tears coursing beneath my eyelashes finding their way down my cheeks, despite my best efforts.

"If that is what you expect of me, so be it," I answered angrily.

There was a moment's silence. Unexpectedly, Cavan took me in his arms and kissed me very gently.

"We are both overwrought and need to view our words more calmly. I will call on you tomorrow, my little love."

Turning from me and, without looking back, he left the room. Soon I heard the sound of horses' hoofs. Sinking onto the nearest chair, my tears flowed freely at last.

"Tomorrow, my little love." The words repeated themselves in my head.

Sadly there was no meeting the following morning, as Roger and I were up early and left on the morning stage-coach. The horses were fresh, neighing and stamping, and we were soon many miles from Toronto.

November 20, 1851

We were up early this morning and attended mass at Notre-Dame church. It is a beautiful building and the de la Hayes are very proud of its fine bells. To my amusement, they refer to the bells by name. Apparently, "le Gros Bourdon," the largest bell of 24,700 pounds, recently developed a crack and ceased to peal so richly. It was recast in 1847, however, and now again delights all with its deep chime.

On coming out of the service, we stopped to speak to a Madame Sévigny and her three small boys. The poor woman was recently widowed. Madame de la Haye told me that the two families have been acquainted for many years. We are expecting the family to dine with us this evening. Her oldest son, Luc, is the same age as Roger's son and attends the same school.

Madame Sévigny spoke kindly to me, hoping that I would enjoy my visit to Montréal. Her accent was one to which I am not at all accustomed and I had great difficulty in following her. I have discovered that there is a variety of accents among the French-Canadian population and some bear scant resemblance to the French I learned with Father Andrew. Indeed, they do not have much in common with Roger's articulation, but he at least can understand them. I feel sorely embarrassed when he translates their French into his for my benefit.

I am adding a note to this before I turn into my bed. The Sévignys were here for the evening according to plan. It seems that Madame Sévigny was a close friend of Roger's late wife. I could not but observe the friendly camaraderie between the two families. The conversation often went to mutual friends and to past shared experiences. Always considerate, Madame de la Haye and Roger would try to include me in the conversation, but I must admit to some relief when the children begged me to join them and to tell them stories.

I have become very popular in my role of story-teller and I thank heaven that I remember many of the tales Darra and I used to make up and act out in our limited free time. Indeed, we used to do our tasks in the guise of some favourite martyr or saint, or perhaps some romantic princess. Darra led and I followed, always in the inferior role! Early on I accepted her superior imagination. The de la Haye children long to meet my sister, so often do I talk of our days together.

"Tell us about you and Darra," they are always demanding, as if our life had some peculiar glamour.

I cannot understand why I do not hear more frequently from Darra. New York seems infinitely further away than our dear Provinces. I try to imagine her here, in this traditional French-Canadian family, where I expect to spend the rest of my life. They are so kind, yet – and here I will admit to it – I feel completely desolate.

November 25, 1851

This has been the most unusual saint's day I have ever had. Saint Catherine is, as most people know, the saint of unmarried women among other groups, and she is also the one who is most popular in the province. Custom decrees that the women of the house make "tire Sainte Catherine," which is a sticky taffy much sought after by the children. Our children were pestering from early in the day and finally we retired to the kitchen to make the syrupy treat. It was difficult to get it twisted and braided into the conventional shape before some eager child fell upon it. One of the maids finally took the broom and chased all the children out, amid much laughter and loud screams from those who felt the touch of the bristles. Later the adults showed as much enthusiasm in devouring the tasty bits as did the children and by nightfall much was gone.

In the evening we attended a "veillée" at a neighbour's house. There was much feasting, music and laughter. Plenty of bonbons were passed around including the "tire Sainte Catherine" which had evidently lasted longer than ours.

Among other tales, one told by Madame de la Haye caught my attention.

"I remember," she said, "the fêtes which we attended on Saint Catherine's day when I was young. I grew up in the country and, in those rural areas, many of the old customs were kept. Even today there is little sympathy for a vieille-fille, or unmarried girl. Of course, in the cities she has opportunities as governess or companion, but on the farm, with our large families, daughters are expected to have a vocation or to attact a suitor as soon as possible."

"Didn't you get a suitor, Bonne-Maman?" asked Marie-Claire with interest.

"Of course I did," replied her grandmother. "Your grandfather was quick to ask for my hand. But that was not the case with my poor sister, Monique. Ooh là! That poor girl had no luck with the young men."

"Why not, Bonne-Maman? Was she ugly?"

"No, she wasn't really ugly. She just had too quick a tongue. She was a bright young girl, the curé's pet, but the boys learned that she was always one up on them. They didn't feel comfortable with her."

"So what happened? Tell us."

"Eh bien! This is what happened. Each year Papa and Maman found new suitors for her, and always she had some complaint. He was stupid or he was too old, or he was ugly. At last Monique was twenty-five years old and still eating our father's bread and still sitting at his table. Her three younger sisters, I being one, and two younger brothers had married ahead of her. Then came the Fête de Sainte Catherine.

Our father spoke to her saying, "This is your last chance, we will have a veillée and if you do not find yourself a husband, then, 'coiffe le bonnet de Sainte Catherine.'" At this point, Madame de la Haye paused significantly and there was an ominous silence.

"Was it then an ugly bonnet?" demanded one of the children.

"No, it was a white bonnet, and it had a white matching apron, but it meant shame. All the unmarried girls over twenty-five were required to wear these bonnets for the evening at a veillée in hopes of proving themselves available to some man who was not yet suited. Imagine their feelings. I remember that Monique went white and just looked at our father."

"So what did she do? Did she wear the white bonnet?"

"No, as a matter of fact she did not. She went privately to our mother and said that she wished to enter the order of the

Congregation of Notre-Dame, a well-known teaching order."

"'For,' she said, 'if I have to obey a man, let it be our Father who is in heaven. Furthermore,' she added, 'the sisters of the congregation are knowledgeable and I will become a teacher.' That is what she did, but I always wondered if she had a vocation or if she could not bear to 'coiffer le bonnet de Sainte Catherine.'"

There was a thoughtful silence and the story was on my mind for the rest of the evening. There is no question about it, life is very hard for a woman who is not blessed with the married state.

December 15, 1851

It is difficult to believe that once again the Christmas season is upon us. When I remember last year at the Kingsley's, I am almost homesick. How ungrateful this sounds. Perhaps it is because the customs we remember as children are always most dear to our hearts.

The de la Hayes always go to the Ile d'Orléans for the season. This charming island lies at the foot of Québec City, but seems an entity all to itself. Roger's brother, Pierre, owns a large farmland plot to which the entire family returns at the end of each year.

We were the first to arrive, having battled the snowy road from Montréal to Québec City in somewhat unpleasant conditions. Winter has set upon us with a vengeance and the snow fell in big tufty flakes, obscuring my view of the St Lawrence River. We passed the farmhouses scattered by the banks, still a reminder of the old strip pattern in which the seigniories were allotted. Twice we stopped at small villages to rest the horses and to stretch our legs.

Once we called in at friends of the de la Hayes and warmed ourselves before the huge fireplace. Ignoring the wintry blasts of air, the children raced about outside, letting off the energy which had been pent up during our hours in the carriage. Snowballs flew and Marie-Claire was accidently hit on the head. The small flushed girl, faced streaked with tears, came to my side and curled up on the couch beside me.

Québec, as seen from the Ile d'Orléans, is situated in dignity above the rocky face which rises from the St Lawrence River. This position made it a difficult city to attack in the days of war between Great Britain and France. I tried to imagine the scene in summer; Wolfe's ships patrolling the waters and above, Montcalm battling the corruptions and jealousies of the local dignitaries. How different the story seemed from the mouths of the de la Hayes.

In winter, the waters form an ice-bridge between the city and the Ile d'Orléans. Once it is sufficiently frozen, one can cross without difficulty or danger. We arrived late, tired and cold and, after battling with the stream of French, and again struggling with accent problems, I retired to bed.

I am treated as the oldest of the de la Haye children, to be taught, cherished and shown the sights. I realise now that New Year's Eve is the traditional gift-giving time for French-Canadians. Many plans are being carried out, some involving skills of the needle, others wood-carving and yet others requiring brush and palette. I am the keeper of many secrets.

I wonder how Darra will spend the season in New York. Her rare notes have now ceased and I am filled with alarm. I try to believe that she has written to Montréal, or that her letter has been mislaid in transit. If only I may hear from her before too long. I have written to Father Andrew, mentioning my concerns and begging for news of St Joseph's. I wonder how Darra will settle into the de la Haye family after my marriage, for Roger has promised to give her a home.

Yes, at last I face the word. I will be married to Roger de la Haye in June. I have hesitated to accept a formal engagement at this time, having made excuses that I am still faltering in my use of French and would like to be more at ease before I face the world as his affianced bride. Madame de la Haye supported me strongly in this and so Roger agreed, although somewhat reluctantly.

Again I wander. To return to Darra. I am sure she would enjoy the solidarity and the warmth of the family. The propriety and strict rule of the church which embraces all would be quite another matter, I fear. Bishop Bourget of Montréal is most ardent in protecting his flock from worldly evil. His dislike of Protestants seems almost un-Christian. Of course, Father Andrew would not want us to forsake our mother church, but even his homilies against the fallen brethren were made in sorrow and not in hatred. The strictures of Bishop Bourget have astonished me in their zealous attacks against the radical Dorian and his party and paper.

In Upper Canada we are aware of a diversity of opinion and, while critical, we accept it as part of our heritage. With Roger I am comfortable but I must admit to feeling alien with some of his friends and their wives.

December 20, 1851

Today, all the family, including Roger's brother, made a trip to see the famous Montmorency Falls. We drove along a gradually ascending plateau from Québec and then came to a small village. Walking behind the houses, we discovered ourselves on the ledge from which the river falls. At first I was disappointed, having expected a more spectacular sight. A young girl came out of one of the houses and, acting as guide, led us to various points of observation. From those, I saw the falls to be lofty and that they cascaded into a charming small bay surrounded by rocky walls.

Putting his arm around me, Roger led me to the glassy shore. "Catherine, ma petite, we must come again when the winter has completed its work. Where now we see a mixture of ice, foam and spray, we will later have a frozen tableau. Look, do you see that cone of ice which is forming by the rocks? ... Attention! Jean-Jacques!" He broke off to call sharply to his son who, with the other children, was venturing towards the slippery mound.

"The children remember coming here last winter in February when the cone had grown into a high mount. Then it is always a popular tobogganing site."

"I don't understand. What causes it?" I laughed, seeing the children slipping and sliding as they tried to climb the little white conical hill.

"It is the structure of the bay combined with the waters freezing against the rocks before they can escape. It is a favourite subject for artists and great fun for children." Roger joined in my laughter as the children cascaded down one after the other.

Soon Marie-Louise came running to us, begging me to slide with her. I hesitated, then with a glance at Roger, I took her hand and followed her to the scene of entertainment. Soon, using the children's toboggan, I slid down the slope, to many cheers.

"Papa, Papa, come and slide."

But Roger refused, laughingly. "I am an old man. Would you have me break my back?"

"Mademoiselle Catherine is sliding with us."

Flushed and elated, I climbed off the toboggan and joined Roger as he stood with the other adults. He looked at me tenderly and turned to his brother.

"Catherine is too young to turn down such games," he remarked.

At that very moment, my heart betrayed me unexpectedly. A group of men and women approached the cone. One stood out, tall, lean, with rusty hair bright against the snowy backdrop. 'Cavan,' my heart cried out, but it was not Cavan. The young man placed his arm about a plump young woman who was with him. Together they clambered up the peak and, climbing onto a large toboggan, they slid down, he in front, she clinging to his waist. I turned from the sight hastily, banishing memories, realizing I was as cold within as I was without.

We hastened back to the village, eager to warm ourselves and to find some refreshment. Here we were most hospitably received by an habitant family (as they call the country people here). They offered us milk and excellent snow-white bread which had been blessed by the priest and, therefore especially intended to be given to visitors.

I looked about me with interest at the spacious rooms, the furniture, which was old-fashioned by Toronto standards, but generally gayer and more original in decoration. I noticed a portrait of Napoleon, who is generally still popular among the common people. A main feature on the wall was a religious text for the month of December, resplendent in a gilt frame.

"They are supplied each month by the parish priest," Roger explained to me.

As we left the village, our attention was drawn by an elegant column which stood all alone on an elevation.

"What is that, Papa?" cried Marie-Louise. "Is it for one of the blessed saints?"

"Come. We will go and see."

Stopping the driver, who pulled up the horses in response to our banging on the window with many gesticulations, we fell out and followed the children who were racing eagerly ahead.

The edifice proved to be a Temperance column, inscribed with stern injunctions, prayers and vows to the Virgin Mary. I looked at it with some astonishment. That would have been a suitable object for Father Andrew to have near the stables to bring old George to a greater state of sobriety, I decided. I used to hate the days when the old groom had appeared with his reddened face, glazed eyes and noxious breath, only to be promptly banished with harsh words by Sister Isobel.

"As with many of the villages, almost all the habitants here have taken the pledge," Roger explained. "The Catholic clergy has great power and has promoted the sale of Temperance crosses, you may have noticed the black cross that was hanging on the wall in the home we visited?"

I thought of the wine that flowed at the parties I had attended with the Kingsleys and later with the Smythes. It seemed to me that, used in moderation, it enhanced the savour of the food.

Breaking into my thoughts, Roger laughed. "The only wine the poor devils can even dream about is that at the Lord's table. The clergy keep that taste for themselves alone." I was glad to know that Roger is no admirer of the conservatism that pervades the French Church in Québec.

After our outing, we drove home in high spirits, the children singing all manner of Christmas songs. On our arrival at the Ile d'Orléans, we learned that two of Roger's sisters and their families were now under the family roof. Again hugs, greetings, tears and exclamations filled the air.

I retired quietly to the stool beside the fire, watched and listened in wonder. I have only Darra, and we are apart. Nothing will ever divide me from her. Indeed, I wonder if I am making this marriage as much on her behalf as mine. I feel guilty that I cannot love Roger as he deserves, but I intend to do everything I can to be a good wife. He will not find me lacking. once we are married, surely at last Darra and I will have the family we long for.

January 3, 1852

Another New Year is upon us, thanks be to God for all His kindness to me. We are back in Montréal, having travelled all day yesterday because Roger must return to his work. Therefore, despite the fact we were at mass on New Year's Eve, and celebrated the event by opening all our gifts, we had to prepare for our departure the following day.

I have suffered from a minor chest infection and, following our expedition to Montmorency Falls, was compelled to spend much time resting. Even now I am troubled by severe bouts of coughing. On our way home, I was careful to keep a handkerchief to my face to avoid further chills. Sister Isobel was very strict about this and I always obeyed. Darra always refused and screamed with temper when she was required to do so. Accordingly, Sister had to smack her soundly. Why does my mind so constantly return to our earlier days? I long for an opportunity to visit Kingston again.

Like a child that has fallen down or has been hurt and runs home, perhaps so it is with me. I received a letter from Mrs Smythe on our return to the de la Haye residence. It was full of news and sent Christmas greetings to us all. But one paragraph stands out clearly in my mind, repeating itself, refusing to disappear from sight.

"You remember Moira Parnell?" I read. "Well! That young lady has surprised us all and become engaged to Major Philip Digby. He has bought extensive lands in the west and hopes to farm after his military service is completed. Meanwhile, a June wedding is planned. Apparently her mother has come around to the event with good grace.

We all expected a wedding to the O'Hara lad, but his father has returned to Ireland and it is said none too soon. I would not mention this to anyone but you, Catherine, knowing you to be

186

discreet. It is said that a certain dalliance involving one of the Jones girls resulted in their father horsewhipping Mr O'Hara! The girl has been sent south to her aunt, and it is said that Mr O'Hara was compelled to give a goodly sum of money for her keep in order not to bring a public scandal."

There was no word of Cavan. How I long to know where he is and how this has affected him. For a moment, I dreamed that he was free, but that is not so, of course. I am still Catherine, a foundling daughter of the New World, with no past and an uncertain heritage to present to a husband. I must not look back, but only ahead to all the advantages I am offered.

Twelfth Night, 1852

The de la Hayes celebrate this night in the old traditional way. There was a special dinner to which the Sévignys were invited. It was the first time we have seen the family since our return and they received a royal welcome. The children greeted "Tante Madeleine" with enthusiasm and then repaired to the back room where they began to make much noise.

Madame de la Haye drew Madame Sévigny to the fireplace with an affectionate embrace. Roger followed and I was struck by the curious intimacy of the scene. Somehow I felt an outsider. Without realising it at the time, I think I made my decision then.

The dinner was sumptuous. The table which was set with all of Madame de la Haye's most valuable china, had come from France at the time of her grandfather's marriage. I admired the glassware especially, with its rose tint and delicate design. The heavy ornate silver was a wedding gift on the occasion of her own marriage.

As course followed course, the children were becoming increasingly impatient. They were waiting for the cake. No cake was as much fun as Twelfth Night's cake! Soon it was carried to the table. A very large cake meant to feed many eager mouths. Hidden inside it were a pea and a bean. When the cake had been divided, the one who won the pea would become queen for the evening and the one who found the bean would be the king. The remaining company would be designated specific roles and would be under the rule of the king and queen.

How the children loved to hold all the power, if only for one night. As Madame Sévigny whispered to me, usually a child drew the honour. A hush fell over the table as Madame de la Haye began to serve the cake. It was as though the children held their breath.

"Catherine. Do you want to be queen?" whispered Marie-Claire.

"Sssh. We must wait and see. Maybe if I get the pea, I will give it to you."

The servings were passed around and there was a sudden joyful cry.

"Papa, Papa. I have it. O! C'est moi qui suis la reine. I am the queen!"

Her face beamed with delight and the usually quiet Marie-Louise held up a pea for all to see. There was a moment's silence while we all searched for the bean.

Again, a cry went up. "Voilà! Here it is. Look. I have it. Now I shall be the king." It was Madame Sévigny's oldest son, Luc, who attracted our attention.

Everyone broke into applause, saluting our new monarchs.

At once, the children began ordering their subjects to fulfill their commands. Roger was called upon to sing for the company, which he did in a fine baritone. Madame de la Haye played one of the children's favourite songs three times, protesting her stiff fingers. Jean-Jacques was sent to the corner by his younger sister and forced to remain there till I pleaded for him.

As we tired of the orders and begged for mercy, Marie-Louise suddenly went over to Madame Sévigny and said, "All right, Tante Madeleine. I will give my last command to you. Stay in our house and be my Maman."

There was an abrupt hush, broken by Jean-Jacques, who said impatiently, "Oh, Marie-Louise, you can't ask for things like that!"

The child looked abashed and glanced uncertainly at Madame Sévigny, whose face had turned rosy-red.

"Tante Madeleine. I didn't mean to do wrong."

The kind woman put her arm around the child and replied, "You are only telling me that you love me and that makes me happy as I love you too."

The embarrassment of the moment passed. The children went off to their own concerns while we retired to the front room where we sat around the fire. Shortly afterwards, the Sévignys took their leave and we all prepared for the night.

I knew that I must speak to Roger and not continue the mistake that we were making. Yet again, I set myself to make my plans.

January 7, 1852

Dear Major and Mrs Kingsley,

I will be returning to Kingston at the end of this month. I've decided not to remain in Montréal, where I've enjoyed the hospitality of Madame de la Haye and her family. It has been a wonderful experience and I was most warmly received. Nevertheless, I realise it is not in my heart to remain here permanently.

Remembering your kindness to me, I am taking the liberty of requesting a position in your home. Or perhaps you would recommend me to an acquaintance who might be in need of my services. I must find a position as soon as possible.

You will have heard of the death of Sister Isobel. This is my first opportunity to return to St Joseph's and to visit her grave.

I hope to see you and relieve you of my quilt. I am embarrassed that it has been in your keeping for so long. My sister would have taken it in the summer, but at that time you were in New York. It is our only remaining heirloom (we suppose it to be from our mother's family), apart from my bracelet of coloured stones and my sister's cross. You will understand that we hold these mementoes dear.

I hope to hear from you soon. I am planning to remain at St Joseph's during the month of February or until I find employment.

It is my fond hope that this letter finds you in good health . . .

Yours most respectfully,

Catherine St Joseph

12

November 26, 1851

So I'm an illegitimate offspring! A bastard! So be it. That's what I told myself last September just before my dinner engagement with Mr Basil Levishon. I studied my wardrobe carefully; the royal-blue sateen, the apricot silk, the daffodil yellow, just like you, dear confidante.

After much pondering, I settled on the new shamrock green costume. It was fashioned of moiré, taken from a magnificent bolt of exclusive watered silk brought in from France, a shamelessly extravagant expenditure but, as the dressmaker reassured me, it did compliment my skin and hair. After the deaths so recently endured, I felt the need of this folly. My unknown mother's brooch shone gallantly from its neckline position.

All I recalled of Mr Levishon from our brief meeting in Toronto so long ago was the image of an older man, somewhat portly in girth but distinguished in his manner of dress. On coming face to face with him, however, I was obliged to remind myself that he was not only wealthy but held out the promise of a New York stage career.

"Ahhh," he wheezed, nodding his almost bald head over my hand, "so you've come to the city of promise to try your wings? That is good."

"It's a pleasure to make your acquaintance once more, Sir," I said.

"A carriage awaits us, m'dear." With that, he offered me his arm and we sailed through the polished wood and brass doors of the Astor, as the concierge and the bellboys hovered respectfully about us. Evidently Mr Levishon is an easily recognizable gentleman in New York society.

The restaurant where we dined that evening, if you could

grace it with such a common name, was different from anything I had encountered before. In the first place, it was located outside the city proper, set back on a large estate with rolling green lawns and well-tended gardens. To the casual passerby, it appeared to be the mansion of some well-to-do family, with its porte-cochère, its rough-hewn stone front and pristine white-painted trim. When our carriage drove into its lane and halted in front of the massive verandah, adorned with smooth white columns, I felt immediate surprise.

Its interior caught me off guard also for, although there was a large reception hall which led off towards the ladies' and gentlemen's restrooms and to what appeared to be a series of private lounges, I could see no sign of a main dining room. The entire place was lit with crystal chandeliers and I imagined myself in an estate as palatial as the courts of France or Russia.

Bade to surrender my wraps to the female attendant who then led me into the ladies' room, I acquiesced silently and followed as though this were a familiar occurrence. The attendant was lean with the look of one who has never had quite enough to eat; she had skin the colour of crème caramel and wide-set almond eyes. I couldn't help but think that, if someone coaxed her into a smile, she would be considered beautiful.

"When y'all ready, Ma'am," she drawled in a voice I can only describe as treacle, "Ah'll take yuh to yurr gennle–maan frien'."

The powder room was exquisite, muted peach-shaded candelabra in each corner and over the tops of the gilt-framed mirrors, swan-white basins shaped like conch shells and, on the walls, an ornate wallpaper patterned in peach, cream and golden stripes. I was enchanted and had no urge to rush away. I dawdled, rinsing my hands beneath the gilt taps in the form of open-mouthed fish, drying them on the thick Turkish, peach-coloured towels provided.

When I could procrastinate no longer, the attendant approached me, bearing a tiny gilt tray filled with an assortment of cut-glass bottles. To my amazement, each one contained a French perfume bearing some famous name.

"They iss floral–ver' sweet lak honeysuckle, and they iss spice lak cinnamon or nutmeg, and they iss what the vendah do call musk–ver' heavy, that one," she informed me in her singsong inflection. "Why type you be, Ma'am?"

I hesitated. I had no idea which bottle to choose.

"Try this one," the younger woman urged. "It smell lak a whole garden filled with blossom."

I took her advice, but applied the scent sparingly, not wanting to draw too much attention to myself. I then followed my attendant to Basil Levishon's dining table.

Once more, I was treated to the unforeseen. Basil awaited me in a private salon. He was seated on a mushroom velvet banquette and, when I walked through the matching velvet-curtained entryway, he rose to greet me.

"Aaaah, there you are," he exclaimed. "Champagne?"

As I nodded my head to indicate agreement, I couldn't help but think that the beverage was becoming less than a luxury lately. I looked about the room admiringly. The décor was all in mushroom-coloured velvet, not only the chairs and couches, but the lampshades and wall panels as well. The table was oval, covered with crisp white linen and laid with gleaming silver, gilt-rimmed china and lead crystal glassware. I felt quite overcome.

"Do you approve?" Basil asked.

"Oh yes, but of course. It's most elegant."

"You have no objection to my keeping your company for my eyes alone?"

"Why no," I said hurriedly, not wanting to allow him to share my surprise. "I was unaware that such dining parlours existed – I mean, I think of dining rooms as having several tables." It was a lame answer, but I hoped it would suffice.

"This charming residence was purchased by a group of business gentlemen who desired a place to retire to for matters of certain secrecy – classified business information, private affairs, matters of diplomacy – ah, er, of delicacy. This little mansion is used by its members and occasional guests. We formed a club. Not everyone has access to it."

I nodded once more, hoping he would continue talking so I would not be forced to expose my ignorance of such matters.

"We call this place Le Rendez-vous, it is only one such residence which we use for our private purposes. Our principal edifice is more of a pleasure palace. You will see it later. It is called Le Club de Versailles. That is where my business acquaintances and I meet for entertainment of a superior variety. It will be an excellent position for you to make your mark in New York."

He paused and looked at me challengingly.

"My mark, Mr Levishon?" I asked. "I'm afraid I don't understand."

"Call me Basil, Darra. You and I are about to become close friends."

I gulped, trying to hide my dismay. I did not think that I liked the direction of our conversation. Nevertheless, it didn't seem prudent to show my apprehension until I knew better what was in his mind.

"Basil," I said faintly, and he smiled at me with encouragement.

"Don't you remember, Darra? I saw you perform in the theatre, when I was visiting Toronto."

"Indeed, Sir," I protested, "on that evening I had no role at all. I was merely one of the veiled dancing-girls in Ali Baba."

"Yes, of course," he said jovially, "and you were marvellous, absolutely marvellous. Didn't I tell you that I foresaw a career on the New York stage for you? And didn't I promise to help you achieve it?"

"Yes, I suppose you did," I admitted reluctantly, "but my interest lies in the drama, Sir, not in light-weight bit parts like those in a chorus line."

"Of course! I understand perfectly. Let us be reasonable; you see, Darra, the competition in New York is severe and, unless you are an experienced and well-trained actress, possibly from Europe or thereabouts, you must begin with lesser roles. If you feel it is beneath you. . ." He shrugged as though to suggest he was only trying to help me.

"Oh no, please forgive me," I stammered. "I didn't understand. I suppose I thought that, since I'd played Lady Teazle in School for Scandal and Kate in The Taming of the Shrew, I was well prepared for the New York stage."

"My dear girl, I'm certain that you are! Consider, however, that in a big city like New York, the audiences don't recognize actresses who have gained their acting experience on the road;

and the colonial road? Oh no! No indeed! Why, our audiences are sophisticated. They'll never have heard of such towns as Peterborough or Kingston. Why, in most cases, they'll not even have heard of Toronto."

"Really? Can it be true?" said I, amazed at such ignorance.

Basil nodded his head sagely. I turned my attention to the exquisitely roasted pheasant on my plate. The dinner was a miracle of culinary delights, but I scarcely noticed, so caught up was I in Basil's strange plans. We had begun with a clear broth the colour of dried parsley with a blob of cream in its centre. This was followed by coral-tinted smoked salmon with capers and then the whole pheasant arrived, complete with its head, standing upright. All the while, a discreet waiter, clad in morning coat and striped trousers, topped up my wine glass. My head felt somewhat dizzy, but I did not stop sipping the bubbling nectar.

"It wouldn't be forever, of course. Most great ladies of the stage begin their careers in lighter parts – dancing – singing – playing lesser roles and waiting for the big break."

"I suppose so," I said in a low voice. I was disappointed. Somehow I hadn't visualised myself as a harem girl, whirling and twirling before an audience of rich, old, lecherous men. It was the dreamer in me, I supposed, always grasping for something which was just beyond reach. My thoughts sank instantly back to my recent interview with Beaufort Powell and the disillusioning confession about my parentage. I sighed, forgetting momentarily that I was not alone in the silence of my bedroom.

"There, there, m'dear. Everything's going to be fine. Basil Levishon will be your patron and your guardian, and Basil Levishon, as anyone will tell you, never lets his girls down."

I couldn't think what he might mean by that statement, but decided hastily not to inquire. I felt I ought to learn something of the payment for such entertainment as he described, but knew not how to phrase the question. Fortunately, Basil had already anticipated my curiosity.

"All the girls who entertain at the Club de Versailles are provided with accommodation on the premises," he said, studying me closely for I knew not what.

"You mean I would have my own room?" I asked, wondering if

I had understood correctly.

"Yes, of course, Darra. Each girl has her own room and, when she wishes to check out for a day or a night or two, she merely makes her arrangements with Madame Blanche."

"Madame Blanche?" The mystery seemed to deepen every minute.

"Yes, she's the – er, châtelaine. She looks after the girls' needs, sees that they're contented, helps them out with all their little problems."

"Oh." I did not visualize any problems which I would want to confide in a strange woman, but perhaps she was like Sister Martha at St Joseph's. Not that the Kingston orphanage matched this situation, I thought. Not at all.

"The salary is not grand, I'm afraid, but I believe you will find that the extras will more than compensate for that."

"Extras?" I asked, feeling foolish for having to make such an inquiry.

"The gentlemen who grace our establishments are generous with their largesse, and think nothing of paying highly for the exclusive entertainment and companionship of Madame Blanche's ladies. It is my belief that you will be a jewel of rare setting in such an establishment."

"Please excuse me, Mr Levishon – er, Basil, but I still feel quite puzzled about the nature of my employment. What exactly will I be expected to do?"

"Very little, m'dear, certainly nothing that you will have any difficulty whatever fulfilling. You will be expected to dance occasionally, but for the most part, you will only be required to converse with our gentlemen, our visitors, be pleasant to them, to act as hostess, so to speak."

"You do realise that I am not a trained dancer, Basil?" I felt more bewildered by the moment, and could not understand why anyone would be willing to pay large sums of money to make conversation with attractive young women when they could probably do the same for nothing in the homes of their own friends.

"The dancing abilities of our young women are of little import, Darra. But come! Don't worry your pretty little head over the details of our business. All in good time," and so saying, he moved his bulk from where he was sitting to a spot closer to me. "You're a beautiful girl, I must say."

With those words, Basil deposited his empty glass on the table in front of us, grabbed me roughly with both hands and forced his thick, wet lips against my own. At first, I struggled but realised quickly that, despite his age and what appeared to be excessive fat, he was strong and determined. The moment I lay still, he plunged his hands inside the bosom of my gown and, squeezing my breasts with undue vigor, he slipped the straining material from my shoulders. Still in shock, it came to me, nevertheless, that his intentions did not match my own. As his egg-like skull lowered in the direction his hands had taken, I hit out as violently as possible.

"Darra," he cried out with a stunned voice, "don't protest! Be good to your patron!"

"Mr Levishon, I do declare that your actions are scarcely those of a gentleman, and that is what you have purported to be." I was breathing heavily and having a mighty struggle to put my frock back into place, where it belonged.

"My apologies, my dear, I was merely overwhelmed by your nearness."

"Then I suggest that you return to the place you were sitting until just a few minutes ago. Think how embarrassed we both would be had the waiter chosen that particular moment to clear the table!"

"The waiters at Le Rendez-vous," he stated pompously, "know better than to enter the private dining room unless summoned."

"You mean this sort of behaviour is common in your club?" I was incredulous.

"Well, not exactly common, m'dear, but the club is most certainly used often by lovers and would-be suitors. Yes, that's true enough. I apologize, Darra, if I have offended you. You're such a delectable morsel. I quite forgot myself. I'll behave. I promise you."

Not knowing what to make of all that had gone before, I accepted his apologies and tried to pretend his attack had never happened. Of course, I was not so naïve as to be unaware of men's most basic instincts. Pursuit of the female was simply a game they could not stop themselves from playing. Perhaps the fault had not been all his. After all, I had dressed myself in a most bewitching manner.

Once Basil had returned to his own chair, he seemed to gain control of himself and the evening passed with no further incident. On the way home, I became somewhat apprehensive again lest in the dark of the carriage, he might once more throw caution to the winds, but he behaved in a most decorous manner.

"Now, Darra," he said, as he escorted me into the Astor, "I feel sure you will agree that we must shortly move you out of this expensive hotel. When do you think you could be ready? It is my intention to prepare a suite of rooms for you at my own town house and, once you are installed and rested, I will accompany you on our initial visit to Madame Blanche at the Club de Versailles."

I hesitated, wondering if it was the thing to do to stay at Mr Levishon's house, but I knew he was correct in his calculation that the Astor was too expensive for me to remain much longer.

Seeing me falter, Basil at once spoke to reassure me. "Please do not worry yourself in any way, m'dear. There is a housekeeper and an entire staff of servants on the premises. You will in no way be compromised."

Reluctantly I agreed. "Very well, Basil. I shall spend tomorrow seeing to the removal of my wardrobe and settling my accounts."

"Your account has already been settled. A carriage will come for you in two days then. I look forward to having you honour my dining room table and pour from my silver tea service."

November 27, 1851

It was the last week of September when I checked out of the Astor and moved into Basil Levishon's house. I was surprised to discover how small it was, but considering that he uses it only as a city address, I thought I understood. Indeed, he was so seldom in the place that I found myself lonesome for someone to talk to.

One week after my arrival in his town house, he left me a note saying that he would call for me that very evening in order that we might visit the Club de Versailles together. I pondered long over a choice of appropriate dress, ruling out my former favourite, the green moiré because of the unfortunate connotations of my second meeting with Basil. A light but continuous drizzle fell outside and, therefore, not wishing to make any faux-pas, I opted for a sombre black velveteen costume. Upon Basil's arrival, he entered briefly and looked me over carefully before helping me with my wrap.

"Is my appearance in keeping with the evening's plans, Sir?" I asked.

"I do wish, Darra, that you would remember to address me as Basil – yes, you look perfectly groomed and enchantingly attractive. I'm sure I will be the envy of every gentleman on the premises."

The drive to the Club de Versailles took at least an hour and, when we drove up to the entrance, I thought we had made an error and returned to Le Rendez-vous. There appeared to be lights illuminating every room of the mansion. When I peered out the carriage window, it looked like a snow castle designed for a fair princess, with sun and moon both shining brightly on its surface and lit from within by a thousand lamps.

"So what do you think, m'dear?" asked Basil, seeing me gaze at the club wide-eyed.

"It's unbelievable. Why, I've never seen so many lights blazing at the same time. Are they all gas lit?"

"Of course, yes. Our members spare no expense in our entertainment palaces." Basil grinned at me roguishly.

A dwarf-sized man, dressed in the same morning dress as the waiters at Le Rendez-vous, handed me down from the carriage and, as he did so, presented me with an open parasol to help keep me dry. Once inside, I looked about me and noted that the décor was similar to that of the other residence.

The grotesquely small servant was disappearing down a hallway with a bundle of wet parasols and umbrellas and I couldn't help but wonder if he was one of the midgets who were reputed to entertain for Mr Barnum and his circus. Basil, however, was urging me towards a tall and stately woman with brilliantly hennaed hair. I could scarcely remove my gaze from it.

"Blanche, m'dear," and he embraced her gustily, "how's business?"

"Can't complain, you old devil," she answered, leering at me in a most strange manner. "I suppose this would be the young lady you were telling me about."

"Yes. Darra St Joseph. Darra, m'dear, I'd like for you to meet my dearest and oldest friend in New York City. Allow me to present you to Madame Blanche."

"Howjado, dearie? Pleased to have you join us, I'm sure."

"How do you do?" I replied. With considerable astonishment, I stared at this picture of coquettish contrasts. She appeared an old harridan with her bright cheeks like apples, her heavily-rouged mouth and the wrinkles on her face running from forehead to chin like rivulets of powdered chalk.

"Come closer, my child," she beckoned. Her long bony fingers reminded me of witches from fairy tales and myths of childhood days. "I need to study you. Walk! Yes, that's alright. Turn in a slow circle. Yes, that's good. Yes, you should do just fine." As she nodded her head up and down, I watched with fascination her high pouffed pompadour as it threatened to collapse.

"Don't fuss, Blanche," said Basil. "Of course she'll do. Best piece of – er, femininity you've seen around here in a dog's age."

"Do you dance, child?" asked the woman, ignoring Basil's interruption. "Sing?"

I was perplexed, wondering how to respond. "I've never received professional training in the dance. As for singing, no, I am not a singer."

"Blanche." Once more Basil interceded. "I have already informed Darra that all she need do is entertain our customers; converse politely with them, and dance occasionally, make them feel at home, so to speak, in this home away from home. Besides, Blanche, I already told you that Darra is to be my own personal hostess during the following weeks."

"Oh you did, did you? What about Goldie, huh?"

"Not now, Blanche. We'll discuss it all later, privately."

Madame Blanche desisted abruptly at that point, so I never did learn what it was all about, or who Goldie might be. That is to say, I didn't learn at that time. My knowledge about such things was to come later, about a month and a half later, to be precise. On that specific September eve, I was ignorant of everything that took place at the Club de Versailles.

My first week at the Club de Versailles was pleasant and certainly not overtaxing, but I still found it mysterious that gentlemen of the type who frequented the premises weren't entertaining themselves with ladies of their own class and background. Although I was fortunate enough to have had a better than average education with the sisters and Father Andrew at St Joseph's, I understood my position in life quite clearly. Every evening I reminded myself of my scandalous heritage and that dear Cat was not after all my sister. It continued to grieve me and yet the harder I steeled myself to put my past behind me, the oftener I gave way to silent tears shed into my pillow at night.

I'd made no friends to date with the other girls who worked at the Club. Every time I attempted to open a conversation with one of them, Madame Blanche appeared and spirited the girl off or I was called on to perform some errand or other. I thought the circumstances unusual. It did not trouble me unduly, however, because none of the girls had any characteristics whatever in common with Cat or the sisters at St Joseph's. Neither were they of the type I had met in Toronto at the Royal Lyceum. Secretly I wondered if the girls considered me unfriendly. Was there something wrong with me?

One evening in October, as I was descending the graciously ornate, curving staircase to the foyer of the Club, I spied Basil and Madame Blanche in what appeared to be an angry conversation. As I approached them, they discontinued their argument abruptly, but too late for me to miss Madame Blanche's last remark.

"Well, old fart," she was saying, her nose almost touching his chin, "you better set her straight tonight, because she ain't pullin' her weight and the other gells is bitchin'."

"Why, Darra," said Basil, smiling smoothly, "there you are."

He extended his hand to me and, simultaneously, Madame Blanche sniffed loudly, spun about and stormed out of the room.

"Good evening, Basil. Is Madame upset?" Such a foolish remark! It was perfectly obvious that she was furious, but what else could I say?

"Blanche? Oh, don't mind her."

"Whom are we entertaining tonight, Basil?"

"Eh?" I could tell his mind was elsewhere, but he turned about and looked me up and down as though trying to make a decision. "Yes. Come, Darra. You and I must needs have a private talk."

"Yes, of course, Basil. Have I done wrong? I'm truly sorry if I have." I knew my dancing wasn't quite up to that of the other girls, but I'd already told Basil that I found it embarrassing and almost immoral to wriggle my hips before all these unknown strangers, as desired by Madame Blanche.

Basil pursed his lips together, but said nothing. He led me into one of the private lounges of the foyer, shut the door, secured it and bade me sit down.

"Yes, Darra, I fear the time has now come. You have been here almost a month and you continue to pretend you are a naïve schoolgirl, straight out of the convent." He glared at me.

"I – I'm sorry, Basil. What would you have me do?"

"Darra . . ." He sighed mightily, looked at me again as though trying to decide how best to break some bad news to me, then commenced pacing back and forth in front of me. "Tell me, m'dear, is the money allowance you were given last weekend sufficient for your needs? Is your wardrobe perfectly satisfactory? Perhaps you are in need of some replacements?"

"Oh Basil, how sweet and kind you are." I didn't admit how relieved I was that all he was worried about was my clothing needs! "I have quite sufficient costumes at the moment. Of course, as the winter closes in, I shall be needing to make a visit to the dressmaker. I still have some money in Kingston which I haven't as yet transferred here and I will, as you have stated, be earning more money soon, when I learn more properly how to entertain the gentlemen. I was wondering if maybe I should take lessons on the piano and in voice. Would that be a good idea?"

Basil had a strange look on his face. "No, it would not be a good idea, Darra. A good idea would be for you to cut out the pretense. Well, I suppose there's no easy way to say this. So be it!

The young ladies who work in this establishment earn their keep by accommodating the visitors who frequent the premises. That is to say, they agree to do exactly what the gentlemen request of them. Now do you understand?"

I was merely baffled. "But Basil, I try. What have I done wrong?"

"Well, for one thing, Darra, last evening a gentleman complained to Madame Blanche that you refused to accompany him to one of the lounges."

"Naturally I refused, Basil," I answered him, remembering the disconcerting incident instantly. "He was no gentleman, I can assure you. He used language no gentleman would use and his suggestion was indecent."

"What do you mean, indecent?"

"He – he wanted me to – he wanted me to go with him and. . ." but I couldn't continue.

"That gentleman, Darra, that gentleman wanted, no – expected that you would accompany him to that lounge. No, let's call a spade a spade, that bedroom and he expected you to have sexual relations with him. Is that correct?"

I stared at him, wide-eyed. Could I have heard correctly?

"Yes." My voice was inaudible. I dropped my eyes to the floor.

"Darra." Basil crossed the room and stood in front of me. "Don't hang your head like that. Look at me and listen carefully." I complied, albeit reluctantly. "This establishment, this pleasure palace is exactly what it is called, and m'dear, entertaining the gentlemen who visit it includes pleasing them with sexual favours. Do you understand?"

My stomach knotted. My head was throbbing. I hoped I would not faint.

"I – I can't," I stammered.

At this juncture, Basil laughed in a cruel manner. "I am now bored with your play acting. In case you are unaware of it, let me inform you that I possess full details of your background. Orphaned bastard, reared by nuns, abandoned by your mother who was, incidentally, also a bastard. And don't try to tell me that you are a virgin! You shared Trevor Vaughn's bed for several months, as did several other besotted would-be actresses before you. What's more, you were the mistress of that notorious crook, Kendall Warrick. You had a miscarriage in Albany, and here you are in New York. Unless I am sorely mistaken, you are not only in need of employment, but you are also hiding out from the law."

"Oh no," I managed to choke out, aghast at the distortions in his account.

"Oh yes, Darra, and if you know what's good for you, you'll toe the line and do as you're instructed."

"You are correct about much, Mr Levishon." At least I needn't call this disgusting man by his Christian name. "I am illegitimate, but that is hardly my fault. It's true I ran off with Trevor, but, and you may not believe this, we did not become intimate. Be that as it may, Trevor was a good man. He was kind to me and I loved him. As for Kendall, he swept me off my feet. He was my first and only real love. His dastardly murder near broke my heart. For all that, I am in no way mixed up in what appears to be some criminal element in his former life."

"Pahhh! You look so appealing when you beg, but I am not taken in by your pretty words. You were with Kendall on the river the last night he was seen alive, meeting a disreputable gambler. I think the police would pay highly for such information. Shall I call them and turn you over for questioning? The jails are not a pleasant place in which to sojourn."

I felt trapped, well and truly. Suppose I were to tell the police I was innocent, that I knew nothing of Kendall's life of crime or background? They would never believe me. Darra St Joseph; a bastard who lied about her name, who ran off from honest employment in Kingston to pursue a theatrical career, and, who later succumbed to the blandishments of a criminal. I could never think of Kendall as a criminal.

"What do you want of me?" I asked, at that moment feeling I had no choice but to comply with any request he might make.

"We will join the others for drinks and dinner and tonight you will make an effort to imitate the deportment of the other girls so that you may behave accordingly in the near future."

The evening passed in a blur of confusion. Now that I realised why Basil had befriended me, I quickly came to the conclusion that I had best behave submissively and bide my time. Again I thanked our dear Lord for bestowing on me the gift of acting. Smiling at Basil's guest and flirting with all outrageously. I believe I gave the performance of my life. I forced myself to behave shamelessly, swaying my lower limbs in a burlesque of what up to now had seemed to me indecent conduct. I even encouraged an old lecher to believe that I might succumb to his amorous designs. The pretence and sham of my action hid my true thoughts from the guests and soon I could see that Basil had ceased to worry.

All through dinner, which was an art as usual, I schemed and plotted my escape from this den of iniquity. Wine flowed as though from taps and I raised my glass frequently to my lips. What no one realized, however, was that I was merely pretending to drink. At every opportunity, I switched glasses with my companion. As midnight approached, Basil joined me and, in order to convey to the others that I was his property, he ran his hand over my bosom in plain view of the company. Instead of shrinking as I wished to do, I forced a smile to my lips and waved goodnight to the other gentlemen.

"Well done, m'dear," Basil exuded, as we moved down the hall together. "I knew you had it in you."

"I only wish to please," I lied. "I did not understand the nature of your establishment, Basil. Truly I did not."

"Good. Then, wench, let us enjoy each other's company tonight and you can prove yourself to me."

How was I going to free myself from this entanglement? My thoughts flew around in my head like bats in the attic. I couldn't run to the door. Someone would be sure to stop me. If only I had made friends with some kind soul in the Club. Frantically, I sought for answers. A powder, to pour into Basil's nightcap, but where could I get it? I shrank from physical violence. I could not see myself hitting him over the head or stabbing him with some sharp instrument!

Meanwhile, we had arrived at the door. Basil opened it and ushered me inside, locking it securely. I noted well as he casually placed the key in his vest pocket.

"Now, Darra, the jig is up. I'm an old man and it's past my bedtime. Off with those clothes and prove yourself once and for all." With that, he draped his jacket and vest over a chair back, sighed and sat on the edge of the bed, all the while stroking the modish coverlet.

"Yes, of course, Basil, but first I must change my attire. Surely you wish to have me come to you properly adorned, in one of those beautiful peach silk and satin negligées?" Anything, I thought, to delay the inevitable.

"All right, if you wish," he agreed, "but mind you don't take long in there or I'll be in to fetch you out!"

As I moved slowly towards the privacy of the bathroom, I noted Basil's eyes following me. Just before I closed the door behind me, he swung his legs up onto the bed and stretched out full length.

Once inside the peach and white room, I turned on the fish-like faucets and stared at the streaming water filling the bowl. What could I do? I knelt by the over-sized bathtub and prayed.

'Hail Mary full of grace, pray for us now and at the hour of our death ...' I repeated the litany over and over, just as I used to do at St Joseph's. After a while, I decided to pour myself a bath.

The water gushed in torrents. I sprinkled liberal amounts of herbs and oils which bubbled frothily on the surface. Before removing my clothing and stepping into the perfumed tub, I checked to make sure the door was securely locked. The water continued to flow into the bath. I eased myself into a comfortable position, wondering as I did so how long it would be before Basil commenced banging on the door. A strange peace descended on me.

How much time elapsed before I decided to climb out of my retreat, I know not. The water had turned tepid. My fingers were wrinkled and pink. Perhaps I had slept. Except for the running water all was silent. Thoughtfully I towelled myself dry and, without consciously thinking about why I did so, I dressed once again in my black velveteen costume.

I crept to the door, scarcely daring to breathe, and slipped the lock from its hasp. Slowly, gently I turned the handle until there was a crack barely large enough to peer through.

'Oh God is merciful,' I thought, at that moment not recognizing how my prayer had been answered. Basil lay on the bed, mouth agape, snoring noisily.

Without further ado, I tiptoed towards his vest, hanging so conveniently on the chair next to the bed. As I reached my destination and slipped my hand inside the pocket where I had seen him secrete the key, Basil gave a great groan and turned on his side. I froze.

"Wurr – uummph – wurr – uummph," issued from his open mouth.

I knew I must move quickly. Basil's body rested so close to the edge of the bed, I felt certain it was only a matter of time till he slipped off onto the floor. Where was the key? My fingers groped blindly. No, it was not in that pocket. Once more, I held my breath. I withdrew my hand promptly and, without a pause, searched the other side-pocket. As my hand encountered cold steel, my heart commenced to beat more loudly than I thought possible.

At last, key in hand, I headed for the door. My ticket to freedom saved me and the key turned easily. The doorknob made no protest as I slipped outside into the empty hall. Swiftly I relocked the door, thinking for one happy moment how surprised Basil would be on awakening. Then, on light feet, I raced the length of the passageway, hesitating every now and again to listen for sounds of activity. I couldn't believe my luck.

'Luck of the Irish,' I encouraged myself. At that very moment, just as I gained a convenient side door onto the verandah, I heard a low laugh. Quickly, I wrapped myself within the folds of the mushroom velvet draperies on either side of the French doors. I listened, but no further noises came my way.

I was outside. The vast lawns spread before me like an endless racetrack. I ran from the shadow of one tree to the next. At every advance, I imagined a giant hand reaching out to grab me and drag me back to pay my dues in the Club de Versailles. The moon was bright except for occasional scudding clouds which the wind pushed across its surface at intervals.

Of a sudden, I spied the roadway. I crouched in the dark of the ditch and pondered which way to head. There were no signs. Which way was New York? Was New York where I wanted to go? At that moment, I made the decision to report to the police.

Surely they would help.

'Please God,' I prayed once more, 'guide me and give me your protection as you have done until now.'

With that, I pulled myself erect, straightened my skirts and hurried down the road.

I wonder how long I groped my way, pausing frequently to rest or to hide from what I imagined to be strange noises in the night. At one point I fell into a disturbed slumber from which I woke shaking from fear and shivering with cold. With the first light of dawn, I encountered settlement and sighed with relief that I had set out in the right direction. By now, I was determined to consult the police and, therefore, studied the road signs in order that I reach Manhattan as quickly as possible.

"Where ye be headin', young lass?"

I turned quickly to note a ragman sitting atop a waggonful of material scraps. He was clad in a worn black-cloth coat and a strange stove-pipe hat which had seen better days.

"Manhattan, Sir," I ventured.

"Well, hop in if you've a mind. Ye may as well ride as walk."

I hesitated only a moment. I was exhausted and so I accepted his kind offer. Once I was seated amid a pile of rags, the man twitched the reins laconically and the poor old nag attached to the waggon set off.

Clump-clump-clackety-clump. The horse was such a bag of bones, I wondered at times if we would arrive at our destination the same day. One thing was certain. I could have walked more quickly, if I hadn't been so tired, that is.

Although it was still early morning, by the time we had reached the part of Manhattan where my driver was headed, the sidewalks and corners were already crowded with vendors.

"Thank you kindly, Sir," I said, jumping off the cart and wishing I had a coin to bestow upon him.

He only nodded his head and continued on his way.

Now all I had to do was find the police station. I looked all around trying to remember where it was located, but before I had need of making inquiries, I spotted a member of the law force standing on a far corner.

"Excuse me, Sir," I began, once I had drawn abreast of him. He turned and looked me up and down in what I considered to be a most insolent manner.

"I am searching for the police station and I wondered if you might direct me?"

"Well now, I might," he said, "but since I am the law myself, why not confide in me?"

"I wish to report some quite unsavoury and, I feel sure, illegal activities." I stammered, wondering how best to present my plight to this barely interested officer.

"And what might these illegal activities be? Murder? Assault? You look a fine strong maiden. Have you been put upon then?"

"I – I was invited, no, lured into accepting an invitation to dine at a place called the Club de Versailles," I began, wondering if the officer might know of its existence. "I was under the impression that I was to be an actress in the place. What transpired was quite different. I was expected to perform different acts." Once again, I hesitated. "The place turned out to be a house of ill-repute." I tried to look away from the broad smile that was spreading from one ear to the other on the officer's face.

"Is that so?" He raised a whistle to his lips and, as the sound went out round the square, two more officers materialised from I know not where.

"What do you think of this lass's sorry tale?" he asked his brother officers. "Tell on, Miss. What did you say your name was?"

"I am Darra St Joseph," I said imperiously and lifted my chin a knotch as I did so.

The policemen stood round me in a semi-circle, staring at me attentively. I repeated what I had just said. My words seemed to instill in them nothing but amusement. One of them guffawed loudly.

"I suppose you're one of them Irish immigrants who keep arriving in the port of New York City and expect to find the roadways paved in gold, are you?"

"Oh, no, Sir," I protested. "I am from the colonies to the north, from the city of Kingston. I came here to be by the side of a dear actor friend who, God bless him, unfortunately died."

"From Kingston, then, are you? I suppose you thought you'd

find fame and fortune on Broadway. Is that it?" His eyes were cold and hard and, instinctively, I tried to hide from their gaze.

"Why yes, I suppose you might say so. I am, after all, a professional actress."

"If that's the case, then why did you agree to perform in the Club de Versailles?"

"I was misinformed. Mr Levishon told me that it would further my acting career."

Once again, the trio laughed delightedly, but I could see nothing funny about my dilemma.

"Levishon then, is it?" one of them said and, so saying, laid his hand on my arm. "May I give you some advice, my beautiful little baggage?"

I nodded my head fearfully, bit my lip and tried to keep my tears in check.

"Every day, there are shiploads of poverty-stricken, starving immigrants arriving, and all of them are looking for work. The numbers this year are higher than they've been in a donkey's age. Now listen, you're young, you're pretty and I'm sure many a gentleman would pay a high price to have you spread your legs for him. So take my advice and return to your patron."

"Oh no," I cried, aghast at his words.

"I'll even arrange transportation for you," said another policeman.

I tried to step backward and break the grip of the man who held my arm, but this caused the three of them to close ranks and I found myself caught in their trap.

"Have you any money?" one of them asked abruptly.

I shook my head. "No. I didn't dare to bring anything with me when I ran away last night."

"You could be arrested for vagrancy." This comment came from the original officer whom I had approached. "Maybe we should take you down to headquarters after all."

By this time, I realised that even the law was corrupt and that I wasn't going to receive any help from this source. I decided to pretend I would return to the Club de Versailles.

"Perhaps you gentlemen are right," I said, using a humble tone. "But first I must rest."

"You look like you could use some food too," said the one nearest me, encircling my waist with his arm. "Come, we will go to the hotel across the street and make arrangements."

"Oh thank you, Sir, but as I said, I've no money." I didn't wish to accompany this policeman any more than I had a desire to share Basil Levishon's bed. "If you'll just hire a cab for me, I'll pay the driver when I reach my destination."

"What a beguiling child you are," he laughed and half-led, half-dragged me towards the hotel. "Once we have eaten, you may have the privilege of paying me in your own way."

'Help me, dear Lord,' I said to myself and scanned the crowd hopelessly. 'Where are you now that I need you?'

At that moment, a carriage, pulled by two galloping horses drove rapidly upon the scene, scattering people and animals in their wake. A shrill cry rent the air and, just before the carriage reached us, I saw a child trip and roll beneath the wheels. My escort, temporarily alerted to the danger, loosened his grip and immediately, I darted to the other side of the road. When I got there, neither did I pause to observe the accident nor did I think where my path might lead. I simply took to my heels and fled.

Such a day as I encountered. Throughout the daylight hours, I spent my time hiding from anyone who looked the least suspicious, and in resting in any inconspicuous place. By evening, I was not only cold but hungry. A group of destitutes were huddled together near an open fire in a sheltered square. I longed to approach them, but fear held me back. As I continued to crouch behind a pile of discarded garbage, however, I came to the conclusion that I must make a move of some sort.

Finally I squared my shoulders and headed towards the group. They scarcely even noticed my arrival, such was their look of defeat.

"Excuse me," I began, addressing my remarks to a young woman who looked close in age to me. "May I please warm my hands by the fire?"

She shrugged. "'Tain't my fire. You're welcome as far as I'm concerned." Having spoke her piece, she lowered her dull eyes to the ground once more.

I moved closer, the heat drawing me as a moth to a flame. A

man squatted near me; he was roasting chestnuts.

"Have some?" he offered and I gratefully accepted his kindness. Alas! When I attempted to swallow the sweet nuts, I felt nauseous of a sudden and was unable to do so.

"When did you last have a meal?" the man asked me.

"Yesterday," I answered, feeling faint and dizzy. My forehead was beaded in perspiration and I reached up my hand to wipe it dry.

The man stood up and, peering at me, spoke again. "You look ill. Ain't got the fever, have you now?"

"Oh, I don't believe so." As I spoke, my whole body was seized with a shaking and shivering of such strength that I felt a necessity to sit down.

"Hey, Rose," I heard someone call, "Bring that extra shawl over here, will you? There's a lass here what's got the fever."

To my utter astonishment, the men and women huddled about the small warm space, tended instantly to my wants. One wrapped me tenderly in a large shawl of many brilliant colours. Another lowered me to the ground, close to the fire, but first she prepared a layer of newspapers for me to sit on.

"She needs to drink something," I heard the woman called Rose say. Before I was able to discern what was happeneing, some vile tasting liquor was forced between my lips. "There, mavourneen, I know it's not to your taste, but 'twill warm your insides."

Strange to say, she was right. The liquor burned all the way down my throat but soon it spread a warmth throughout my body and caused me to feel quite light-headed. I remember, later on that evening, the same woman spooning hot broth into me. I kept giving in to sleep and then, upon awakening, being forced to drink again. The entire experience was strange and somehow unreal.

At one point, when I was finally awake, Rose asked me where I was from and what had happened to me. In a desperate move, I confessed all and begged her to tell me of where I might find employment.

"You are not alone, my child," the woman said. "Many young Irish girls have been enslaved in the bawdy houses. Some go willingly; others are dragged there. Once caught, they find it difficult to escape. There is very little else open to them. I've been here six months and so I know."

"I'm willing to seek honest employment," I insisted. "I was a maid in the home of gentlefolk, and I would go into service again. Can't you tell me where to look?"

"Perhaps when you have recovered," she said, looking at me with great pity. "Right now, you're in no fit state to work at anything."

Lying back among these poor but honest people, I was overcome with a deep appreciation of my own fortunate up-bringing. Why, I suddenly realised, this is how it must have been for Noreen, the unfortunate girl who sailed from Ireland with a babe in her arms. She had been alone in the world. How brave she was. Perhaps her plight had been similar to that of the woman, Rose.

'Dear Lord,' I prayed silently, 'thank you for revealing my mother's true character to me, and help me grow to better understanding of those less fortunate than I.' Once more, I allowed myself to surrender to sleep.

Those dear immigrants, destitute though they were, cared for me as if I were their own for several days and nights. When I felt stronger, I approached the subject of my future once again.

"I must not continue to burden you thus," I said. "You have all been so kind. I know not how to thank you, but I must seek employment and fend for myself."

The woman looked at me, shook her head with resignation and spoke. "There is only one piece of advice which I have to offer you, child, and that is that you return from whence you came. While you were feverish and sick, you spoke of many things. Your mind was rambling and it is clear to me that you are a dreamer. You spoke of a place called St Joseph's and of kindly people by the name of Sister Martha and Father Andrew. You also wept over the loss of your dear sister, Catherine by name."

"Oh, you must forgive me," I burst forth agitatedly. "I did not mean to burden you with my troubles."

"Och, 'tis nothing," she continued blithely. "You should return to this place. I feel sure your homecoming would be greeted with cries of joy."

"I can't." As I said the words, their full meaning settled upon me. How could I go back to Kingston? How could I abandon all my dreams and ambitions? My situation was impossible. The kindnesses of Sister Martha and Father Andrew should not be taken for granted. Besides, I must stay far away from Cat in order that she at least be allowed to accept her rightful place in society as the daughter of Major Kingsley.

"Fiddlesticks. Faith and begorra, child, ye can't stay here. There's little enough work for those who are strong and brawny, and I'll not see you go back to that house of ill-repute. It's back to St Joseph's with you."

"How can I go back?" Rose seemed insistent and I began to wonder if perhaps she had a magic solution. "The passage is expensive. When I left the Club de Versailles, I abandoned all my worldly goods, my wardrobe, my money, I have nothing." Once again I felt despair.

"Your only hope is the Church," she announced determinedly. "You must seek solace in the Church. Don't think that because you feel somewhat better today that you are completely well. It will be several weeks before you are returned to normal. You must needs rest and eat proper food. The nuns will see to it."

December 18, 1851

I am resting on a cot in a small room at the Mother House of Sister Agnes. The room is dull, its walls grey, its curtainless windows barred like in a cell. Except for the cot, a prie-dieu and a wash basin, the room is bare. Only a small crucifix adorns the walls, our Saviour suffering for the sinners of the world.

I arrived here in the early twilight hours on that fateful day when the dear immigrants persuaded me what I must do. The woman who had nursed me so lovingly, made the arrangements. Soon I was bundled into a cart laden with garbage, which had to be disposed of outside the city. The driver, who spoke nary a word during the entire journey, let me off on a corner and pointed to a small church in the near distance. I thanked him and limped down the road, pausing frequently when I broke into a cold sweat. I knew that my body was merely reacting to the strain of excessive physical activity after my illness; nevertheless, I was relieved to finally reach the door of my destination.

Once inside the chapel, I moved with dazed footsteps to the altar bench, knelt down and thanked Mary for continuing to care for me. My thoughts took me straight back to St Joseph's where, as a child, I'd spent so many hours on my knees atoning for my sins. Here I was once more.

Hail Mary full of grace pray for us sinners now and at the hour of our death, I repeated it over and over again. At some point along the way, I must have lost consciousness for the next thing I became aware of was a soft voice and a kind figure in a black habit bending over me.

"She's coming to now," I heard her say and I blinked my eyes, trying to make sense out of what was happening. Where was I? Suddenly I remembered everything; the terror of the Club de Versailles and Basil and the frightening Madame Blanche; the kindness and sympathy of the Irish immigrants who found New York hostile and disinterested in their plight; my illness and the drive here in a garbage cart. I tried to contain my desolation and my tears and then I glimpsed the blessed sight of the nun in her black habit again.

"Where am I?" I murmured, hoping she did not think that I had assumed faintness in their chapel, for my own ends.

"This is the Mother House of Sister Agnes. We found you in the chapel where you had fainted and fallen onto the floor. Have you been ill recently, my child?"

"Yes, Sister, in Manhattan. I caught a chill in a rainstorm one night when I had no place to sleep. Some Irish immigrants cared for me, even though their own condition was far from assured."

"And how came you here?" she asked.

"A garbageman drove me to within sight of the church," I confessed.

"Rest now," she said. "I shall bring you some broth anon. Then you can tell us your name so that we can get in touch with your family. They must be worried about you."

Immediately I felt fear again. The sister looked so full of concern and yet, were I to confess my past and my theatrical ambitions, she would, I felt certain, lose all respect for me.

A day and a night passed before the serene little nun questioned me again.

"I have no family," I admitted. "Please forgive me for putting you to so much trouble. As soon as I am able to be up and about, I shall seek employment and trouble you no further."

"Silence my child, you are no trouble at all. We only wish to help you. You are still tired and far from recovered. You must not overtax yourself. Sleep now."

It was not difficult to follow her suggestions, so I closed my eyes once more and surrendered myself up to the land of non-memory. Now, two weeks later, I am much strengthened and soon I must come to a decision as to my future.

Last week, having first asked the sweet sister to call me Catherine, I allowed as that was not my name at all. I then told her, with great misgiving, that I was Darra and that I came from St Joseph's Orphanage in Kingston. To my surprise and relief, I found that she was well acquainted with it.

"We must contact Father Andrew and inform him of your plight," she said sympathetically.

"Oh no, Sister, I am undeserving of their love. I am a sinner and have betrayed them in all my ambitions."

Sister Marguerite (for that was her name) looked at me in alarm and tried to reassure me. "Our Father in heaven forgives all," she said piously, but, at that time, I felt in my heart that I did not deserve to be forgiven.

December 31, 1851

I am going home. Sister Marguerite has shown me the letter she has just received from Father Andrew and Sister Martha, written in haste from St Joseph's.

"Dear Sister," it said in part, "Please arrange passage for Darra as soon as you feel she is well enough to travel. Assure her we love her dearly and long to have her back in the fold with us."

When I read the letter, I wept. It was such a relief to let the tears flow from beneath my eyelids. I had denied myself the pleasure of surrendering to grief for too long. Up till that moment I had been frozen like a stone in the field, unable to give way to any human emotion. Father Andrew's and Sister Martha's understanding and sympathy reached my heart and now that I have cried long and hard, I believe I will be able to face the future once more.

Tomorrow is the first day of a new year. I have resolved to devote myself to the work of the Lord and to turn aside from vanity and greed.

13

Now that I have been back at St Joseph's for three days, I will steal an hour from my chores and record the astonishing events that have come to pass. January went slowly as, once I had determined to leave the de la Hayes, it seemed that I could not wait to return to Kingston. It was as if some strong cord was pulling me. To my chagrin, there was no response from the Kingsleys.

Sister Martha, however, wrote most eagerly. "My child, it is as if you have read my thoughts. I long to see you again and Father Andrew joins me in sending his love. You will find that he has aged rather rapidly since dear Isobel was called to the Lord. I believe that, to him, she was always a younger sister, and it made her passing more painful. I have been blessed with having help with the young children, but more of that when you arrive. The good Lord moves in mysterious ways."

The journey was tedious, perhaps because I have not fully gathered my strength since I fell ill over the Christmas season. The roads were slow and difficult after recent snowfalls. This resulted in delays and chillsome waits. I welcomed our stops at inns, farmhouses and hotels. When we finally arrived in Kingston, dark had fallen.

I could not carry my bags to St Joseph's and, seeing no familiar face, I hired a cab to take me to the door. I walked up the familiar path slowly, looking for each remembered feature of the grounds. Inside, lamps were burning and the soft warm glow seeped through the curtains. When I knocked, I waited a lengthy time. A lanky girl of about twelve years of age opened the door.

"Yes, Miss?"

"Am I not expected? It's Catherine. I know – "

A cry of joy, and Sister Martha came bustling forward. "My

dearest child, we did not expect you till tomorrow. The coach did not arrive and we thought you'd spent another night on the way."

I was enveloped in a huge embrace. I heard Father Andrew's voice and he advanced to welcome me.

Sister Martha turned on the luckless girl who was standing gawking. "Get moving, Ursula, you silly child. Can't you see that Catherine needs refreshment?"

The child turned and ran towards the kitchen. I imagined I heard a confusion of voices, as in the past.

Later, when I had eaten and drunk the hot beverage prepared for me, we sat and talked long hours. I confessed all my difficulties and even my forbidden love for the young Irish officer.

"Ah, you girls," sighed Sister Martha.

Speaking of my prospects of employment, I remarked on my disappointment at not hearing from the Kingsleys.

"Why, Catherine, I do believe that they are still away," the sister observed. "You are far too inclined to take these matters to heart."

"Did they go to New York again?" I remembered that they had spent the summer with her family.

"No, my dear. The major's mother has been poorly for some time and they returned to England to solace her on her death-bed. I believe the poor soul was called from this world a few weeks after their arrival. Mrs Gildersleeve came by to leave some clothing for the girls and told me that the Kingsleys were due back this spring and that Mrs Kingsley was most eager to return.

I listened with much interest, knowing that Sister Martha had no objection to hearing all the gossip, though she was kindly in repeating it.

"Did Mrs Gildersleeve have any other news?"

"Well, my dear, I wouldn't wish to repeat idle talk but I do remember that she said she thought Mrs Kingsley found it hard to be compared to the first wife, who apparently had been quite a favourite. The poor woman died on her way here to join her husband and so, they said, did the little daughter." Sister Martha looked at me reflectively, "but I expect you remember that, for you became very fond of the family, didn't you?"

"Yes, indeed I did. Major Kingsley is a fine man and I got used to his wife's ways. I look forward to seeing them again."

"Well, no doubt you will, and now, my dear, I think it is high time that we went to bed."

She led me to the room that I had shared with Darra for so many years. I stood outside the door for a minute, and turning to Sister Martha with a slight sob, I said, "It has been perfect coming back, seeing you again, except that I miss Sister Isobel and – oh, Darra! When will I ever see her again?"

Sister Martha gave me a brisk kiss and answered, "If the Lord wills it, very soon." Giving me a little push towards the room, she turned and walked down the passage towards the children's dormitory.

I opened the door and immediately noted a lamp burning. There was Darra's bed and on it was . . . Darra!

For a moment, I stood speechless, not believing my eyes. She looked at me, her eyes filled with tears. Running over to the bed, I flung my arms round her and we clung to each other as if we'd never let go.

"Darra! I thought you were in New York. Why didn't you write? Or if you did, I never received your letters."

"Oh, Cat. Cat." She held me closely, sobbing. I realised that she was not lit with the same joy that enveloped me and I cried out in terror.

"Darra! What is it? What has happened? I can sense something different in you. What is it?"

Whatever I might have expected her to say, it was not the words that followed.

"Oh, Cat, I'm not your sister," she cried.

I couldn't believe what I was hearing. "Darra, of course you are my sister. Whatever are you saying?"

"Cat, listen to me." Sitting up, Darra pulled herself away from me and began to speak. She poured out all that had been told her by someone with the name of Beaufort Powell, the while choking with sobs. She ended forlornly, "and so it is certain that I am Noreen's child and no one knows who my father may have been."

I reeled, remained silent a minute and then said, "In that case, whose child am I?"

You could have heard a pin drop. After a minute, Darra's eyes met mine with a look of infinite affection and a faint smile shimmered in the tear-wet green depths. "Such wonderful news! You will never believe it, but you already know your father. He is Major Kingsley and, of course, his first wife was your mother. She sailed on the same boat as did mine." She went on to tell all that Mr Powell had told her.

It was difficult for me to deal with so many conflicting emotions, so many new ideas. They swirled inside me. One emotion, however, dominated all the rest.

"Darra. I'll never tell him, or if I do, it will only be if you are welcomed as my sister. Darra, nothing can divide us. You mean too much to me. My home will always be yours. No one who fails to love you, will be anything to me." I spoke the truth. Darra and I had shared so much together, and being with her at that moment only reminded me how sorely I had missed her.

"Cat, that is not all." She looked down, hesitating. "Sister Martha said I have no need to upset you with all this but I cannot hide it from you." She shuddered, and I realised that some terrible, damaging thing had almost extinguished my sister's inner flame, her vitality.

It made me feel protective. I flung my arms around her, exclaiming, "You tell me, or you don't tell me, as you wish. All I know is that we are back together. I hate anyone who has hurt you."

"I should have had a baby, Cat, and I lost my little son. At least, I think it was a son," she wept.

"Oh, Darra!" I gasped, despite myself. All at once, my own past difficulties seemed minor.

"When I was in New York," she continued, "I was tricked into working in a house of ill-repute. I ran away and then I became ill."

I listened, appalled as she described the machinations of that villain, Levishon, or some such name. I could not imagine the "palaces of pleasure" she described, nor did I want to believe that men could be so vile.

"Sister Martha?" I enquired cautiously after Darra had completed her sorry tale. "What did she say? Did you tell her?"

"I told her everything, except . . ." There was a faint twinkle, more like the old Darra. "I didn't tell her how really fine I looked in some of those clothes."

"But whatever did she say?"

"She was so kind and good. 'Darra,' she admonished me, 'you are genuinely sorry, that I can tell. I think your sufferings have been punishment enough. The past is now behind you and I must urge you not to over-indulge yourself in guilt. I do not wish to hear any more. You should not think further about these matters. Kindly accept the sacrament of absolution in the spirit our Lord means you to.'"

I couldn't help laughing. "That sounds like her, dear Sister Martha. Our Mother and the best one we could have."

Darra glanced up at me and we both smiled. The past months disappeared and, for a moment, we were together again as if time and fate had not intervened.

February 16, 1852

The past two weeks have been placid and Darra and I have built ourselves a routine. We get up, attend prayers, help with the household affairs, or perhaps settle the children for their morning lessons. We are at Sister Martha's call and we remind Father Andrew of his messages. Neither of us discusses the future, nor what it may hold. I am awaiting the Kingsley's return, wondering how I will be received. At all events, I am determined to make my own life and will seek employment at a later date.

In the afternoons we ply our needles, take the children for their daily walk and perhaps read or study. Darra is slowly regaining her confidence, though at times I find her sitting silently in the chapel, perhaps in tears. Sister Martha does not allow this "self-indulgence" but I find a period of reflection to be a healthy thing. As the body grows in strength, so must the mind rest and then rise and seek answers.

I slip in beside her and, kneeling for a minute, whisper, "Darra, are you feeling better?"

"Yes," she whispers back, and we cross ourselves and leave together.

At the best of times, February is a difficult month. The memory of intense cold, bitter winds, heavy robes and boots tend to discourage us from outdoor activity. Indoors, the fire burns but, away from it, cold draughts frisk about in all the corners of the room. Yet the February sun has a warmth to it that is heartening. Darra and I are closer in thought and emotion to each other, and the pain we have, each in our own way, experienced is beginning to soften round the edges.

Sister Martha seldom chides Darra now about "moping" in the chapel and has been heard complaining that, since she came home, the little ones can think of nothing but stories. I too have been busy in the schoolroom, trying to capture some of the eager, listening faces with my brush.

"What next, Darra, what next?" they cry if my sister so much as pauses for breath. Once, when I became caught up in the tale, her lilting voice carried me back to childhood delights and the stories we loved. Almost unaware, my fingers lightly sketched the princess, her carriage and the prince.

The children gathered around, calling, "Look, oh look, clever Cat has drawn the princess and – look! Why, she looks just like Darra," and so she did.

Today I received a letter from Roger in the post. It brought a surge of memories, some joyful, some painful.

My dear Catherine,
    You will not be surprised, I think, to hear that Madeleine Sévigny and I are to be married. We want you to be the first to know. The children are delighted and cannot wait for us to be installed in one household. It is our sincere wish that you will consider our home yours and that you will not hesitate to visit us.
    I hope, dear Catherine, that happiness lies ahead for you and I will always remember you with love and respect. Roger.

So many unexpected endings. Moira Parnell, engaged to be married, and now Roger and Madame Sévigny to say their vows. Only Darra and I are back where we began. Darra, who seems wonderfully contented at the moment, says that she is reborn. Sister Martha gives her a quick look to see if she is dramatising.

But I? I feel restless and experience a need to take up my life anew, now that I am fortified by my days at home.

March 30, 1852

I have neglected my journal lately. At first, there seemed little news to write of and then. . .

It must have been the first day of spring when Sister Martha sent Darra to the drygoods store to choose fabric for our summer needs.

"It will do you good to get out," she said, "and you may choose some extra yardage in case you have any invitations from young men. I do not expect you and Catherine to sit about like nuns. Nor does Catherine need to look like a charity case when her father returns."

Darra and I exchanged glances. She is still reluctant to enter the world of eligibility and marriage, and I am fearful of my reception at the Kingsleys'. There was no arguing with Sister Martha, however, so Darra selected her light cloak and, asking me my colour preferences, was on her way. When she did not return in time for the midday meal, Sister Martha was extremely put out.

"I did not ask Darra to prepare a wardrobe for our good Queen," she pointed out, "and I fail to see that the decisions of buttons and bows should be that time-consuming."

When Darra did return, she was flushed and excited. She murmured excuses about meeting an acquaintance from Toronto and begged leave to return to the stores with me that afternoon.

"I have need of Catherine," she pleaded. "There are some decisions that I cannot make for Cat. Please let us go together."

"Well, it is true that girls like to plan their wardrobe themselves," concurred Sister Martha. "Off you go then, and, at the same time, buy me a pound of arrowroot as our stock is low. Some of the children still cling to their winter coughs and need extra nourishment."

The two of us set out. Darra seemed unusually gay and strangely vague about the problems of dress we were to settle. Instead of turning towards the drygoods store, she said, "Cat, let us go to the tearoom. I feel an astonishing thirst and need to rest my legs."

I looked at her in some concern, then with suspicion. "Darra, in the past, you have often advised me on my dress and seen better than I what colour or style will become me. Why is my presence now so necessary? Furthermore, we have just finished dining."

Darra merely laughed and said, "It is so long since we have sat and enjoyed the tearoom cakes together. Do let's go."

It's true that St Joseph's fare is plain, though nutritious, and the memory of the tearoom cakes rose in my mind.

"Why not? I would enjoy it."

We walked slowly, enjoying the milder air. The robins had returned, their shrill cries heard from time to time as the wary cats slunk by. The trees were in bud and spring flowers appeared tentatively in the sunnier beds. Passers-by were dressed in lighter attire, some men were hatless.

The tearoom was enjoying a brisk trade. Darra hastened in eagerly. I following in her wake. She headed towards an alcove at the back. I wondered why, for it seemed already occupied by a young man. He appeared to be sitting as though waiting for someone. Unwillingly, I thought of Cavan. Indeed, the man was very reminiscent of – it was Cavan!

I stopped, unable to take another step. He rose and came towards us, his eyes fixed on my face.

"Catherine!"

"I will leave you now," Darra murmured as she stirred beside me. "Don't disappoint me." Turning gracefully, she disappeared from the tearoom.

I stood still, warmth flooding my cheeks, my eyes lowered before the longing in his gaze. It can only have been a moment before he led me to a seat and placed himself across from me.

"Catherine! My love. This morning, when I saw Darra about her errands, I recognized her at once as the charming young actress I had met in Toronto last year. She told me you were back, that you had left the de la Hayes. We talked of many things; she'll tell you about it later. Cat, I have so much to say to you, but not here, not before all the world. May we take a drive? I'll hire a cab. It is such a lovely spring day."

I looked into his hazel eyes, green sparks dancing with mischief.

"I recall, Cat, a most pleasurable time I spent with you in a cab on another occasion."

"Sir, you forget yourself," I rallied boldly. "I am not at all sure I should risk my life in your hands. Besides, Darra awaits me."

"No, allanna. Darra goes back to St Joseph to ask Father Andrew to grant me an interview tonight."

"For whatever reason?"

"Come, my sweetheart, let us find a cab and I will make my reason clear."

Taking my arm, Cavan led me out and I, accepting as if in a dream, followed his lead. Helping me onto the seat, Cavan gave the driver some directions and climbed in beside me. Without speaking, he slid his arm round my waist. I leaned against him, my head resting on his shoulder. Our hands locked. It was as though we belonged together.

Then Cavan raised my face and kissed me tenderly on the lips.

"My dearest love, I have news for you. I have been given honourable discharge from the army on account of that silly accident I suffered last year. No! No!" He exclaimed, seeing my look of alarm. "Do not fear. My health improves daily. There is but one thing I need to restore me to my former strength."

"What is that, Cavan? What has your physician recommended?"

"He has recommended marriage, my love. He suggested I find some pretty girl who would be willing to take me on. Unfortunately, I have not won the lady of my choice." His hand slid caressingly under my cloak. I looked up into the ardent face bent to mine.

"I am sorry to hear that, Sir, perhaps you were a little too forward in your approach, as you certainly are now!" Teasingly, I removed the errant hand. "Tell me something of this woman of your choice?"

"She is little and beautifully formed. Her eyes are cornflowers, her hair is flax. She walks with grace and dignity. More than that, she is loyal and kind."

"She sounds a paragon, Sir, and why has this lovely not accepted your hand?"

"Pride, Catherine. Her pride."

At that moment, the carriage stopped. I had been giving scant attention to our route and now found that we were out of Kingston, the river to our left and, to our right, a gate leading to a small farmhouse. Beyond the house lay as lovely a vista of rolling land, field, and coppice as I had ever seen.

"Where is this, Cavan?" I asked in surprise.

"This is Fairlee Farm, Cat. It comprises 100 acres and is currently for sale. I find it to my taste. Do you like it?"

Taking my hand, Cavan helped me from the cab and we paced carefully down the road. Then, turning me towards him, Cavan raised my hand to his mouth, kissing each finger in an old remembered gesture.

"Allanna," he asked softly, "will you marry me? I've loved you for so long. Be my wife and grace my home, will you? Come and live with me at Fairlee Farm."

I answered without hesitation. "Yes please, Cavan."

Folding me in his arms, our bodies blended as one, our lips met sweetly. Time ceased, eternity was ours.

I have paused, for the memory of those moments will be with me always. Sometime later, we wandered back to the cab and, seating ourselves inside, settled back to enjoy our dreams of the future. The trip home passed quickly and soon we arrived at St Joseph's. Cavan and I walked up the path, hand in hand. As we entered, Darra peeped from the parlour door and, seeing our smiles, rushed up to me and threw her arms around my neck.

Father Andrew stood up to greet us, saying, "What is all this, my child? Who is this young man? Introduce me, please."

Leaving the two men to discuss business affairs, Sister Martha, Darra and I retired to the kitchen, where we exchanged embraces and, I must admit it, shed some tears.

"Our first wedding," sighed Sister Martha.

Turning to more practical matters, we prepared refreshments, it being taken for granted that Cavan would spend the evening.

We dined apart from the children. Father Andrew and Cavan seemed in good accord and Sister Martha beamed on us as if all were of her making. Darra sparkled, teased and laughed without a care in the world. I thought how admirably she and Cavan agreed, their puckish humour providing foils for each other.

After dinner, Father Andrew and Sister Martha excused themselves and left the three of us to our own devices. Cavan settled himself beside me on the horsehair couch and Darra curled up in the big armchair beside the fireplace.

"Since it is only family, Sister Martha cannot tell me to sit up properly," she remarked.

"That is true, Darra," Cavan remarked, "But, sister mine, you should show a little respect to your older brother and his affianced bride."

Darra laughed and, just as she was about to say something, I broke in, "Oh Cavan, I am so glad you already feel that Darra is a sister. I couldn't marry you if you did not."

Cavan turned to me very seriously. "Cat, Darra has been patient, but she has something to tell you."

Puzzled by his tone, then alarmed, I turned to Darra hastily.

"Oh Darra, what is it?"

"Don't sound so worried, Cat. I have good news, but I didn't want to tell you about it too soon. Believe it or not, I have found my father, but the best part of the whole story is that I have also gained a brother!"

I gazed at her incredulously. Darra had found her father? And a brother? For a moment, some selfish impulse made me afraid. Would these strangers alienate her from me?

All at once, the realisation of what this meant to my sister came to me and, jumping up, I ran over, threw my arms about her and demanded, "Why have you kept it from me? Where are they? Who are they? When will I meet them?"

Darra rose, pushing me aside. With great dignity and presence, she crossed the room to where Cavan was sitting. Regally, she waved him to his feet. "Miss St Joseph, may I present my brother, Cavan O'Hara?"

I opened my mouth to protest in astonishment, then closed it again. I saw Darra's red curls dancing just below the russet locks of my love; two pairs of mischievous slanted eyes, green lights flashing, two straight noses above the mobile mouths. How much the two looked alike!

Seeing my utter bewilderment, Cavan took me in his arms and pulled me back to the couch. "Sit, my love. We will explain it all to you." Then, with my head resting against him, secure in the cradle of his arm, I listened to Darra's arresting tale.

"When Cavan ran into me on the street, we stopped to exchange greetings. Of course, I thought of you, Cat, and wanted to detain him so that I could discover what was going on. I was determined that his presence in Kingston would not mean further hurt for you."

"And I," broke in Cavan, "could not believe my good luck. There was my long-lost love's sister, all smiles and charm and ready to confide in me."

"Silence," Darra interrupted imperiously. "I turned on my wiles fully and the gentleman quickly succumbed to the honour of accompanying me to the tearoom. At first, all he could talk about was my sister, her charms, her cruelty and so on. I was becoming a bit bored with it all. Suddenly I saw his gaze riveted on my maidenly form. Why, he even ceased talking."

"Darra!" I objected.

"Next," she continued, ignoring me, "he leaned forward and demanded, 'Where did you get that brooch?'" She fingered the lovely emerald, gold-entwined ornament which Beaufort Powell had given her at their last meeting.

"Your mother's brooch?" I asked, recalling the happines with which she had shown it to me on our reunion.

"Indeed yes. He could not take his eyes off it."

"It just happens," interjected Cavan, "that it was a perfect match to a set of my mother's. She received it on the occasion of her marriage. The set includes a necklace, pendant, ring, brooch and earrings. My mother scarcely wore the pieces, declaring that green was not her colour. I remember one evening when my father demanded that she wear the set and there was a quarrel. Eventually, my mother appeared without the brooch. She said it was lost. My father was furious and wanted to call in the servants. My mother cursed him and admitted that she had given the brooch to the maid. 'You know why she left, Timothy. You gave her something,' my mother insisted, 'so why should I not do so also?' With that, she stalked out of the room.

"I was interested in the whole story, all the estate knew that the girl was pregnant by my father. I remember her. Noreen. She was a cheerful, young thing of Darra's general build and colouring."

"Well," picked up Darra, "I told him all that Mr Powell had revealed to me. We compared notes, we compared features and we decided that we were related."

"Indeed," remarked Cavan, "we were both amazed, but it pleases us greatly. In order to complete our happiness, we decided that I should marry you so that you would in reality, and in law, have Darra as a sister."

"We arranged to have you meet Cavan at the tearoom," Darra continued, "and everything went just as planned. Oh, Cat. . ." The tone of her voice abruptly changed in emotion. "Isn't it wonderful? I can scarcely take it all in. You and Cavan and I. A real family at last."

As I record this, I am still filled with amazement and joy. Each day brings the three of us closer together. The only cloud which mars my happiness is my forthcoming meeting with the Kingsleys.

April 2, 1852

It is general knowledge that the Kingsleys arrive back in Kingston tomorrow. I become increasingly fearful. Cavan, Darra and I have held endless discussions as to how I should be introduced as the rightful daughter of the household. Finally we decided that Cavan would ride over in the afternoon and initiate the subject while Darra and I wait here. Cavan can then proceed as he sees fit.

Cavan and I have decided on a June wedding. How greatly I wish to grace his home as Catherine Kingsley! I am not, however, unaware that much will depend on Kingston's acceptance of my arrival into society by so unusual a route. Whatever will Mrs Kingsley think? I fear that Darra is right when she says, 'Dear Agatha will agree with whatever seems most acceptable to the social élite.'

Cavan will not allow me to dwell unduly on the subject and I must end my scribbling. Even now, he urges me to join him in a drive to Fairlee Farm. The purchase is now complete and we had the pleasure of taking Darra to view the property. She was utterly delighted and vows that she will spend all her free time with us.

April 4, 1852

I am writing this in the nursery at the Kingsleys', in my father's home. Last night there was no persuading them that I should return to St Joseph's for the night. Indeed, after so traumatic a day, I was more than ready to refresh my strained emotions with sleep.

Cavan left us shortly after three in the afternoon, kissing me roundly, and ordering Darra not to allow me to give in to my fears. We withdrew to the parlor and speculated endlessly on what could be occurring. At the point of despair, wondering how much longer I could endure the tension, we heard the sound of hoofs.

Darra raced to the window and, peeping from behind the curtains, called out, "Oh, Cat, it's Major Kingsley's carriage! He's leaping out and hastening up the path!"

At that very moment, the door bell pealed. Darra was out of the room in a flash, but I stood motionless. Major Kingsley, my father, rushed into the room, almost preceding Darra in his anxiety. He stopped. We gazed at each other. Finally he stepped forward and embraced me.

"Catherine! My dear child. How could I have not suspected something? You are so much like your mother."

By then I found that I was crying and the next few minutes passed in confusion. Darra wiped her eyes, went running to brew fresh tea and called for Sister Martha.

I will never forget the next half hour. Father Andrew slipped in to receive Major Kingsley's gratitude for having cared for me. Sister Martha shed a few tears.

"If only dear Isobel could have been here to witness this," she said.

Turning to them, Major Kingsley spoke. "May I beg permission to take my daughter back with me? I assure you that I shall make a tangible donation to St Joseph's in appreciation of all you have done for Catherine. Meanwhile, I should return home."

Wondering about Cavan's whereabouts, and assuming he had preferred to allow my father to come on his own, I ventured to inquire, "Where is Cavan, Father? Is he waiting outside?"

"He is at our house," replied the major, "attending to Mrs Kingsley. The news was rather a shock for her."

Darra and I exchanged glances.

"I do hope she will not mind too much," I murmured.

My father cleared his throat. "I think you know that Agatha is highly strung, my dear. I have no doubt that she will come to her senses shortly. Your young man seems to have the situation in hand."

We rose to leave and Darra stood aside in silence. I opened my mouth to ask my father's permission for her to accompany us.

"Come along, Darra," the major said, tapping her on the arm. "Cavan has told me that you are related to him. That's quite a story, my girl. In all events, I would as soon have two daughters as one. Get your cloak and don't let us delay."

Darra glanced at him incredulously but, seeing the smile on his lips, she broke into smiles and almost danced out of the room.

I pressed his arm, whispering, "Thank you. Thank you so much."

Soon the three of us were installed in the carriage, filling in the missing pieces of the story.

"Did you not receive my note?" asked Darra. "I thought when you saw the quilt that you would know at once."

"Mrs Kingsley and I received it when we were in England. We could not understand it at all. Then, with other worries on our minds, we put it out of our thoughts. Of course, we would have checked at some point. In fact," he remarked, looking somewhat puzzled, "I still do not know what relevance it has. We will unroll it once we are home."

When the carriage drew up at the Kingsley house, I was struck by the irony of my arrival as daughter, where previously I had been maid, then companion.

Cavan greeted us at the door, saying quite matter-of-factly to my father, "Mrs Kingsley is in the parlour, Sir."

My father strode ahead. I followed. Cavan and Darra took up the rear amid whispers and low-key laughter.

Mrs Kingsley lay draped across the couch, her smelling salts on the table. Her face was red with much weeping.

At the sight of me, she burst out, "This is most inconsiderate of you, Catherine. You know very well how sensitive I am."

"Madam, I am very sorry," I answered as was my habit.

Mrs Kingsley raised her handkerchief to her face and allowed a few sobs to escape her.

"What will the town say?"

"The town will rejoice in our good fortune, my dear."

"We will be having a most fashionable wedding," added Cavan, grinning at me in a teasing manner. "We hope you will honour us with your presence."

Mrs Kingsley rang the bell and demanded a fresh brew of camomile tea. Oonagh, who answered the bell, stared at Darra and me in open amazement.

"What are you staring at, girl?" demanded Mrs Kingsley in a new burst of temper. "Get me a fresh brew and keep your mouth shut."

Darra and I smiled at Oonagh sympathetically as she hurried from the room.

"My dear," my father was speaking firmly. "I must ask you to take a strong hand on yourself. You have two new daughters. Catherine, beloved child of my first wife, and Darra, Cavan's sister."

"That little piece! How can you, Edward?" With a low cry, Mrs Kingsley once more swooned on the couch. Cavan raised the smelling salts to her nose with a briskness that caused her to gasp.

"I believe your opinion to be quite mistaken," he spoke up. "You have here two of the loveliest young women in Kingston for daughters. They have been brought up with great respectability. In opening your home to them, you set a fine example to society. I have no doubt that you will be much admired."

"Do you think so?" was her doubtful response.

"I am sure of it, my dear," added the major. "Let us plan a small dinner for a select few to celebrate our daughter's engagement. There is no doubt that the wedding will cause quite a stir, with the arrival of Catherine's friends from Government circles. Of course, the Gildersleeves will expect to be invited."

Mrs Kingsley looked thoughtful. "Catherine, my dear, as I have said all along, it was inconsiderate of you to give us so little time to prepare for a wedding." She looked resentfully at Darra. "I hope you too are not expecting me to wear myself to the bone in preparation of a second marriage for you."

"Indeed! No, Madam," said Darra, shocked. "I expect to take the veil . . . Sister Martha, however, considers me still unready."

All heads turned to her in surprise.

"Oh Darra!" Cavan and I spoke simultaneously.

"Most unready! Most unsuitable, I should say," said Mrs Kingsley unkindly. "Besides, I will expect help with all that is going to fall on my shoulders. Men have no idea what a wedding involves."

"I'm most anxious to help you, Mrs Kingsley. I am much more experienced in gracious living now. You will find me far less flighty," Darra hastened to reassure my stepmother.

"Enough, enough, girl. Fetch me my blue shawl from the bedroom. I have a chill, my nerves being so badly shaken. If I must have two girls around, at least be of some use."

Cavan winked at Darra as she went dutifully in search of the shawl. At the same time, my father left the room and soon returned with the quilt.

"Let us unroll it together," he said.

My heart contracted when I saw the bundle again after so many months. We untied the strings, carefully laid it out on the floor and all the old remembered patches shone up at me. My eye wandered from one old favourite to another.

"Of course," said my father in wonder.

"Why, Edward, it is exactly like the one that was in your mother's room," cried Mrs Kingsley.

"Yes. She made several and gave one to Frances for the baby, for Catherine. Oh, my dear," he said, turning to me, "if only I had looked at this when you left it behind last year."

Later Darra declared it time to return to St Joseph's or she would be unable to attend to her duties with the children the next morning. Cavan drove her home, but not before she and I exchanged hugs and kisses and my father gathered her into his embrace, reassuring her that his home was hers.

Mrs Kingsley sniffed and reminded Darra to call on her in order that they might discuss the luncheon for Catherine's engagement.

"I cannot be expected to do all the planning," she complained, "and get out all the invitations in my state of health."

Cavan bade her farewell, insisting he would be the envy of all his friends, having won so young and chic a mother-in-law.

Mrs Kingsley bridled somewhat, then rallied, "Enough of that, young man. I am, of course, far too young for Catherine to be my own child." Somewhat mollified, she rose and accompanied them to the door.

My father took her arm, saying, "I am proud and grateful, Agatha. You have borne the shock of this admirably. Let us now see Catherine to her room."

Once in bed, I slept peacefully. This morning, when I woke early, I began writing in my journal instantly. What a long way Darra and I have come since the day we left St Joseph's to go into service.

June 24, 1852

Tomorrow is my wedding day. Never again will I write in my journal as a single woman. Indeed, the pages are exhausted and I have barely room to paste in one of the wedding invitations.

My wedding gown, of pure silk, is hanging in the wardrobe. It is plain but for a delicate border of embroidered pansies encircling the bodice, cuffs and full skirt. Mrs Kingsley has lent me the blue garter which she wore at her own wedding. Darra's cross awaits me on the chest of drawers. I shall return it before Cavan and I leave for our honeymoon. My veil is of Brussels lace, stitched to a neat Juliet cap.

We are expecting a large number of guests since Agatha, as I must remember to call her ("I'm far too young to be called Mother," she told me), insisted that this must be the season's most fashionable wedding. I had hoped for a more intimate ceremony but was over-ruled by Agatha.

"Good gracious, Catherine," she protested, "we do not want the world to think that we have anything to hide."

My stepmother was much elated at the luncheon she gave in my honour. It was attended by the cream of Kingston society, headed by Mrs Gildersleeve.

"My dear Catherine," she said, crushing me to her bosom, "this is the most romantic story I have ever heard. I vow I wept when I was told how you were restored to your father. Agatha," she added, "you are fortunate woman to be part of such a touching tale."

"It was not as surprising to me as you may think," my stepmother responded. "I always said to Edward that there was something different about Catherine. 'That child has something special in her,' I told him. 'We must do all we can to help her.'"

This theme was oft-repeated and, listening to the kindly interest of the guests, Agatha was soon convinced that I was virtually her discovery. Accepting Darra was more difficult, but seeing that she was Cavan's sister, Agatha had no recourse but to acknowledge her to the guests.

"Yes," I heard her say. "The girl's father and mother are overseas and I told Edward that it behooved us to act as parents in their absence. 'Our home is yours,' I told her.

"You are so kind, Agatha," one of the guests said.

"Why, I only do my duty, as any Christian would."

Towards the end of the afternoon, Mrs Gildersleeve approached me.

"I must admit to being quite vexed with this young man for stealing your heart just at this time," she chided me.

"What do you mean?" I asked, smiling.

"My husband and I are travelling to Europe shortly. He is called upon to do some business with Her Majesty's government. I will be on my own a great deal of the time. Of course, we have friends and I will have introductions, but I had counted on taking a companion with me. You would have been ideal, Catherine. I really do not know who would suit me as well."

A merry peal of laughter rang out at just that moment and my eyes turned towards my sister. How sweetly she rejoiced in good fortune, when most of her dreams had turned to grief. While my future lay, God willing, secure at Fairlee Farm with Cavan at my side, what lay ahead for her?

I spoke impulsively. "Oh, Mrs Gildersleeve, would you consider taking Darra? I know my sister is free to go and I am sure you would find her a most pleasant companion."

Mrs Gildersleeve turned and looked towards Darra, who was deftly helping Agatha. With a smile here, a word there, she moved among the guests, a study of grace, conspicuous with her bobbing red curls.

"That just might be a happy solution, Catherine," the older woman agreed. "I will think on it."

A week later, Darra came to me saying that Mrs Gildersleeve had discussed the matter with Sister Martha and received her full approval. They expected to leave in four weeks' time and would be away at least three months. Everything would depend upon the success of Mr Gildersleeve's business negotiations.

My sister and I will, therefore, be parted again, but this time the separation holds no fears. Our letters will continue to cross the land and the waters. By Christmas, Cavan and I should be well settled at Fairlee and Darra will be back to visit us.

Darra is calling me to prepare for sleep, chiding me gently for keeping late hours on the eve of my wedding. And so I reluctantly put aside my pen.

"We must both take our beauty rest, Cat, you to prepare yourself as a wife, and I? Why, I am off to Europe, perchance to meet the Queen."